Rising Star

A Starstruck Romance

Rising Star

USA TODAY BESTSELLING AUTHOR
SUSANNAH NIX

Haver Street Press

FIRST EDITION: November 2018

ISBN: 978-0-9990948-8-4

Haver Street Press | 448 W. 19th St., Suite 407 | Houston, TX 77008

Edited by Julia Ganis, www.juliaedits.com

Cover Design by Cover Ever After

For everyone who's ever been afraid to speak up because you knew you wouldn't be believed.

one

ALICE CARLISLE PRESSED an ear against her bedroom door, listening for sounds of life on the other side. All appeared quiet in the apartment beyond. *Good.* Hopefully her roommate was still fast asleep.

She slipped out of her room, quietly pulling the door shut before tiptoeing down the hall to the kitchen where—

A mostly-naked man stood at the stove with his back to her.

He was hot enough to be a model, flipping pancakes in nothing but a pair of striped boxer briefs that clung to his taut buttocks and muscular brown legs. It could have been a scene straight out of one of Alice's more X-rated fantasies, if only the pancake flipper in question were straight and single. Alas, the beautiful Diego was very gay—and very much in a relationship with Alice's roommate, Isaac.

"I'm totally saving some of this maple syrup to lick off you later," Diego said without turning around, obviously not realizing it was Alice who'd come into the room.

"Careful," she replied as she walked past him. "I've heard food play can increase the risk of bacterial infection in sensitive areas."

Diego glanced over his shoulder, his lip curling in an expression of distaste. "Oh. It's you."

"Good morning to you too." Alice jerked open a cabinet to retrieve a travel mug.

"Isaac!" Diego shouted, turning back to the stove. "She's up."

Shit. Alice shoved the mug back into the cabinet, electing to make a hasty exit rather than wait around for her coffee to brew. Her caffeine fix could wait until she got to work. Better that than—

"Hey." Isaac wandered out into the living room in a rumpled T-shirt and a pair of tropical-themed boxers.

"Morning," Alice mumbled as she grabbed a packet of cherry Pop-Tarts out of the box in the pantry.

Isaac ran his palm over the stubble on his chin. "I need to talk to you."

"No time." She tore the foil Pop-Tart packet open as she headed for the front door. "Running late for work."

"Alice—"

"Later, okay?"

"You keep saying later, but you don't get in until after midnight most nights and you're usually gone again before I'm up in the morning."

She turned her back on him and pulled open the apartment door. "I know! Work's just been really crazy this week."

"This can't wait anymore."

"Sorry!" Alice said, stepping into the hall.

"You can't keep running away!" Isaac shouted as she pulled the door closed behind her.

Sure I can.

Alice had practically elevated running away into an art form. Besides, she already knew what he wanted to talk to her about, and the longer she could put him off the better.

A few weeks ago, Isaac had asked her to move out so Diego

could move in. Not that he wasn't already camped out here full time, but apparently Diego wanted her bedroom to use as a home office for his burgeoning graphic design business. Nice, huh?

Alice assumed Isaac wanted to know how much longer it would be before she was gone. The problem was, she hadn't been able to find a new place yet—though not for lack of trying. It just wasn't that easy, given her financial circumstances and the current state of the economy. Times were tough all over, and everyone else in the greater Los Angeles area was looking for affordable housing too.

In a way, she'd brought all this on herself. Isaac had been a great roommate before he'd met Diego. She was the genius who'd encouraged him to try online dating, and inadvertently cemented her status as an unwanted third wheel.

Alice started her car and fired up her favorite true crime podcast for the commute from Silver Lake to Burbank. As she was merging onto the 5, her podcast paused for an incoming call from Isaac. She declined it, and a minute later her phone chimed to let her know she had a new voicemail. *Fantastic.*

She didn't listen to the message until she was making the long walk from her assigned parking lot into work.

Hey, Alice, it's Isaac. I didn't want to do it this way, but I told you it couldn't wait anymore. It's been a month since I asked you to move out, which is more than fair. Diego's lease is up on the thirty-first and he has to move his stuff out before that, so I'm giving you a hard deadline of March twenty-third. You need to have all your things out of the apartment by then and give me back the key. I didn't want to do this, but you haven't given me any other choice. Sorry.

He didn't sound sorry. He sounded annoyed, and eager to get rid of her. And Alice had actually thought Isaac was her friend. At first they'd just been roommates—someone she'd found through a friend of a friend—but they'd gotten pretty close there for a while. Until Diego came on the scene. As soon as he got himself a boyfriend, Isaac had chucked Alice like last week's avocados.

That was what you got for trusting someone. Alice didn't make friends easily, and this was exactly why. When you let your guard down, it made it easier for people to stab you in the back.

Sighing, she flashed her badge at the security guard and went in search of a much-needed caffeine infusion.

Two hours and three cups of coffee later, Alice was still wondering how the hell she was going to find another apartment on Isaac's timetable as she stared at the gaping chest wound on the gurney in front of her.

"Chest is full of blood," said the man beside her in doctor's scrubs. He was handsome on a whole other level than most mortals—dark blond hair, bright blue eyes, muscles for days—but Alice paid him no special attention as she fumbled with the IV line on the patient's arm.

Nine months at this job had inured her to both the gore—which smelled weirdly like Orange Glo—and her coworkers' aesthetic perfection. Symmetrical faces, winning smiles, and rock-hard bodies were so de rigueur in her current workplace that she barely even registered them anymore.

Alice wasn't in their league, but she was attractive enough, in a Scandinavian farm girl sort of way, that she'd occasionally been the target of unpleasant comments in school and at other jobs. "You're smarter than you look," "No one will ever take you seriously looking the way you do," and much worse had been flung at her various times over the years, in both academic and professional settings. She loved that she was far from the most attractive person at her current job, because it allowed her to feel invisible. In fact, part of her job was to *be* invisible, which suited her just fine.

Anyway, she had more important things on her mind than

admiring her handsome coworkers, like the fact that in a little over two weeks she'd be homeless.

Isaac's timing was terrible. It was mid-semester, so there was nothing available near the university. Even worse, her current job was ending in just a few weeks, which meant she'd be saying goodbye to a regular paycheck. She'd tried to be good about saving, but those savings weren't going to last her long if she had to cough up a brand-new security deposit.

"Pressure's down to sixty," said a nurse with a Screen Actors Guild card and a more flattering set of scrubs than Alice's plain pink ones.

"Must have nicked an artery," Dr. Handsome said beside her, and Alice leaned forward, pretending to suction the chest cavity for him.

The grizzled TV veteran working across the table from them plunged his gloved hands into the patient's chest. "Call the OR and tell them we're on our way."

Even if the casting agency found Alice another job, studio apartments in her budget were few and far between—and usually next door to a meth lab. She'd been hoping something would turn up before Isaac lost patience and gave her an ulti-matum, but that ship had pulled anchor. Her only option at this point was the one she'd been hoping to avoid: the dreaded Craigslist roommate.

Just the thought of it made her shudder. Who knew what kind of weirdo she'd wind up living with?

"He's unresponsive," the nurse with the cute scrubs said.

The hot doctor beside Alice—better known to television audiences as the adorably charming Dr. Ethan Convey—bent over to check the patient's chest drainage unit. "Chest tube output is twelve-hundred cc's. Prep for thoracotomy."

His hip bumped against Alice's, and she shuffled aside to give him more room. They were working in tight quarters, and part of her job was to stay out of everyone else's way. But as she reached for a scalpel on the tray of instruments beside her, she misjudged how close it was and knocked the whole thing over, sending hemostats, forceps, and scalpels flying with a deafening clatter.

"Ow!" the man dying on the gurney cried out as he flinched away from the flying medical equipment.

"Shit. Sorry," Alice muttered. Good thing their scalpels weren't actually sharp.

"Cut!"

The director ripped off his headset and approached with a thunderous expression on his face. It was Dean Harwell's first time in the director's chair on *Las Vegas General*, and the technical challenges of filming the show's complicated trauma scenes had been giving him fits all week. Dean was moonlighting from his regular job as star of *Las Vegas General*'s better-rated lead-in, and had only ever directed two episodes of his own show before this. The producers had done him a favor letting him direct, but at this point it was clear to everyone that they'd made a grievous mistake. The guy was in way over his head, and had been taking it out on anyone and everyone with the misfortune to attract his attention.

Alice's feet weren't the only ones that shifted nervously as Dean stormed toward them. The other two nurses in the scene —a background actor named Diane and a minor recurring cast member named Abby—shrank back and hung their heads. Even Griffin Beach—who was in his seventh season as series regular Ethan Convey and had recently blown up the box office in the fourth installment of the blockbuster *Troublemakers* franchise—visibly winced. Only Alfie Crosby, a forty-year veteran of stage and screen sitting comfortably at the top of the call sheet seemed unfazed by the oncoming tantrum.

"Why is the dead guy talking?" Dean demanded, red-faced under his backward Yankees cap. *"And moving?"*

Once upon a time, Alice had actually thought Dean was

hot, but that was before she'd had the pleasure of working with him. Funny how much less attractive some people became once you got to know them.

"He's not dead yet," Alfie said, looking more amused than anything. "There's another page of dialogue before he codes." According to *The Hollywood Reporter*, Alfie was being paid a cool half million per episode, so he could afford to be amused.

"She threw a tray of sharp instruments at my face," the not-dead-yet actor mumbled in his own defense.

"Sorry," Alice said again. In an entire season working background, this was the first time she'd ever ruined a take—but of course Dean didn't know that.

"*Background are supposed to be seen and not fucking heard!*" he shouted. "It's right there in the goddamn name: *background!*"

All the extras on his own show despised him. Alice had talked to some of them in the commissary last week, and they'd offered their condolences over Dean's guest directing stint on *LV Gen*. Now she knew why.

Dean started to take a menacing step toward Alice, but Griffin Beach inserted himself between them. "It was my fault," he said, facing down Dean with a level stare. "I bumped into her and made her knock the tray over. If you're gonna be pissed at someone, be pissed at me."

Alice could have hugged him for taking the bullet for her. Not that she ever would. There was a strict caste system in place on set. Extras who got too familiar with the talent would quickly find themselves out of a job and unlikely to be assigned a new one by the casting agency.

She hid gratefully behind Griffin's broad shoulders and kept her mouth shut while Dean railed about professionalism and the fact that it was only eleven a.m. on Wednesday and they were already four hours and ten pages behind schedule. Someone might have pointed out that they were only behind because of Dean's inexperience and repeated tantrums—this was his second outburst of the day and they were still hours away from lunch—but no one did, because it would only antagonize him and lengthen the duration of his tirade.

It was a full five minutes before he lost steam and stalked back to the monitors.

"Thank you," Alice whispered to Griffin as soon as Dean was out of earshot.

Griffin gave her a wink so devastatingly sexy she felt her knees go wobbly. So much for not paying attention to how attractive he was.

"Don't worry about that apple-faced goon," he whispered back, covering the mic tucked under his shirt as he leaned toward her. "He's not even qualified to be the assistant manager at PetSmart."

Alice swallowed, momentarily paralyzed by the perfect storm of Griffin's kindness and sexy proximity, combined with her own overwhelming gratitude and embarrassment.

"Boy, what a dickhead," Alfie announced loudly, not caring who heard him. "Who told that moron he could direct?"

Griffin snorted and wandered back to his mark, leaving Alice to pull herself together and reapply her veneer of detached professionalism.

Props came through and reset the scene, Dean called action, and they started again from the top.

This time, Alice managed not to throw a tray of scalpels at anyone.

two

GRIFFIN BEACH WINKED at a passing PA as he stepped out of Stage Ten on the Kenwood Studios backlot and slipped his phone out of the pocket of his scrubs. The scrubs might actually be the thing he'd miss most after *Las Vegas General* filmed its last episode in a few weeks. There were a lot of things to like about this job, but getting to wear what were essentially pajamas most days was a definite perk.

No, he amended as he exchanged greetings with one of the grips, he was going to miss the cast and crew most of all. After seven seasons, this stupid show and the people who worked on it were the closest thing he had to a family. But that would all be over in a few weeks, and he'd have to say goodbye to this place that had become his second home.

Griffin was having a hard time adjusting to the idea. Even though he knew moving on was the best thing for his career right now, he hated change. But his agent was right: he'd gotten too comfortable here. At this point, he could pretty much play Ethan Convey in his sleep. He needed to stretch himself. Show the world that Griffin Beach was more than just a dimpled smile in a pair of scrubs.

He'd taken the first step two years ago when he'd landed his first big film role in *Troublemakers 4*. Even though he'd been fifth on the call sheet in an ensemble action movie already packed with big-name talent, the world had taken notice of Griffin's newly bulked-up physique, comic timing, and action hero potential. The film went on to earn higher grosses than its last two predecessors in the franchise, and more than one review had credited it to Griffin's likable new addition to the cast.

A string of magazine covers had followed, along with a meaty starring role in an indie drama last summer. He was on his way to becoming a household name, but he needed to throw off the shackles of his television shooting schedule and focus on films full time if he wanted to reach the next level. That meant saying goodbye to the job that had launched his acting career.

That reminded him, his agent had sent a text asking him to call her. Sabrina Keeling had worked miracles for Griffin since she'd started representing him three years ago. He'd always be grateful to his first agent for getting him onto *Las Vegas General* when he was an unknown with only a few commercials under his belt, but switching to Sabrina was the best decision Griffin had ever made for his career. She'd gotten him into *Trouble-makers 4* and set him up with a publicist to maximize the resulting press. Sabrina had also encouraged him to follow it up with a smaller indie drama to show off his range. Most importantly, she'd worked her magic to get him his next part: a starring role in *Prepare for War*, a big-budget studio project helmed by none other than Jerry Duncan. With Sabrina in his corner, all Griffin's professional dreams were finally coming true. Which meant when she called, he called her back right away.

He hit Sabrina's speed dial number—she was number one,

at the very top of his contacts—on the walk back to his trailer. "You beckoned," he said when she answered.

"How's my favorite client doing today?"

"I don't know, you'll have to ask Chris Pine yourself." Griffin flashed a smile as he passed one of the wardrobe assistants.

"So funny," Sabrina replied with her trademark British dryness. "Love that sense of humor. How's Dean's directorial debut on *Las Vegas General* going?"

"Horrendous."

"Shocking. Who could have predicted?"

"You did."

Sabrina had been Dean's agent several years ago, until they'd mutually agreed to part ways—which Griffin assumed meant she'd fired him for being an uncooperative asshole.

"Well, I've got good news to brighten your day. You're on the short list for the *Buckaroo Banzai* remake."

Griffin felt a flicker of unease. "You told me that yesterday."

"Did I?"

"Yes. You're using your good news/bad news voice." Sabrina never gave him bad news without first giving him some good news to soften the blow—even if the good news happened to be a rerun. "Just get to the bad part," he said, feeling his stomach clench in anticipation.

"It's just a little thing. I don't want you getting stressed."

"I don't get stressed," Griffin insisted as his stomach acids churned like a jacuzzi tub. "You know me, I'm easygoing."

"I know I told you I'd set you up with my dog sitter while you're in Atlanta, but it's a no-go. Turns out she's moving back to Michigan."

Griffin came to a stop. "Oh."

As soon as *LV Gen* wrapped, he was flying to Atlanta to shoot *Prepare for War*. He'd been planning to leave his dog here, in the care of Sabrina's dog sitter, so he wouldn't have any distractions on set.

"We'll figure something out," Sabrina told him.

One of the studio bicycles whipped around him, and the writers' assistant called out a greeting as she passed.

Griffin waved back, forcing a smile. "Don't worry about it," he said into the phone.

"I've already got my assistant asking around the office. Someone's bound to have a good dog sitter they can recommend."

Griffin started walking toward his trailer again. "Someone who's available on a few weeks' notice?"

"Sure, why not?"

Because dog sitters were in high demand in LA. Especially the ones with excellent references who could be trusted in a celebrity's home.

"If it makes you feel any better, I've got to find a new dog sitter too."

"It's fine," Griffin said, grinding his molars together. "I'll find someone else." He preferred to handle it himself; it was one thing to take Sabrina's personal recommendation, but he wasn't so keen to hire someone based on a secondhand reference. Not when he was going to be away for three whole months.

He couldn't leave his dog with just anyone. Taco was his best friend, and the little guy depended on Griffin to take care of him. It had to be someone Griffin knew well enough to entrust him to. Someone who would care for him the way he deserved to be cared for.

Sabrina offered an apology which Griffin assured her wasn't necessary, and he bid her goodbye as he reached his trailer. At the sound of Griffin's voice, Taco yipped a greeting through the door, his nails tapping an ecstatic rhythm on the linoleum inside.

Griffin had rescued him five years ago, after seeing someone toss a puppy out of their car and drive off. Seriously, what kind of monster threw a puppy out of a moving car? Griffin had taken the scared little mutt to the vet and then brought him home to the big empty house he'd just bought himself two months before. He hoped the asshole who'd mistreated Taco was rotting in hell, but Griffin felt like fate had delivered a blessing to him in a scruffy, flea-bitten package.

"Hey, buddy," he said, leaning down to keep the dog from escaping as he opened his trailer door. Taco spun in excited circles, wagging his whole body along with his tail, and Griffin scooped him up as he pulled the door shut behind him. "You miss me?"

In reply, the little terrier mix licked Griffin's face with enthusiasm.

"Gross, man. No Frenching." He set Taco on the couch and dropped down beside him, ruffling the dog's ears. "What am I gonna do with you this summer, huh?"

He was already feeling guilty about leaving him behind while he was in Atlanta. Maybe he should just take him with him. But that would create a whole new set of problems. For one thing, Griffin hadn't told the production manager he'd be bringing a dog, and the housing they'd arranged for him might not allow pets. For another, he wasn't sure it was a good idea to bring a dog with him onto a Jerry Duncan set every day.

This was Griffin's first time at the top of the call sheet on a major studio production, and he was already feeling the pressure. Jerry Duncan was one of the most successful directors in the business—but also one of the most feared. He was notoriously demanding and bad-tempered, bringing his huge productions in on schedule and under budget by ruthlessly pushing his actors and crew almost to the breaking point. Griffin fully expected it to be three months of hell, but if this movie was as successful as Duncan's other pictures, it would make his career.

He didn't need the added stress of taking care of a dog in a strange city on top of the grueling work schedule. As much as he was going to miss his little buddy, he preferred to leave him here, in a familiar place, with someone he trusted.

But who? How the hell was he going to find someone on such short notice?

three

TODAY WAS TURNING out to be a real steaming shit
pile of a day.

As Alice stared at the new email in her inbox, she felt the
rumble of a stress headache coming on.

From: Dr. Regina Frazier
Subject: Just checking in (again)!

The cheerful exclamation point her dissertation committee
chair had tacked on didn't quite manage to counteract the
passive-aggressiveness of the parenthetical.

Alice didn't need to read the body of the email to know
what it said. Undoubtedly something similar to the last two
emails Dr. Frazier had sent. With a quick finger swipe across
her phone's screen, she archived the message unread. Out of
sight, out of mind.

Too bad the real world didn't work like a smartphone. If
only you could make problems disappear as easily as swiping
away an annoying alert on your phone screen. *Poof!* Gone!
Never to trouble you again.

Unfortunately, this wasn't a problem that would go away so easily.

The reason Alice was ignoring her dissertation advisor's emails was that she'd been ignoring her dissertation. For months. Like, the last nine months.

It had been easy to stay off the professor's radar at first. Dr. Frazier had been on sabbatical last summer and fall, and only checked in a few times. Since Alice was in the fifth year of her PhD program and had been a great student and self-starter up until then, Dr. Frazier had no reason to suspect she wouldn't be just fine on her own for a few months. Especially since Alice had responded to all her early emails with assurances that everything was proceeding apace.

But now it was the spring semester. Dr. Frazier was back from sabbatical, and a few weeks after the start of classes, she'd sent an email asking for an update on Alice's progress. Which Alice had ignored. A few weeks later she'd sent another email, which Alice had also ignored. And now this one. Alice knew she couldn't put her off forever. By now, Dr. Frazier had almost certainly asked around the sociology department and discovered Alice hadn't been seen on campus in months—not since the previous June, to be exact.

Sooner rather than later, Alice was going to have to face the music and explain herself.

There was a good reason she hadn't set foot on campus in two semesters, and that reason was named Dr. Gilchrist. He was a member of Alice's dissertation committee specializing in criminal recidivism, and the department expert in network analysis. One of the key components of the dissertation prospectus her committee had approved was a chapter applying network analysis to her data. Alice didn't know how to do network analysis, so her adviser had recruited Dr. Gilchrist to walk her through it.

At first, Alice had liked Dr. Gilchrist—or Neil, as he'd

cheerfully insisted upon being called. She'd enjoyed the inter-actions she'd had with him in the past, and had been excited when he'd agreed to be on her committee and work with her on the network analysis. He was personable, generous with his time, and had a lot of knowledge he seemed eager to share.

Or so she'd thought.

Their first meeting had gone well enough, but he started to make her uncomfortable the second time she'd come to his office. For one thing, he'd closed the door, which he hadn't done before. Once they were alone, his friendliness became more pronounced, to a degree that set her on edge. More than once, she caught him staring at her breasts.

But he hadn't done anything overtly wrong—nothing she could describe to someone else in a way that would be incon-trovertible—so she convinced herself she'd let her imagination get the better of her.

She continued meeting with him, even as his so-called friendliness moved farther over the line. He started touching her casually on the shoulder or the knee. Making offhand comments on the appearance of other female students in the department. Once, as he was showing Alice something on his computer, he tabbed past a porn website. He started intro-ducing sexual subjects into the conversation, asking Alice about her sexual history and preferences, and sharing inappropriate information about his own.

She spent a lot of time shifting out of his reach and pretending to laugh off his comments. The shame shouldn't have belonged to her, but she was the one left feeling guilty and unclean.

It occurred to her that he was intentionally dragging his feet and withholding the knowledge she needed in order to keep her coming back, but what could she do? She needed him, and Dr. Frazier was away, unable to help—even assuming she'd believe Alice, which was by no means a given. She was, after all, the one who'd sent Alice to Dr. Gilchrist in the first place.

And he hadn't done anything *that* far over the line. Professors were friendly and informal with graduate students all the time. Nothing had actually happened, right? Alice was just constantly uncomfortable, feeling like she needed to play defense around him.

Her anxiety increased as Dr. Gilchrist's "flirting" became more aggressive. He regularly complimented her body and reminded her how much influence he could have over her future in academia—though not in the same sentence, of course. The two statements were linked only by inference, but infer from them she did. He invited her out for drinks repeatedly, which she was forced to decline repeatedly. Once, he attempted to give her a shoulder rub.

It wasn't any one thing that finally crossed the line into too much. It was more like a steady, progressive increase in her baseline level of dread, until it reached a point that became paralyzing. Alice left Gilchrist's office one day, her skin crawling from the feel of his eyes on her, and simply never went back. She begged off their next scheduled meeting and stopped answering his emails altogether.

That was nine months ago, and she hadn't set foot on campus since. She hadn't touched her dissertation either. Even thinking about it made her feel queasy.

Writing a dissertation was supposed to be stressful, but it was the harassment that had kept her up nights, made her feel like she was getting a stomach ulcer, and brought her to tears unexpectedly. It was Gilchrist's predatory attentions that had sent her into hiding and brought her academic aspirations to a humiliating and unplanned halt.

She was twenty-seven and she'd been in school her whole life—she should be graduating in June and starting her job search. Instead, just when her career should have been taking off finally, it was over, and Alice had nothing to show for her years of work. No PhD, no plan, and no aspirations. Nothing but a temporary job she'd never intended to keep for so long, on a television show that had been canceled.

Alice swiped to her phone's browser and typed *Craigslist* in the search bar. She'd have to reply to Dr. Frazier soon, but not today. Her stomach already felt like a garbage disposal choking on a chicken bone, and anyway she had the more pressing problem of her impending homelessness to deal with. Her dissertation had already waited nine months; it could wait a few more weeks until her current housing crisis had resolved.

While everyone else ate lunch in the catering tent, Alice sat alone with her burger and fries at one of the picnic tables on the other side of the soundstage and browsed the room-mate-wanted listings. She'd already asked all the other extras and production assistants if they knew anyone in need of a roommate or sublet. Unfortunately, no one had, and her earlier Zillow search had turned up nothing but a dire-looking studio in Reseda she could just barely afford, with the toilet literally in the living room with no walls or doors around it.

It left her no choice but to throw herself on the mercy of internet strangers.

As she scanned through the classified ads, Alice grew increasingly depressed. Repulsive as the living room toilet was, most of the roommate situations seemed even worse...

420 friendly house. Must be okay with snakes.

Biggest of nopes on the House of Reptiles.

Happy, healthy vegan couple looking for bi roommate to share house & fun with.

Clearly a poly couple in search of a live-in third. She wished them luck in their endeavors, but no way.

Looking for housemates for an intentional community centered on spiritual and prayerful living.

Definitely a cult.

I am 35 yo nudist professional male and prefer if you also are a nudist. Females only.

Gross.

For the right attractive female I have no problem taking care of your chores. ;) Let's exchange pics and get to know each other.

Alice groaned and folded forward, resting her forehead on the picnic table. Was everybody looking for a roommate in Los Angeles some kind of perv? She was going to end up with the living room toilet in Reseda, wasn't she? She supposed as long as none of her guests ever needed to pee, she could learn to live with it. Or maybe she'd just never invite anyone over at all —it was hard to imagine offering someone a drink with her toilet sitting out in the open a few feet away.

Something cold and wet nuzzled against Alice's ankle and she startled upright. Griffin Beach's dog Taco gazed up at her with his comical underbite and wide doggy eyes.

Taco's owner stood a few feet away, holding a smoothie shaker in his hand. "You okay?" he asked, tilting his head as he studied her face.

He was still wearing his blue doctor's scrubs, which had been custom tailored by wardrobe to look far better on him than scrubs had any right to do. Griffin had been a lot skinnier and less muscular the first few seasons of the show, but he'd bulked up so much for *Troublemakers 4* that they'd had to write an explanation for his upgraded bod into his character's story-line on *Las Vegas General*.

"Yep. Fine," Alice said quickly as she reached down to pet Taco. He wagged his tail and whined hopefully, so she gave in and lifted him onto her lap.

Griffin shook his head, grinning as Taco licked Alice's chin. "Found a sucker with a lap, did you, buddy?"

Alice pushed Taco away from her face and glanced at Griffin without quite meeting his eye. "Thanks for earlier. I'm sorry you had to step in."

He gave a one-shouldered shrug. *"De nada."*

She'd always liked Griffin, but she was also a little wary around him, and not just because background had to tread carefully around the talent. He was nicer to the extras than some of the other actors, but he could also be kind of…flirty. Which wasn't *necessarily* a bad thing. A lot of actors could be like that, and sometimes it was just a harmless side effect of their people-pleasing personalities. The profession tended to attract certain types: attention-starved middle children, class clowns who needed to be liked, and extroverts who drew energy from interacting with others. There were plenty of introvert actors too, but they seemed far less comfortable with the fame and attention that came with success.

Guys like Griffin, on the other hand, seemed to eat all that stuff up. And while his friendliness was certainly preferable to the raging asshole prima donnas who threw a tantrum if you made eye contact with them—like Dean Harwell—Alice's recent experiences had left her distrustful of friendly men.

Not that she'd ever heard a bad word against Griffin, beyond his reputation as something of a manwhore. According to the set grapevine, his workplace conquests numbered in the double digits, including at least three of his costars and two members of the makeup department. If you believed the gossip sites, his romantic past was littered with an endless string of C-list actresses and models, none of whom had lasted more than a week or two. One of the less reliable sites even claimed he had a penchant for picking up starry-eyed fans in bars, which Alice wasn't sure she believed, but wasn't sure she *dis*believed either.

She wasn't being judgy. As long as all parties were consenting—and she'd never once heard anyone imply other-wise—how Griffin Beach chose to conduct his private life was totally his business. Alice simply had no interest in drawing his attention—or anyone else's for that matter. At this particular point in her life, she didn't want anything to do with *any* men, no matter how nice or gorgeous.

"I feel like such an idiot," she said, scratching Taco in his favorite spot under his chin. "I've never messed up that bad before."

"Seriously, don't worry about it." Griffin threw his leg over the bench across from her and sat down, propping his forearms on the table. "It happens to the best of us. On my very first speaking part, I poured a pot of coffee all over the table instead of into my cup. Forget Dean. He was in a pissy mood long before you threw a tray of knives at Brent."

"I know." Alice sighed and reached for a cold french fry, which she broke in half to share with Taco. "Dean isn't even my biggest problem right now."

Griffin's eyebrows lifted in inquiry. "What's up?"

The dissertation hanging over her head wasn't something she liked to talk about, so she stuck to the more emergent housing problem. "I'm being kicked out of my apartment so my roommate's boyfriend can move in."

"Ouch."

"Yeah, and the apartment search isn't going well."

"Slim pickings?"

"See for yourself." She unlocked her phone and slid it across the table with the Craigslist page open.

Griffin's eyes widened as he scanned the listings. "*Female coed wanted for rent-free situation,*" he read aloud. *"Must be open minded and a good listener who enjoys a mature man. Light cleaning and cooking expected."* He looked up at her, grinning. "What? You don't want to be a sex-slave-slash-therapist-slash-housekeeper for some creepy old dude?"

"I'm not that desperate—yet. But ask me again when I'm living in my car." Taco lay down with his head on his paws, and Alice laid her hand on his head, smiling at the blissful way his eyes rolled. When she looked up again, Griffin was staring at her with a weird expression on his face. "What?" she asked, warily.

"Nothing." He reached for his smoothie shaker and took a drink of whatever beige liquid was inside. "I was just thinking..." He wiped his mouth with the back of his hand. "You could move in with me."

Alice's mouth fell open. "Uhhh..." Had Griffin Beach seriously just asked her to move in with him? Because that was crazy. Big time movie-slash-TV stars didn't invite lowly extras to move in with them out of the kindness of their own hearts. That was definitely taking nice *way* too far.

"I didn't mean move *in* with me, move in with me," Griffin clarified without making things any clearer.

"What...did you mean?" Alice glanced around apprehensively, and was discouraged to find no one else in sight. She and Griffin were effectively alone on this side of the building.

"I just—" He ran a hand through his hair, almost like he was...nervous? She'd never seen him act nervous before—he usually oozed easygoing confidence. "I need a dog sitter. As soon as we wrap next month, I'm leaving for a three-month shoot in Atlanta, and I've been trying to find someone to take care of Taco for me while I'm gone."

"Oh." Alice relaxed a microfraction. That was *slightly* less crazy.

"Three months is a long time to trust him with a stranger," Griffin went on. "But he loves you, and you're great with him. You could house sit for me and look after both him and the house while I'm gone. It's win-win. And I'll pay you, obviously."

"Really?" Alice said in disbelief. "I mean, you barely know me. You sure you want to let me live in your house while you're away?"

It seemed like an awful lot to trust her with on their limited professional acquaintance. They chatted occasionally, sure, but it wasn't like they really knew anything about each other. For all he knew, she could be a crazed dognapper who was just waiting until the right opportunity presented itself.

Okay, maybe that was a little far-fetched.

"We've worked together almost every day for an entire season," Griffin pointed out. "Which is long enough to know you're reliable and professional on the job. You already look after him for me sometimes when I'm on set, and I've let you go into my trailer when I'm not there."

That was all true. On more than one occasion Griffin had asked her to take Taco back to his trailer—or go get Taco from his trailer and take him for a walk. He used to ask the PAs to do it, but once he saw how much Alice liked Taco, he'd started asking her sometimes too.

"You've never once stolen my laptop or sold my email to TMZ," Griffin said with a shrug.

"That you know of," Alice said. "I could be biding my time until your next movie hits to drive the price up."

He smiled. "I'm taking my laptop to Atlanta with me, but if you want to sell my old socks on eBay, go nuts...unless you're not interested in being a dog sitter? Which I would totally understand." He gestured at Taco. "This guy can be a real diva. Insists on having his kibble sorted by color, pees on the floor if his mochaccino isn't hot enough. That sort of thing."

Alice chewed her lip as she tried to imagine it. Griffin probably had a hella nice house. Having it all to herself for three months would be like a vacation getaway—but with a bonus dog to snuggle. Not to mention how great it would be not to have to pay rent for a while. She could save her money while she took the next three months to find a new place and a new job. Maybe even use the alone time to get back to work on her dissertation. If she could just finish the damn thing, she could put graduate school behind her and stop feeling like a failure.

There was only one problem...

"I have to be out of my place by the twenty-third," Alice said.

"Of *this* month?"

"Yeah."

Griffin tapped his fingers against his shaker as he seemed to think about it. "Okay. Well. What if you moved in now? It's only a month until I leave. We could be roommates for a month."

He didn't look entirely sold on the idea, and neither was she. *Living together?* In his house. Like roommates, except in this case Alice's roommate would be her landlord *and* her employer, and also someone rich and famous who was used to getting his way and being catered to.

All the alarm bells ringing in her head made her headache kick into a higher gear.

"Well?" Griffin said. "What do you think?"

Alice wished she could accept his offer. It would be the solution to so many of her problems. If one of the female cast members had proposed it, she would have said yes in a hot second. But moving in with Griffin Beach? She just couldn't see herself doing it. The more she thought about it, the more her insides knotted up.

Sure, he palled around with the crew and extras like he was just one of the guys, but Griffin Beach wasn't just one of the guys. He was someone who made twenty times her salary and could get her fired with a phone call. Not just from *Las Vegas General*—he could call her agency and make sure she never set foot on a set again. As an extra, she always had to be careful around the talent: don't distract them, don't get in their way, don't speak to them unless they speak to you first. There was a hierarchy that enforced the power imbalance on set. Did she really want to take that power imbalance home with her at the end of every day?

Maybe it would be fine. Griffin genuinely *seemed* nice. But so had Dr. Gilchrist. Alice had learned the hard way that nice could be deceiving. Sometimes men only acted nice to get you to let your guard down. To make you think you could trust them. It was only later, once they'd gotten past your defenses, that they showed their true selves. When you'd put yourself in a vulnerable position that was hard to get out of, and they could use their power over you to their advantage.

It was possible she was just being paranoid—probable, even. Maybe Griffin was exactly as great as he seemed and was just looking for someone to take care of his dog and nothing else. But Alice had heard too many stories about rich, good-looking actors who were used to taking what they wanted from the women around them. If she moved in with him she'd be completely at his mercy, with no backup plan and nowhere to go if things went bad. Not to mention, he was a *lot* bigger and stronger than her.

She'd already endured unwanted advances from one man in a position of authority over her. No way was she putting herself in a position for it to happen again. It had been bad enough dealing with it on campus, but to put up with something like that at home, where she couldn't get away from it, was unthinkable. Even if her fears were totally unfounded, she just couldn't take the chance.

"I appreciate the offer," she said, shifting uncomfortably, "but I don't think so."

Disappointment splashed over Griffin's features. "You don't want to be a dog sitter."

"It's not that, it's just…" She couldn't think of a normal-sounding reason to give him. *I'm afraid to be alone in your house with you? Actually, I'm afraid to be alone with any man. I've been burned before and now I'm sort of broken, so I can't bring myself to accept your very sweet offer. Sorry about that!*

"No worries," he said, letting her off the hook. "I'll find someone else."

"I'm sorry." Alice looked at Taco, feeling like she'd let him down.

"It's cool." Griffin grabbed his smoothie shaker and stood up. "Come on, Taco." He whistled, and the dog jumped down from Alice's lap.

"Good luck with your dog sitter search," Alice offered.

"Good luck with your apartment search," Griffin called over his shoulder.

She watched morosely as the best housing offer she was ever likely to get walked away. Was she crazy for turning it down?

Probably.

That was what that creep Gilchrist had done to her. In addition to ruining her academic career, he'd left her too broken and distrustful to accept kindness when it was offered to her.

four

"BANG."

Alice pretended to flinch at the second assistant director's monotone impression of a gun firing. The other extras around her dropped to the floor in halfhearted impressions of panic, but she stayed where she was. She was playing a patient today instead of a nurse, stuck on a gurney with her regular clothes hidden under a hospital blanket, and she was supposed to stay put when the gunfire started.

It was just as well. Unlike most of the other extras, Alice hadn't gotten into background work because she wanted to be an actor. Let the rest of them have their spotlight and put their acting lessons to good use throwing themselves to the floor. She was content to lie on her gurney with her back to the camera, mostly hidden from view.

The soundstage was crowded this morning, and the cast hadn't even showed up yet. There were even more crew on set than usual because of the firearms they were using today, which required armorers and additional makeup and safety personnel as well as a stunt team.

"Alice."

Her stomach lurched as Robert, the second AD, approached her. *Did I not flinch well enough?* She bit down on her fingernail as he picked his way through the extras huddled on the floor.

"Ethan will be standing here examining you at the start of the scene," Robert told her, "and when the gun goes off, he's going to shield you with his body. Okay?"

Alice's eyes widened. Ethan was Griffin's character. And he was going to be *shielding her with his body?*

She gave Robert what she hoped was a convincing thumbs-up. "Got it."

So much for lying on her gurney unnoticed. Now she was going to have a member of the principal cast—a very muscular, very attractive, very *male* member of the principal cast—sprawled on top of her.

"Our gunman's got a couple lines of dialogue," Robert went on, flipping to the next page of his script sides. "Then Gary the security guard shows up on the scene, yada yada. After their exchange, Alfie enters from here." He pointed to one of the doorways. "When he starts talking, I want some of you to start crawling to safety."

Robert picked out a few extras and assigned them a specific dialogue cue and a direction to exit during the three-way exchange between Alfie, the security guard, and the gunman.

"While you're doing that," he said, moving on, "the heroic Dr. Convey is going to wheel Alice's gurney out of frame, so make sure you stay out of his way and watch your fingers and toes. That gets us to page twenty-two, when the gunman shoots good old Gary the security guard."

Alice had been pretty sad about that when she'd seen this script. Gary had been playing a security guard on the show for most of its run. It was nice that he was getting a little bit of a spotlight in the show's final season, but killing him off in episode eighteen meant he wouldn't be around for the series finale.

Robert went through the rest of the scene, but since she would be off camera by then, Alice didn't bother paying attention. It was a pretty sweet gig being on a gurney. She got to lie down for the whole scene, and there was no chance of her tripping or dropping something, which was what she spent most of her on-camera time worrying about. Since her screwup the other day, she'd been even more paranoid about it.

By the time Robert had finished choreographing the background action, the cast had started wandering onto set. Gary the security guard was joking around with the guest actor who was about to kill him, while the other extras loitered on their marks. Alice lay back on her gurney and pulled out her phone to check her email, in case there'd been a response to any of the dozens of apartment inquiries she'd sent out.

She'd devoted every free moment of the last four days to looking for a place to live, scouring all the online classifieds sites she could find and responding to every non-crazy-sounding female roommate situation out there. So far, the few who'd bothered to contact her had either been filled already, or wouldn't be available soon enough to save her bacon. She'd even spent hours over the weekend driving around apartment-heavy neighborhoods looking for *For Rent* signs and calling leasing agents, but everything had been out of her price range. Even the toilet studio in Reseda had been snatched up. And yes, she'd actually called on that one, because that was how desperate she was.

What she wasn't yet desperate enough to do was consider a male roommate, and unfortunately the majority of the roommates classifieds had been placed by men. It probably shouldn't be surprising that more men than women were willing to let a stranger from the internet move in with them.

To her disappointment, she had no new emails or phone

calls since the last time she'd checked twenty minutes ago. She wondered what would happen if she begged Isaac for more time. He'd have to give it to her, wouldn't he? What was the alternative? Putting her stuff out on the curb and changing the locks? Surely he wouldn't go that far if she made it clear how hard she was trying to find a new place. Maybe if she offered to pay for Diego to put his stuff in storage for a month? Not that she could afford to do that.

Honestly, at this point she wanted to move out as badly as Isaac and Diego wanted her gone. Whenever she was around the two of them, she could feel the resentment pouring off them in waves. Feeling unwanted in her own home totally sucked donkey balls.

"Hey!" Griffin said, appearing beside her gurney in his doctor's scrubs.

Alice looked up from her phone and attempted to return his smile. "Hey." They hadn't interacted much since she'd turned down his offer last week, and she still felt awkward about it.

"Looks like we're scene partners this morning."

"Looks like it."

"Cool." He took the stethoscope from around his neck and put it in his ears. "Where would you like to be examined?"

Alice stared at him. "What?"

"I'm supposed to be examining you when the bullets start flying." He waggled the stethoscope at her. "What's your complaint? What brought you to the hospital today, ma'am?"

Right, the scene. He needed a reason to be standing here next to her when the shooting started. "I dunno," she said. "You're the doctor-actor. What do you want to do?"

Alice didn't usually put much thought into her scenes. She wasn't ever chosen for the featured background roles that required actual acting, so most days it was just a matter of walking from one place to another, or handing a particular instrument to one of the doctors. Some of the extras invented elaborate backstories and motivations for their presence in the scene, but Alice had never bothered going that deep.

Griffin's mouth tugged to one side as he thought about it. "You could have some kind of wound, like a scalp lac, that I'm looking at. Or if you've got the flu, I could feel your glands."

Alice narrowed her eyes at him. "Which glands exactly?"

He rolled his eyes. "The glands in your throat, knucklehead."

"That's okay, I guess. As long as we keep it outside the bathing suit area, I'm cool."

"Bikini or one-piece?"

"One-piece."

He nodded and hung his stethoscope around the back of his neck. "So no palpating your abdomen. You're on your own if you have internal injuries."

The sad thing was, Alice wouldn't actually mind being palpated by Griffin Beach in a perfect world. It was pretty pathetic that she couldn't even enjoy being in this scene with him. But when Griffin was looming over her about to play doctor for the camera, the reality was a lot more intimidating than the fantasy.

Alice hadn't played many patients—patients tended to have lines, which required SAG cards and SAG pay scale—but she'd always thought it must be hella weird to have all those people standing over you, touching different parts of your body. The trauma and surgery patients really got manhandled sometimes, and in places Alice generally preferred not to be manhandled by coworkers. Workplace norms were different for actors though. Their bodies were their instruments, and they were freer with them than the average person.

Too bad Alice wasn't an actor. She was just a sociology grad student trying to pay her rent, and she wasn't chill about getting physically intimate with people she wasn't dating.

"That shirt looks hideous on camera," Dean Harwell shouted at the costume supervisor as he gestured at the actor playing the gunman. "Why is he wearing that thing?"

"It's the shirt you insisted on last week," she replied through clenched teeth.

Griffin rolled his eyes and twisted his face into an impressive approximation of Harwell's scowl. "Why did you let me insist on such a butt-ugly shirt, Carmen?" he mocked under his breath. "Don't you know I'm incompetent?"

Alice bit her lip to stifle a laugh and Griffin grinned at her.

"Budge over." He gave Alice's foot a poke. "It looks like we're gonna be waiting a while."

She pulled her knees up to her chest to make room for him, and he hoisted himself onto the edge of her gurney. It felt weird lying down when he was sitting next to her, so she sat up and scooted her back against the wall. After a moment, Griffin followed suit, scooching back to lean against the wall beside her. Their legs stuck out in front of them, Griffin's scrub pants and vintage Adidas next to Alice's jeans and plaid Toms.

"Cool shoes," he said.

She clicked her feet together like Dorothy in Oz. "Thank you."

"Did you find a place to live yet?"

"Nope. Still looking."

"You'll find something."

She glanced over at him. "Did you ever find a dog sitter?"

He shook his head. "Still looking. I interviewed a couple prospects this weekend, but…" He trailed off, shrugging.

"You didn't like them?"

"They were fine. My agent's assistant got their names from a service and I'm sure they're great, but I'd rather go with a person recommended by somebody I know—someone who's used them before and knows they did a good job." He shrugged again. "My agent says I have trust issues."

"Taco's your family," Alice said. "And you're his whole world. You can't leave him with just anyone."

Griffin looked over at her and smiled. "Exactly."

Guilt pooled in the pit of Alice's stomach. "I'm sorry I couldn't—"

"Hey, don't worry about it. It's fine."

She still felt bad. It would be nice to help him out—and even nicer to be able to take him up on his offer and not have to worry about finding a place to live anymore. But she had a few trust issues of her own. "So what's the movie in Atlanta?" she asked, changing the subject.

"It's called *Prepare for War*. I play an ex-marine SWAT rescue specialist who has to save his daughter after she's kidnapped by a Mexican drug cartel."

"Sounds great."

He shot her a cynical look. "Liar. It sounds like a piece of shit. But it's a piece of shit costarring Kimberleigh Cress and directed by Jerry Duncan, which isn't bad for my first leading role in a major studio picture."

By Hollywood calculus, Griffin's piece of shit had all the earmarks of a blockbuster. Jerry Duncan's movies usually starred actors like Tom Cruise or The Rock and always broke box office records on opening weekend, and Kimberleigh Cress was just coming off the success of a breakaway hit trilogy based on a popular young adult book series.

"That's awesome," Alice said. "You're gonna be great."

"Can we get this walk-through started sometime today?" Dean Harwell shouted, as if anyone but him was causing the delays.

"Twenty bucks says that vein in his forehead bursts by lunchtime," Griffin whispered as he hopped off the gurney.

Alice snort-laughed, clapping her hand over her mouth, and Griffin grinned at her.

"Stop it," she whispered as she lay back down on the gurney. "You're going to get me in trouble."

The other actors and extras shuffled to their positions with the peppiness of a slow-moving zombie horde—six days of working with Harwell had taken its toll on morale. When Robert cued the background, Griffin shifted smoothly into serious doctor mode, grabbing the chart hanging off the side of Alice's gurney. She didn't have anything to do, so she watched him as he flipped through the chart pretending to read it. His eyes were really strikingly blue, and framed by crazy long lashes that contributed to his boyish appeal. And the costume department had expertly tailored his scrubs to emphasize the bulginess of his biceps. Well done to them.

The other extras moved around them, pretending to do bits of business. Behind her, Alice heard the actor playing the gunman start his dialogue.

Griffin set the chart down and shook his head at her gravely. "I've never seen a case of athlete's foot this disgusting."

She pressed her lips together, trying not to smile. Background were only supposed to *pretend* to talk, but Griffin wasn't background, and he wasn't miked for this scene, so she supposed he could do what he wanted.

He lifted up her right foot, prodding it gently as he pretended to examine it. "I'm afraid we're going to have to amputate."

Alice struggled to keep a straight face as he grinned at her, waggling his eyebrows like Groucho Marx.

"*Bang!*" Robert shouted.

Griffin dropped Alice's foot and threw his body across hers.

Even though she'd known it was coming, she wasn't prepared for it. He was heavy and firm, all hard muscles and warm skin, and did she mention *heavy*? She let out an embarrassing squeak of surprise as the breath rushed out of her lungs.

"Am I hurting you?" he whispered. His lips were next to her ear, and his breath tickled her neck.

She shook her head. It was fortunate she wasn't supposed to talk, because at the moment she wasn't sure she'd be able to. She lay frozen beneath him, hyperconscious of every place his body touched hers, which was pretty much *everywhere*. Although his IMDb bio claimed he was six feet, Alice put him closer to five ten—but it was five feet ten inches of concentrated muscle mass that radiated heat like a furnace.

Griffin shifted on top of her and she tensed—until she realized he was just trying to move some of his weight off her. "Better?"

She managed a small nod and let out a slow, careful breath, forcing herself to relax. This was just part of the job. He did this and way worse than this with other actors all the time. It was nothing to him.

Any normal woman in her right mind would be thrilled to have Griffin Beach's amazing body on top of her. Hell, Isaac would expire from jealousy if he knew. Alice knew she should be enjoying it, but instead she was trying to fend off a panic attack.

Griffin turned his head to watch the scene unfolding down the hall. She couldn't see anything, but she could hear the actors reciting their dialogue. Gary the security guard had arrived and was shouting at the gunman to stand down.

Alice squeezed her eyes shut and concentrated on slowing her breathing. Relaxing her limbs one by one. Just when she was finally starting to unclench a little, Griffin slid off her and pushed the gurney away from the gunman through the closest open doorway.

When they came to a stop off camera, Alice bolted upright. She was still breathing a little heavily, and she had a bad feeling her face was as red as a beet.

"Sorry if I crushed you," Griffin said. "I'll try to be more gentle."

"It's fine," she told him. Better for him to think he'd squished her than the truth—that she was freaked out by a little innocent physical contact with an actor filming a scene. Fuck Dr. Gilchrist for doing this to her. She should be having the time of her life right now, and he'd ruined it for her.

"*Bang bang*," Robert shouted from the next room. "*Bang.*"

"Poor Gary," Alice said.

Griffin bowed his head. "May he rest in peace."

"Back to one!" the first assistant director shouted when the scene was over. "This time's the real deal."

One of the crew guys came and wheeled Alice back into place, and she arranged the blanket over her so none of her street clothes showed.

Griffin wandered back over to her side and gave the blanket a tug. "You should probably take your shoe off. If I'm examining your foot, I wouldn't do it through your shoe, and it might be visible on camera."

"Right. Sorry." She sat up and pulled her shoe off, thanking the gods of personal grooming that she'd made time for a pedicure last week.

Griffin leaned his hip against the gurney, sucking on an Altoid as he watched the crew work around them. He glanced down at her foot with its bright blue nail polish, then away again. "You're not ticklish, are you?"

"Nope." *Thank god.*

A crew member came by to pass out ear protection because of the firearms and admonish them to wear it during every single take unless they wanted to suffer permanent, high-frequency hearing loss.

The crew finished setting up, and when Harwell called action, Griffin flicked aside the blanket and laid his hand on Alice's bare foot. He frowned as he manipulated her ankle like he was checking for a sprain, then his fingers squeezed her big toe. "This little piggy went to market." He moved on to her other toes, one at a time. "This little piggy stayed home and ordered pizza. This little piggy picked up a double-double with cheese after work. This little piggy had none because he was on a water cut for a shirtless scene he had to shoot the next day."

By then, Alice was biting down hard on her lip to keep from laughing, and Griffin was clearly enjoying her struggles to keep a straight face as he wiggled her pinky toe.

"And this little piggy—"

BANG.

She didn't have to pretend to flinch this time. The gunshot was so loud that even with ear protection, it legit scared the shit out of her. In the midst of her adrenaline spike, Griffin threw himself on top of her. He didn't crush her with his weight as much this time, but his body lay draped half over hers with his arm across her chest and his face pressed next to her ear.

"You okay?" he whispered, and she nodded as her heart raced at Mach 2 in her chest.

The unexpected shock of the gunshot had diverted all mental resources away from her tension at Griffin's proximity. In fact, the reassuring weight of his body actually made her feel calmer. It was almost sort of comforting, like the lead apron they laid over you at the dentist for x-rays. If this were a real active shooter situation, she'd be thankful to have him there.

They lay there for a few more moments, until Griffin's cue came to wheel her out of danger. Once they were safely off camera, he gave her a sympathetic look. "It's always a lot louder than you think it's going to be."

Alice sat up and hugged her knees to her chest. "I thought I was ready for it, but apparently not."

"Hang on, there are more coming."

Three more shots rang out as Gary the security guard was

gunned down, but this time they didn't startle her nearly as much.

The scene ended, Alice's gurney was wheeled back into position, and the armorer and his team reset the weapons so they could do it all again from the top. And again. And again.

Each and every take, Griffin would make a new joke as he pretended to examine her:

"I've identified the problem: you have two left feet. Literally."

"According to your chart, you're missing a kidney. Do you happen to remember where you left it?"

"We're going to have to do a brain transplant. Unfortunately, the only brain we have in stock is a baboon brain. You don't have a problem with that, do you?"

And each and every time, Alice would struggle to maintain a straight face.

By the fourth take, she wasn't startling at the gunshot anymore. By the fifth take, she'd gotten almost blasé about the physical contact with Griffin. When he flopped across her, she just rolled with it.

Somewhere around the tenth take, as Griffin lay with one leg hooked over hers, his arm across her waist, and his nose pressed into the side of her neck, she started to reconsider his dog-sitting offer.

He'd been nothing but sweet and respectful all day, without once taking advantage of this totally weird situation they were in or making her feel more uncomfortable. She'd actually had fun, once she stopped being so nervous. He was perfectly easy to get along with, and his goofy jokes had eased some of the tedium. Would it really be that bad, living with him for a few weeks? Sure, it might be weird at first, but just like today, she'd get used to it.

As Alice lay there pinned beneath Griffin's body, it seemed silly to be so paranoid about sharing a house with him.

On the next break in between takes, she worked up the courage to broach the subject. "Listen, about that offer you made me the other day…"

Griffin turned to look at her, eyebrows arched. "Yeah?"

"Is it still on the table? I mean, have you decided on another dog sitter yet?"

He reached up to rub the back of his neck, and she tried not to notice the way his biceps flexed. "No." He winced and shook his head. "I mean yes, the offer is still good. I haven't found anyone else yet."

"I'll do it, then. If you still want me."

"Yeah, definitely."

"Okay." She let out a nervous laugh. "Thank you. I really appreciate it."

He broke into a smile. "Shit, that's a load off my mind. You have no idea."

"For me too." She bit her lower lip. "Is it still okay if I move in this weekend?"

"Absolutely." He stuck out his hand. "Roomie."

She took a deep breath before returning his handshake. "Roomies."

five

GRIFFIN LIVED IN STUDIO CITY, up in the hills south of Ventura Boulevard. As Alice wound through the streets lined with million-dollar homes, she felt conspicuously impoverished in her dented, eight-year-old Toyota Corolla.

After half a mile, she slowed to a stop in front of an inconspicuous private drive and grabbed her phone to double-check the directions Griffin had texted. Squinting at the curb, she found a numbered mailbox peeking out of an overgrown Mexican sage, just like he'd described. The white vinyl numbers stuck to the front matched the address he'd given her. This was it, apparently.

She swallowed her trepidation and steered her car down the narrow drive wedged between a vine-covered fence on one side and a thick row of scraggly cypress trees on the other. From the street it looked shabby and abandoned, but she imagined people paid premium prices for this kind of privacy.

After twenty feet or so, the trees on the right gave way to a white-painted brick wall. Just beyond, she could see the eave of a low-roofed white brick house. As she continued, the drive widened, opening up to a double carport painted a cheerful turquoise. Alice parked alongside a black Range Rover she hoped to god belonged to Griffin, and got out of her car to take in her new temporary home.

This was more like what she'd expected. Just beyond the carport, the hill dropped away to expose a stunning view of the city. A flat green lawn stretched out next to her, sloping down to a line of well-manicured bushes that screened the neighboring property on the hillside below. At the top of the lawn, a wide, stained deck lined a modest midcentury house with floor-to-ceiling windows looking out over the yard and the gorgeous view.

As Alice was staring at the house, a sliding door opened and Taco came shooting across the lawn toward her. Reassured that she'd come to the right house, she let out a relieved breath and dropped to her knees to greet the excited dog, who leapt into her arms.

"You found it," Griffin said as he strolled toward her in flip-flops, athletic shorts, and a Nike T-shirt.

"I did." Alice stood up with Taco cradled in her arms. "You're right, it's pretty hidden back here."

"Keeps the riffraff out."

"Thank you again for letting me stay with you."

He waved a hand. "It's nothing. You're saving my ass by taking care of this doofus for me while I'm gone."

Her eyes traveled to the house again. "Nice place." The deck was furnished with a high-end barbecue grill and expensive-looking outdoor patio furniture, with pots of flowering plants and herbs arranged attractively around the edges.

He swiveled his head, following her gaze to the house. "It's not bad. Who would have thought, when I was living out of my car nine years ago, that I'd end up with a place like this?"

Alice turned to him in surprise. "You lived in your car?"

"Just for a few weeks once when I was between crash pads. I did a lot of couch surfing in those days."

She wondered if that was why he'd offered to let her live here. Because he remembered what it was like to be poor and in need of a place to live.

Or maybe not. Maybe he just needed a dog sitter and she was reading too much into it.

"Come on." He jerked his head toward the house. "I'll show you around, and then we can get your stuff moved in."

Griffin had told her his guest room was fully furnished, so she'd put most of her belongings into a storage pod for the time being. Isaac and Diego had been so thrilled to be rid of her, they'd gladly carried her bed and dresser downstairs and loaded them into the pod for her. All she'd brought with her to Griffin's was her clothes, her books, and a few other sundries, which had easily fit into one carload.

Alice followed him across the lawn and through the sliding door, which led to an airy living room with an arched ceiling. A large sectional couch sat in one corner of the room, across from a huge television beside a central fireplace that divided the open space in half. On the far side of the fireplace was a dining room, and past that a hallway that presumably led to the bedrooms.

There wasn't a lot in the way of furniture or decorations, but what there was appeared carefully chosen to complement the space. Black and white patterned throw pillows livened up the neutral gray couch, with a couple of solid yellow ones thrown in to lend a pop of color that perfectly coordinated with a yellow vase squatting on a nearby console table. The cushions on the deck furniture were also yellow, bringing the outside indoors to make the space look bigger. It was all very HGTV, but it didn't have a lot of personality. There were no knickknacks or photographs, and very little of the sort of clutter that tended to build up in a lived-in home. The only signs the house was actually occupied were a dirty coffee mug and smoothie shaker on the coffee table, and a few scattered dog toys on the floor.

"It's gorgeous," Alice said, ruffling Taco's ears as her eyes traveled over the stylish but impersonal space.

Griffin shrugged like he didn't have an opinion. "I hired a decorator. We were midseason on *LV Gen* when I moved in and I didn't have time to furnish the place myself. Between work and the gym, I don't get to spend all that much time here, to be honest."

That explained why it felt more like a staged TV set than a real home. Alice was reassured to hear that he didn't spend much time at home. The less he was around, the less awkward she'd have to feel about intruding on his personal space.

He headed into the open-plan kitchen that was separated from the living room by a breakfast bar and gestured around him. "This is the kitchen, obviously."

That part of the house looked a little more lived in. There were dirty dishes in the sink and a fat tub of something called Stacked Protein on the counter next to the coffeemaker. The kitchen had been fully updated with shiny new appliances, stainless steel counters, and beechwood cabinets, and there was a breakfast nook at one end with booth seating around a small white table.

Taco started wriggling in Alice's arms, so she set him down on the tile floor. He sat himself at attention in the middle of the kitchen with his tail swishing like a windshield wiper and his attention focused intently on his owner.

"He thinks he's getting dinner," Griffin explained. "But he's not. It's too early." He reached into a canister on the counter and extracted a dog biscuit, waving it over Taco's head. "This is all you get, you glutton."

He tossed the biscuit in the air and Taco leaped up to catch it in his mouth.

"Anyway," Griffin said, pulling open the large Viking refrigerator as Taco wolfed down his treat, "I cleared some space for you in the fridge." The two bottom shelves were lined with matching plastic containers that all bore handwritten labels, but the one above it was empty. "The studio's got me on a diet for this movie I'm shooting next month, so I have these nutritionist-prepared meals delivered."

"That's pretty cool," Alice said. "Saves you from cooking."

"It's not as cool as it sounds. They're mostly unsalted chicken breasts and plain vegetables. Maybe a little quinoa if I'm really lucky. Do not recommend."

"So they're not worth stealing. Noted."

He pulled open the pantry door. "I cleared some space for you in here too. That's where I keep Taco's food, so he gets real excited whenever you open it. Just FYI."

Indeed, the dog had begun spinning in excited circles, racing from the pantry to his food bowl and back again.

"How often do you feed him?" Alice asked.

"Twice a day, but you don't have to worry about that yet. I'll do it until I leave."

"I can start helping out now that I'm here."

"Nah, don't worry about it." Griffin shut the pantry and strode out of the kitchen. "Your room's this way."

Alice followed him through the dining room and down a hallway to the back of the house. "My room's down there," he said, pointing to a doorway at the far end of the hall. "Laundry room's the second door on the right." He turned to face her, hooking a thumb at the open door on his immediate right. "The guest bathroom is yours. Towels are in the cabinet next to the shower."

Alice peeked through the doorway and caught a glimpse of clean white lines and shiny jade green counters. A glass door at the far end of the bathroom opened directly onto the deck, presumably affording the same stunning view as the living room and dining room when the shade was raised. Alice would not be raising the shade.

"And this is your room." Griffin opened the door directly across from the bathroom and she followed him into the guest bedroom she'd be living in for the next four months. "It's not the biggest or the brightest room in the house, but I hope it's okay."

The single window was high and narrow above a double bed topped with a crisp white duvet and cheerful turquoise pillow shams. There was a Scandinavian-style dresser on one wall and a small matching desk opposite, beside a pair of frosted-glass closet doors. Like the rest of the house, it was attractive, but in a sterile, elegant way, like a hip boutique hotel.

"It's amazing," Alice said. "Seriously. I love it."

"Cool. Let's go get your stuff, then."

Thirty minutes later, the two of them had carried all of Alice's stuff into Griffin's house. Boxes of books, food, toiletries, and shoes cluttered the floor of the formerly neat little guest room, while mountains of clothes and plastic coat hangers covered the bed. Griffin leaned in the doorway, surveying the chaos.

"Don't worry," Alice told him, unzipping a suitcase stuffed with hoodies and T-shirts. "I'll have it cleaned up by tomorrow."

"Whatever," he said with a shrug. "It's your room. You can do what you want with it."

"Thank you for your help. And for letting me stay here."

"You're gonna stop thanking me at some point, right?"

"Probably not."

He shook his head, smiling. "Okay, well, make yourself at home. And let me know if you need anything."

Alice spent the whole afternoon and evening in her room unpacking, venturing out only a couple times to get herself a glass of water and use the bathroom. Griffin spent most of the day watching basketball in the living room, then went outside to sit on the deck. He was out there when she went into the bathroom, and she heard him muttering to himself. Peeking through the window in the door, she saw him sitting with his back to her, holding a script in his hand—memorizing his lines apparently.

At ten thirty he retired to his room, calling out a good night as he passed her door. Alice waited five more minutes before padding quietly out of her room. Griffin's door was cracked, and yellow lamplight spilled out into the darkened hall from his bedroom. She ducked into the guest bathroom to brush her teeth and wash her face, then scurried back to her room, closing and locking the door behind her before changing into pajamas and getting in bed.

Alice lay in the strange bed in the strange room of the strange house and tried to make herself relax. She was used to hearing the noise of the city around her, but it was eerily quiet up here in the hills. No, not quiet, she amended as an owl hooted somewhere outside. All this nature around her made a different kind of noise than she was used to: trees rustled in the wind, crickets chirped, and some sort of night bird tweeted its head off outside her window. It was going to take some getting used to—along with everything else.

It was weird to think about the fact that Griffin Beach was lying in his bed just down the hall. She wondered if he slept in pajamas or just his underwear—or maybe naked. Surely he wouldn't do that with her in the house, would he? Not with his door open, anyway.

Wind rattled the window above the bed, and Alice pulled the duvet up under her chin, trying to shake off the sense of unease. She suspected she wouldn't be able to fully relax until Griffin left in a few weeks.

She heard the click-clack of Taco's paws on the hardwood

floor outside her room, followed by a snuffling at the crack under the door. He pawed at the wood and let out a pitiful whine.

"Taco! Cut it out!" Griffin called from his room. "Let her alone."

Alice rolled over on her side, pulling her knees up to her chest, and tried to sleep.

IT'S NOT LIKE YOU'VE NEVER HAD A ROOMMATE BEFORE, ALICE reminded herself as she lay in bed on her first morning in Griffin's house. She'd been awake since the crack of dawn, thanks to the damn birds that had started chirping at some ungodly hour, as if they were calling forth the sun with their cacophonous racket.

She hadn't wanted to be the first one up for fear of waking Griffin, so she'd stayed in bed, trying to pretend everything was normal. Except nothing about this was normal. Griffin was a heck of a lot richer, and hotter, and more famous than any roommate she'd ever had. How was she supposed to act normal around all that?

It was one thing to interact with him at work—literally her whole job consisted of pretending to act normal around actors —but that was in a controlled setting where there were rules in place to guide everyone's behavior and she knew exactly what was expected of her. It was also for a limited amount of time each day. Sure, when the shooting days stretched to fourteen hours it could feel like forever, but there was always an end in sight, when she could go home and relax.

There was no more relaxing for her at home now. There was just more tiptoeing around and trying not to get in Griffin's way, stretching out forever.

No, not forever. Just for a few more weeks, until he left for

Atlanta. Then she'd have this awesome house all to herself. Three whole months on her own, living in luxury without the stress of paying rent. She just had to survive the next few weeks first.

She heard Taco scurry down the hall past her bedroom, followed a moment later by Griffin's shuffling footsteps. Alice got up and quietly made her bed, laying out the pillows exactly as they'd been arranged yesterday when she arrived. The kitchen shared a wall with her bedroom closet, and she could hear Griffin opening and closing cabinets on the other side. She sat on the corner of the bed and tried to psych herself up to leave her room. Was she willing to walk around in front of him in her pajamas, or should she get dressed before going out there? Or maybe she should try to sneak into the bathroom first so she could take a shower before she had to interact with him?

While she was still deliberating, Griffin walked past her room again on his way back to his bedroom. Shortly thereafter, she heard water rushing through the pipes in the attic, which probably meant he'd started up his shower. Now was the perfect time for her to dash to the bathroom for a pee, which she really needed quite badly at this point. Once she was safely locked in the bathroom, she could hang out in there until she heard his water shut off, then take her own shower and get dressed for the day before she had to face him. It was the perfect plan.

Alice grabbed her clothes and a shower tote with all the toiletries she'd need, stepped out into the hall—and found herself face to face with Griffin.

Wearing nothing but a towel.

A towel that was sagging *dangerously* low on his hips and only just barely covering his man bits.

She froze, so startled she let the shower tote tip, dumping its contents all over the floor. "Damn," she muttered as she dropped to her knees to gather up her things, which at least gave her something to look at that wasn't Griffin and his sagging towel.

"Hey," he said sheepishly. "Morning."

"Morning," she said, trying to ignore his mostly naked— and extremely impressive—body.

Settle down. It's not like it's the first time you've seen his abs.

He'd done plenty of shirtless scenes on *Las Vegas General*, not to mention a cover of *Men's Health* last year that she may or may not have drooled over at the checkout stand.

This was just the first time she'd seen his abs *in person*— most of his shirtless scenes on *LV Gen* had been love scenes that didn't require background, so she'd only seen them when they aired on TV later. Turned out it was one thing to see Griffin Beach's abs on-screen or in an airbrushed photo, and something else entirely to see them standing two feet away from her *in the flesh*, with mere millimeters of sagging terrycloth hiding his unmentionables. Apparently they hadn't done that much airbrushing for the magazine cover. His six-pack was very real, as was his Adonis belt and the vein leading down to his —yeah. *Wow.*

Griffin squatted down to help her pick up her things, which unfortunately caused his towel to gap, exposing an alarming amount of skin on his muscular upper leg, all the way up to—

Alice tore her eyes away again, hoping he didn't notice her blushing as she accepted the bottle of shampoo he held out. She hurriedly shoved the rest of her stuff back into her tote and stood, trying to keep her eyes averted.

"Sorry." As Griffin got to his feet, he finally seemed to notice his towel wasn't covering him as well as it could and tugged it up higher on his hips, grimacing. "I promise I won't make a habit of parading around the house in a towel. I just realized as I was about to get in the shower that I left my clothes in the dryer."

"It's fine." Alice shuffled her feet, looking everywhere but at Griffin.

"I put on a pot a coffee. Help yourself when it's ready."

"Cool. Thanks."

"I'm just gonna—" He hooked a thumb over his shoulder, backing away toward the laundry room.

"Yep," Alice said, "me too," and fled into the bathroom.

six

WELL, *fuck.*

So much for trying not to make Alice uncomfortable.

He'd practically flashed her on her first morning here. *Great job, asshole.* The way her face had gone gray, she'd probably decided he was as much of a creeper as those freaks on Craigslist.

He really had not intended to strut around in front of her mostly naked. He just wasn't used to sharing his house with anyone. He'd lived alone for seven years and gotten used to doing things a certain way—like leaving his clean clothes in the laundry room.

He'd just have to be more careful, now that Alice was living here.

When Griffin reemerged from his bedroom fifteen minutes later—freshly showered and *fully* dressed this time—he heard the shower running in the guest bathroom and caught a whiff of something pleasant and tropical-smelling as he walked past the door. Mango, maybe, or peaches. Whatever it was, it smelled nice.

Still feeling like a bit of a heel, he went into the kitchen, poured himself a cup of coffee, and added a dollop of the depressing coconut milk creamer that was all he was allowed these days. God, he missed dairy. And sugar. And soft, fluffy white bread oozing with butter.

He spent a lot of time thinking about food these days. This diet the studio had him on was brutal. He'd foolishly thought he looked pretty good when he went up for this part—he'd kept off the weight he'd lost for *Troublemakers 4* and retained most of the muscle—but not good enough, apparently. They wanted even less body fat and more muscle definition, which meant force-feeding himself a lot of protein and not much else, on top of an aggressive bodybuilding program in the gym.

As he made his usual, depressing breakfast of poached eggs and sautéed spinach, Griffin reminded himself how much this project would do for his career. A *Jerry Duncan* film. Most actors would kill for a part in one of Duncan's movies. This project would make him or break him. If it was a hit, he'd be able to ride it to the next level of his career—but if it tanked, he'd be marked as box office poison and his film career would be over at thirty, before it had really gotten going.

No pressure or anything.

At least he had someone to look after Taco while he was away. That was one less thing to weigh on his mind—assuming he didn't scare Alice off before he left for Atlanta.

They only had to put up with each other for a few weeks, and then he'd be gone and she could have the house to herself. Surely he could cohabitate with someone for a few weeks.

Except he'd never lived with a woman before—not since his mom, anyway. All his previous roommates had been guys, and he'd never even had a girlfriend that lasted more than a few months.

Griffin didn't have room in his life for a full-time girlfriend, as he'd been angrily informed by the last two women he'd tried to have a relationship with. They'd both accused him of being selfish and self-involved, of ignoring their needs and putting them last. They hadn't been wrong either. He had done those things. He was a shitty boyfriend. But he wasn't willing to change his ways.

His career was his number-one priority and it demanded one hundred percent of his focus. Everything else had to come second. He barely had room in his life for a dog; no way did he need all the added trouble and obligations of a girlfriend. Besides, he liked being on his own without having to answer to anyone else. Why would he want to give up all that freedom?

These days Griffin kept his "relationships" to fleeting encounters and temporary hookups. He rarely even brought the women he slept with back to his house—he had to be careful who he gave his address and wifi password to—but it wasn't like he was a dick about it. He always made it clear right off the bat that he wasn't looking for anything serious or long term, and sought out women who were fine with that.

Maybe one day he'd be ready to settle down, but not now. He was only thirty, and he had other priorities. It wasn't fair to invite someone into his life, then expect her to be okay with taking a back seat to everything else—so he simply didn't invite women into his life.

The irony that he had literally just invited a woman to move in wasn't lost on him. But he wasn't inviting her into his *life*. Just his guest room—and just temporarily. It was a mutually beneficial business arrangement, that was all.

When he noticed Taco rouse himself from his post-breakfast nap and scamper across the kitchen floor, Griffin threw a glance over his shoulder and saw Alice standing by the pantry. "Hey."

"Hey," she answered back, bending over to pet the dog butting against her legs. Her long blonde hair was still wet, and hung in damp waves around her face.

Griffin turned back to the stove, pushing his spinach around the pan. "You sleep okay?"

"Yeah. Great."

"The bed's comfortable enough for you?"

"It's awesome. Better than mine."

He set the spatula down and turned to face her, ready to eat crow. "I'm really sorry about this morning. It won't happen again."

She turned her face away, but not quick enough to hide the blush that spread across her freckled cheeks. "It's no big deal."

He hoped she wasn't trying to use background work to break into acting, because that poker face of hers was going to be a real obstacle. "I'm not used to having another person around," he said. "But I'll try to quit leaving my clothes in the laundry room."

"It's fine. Whatever."

Griffin turned back to the stove and pushed his spinach around some more. "There's coffee if you want it."

"Cool. Thanks."

"Mugs are in the cabinet to the left of the sink." He watched Alice as she picked out a mug. Her wide blue eyes and heart-shaped face were strikingly pretty, but she didn't carry herself like someone who thought she was beautiful. Instead, she acted like someone who preferred not to be noticed at all. "I don't have any dairy," he said, looking back down at his spinach, "but there's coconut milk creamer in the fridge."

"I usually take it black."

"Smart. The coconut creamer tastes like children's tears and shattered dreams."

Griffin was pretty sure he almost caught a glimpse of a smile before Alice hid it behind her coffee mug, which he took as a promising sign he hadn't scarred her forever.

"You want some eggs?" he offered. "I can throw another couple in to poach if you want."

"No thanks, I'm good." Alice took a packet of off-brand toaster pastries out of the pantry and ripped it open.

"*That's* your breakfast?" he said with undisguised horror. "Pop-Tarts?"

"Yeah." She tore off a paper towel and carried it, her fake Pop-Tarts, and her coffee to the breakfast table, with Taco trotting hopefully at her heels.

Griffin dished his six poached eggs and spinach onto a plate and joined her at the table. He felt Alice's eyes on him as he dug into his breakfast. When he glanced at her, she quickly glanced away.

The silence between them set him on edge. He always felt the need to fill silences when he was around other people, and he resented having to do it over breakfast in his own kitchen. Especially when he wasn't even sure it would be appreciated.

Alice had never seemed to want all that much to do with him, to be honest. Not that she was unfriendly, exactly. Just…indifferent.

Griffin wasn't used to indifference—particularly from women. His presence usually inspired a lot more gushing, eyelash batting, and hopeful flirting than the polite distance Alice projected at him. It was unnerving. Not that he expected every straight woman he met to throw herself at him, but… well…they kind of did. He was a friendly, flirty guy, and people usually responded to that. It wasn't just the opposite sex either. He was likable, dammit. Everyone liked him.

Alice was a tougher nut to crack. He couldn't figure out how she felt about him. She was so reserved most of the time —almost wary, like she was expecting him to turn into an asshole at any moment. It made him want to win her over. To show her what a great guy he was. Prove to her how cool and approachable he was.

He'd been told by a therapist once that he suffered from a pathological need to please, stemming from childhood abandonment issues. Whatever. It bugged him that Alice didn't seem to like him and he didn't understand why.

That was part of the reason he'd started asking her to walk Taco in the first place. She was crazy about the damn dog. Whenever Griffin brought Taco around, Alice went from merely polite to downright enthusiastic. She cooed and cuddled and doted on that dumb dog. It felt like a win every time the dog got a smile out of her.

She didn't have to like him as long as she liked Taco, and she *loved* Taco.

"You sure you don't want some?" Griffin asked, twirling soggy green tendrils of spinach on his fork. "There's more spinach on the stove."

Alice made a face. "Not everyone likes spinach for breakfast, Popeye."

"Believe me, this isn't by choice."

"I don't know how you stand it."

He shrugged. He definitely didn't love all the dieting, but he could still remember what it felt like not to know where his next paycheck was coming from. It made it hard to consider his current situation a hardship. "It helps that I get paid a lot of money to stand it. You can get used to anything if you have to."

Alice looked down at her shitty Pop-Tart guiltily. "Having my food around the house isn't going to make it harder for you, is it? I don't want to lead you into temptation or anything."

Griffin snorted as he scooped up a bite of eggs. "Believe me, your sad, knockoff Pop-Tarts aren't that much of a temptation."

"Well, just let me know if it ever bothers you."

"I'm more bothered by what you're doing to your body eating that crap."

She stiffened like he'd hit a nerve. "My body is my own business."

He held his hands up in a gesture of surrender. "Fair enough. I'm just saying, if you ever want to borrow any protein or vegetables or actual food or anything, just let me know."

"Believe it or not, your sad breakfast spinach isn't much of a temptation."

They fell into another silence, and this time Griffin decided to just roll with it without forcing conversation. It was Alice who spoke up a minute later.

"Hey, um…"

He looked up, his mouth full of egg.

"Is it okay if we don't tell anyone at work about this arrangement?"

He swallowed. "Yeah, sure. If that's what you want."

"It's just that it might be kind of weird. I don't want anyone to start treating me different or anything."

"Of course. Mum's the word." He made a zipping motion across his lips. "Secret roommates it is."

After he'd forced himself to eat as much as he could stand, Griffin carried his plate to the sink and scraped the remains down the drain. He flipped on the disposal, but instead of grinding, it made a dull humming sound. He flipped it off and leaned over to peer down the drain. Flipped it on again. More humming but no grinding.

"Dammit." He flipped the switch on and off a few more times, hoping it would magically fix itself.

"What's wrong?" Alice asked.

"Damn disposal's broken." He peered down into the drain again, but couldn't see anything past the spinach.

She shoved the last bite of Pop-Tart in her mouth and came over to stand next to him at the sink. "Is something stuck in there?"

Griffin shook his head, straightening. "Not that I can see."

As Alice leaned over to peer into the drain, he got another whiff of that fruity shampoo she used. Definitely peaches.

He edged away before she noticed his gratuitous hair sniff-ing. "I'll have to call a plumber." Which was going to be a pain in the ass because he was on the call sheet every day this week and wouldn't be home to let a plumber in, which meant they'd have to live with a broken disposal until his next day off.

"I might be able to fix it."

"Really?" Griffin asked, hopeful but also skeptical.

"Maybe." Alice waved him away from the sink so she could open the cabinet underneath. "Don't suppose you know where the wrench that came with this thing is?"

He was embarrassed to admit that he had no idea his garbage disposal was supposed to come with a wrench, but he did remember a bunch of random hardware and instruction manuals that had been left in a drawer when he moved in. He dug around in it until he found a silver Allen wrench. "This it?" he asked, holding it out to Alice, who knelt on the floor, clearing a space around the disposal.

"That's it." She extended a hand and he slapped it into her palm the way she'd done dozens of times to him on set with medical instruments.

Twisting around so she was lying on her back with her head in the cabinet, she stuck the wrench into the underside of the disposal. Griffin squatted beside her for a better look as he kept Taco from climbing into the cabinet with her, but couldn't really see what she was doing. After a minute or two of fiddling, she nodded at him and said, "Try it now."

He flipped the switch and the disposal roared to life. "What kind of witchcraft?" he asked in amazement.

She squirmed out from under the sink. "It's an easy fix, actually."

"How?" He held out a hand to help her off the floor, and she let him pull her upright.

"There's a socket on the underside that you can use to

unjam the flywheel." She gave him back the Allen wrench with a shrug.

"Are you kidding me?" He shook his head as he dropped the wrench back in the drawer, amazed that the solution had been in there all along, unbeknownst to him. "Last time that happened I paid a plumber two hundred bucks to come out and fix it."

"Then you got screwed out of two hundred bucks."

"No shit." He smiled. "Thanks."

Alice smiled back and saluted him with her coffee cup. "No problem."

Griffin watched her shuffle out of the room, feeling like he'd just won his first game in a tennis match.

ONCE THE WORK WEEK STARTED, ALICE DIDN'T ACTUALLY SEE all that much of Griffin around the house—which was perfectly fine with her.

Monday morning, for example, Alice was up and gone by seven before Griffin had even stirred. He rolled on set around lunchtime, she was released at four in the afternoon, and he didn't get home until nearly midnight when she was already in bed. The next day was the opposite: Griffin was already gone at nine a.m. when Alice got up, and she didn't see him until her call time a few hours later. He wrapped for the day at six, she was stuck on set for another five hours, and by the time she got home he was snoring away in his bedroom. That was one of the only things she'd learned about him in their first few days as roommates: Griffin Beach snored.

It went on like that for pretty much the whole week, with the two of them passing like trains headed in opposite directions. Even when their shooting schedules overlapped, they didn't see each other much because, true to his word, Griffin kept his distance from her at work and didn't let on that they were roommates.

Alice took full advantage of the times she had the house to herself by poking around and getting more comfortable with the place. She learned her way around Griffin's kitchen, figured out how to work the television and sound system, and got up close and personal with his washer and dryer. The only place she didn't venture was into his bedroom. Not that she wasn't curious, but if she wanted him to respect her privacy, she should probably respect his.

Their main form of communication was via Post-it notes that Griffin left in the kitchen for her:

There's hot coffee in the thermos.

Went to the gym. Back in an hour.

The cleaning lady is coming today at 9:00. Don't be naked!

Alice responded by leaving her own Post-its for him:

Picked up more of that coconut milk creamer you love so much.

I fed Taco already. Don't let him talk you into 2nd breakfast.

The house smells like vinegar because I descaled the coffeemaker.

Making herself helpful around the house was her way of saying thank you and apologizing for invading his space. It was the best way she could think of to show her appreciation for the favor he'd done her by letting her move in with him. She'd never learned to cook, but she was handy in other ways. She figured as long as she could keep making herself useful, maybe her presence wouldn't be too much of an imposition.

The more familiar she got with the house, the more she found to do. And for each task completed, she left another Post-it to keep Griffin in the loop:

Gave Taco a bath.

Replaced the water filter in the fridge.

Cleaned the exhaust fan above the stove.

Her Post-its disappeared without provoking a negative response, so she assumed he didn't mind. She *hoped* he was pleased.

By Saturday morning, Alice was feeling more settled as she sat on the back deck enjoying the view over her morning coffee. Griffin had yet to arise, since he'd been stuck shooting on location until some ungodly hour. She'd heard him creep past her bedroom when he finally made it home in the wee hours, his efforts at stealth undermined by the excited pitter-patter of Taco's claws on the hardwood.

The dog was currently dozing beside her after running around peeing on every bush in the yard earlier. Alice stretched her legs out, pointing her toes as she lay back in the comfy lounge chair. Her laptop sat untouched on the table beside her, glowering at her as she sipped her coffee.

She'd finally worked up the courage to respond to Dr. Frazier's last email. Now that her living situation was settled, it was time for Alice to deal with her dissertation—and that meant facing her advisor. They were meeting on Monday morning first thing, and sometime between now and then Alice needed to dust off the research she'd been ignoring for months and reorient herself. At this point she couldn't even remember where she'd left off or how much she still had to do. She needed to be prepared to answer Dr. Frazier's questions and explain why she hadn't made any progress.

Easier said than done. Alice still had no idea what she was going to say when they met on Monday. The truth? Which could spark a Title IX investigation that would drag on for months, putting Alice through hell and making her the center of a maelstrom of negative attention that could possibly end her academic career before it started. Or some sort of lie? Which was a coward's way out that would allow Gilchrist to go right on doing what he was doing and getting away with it.

Both options made Alice feel sick to her stomach.

She was on her second cup of coffee without yet working up the courage to open her laptop when the sliding door to her right opened. Taco scampered over as Griffin stepped out of his bedroom, squinting at the bright sunlight in a rumpled white T-shirt and pair of plaid pajama pants—which answered her speculation about his sleep attire of choice. *Whew.*

"Hey." His sleep-roughened voice was an octave lower than usual, and far sexier than Alice was prepared for. The whole *just rolled out of bed* package was a lot to take in, frankly. How many women would give their left arm for a glimpse of him like this? And here Alice was with a front-row seat that was totally wasted on her.

"I didn't wake you, did I?" She'd tried to be quiet, but the only thing standing between her and his bedroom was five millimeters of sliding safety glass.

"Nah. You're fine." He straightened from petting Taco and sank into the chair next to Alice with a groan.

"What time did you wrap last night?" she asked.

He leaned back in the lounge chair and closed his eyes as he stretched his arms overhead. "Like three or something. Late."

It was impossible not to notice his bulging triceps—or the

rest of his body for that matter—when he was stretched out beside her like a centerfold model, in a T-shirt so thin it was practically transparent. Her gaze wandered over his torso, catching on a sliver of exposed stomach that reminded her of the magnificent abs that had been on full display her first morning in the house.

Alice looked away, feeling guilty for ogling Griffin when his guard was down. "You want some coffee? I made a pot."

He shook his head, sitting up as he rubbed his eyes. "I can get it."

She got to her feet and snatched her half-full cup off the table before he could move. "I need a refill anyway. Back in a mo."

As soon as she was safely inside, she blew out a long breath. *Act normal*, she instructed herself as she poured Griffin's coffee and added a dollop of coconut milk creamer. *You can do this. Just treat him like any other roommate.*

Except he wasn't like any other roommate. Aside from his unreasonable attractiveness, they weren't really roommates at all. Alice was the help, only here because she was doing a job for him. She occupied a second-class position in his house, just like she did on set. His employee, not his guest or his friend.

The work week had offered a nice respite, but now that it was the weekend they'd both be around the house for the next two days. Together. She needed to make some rules to help her cope.

Rule Number One was *no ogling him*. In addition to being not cool, it made it harder for her to *act normal*, which was Rule Number Two. No making this weirder than it already was by letting him know how uncomfortable she was. Just be cool. And Rule Number Three was *don't be a nuisance*. The more she could stay out of his way or at least make his life easier, the better.

When her pep talk was done, Alice carried the two fresh cups of coffee out to the deck. The urge to gather up her stuff and retreat to her room was strong, but she was afraid it would seem rude if she abandoned the deck as soon as he'd joined her. Besides, she couldn't hide in her room all weekend. She would have to interact with Griffin around the house sometimes, and now—when he clearly wasn't doing anything important—was as good a time as any.

"Thanks," he said when she set his coffee down next to him.

"You're welcome." She sank back onto the lounge chair, clutching her own mug in both hands.

His eyes slid her way as he reached for his coffee, lingering on her for what felt like an unnaturally long time before he settled back to gaze at the view in front of them. As soon as his eyes were off her, Alice let out a slow, silent breath.

"You making yourself at home?" Griffin asked after a short silence.

"Yeah."

"Good."

Another silence ballooned between them, feeling heavy and uncomfortable. They'd never had trouble making conversation on set, but Griffin was usually the effusive one. She didn't know what to do with this more subdued version of him.

"It's nice out here," Alice said, flailing to fill the silence before it became a *thing*.

"Yeah, it is. I don't get to enjoy it enough."

Was that a hint for her to shut up and go away? She eyed her computer, wondering if she should pack up and go inside. Or maybe she should open it up and pretend to work. Would that be rude? Or would it let him off the hook? She didn't want him to feel like he had to spend time with her or make conversation.

Ugh. Why were interpersonal interactions so hard?

"Hey, Alice?"

When she glanced his way there was a frown on his face. She swallowed. "Yeah?"

"You don't have to keep doing all that stuff around the house for me."

Shit. She'd already failed Rule Number Three apparently.

"Do you not like it?"

He sat up and swung his legs to the side so he was facing her. "No, it's great—but you don't have to do it. You know that, right?"

She lowered her eyes to her coffee cup, finding it too difficult to follow Rules One and Two with him looking at her like that. "You're not charging me rent. I have to do something to earn my keep." On top of giving her a place to live, Griffin had insisted on paying her for her dog-sitting duties once he left for Atlanta—at a rate far higher than she felt she deserved.

"You're going to be taking care of Taco and the whole house for me while I'm gone," he said. "That's plenty."

"Not for another month. I'm just trying to be helpful."

"I know, and I appreciate it, but I don't want you to think you *have* to."

"I don't want to be an imposition."

"You're not." He leaned across the distance between their chairs and tilted his head to catch her eye. "Okay?"

It was impossible not to smile with all that handsome earnestness directed right at her. "Okay."

"Cool." He pushed himself to his feet and stood up. "Thanks for the coffee. I'm gonna change and hit the gym."

Alice watched Griffin go back into his bedroom, realizing too late that she was staring at his ass in flagrant violation of Rule Number One—and right after he'd gone out of his way to be nice to her. There were only three rules, and so far she was failing massively at all of them.

Five minutes later, he reemerged through the living room door. He'd changed into a tank top and baggy athletic shorts, and had one of his ever-present smoothie shakers in his hand. He twirled his car keys on his index finger as he strode past on the way to his car. "Later."

"Have fun," Alice said, refusing to let herself stare at his exposed arms and shoulders.

"I definitely will not," he replied, throwing a wry grin over his shoulder. "But then it'll be done, and I can spend the rest of the day on the couch watching basketball."

That was exactly what he did when he came back three hours later. Alice was still outside, up to her eyeballs in the dissertation research she'd finally dived into—although she'd moved to the shade of the picnic table by then. Griffin greeted her as he walked into the house, and she managed not to gawk at the sweat glistening on his pumped-up muscles. He disappeared into his room, then reappeared freshly showered ten minutes later and collapsed onto the couch—where he stayed for pretty much the rest of the day.

The patio door was open between them, and the sound of the game floated outside to where Alice sat hunched over her computer on the scenic deck. Her dissertation might be a disaster, but she was lucky to have such a nice, peaceful place to work on it.

And her dissertation definitely *was* a disaster. So far, going back over it all had simply reinforced what she'd already known the last time she gave up: she was totally screwed.

There was no getting around the network analysis. Without it, she wouldn't be allowed to defend, much less pass. But she didn't know how to do it. Even after weeks of meeting with Gilchrist and enduring his gross attentions, she hadn't been any closer to grasping it. Every time she'd felt like she was starting to get it, he'd pointed out new problems in her data that would only succeed in confusing her more. Frankly, even if he hadn't turned out to be a disgusting human being, she wasn't sure she ever would have gotten the hang of it.

Maybe she was just stupid. Or had chosen the wrong field. Or been a fool to think she could handle a PhD in any field. Possibly all three.

Or maybe making her feel that way had been part of Gilchrist's plan all along. Maybe he'd hoarded his knowledge and made her confused to cement her dependency and guarantee she kept coming back.

Only she wasn't going back. If it was going to get done, she'd have to figure it out herself.

She could figure out complex social network modeling on her own in a weekend, right? Because that's what she was going to have to do. It was either that or quit.

And she wasn't ready to quit.

seven

GRIFFIN WAS HAVING A STRESS DREAM. It was the same one he always had, about being on set with the cameras rolling and not knowing any of his lines. When the director started shouting at him, he shot awake in his own bed, his heart racing and the pressure of an oncoming headache in his sinuses.

A glance at his phone told him it was four in the morning. Only two hours before he had to get up to make his early call. He rolled over, trying to get comfortable and will his body back to sleep, even though he knew it was probably hopeless at this point. That was when he noticed Taco wasn't in his usual spot on the bed.

As Griffin lay in the dark imagining all the trouble his dog might be getting into and debating whether to get up and investigate, he heard the sound of someone moving around in the kitchen. Followed by the excited patter of Taco's paws on the hardwood and a soft shush.

Alice must be up. But at four in the morning? He was pretty sure background weren't on the call sheet until the afternoon, so what was she doing awake this early?

Giving up his futile quest for more sleep, Griffin pushed himself upright and wandered out to the kitchen. Alice was ensconced in the booth at the breakfast table with her laptop open in front of her, just like it had been for most of the weekend.

Instead of looking up when Taco jumped up to greet Griffin, she turned her face away and swiped at her eyes. "Shit," she muttered in a rough voice. "I woke you up. I'm sorry."

Oh, no. Was she *crying*? Please, no. He wasn't prepared to deal with a woman he barely knew crying in his kitchen at four in the morning.

Silently cursing himself for not staying in bed, Griffin lifted his hand to cover a yawn and pretended not to notice the way Alice was hiding her face from him. "Nope. I've got stress dreams to thank for that." He turned his attention to the coffeemaker to avoid looking directly at her. "Is that coffee I smell?"

She nodded and started to get up. "I'll get you some."

He waved her off. "What'd I say about that? You don't need to wait on me." Every time she did something for him, it made him feel guilty, like he was taking advantage. She was supposed to be his guest, not his handyman or his housekeeper.

"Sorry."

He wished she'd stop apologizing too. It felt like she was apologizing for her existence, which made him worry that he'd given her reason to think she needed to. She had nothing to apologize for; she was already the most considerate, unobtrusive roommate he'd ever had. He just wanted her to relax, so he didn't have to add her to the list of things he was worried about.

Except now she was in his kitchen crying, and he had no idea what he was supposed to do about that. Ask her what was wrong? Or respect her privacy by acting like he hadn't noticed? What exactly was his obligation here?

See, this was why he preferred living alone.

Griffin rubbed his chest irritably as he selected a mug from the cabinet, still unused to sleeping in so many clothes. Normally, he preferred to sleep in the buff, but he'd adopted the T-shirt and pajamas when Alice moved in. If there was some kind of emergency in the middle of the night, he figured she didn't need him running around in his birthday suit.

"What's got you up so early?" he asked as he poured himself a cup of coffee. "Your call time's not until the afternoon." There. That would give her an opening to talk if she wanted to take it. Or not, if she preferred to keep her problems to herself.

"Couldn't sleep."

He heard a muffled sniffle as he added creamer to his cup —definitely crying, then—but by the time he slid into the seat across from her, the only evidence of tears was a slight pinkness around her nose and eyes. Sticking with plausible deniability, Griffin lifted his coffee cup and nodded at Alice's laptop as if he hadn't noticed the crying. "What're you working on?"

Her eyes lowered to the table. "My dissertation. I've got a meeting with my committee chair this morning."

Which could very well explain the crying. Griffin had never been much of a student, but he'd probably cry daily if he was expected to write a million-page research paper or whatever the fuck was involved in a dissertation.

Alice cast a quick glance at him before staring back down at the tabletop. "It's our first meeting in months, and I'm dreading it."

He leaned over to scratch Taco's back. "Why?"

"Because I haven't made any progress since the last time we met, which was…way too long ago."

"What's it on?"

Alice sighed, pushing her laptop away. "Gender differences

in language used to describe political candidates in newspaper articles."

"Impressive."

"It might be, except I can't finish it."

"Why not?"

Her shoulders lifted in a tense shrug. "A lot of reasons."

Griffin debated whether to drop the subject or keep pressing. How involved did he really want to get in Alice's problems? This was just meant to be a temporary, mutually beneficial business arrangement. The less they knew about each other, the better, maybe. He had enough anxiety without taking on hers too.

Except he wasn't a total selfish prick, despite what his last girlfriend thought of him—or at least he liked to think he wasn't. Did he really want to be a guy who turned his back on a crying woman at four o'clock in the morning?

He set his coffee mug down and tilted his head to catch Alice's eye. "I know I'm not smart enough to understand it, but you could try explaining the problem to me anyway. It might help to talk it through with someone."

"It's not that complicated, really. It's…" She trailed off and pressed her lips together, turning her face to the window.

"What?"

"There's this professor on my dissertation committee, and I need his help to finish some of the models, but I can't work with him anymore."

"Why not?"

Her fingers gripped the edge of the table, but she didn't say anything.

Griffin took a stab in the dark. "Were you two…involved?"

Her lip curled in revulsion. "No."

"Did he do something to you?"

"Not exactly."

Griffin sipped his coffee and waited.

"He makes me uncomfortable," Alice said finally.

"What do you mean?"

She got up to pour herself more coffee and Taco followed her. "He seemed nice at first. Really friendly and helpful. My advisor was on sabbatical last year, and Dr. Gilchrist agreed to work with me while she was gone. I needed his help to do a network analysis for my dissertation, and he's the network analysis expert in the department. We'd meet in his office once a week to talk. It was fine the first few times. He had a lot of helpful advice. But then he started to get too friendly." Her shoulders hunched, heavy with tension.

Griffin felt a knot form in his stomach. "Too friendly how?"

She turned to face him, clutching her coffee mug in front of her, but didn't meet his eye. "Resting his hand on my shoulder or my knee. Complimenting me on what a good job I did 'taking care of' my body. Telling me stories about his sex life and asking questions about mine."

"Gross." Griffin had been the subject of some unwanted touching and uncomfortable compliments in the course of his acting career and knew how unsettling it could be. "What a pig."

Alice nodded, keeping her eyes on the dog who sat at her feet wagging his tail. "I tried to laugh it all off so he wouldn't be offended, and I hated myself for it. I felt so ashamed that I was sitting there pretending to laugh when I really wanted to scream at him to get the fuck away from me. It got to where I was terrified of being alone with him, which made me feel even more ashamed. Eventually I just stopped going —to his meetings, to campus, to all of it. I tried to keep working on my dissertation but I still needed his help to finish, and by that point the whole thing made me feel sick. Even just looking at the data files made me nauseous. So I quit. I let him make me quit. And that made me even more ashamed."

Griffin swallowed, at a loss for what to say. "Did you tell anyone what was going on?"

She let out a bitter laugh. "Tell them what? That he was flirting with me? It's not exactly a crime."

"It doesn't sound like flirting to me. Flirting's not supposed to make you feel bad."

"No, it's not." Alice shook her head. "It's not that easy to explain though. It's like death by a thousand paper cuts. No one single thing he ever did was that bad, so you have to keep asking yourself if you're overreacting. It's just a little thing, right? It's not *that* big a deal. But when it keeps happening, you start to wonder if it's all in your head, or if it's your fault somehow."

"It's definitely not your fault."

She was silent, gazing into the coffee mug she'd refilled and had yet to drink from.

"Alice." He waited for her to look at him. "It's not your fault," Griffin repeated. "And it's not in your head."

For a second he thought she was going to start crying again. Instead she turned around and dumped her coffee in the sink. "I can't drink any more caffeine. I'm giving myself heart palpitations."

Griffin waited while she washed the mug out, dried it, and put it back in the cabinet. When she was done, she came back and sat down across from him. Taco followed her and lay down on the floor at their feet.

"What are you going to do?" Griffin asked when Alice didn't say anything else.

"I don't know. I thought maybe I could teach myself what I needed to know to run the remaining models. That's what I've been trying to do all weekend. But I can't get them to work right and I have no idea why. I'm screwed."

"And you haven't told your advisor about any of this?"

"She was on sabbatical. I've been avoiding her since she got back."

"But you're meeting with her today, right? Are you going to tell her?"

Alice stared out the window. The sky was just starting to lighten in the east, revealing the silhouette of the trees outside. "I don't know. I don't know what she'll do, or if she'll even believe me. But I don't know what else to tell her either. I think I might just quit."

"You mean drop out of graduate school?"

Alice raised one shoulder and let it fall in a halfhearted shrug. "I don't want to stay in academia anymore, so what's the point?"

"To finish your PhD so you can make everyone call you Dr. Carlisle, obviously. Haven't you been working toward this for like four years?"

She pressed her lips together. "Five. Plus four years of undergrad."

Griffin tapped his fingers against his coffee mug. He definitely didn't think Alice should let this one asshole make her quit school and give up on her dreams, but he wasn't sure what she should do instead. The whole situation was seriously shitty. "Is your advisor friends with this guy?"

"I don't know. Maybe. They're in the same department."

"You think she'll try to defend him?"

"I don't know."

The agitation in Alice's tone made Griffin pause before asking his next question. "What's the worst that could happen if you tell her?"

"I won't graduate."

"You're dropping out anyway. What do you have to lose?" Maybe it wasn't his place to question her, but she'd opened up to him. He couldn't help feeling she needed to talk all this through with someone. That part of the reason it had paralyzed her was that she hadn't felt able to tell anyone what she was going through. If she could talk to him about it, maybe she could talk to her advisor too. Maybe someone would do something to put a stop to this guy.

Alice's shoulder shifted in an uncomfortable fidget. "If she does believe me, she could initiate a Title IX investigation."

Griffin was confused. "Isn't that good? Don't you want him investigated?"

"Do you know what an investigation is like?"

"No."

"They'll interview me, him, and everyone we know. All my professors and the rest of my cohort, all his colleagues and friends on campus. They'll all know what's going on, and be asked to give an official statement about it. What they think of me, what they think of him. Who they believe. And then you know what'll happen?"

She paused for him to answer, and Griffin shook his head. He had no clue how these things worked.

"Nothing." Alice practically spat the word out. "They'll decide they don't have enough information to support the report, because it's just my word against his, and that'll be the end of it." She scowled down at the table. "My academic career will be ruined, and his will barely even be tarnished."

Griffin didn't know what to say, so he didn't say anything. Instead, he got up and went to the pantry. He got out a canister of flour and the baking powder, and carried them over to the counter. Then he went to the fridge for eggs, milk, and butter.

"What are you doing?" Alice asked when he got down his mother's old batter bowl and started measuring out the flour.

"I'm making you pancakes." He dropped four tablespoons of butter into a small glass bowl and threw a glance over his shoulder. "You like pancakes, don't you?"

Alice came over to stand beside him at the counter where he was working. "You don't have to do that."

"I know." He started for the microwave but she stepped in front of him.

"Griffin." She was frowning at him.

He waved her away impatiently. "Whenever I was upset about something, my mom would always make me pancakes. I may not be able to eat pancakes, but I can still cook 'em. And you seem like you could use some pancakes this morning."

Alice stared at him for a long moment like she wasn't sure what to say. Then she stepped aside so he could get to the microwave. He moved past her and put the butter in to melt.

"Can I at least help?"

"Can you cook?" Griffin asked. Not that he planned to let her help; he was just curious.

"Not really."

He grinned and nodded at the fridge. "Why don't you get out the syrup and let me handle the rest."

Alice retrieved the bottle of maple syrup from the door of the fridge and carried it to the table. While Griffin preheated the griddle and finished measuring out the ingredients, she sat back down and watched him in silence.

At least now he knew why she'd always seemed so stand-offish with him. He felt bad about all the times he'd innocently flirted with her. He hadn't meant anything by it. He'd just wanted her to like him. But now he worried he might have touched her on the arm or the shoulder without considering whether it was welcome. He didn't think so, but he couldn't be sure. He was a toucher by nature, and he had a tendency to touch his friends when he talked to them. He'd never really thought about how an innocent gesture could be used to coerce or intimidate someone. How a woman who'd experienced harassment might see his actions as a threat.

"So all this stuff," Griffin said as he stirred the pancake batter, "this guy. That's why you were so reluctant to move in here, right? You were nervous about living with me."

"I guess." When he looked over at her she was chewing on her thumbnail. Alice didn't wear fingernail polish like most of the other extras and actresses. Her fingernails were always short and bare and plain. Natural.

He poured two pancakes out on the griddle. "I don't think you should drop out of school," he ventured while he waited for the bubbles to appear around the edge. "Whatever you decide to do, I don't think it should be that."

There was a long silence, broken only by the sound of the pancakes sizzling on the griddle. Griffin got a fork and knife out of the drawer, and carried them over to the table along with the butter.

"Do you think I should tell my advisor the truth?" Alice asked, looking up at him.

He shrugged one of his shoulders. "Only you can make that call."

"What if she doesn't believe me? Or tells Dr. Gilchrist what I said about him? I'll be finished in my field before I even graduate."

"More finished than you'd be if you quit on your own?"

Her chin jutted out. "At least I'd be quitting on my own terms."

"What do you think the odds are this is the first time this guy has ever done this to a student?"

Alice looked away, and Griffin went back to the stove. When the pancakes were ready, he put them on a plate and set it down in front of her.

She bit down on her lower lip as she stared at them. "Thank you."

"It's nothing," he said with a shrug. "Really. Pancakes are easy. And I like to cook, even when I can't eat." He went back to the stove and poured two more pancakes out on the griddle. He figured he'd make the whole batch and Alice could freeze whatever she didn't eat for later.

While the pancakes were cooking, Griffin went and sat down across from her at the table.

He ran his thumb around the rim of his coffee mug as he watched her eat. "You're not scared of *me*, are you?"

She stabbed at her pancakes and shook her head. "Course not."

"Alice," he said quietly, and she looked up at him. "I'm not like that creepy professor guy. I would never do something like that to you. I just want to make sure you know that."

Her teeth worried at her lower lip as she nodded. "I know."

"If I ever do *anything* that makes you feel the slightest bit uncomfortable, I want you to tell me, and I promise I'll stop. Deal?"

She nodded again. "Deal." Her mouth curved in a faint smile and she gestured at her plate with her fork. "These are really good pancakes."

"I know. I happen to be an awesome cook." He got to his feet again and went to flip the pancakes.

"You're a pretty awesome roommate too."

"Damn right I am." He smiled to himself as he finished cooking up the rest of the pancake batter.

eight

ALICE'S HEART started racing as soon as she pulled into the student parking lot. She could see the building that housed the sociology offices from here: Eaton Hall. That was where Dr. Frazier's office was, on the second floor.

And at the far end of the corridor, eight offices away, was Dr. Gilchrist's office.

This was a huge mistake. She never should have agreed to come here. She should have asked Dr. Frazier to meet her for coffee off campus instead. She could have pled work obligations, or made up some sort of personal hardship. She could have gotten a pair of crutches and one of those medical boots and said she'd broken her ankle. That all the walking and stairs on campus were too much for her. Maybe she'd been mugged and that's why she'd been truant. She could say she was still traumatized.

She *was* still traumatized. That much was clear from the fact that she'd been sitting in her car for five minutes, clenching the steering wheel in a white-knuckled grip as she made up increasingly ridiculous excuses not to be here.

But she was here. She'd come this far. It was too late to get out of it. She was already doing it. She just needed to take the last few steps.

Step one: get out of the car.

She tried to hold on to what Griffin had said this morning —what was the worst that could happen? Could it really be any worse than it already was? No matter what the outcome was, she had to think she'd feel better once she'd faced the problem. Close the chapter and move on, one way or another.

Talking it through with someone finally after months of keeping it bottled up had helped a little. Alice already felt better after opening up to Griffin. Maybe even strong enough to face whatever happened after today's meeting.

As soon as she opened her car door, the familiar smell of campus hit her like a face full of cold water. The air had always smelled different around the university. Maybe it was all the green spaces and limited traffic, or maybe it was the food processing plant a half mile away. Whatever it was, Alice had used to love it. It had smelled like academia to her. Lectures and syllabi and bibliographies—all the things that had made her want to go to graduate school.

Now it smelled like dread. Dr. Gilchrist had soured it for her. Twisted it into something that made her feel sick.

But she was out of the car. She was standing in the parking lot with her bag on her shoulder. Progress. Now for step two: walking to the sociology building.

That part wasn't too bad. It was a pleasant walk on a pleasant morning, with a pleasant backdrop of hills spread out in front of her. They dwarfed Eaton Hall, making it seem small and insignificant by comparison.

Alice used the short walk to calm herself down. Concentrating on the repetition of her stride, she took long, slow breaths of fresh air. It helped a little, but the walk wasn't long enough for her to fully get out of her own head. She was at the door to Eaton Hall before she knew it.

She might have stood there for a long time trying to work up the courage to go in, except someone happened to come out just as she was approaching the door, and they held it open for her. It was a student, but no one she'd ever seen before. A whole new freshman class and graduate cohort had arrived since the last time Alice had set foot on campus.

Inside the building, she felt a fresh wave of nausea at the familiar, musty office smell. Her anxiety only increased as she stepped into the stairway and trudged up to the second floor. She was terrified of meeting someone she knew—someone who would ask her where she'd been. Fortunately, it was still an hour before the first classes of the morning started, and the halls were mostly deserted.

She took the long way around to avoid walking past Gilchrist's office. Most of the office doors were closed. Not many professors were in yet this time of morning. Dr. Frazier's door was one of the only ones open. Alice paused just outside and knocked on the doorframe.

Dr. Regina Frazier looked up and smiled. "Alice." She'd changed her hair over sabbatical. It used to be cut in a short afro shot through with gray, but now she wore long black braids that were gathered into a ponytail at the back of her neck.

"Hi," Alice said meekly.

"Come in. Sit down." Dr. Frazier motioned to a chair.

Alice took one of the hard wooden chairs in front of the desk. It felt like being in an interrogation room. Like there should be a bare light bulb casting harsh shadows and a panel of one-way glass set into the wall. Except the lights were the same dull fluorescents as the rest of the building, and the walls of Dr. Frazier's office were covered with framed diplomas and artwork drawn by her kids.

"I've been worried about you." Dr. Frazier leaned back in her chair, offering a kind smile. "You disappeared on us." Her face was soft and round, and her ebony skin glowed warmly in the sunlight filtering in through the narrow office window.

"Sorry." Alice dropped her eyes to the floor. "I had some personal stuff."

"So you mentioned in your email. Are you okay?"

"Yeah. It's just been hard to prioritize school." That wasn't a lie, technically. It had been hard to prioritize school over her fear of coming to school.

Dr. Frazier nodded and threaded her fingers together in front of her on the desk. "How can I help? What can we do to get you back on track?"

"Um…" Alice had rehearsed what she was going to say a dozen times in her head, but now that she was here the words stuck in her throat.

Dr. Frazier leaned forward, eyebrows slightly raised, and waited.

"Actually…" Alice took a breath and tried to will her voice to steadiness. "I think I need to drop out of the program."

She'd been going back and forth on it all morning, and that was what she'd finally decided. She felt like a coward, especially after Griffin had encouraged her not to quit school, but she just didn't want to deal with any of this anymore. She was tired of living with this big black cloud hanging over her. She wanted to be free of it, even if that meant taking the quitter's way out.

Dr. Frazier blinked and pulled her head back. "Why?"

"It's complicated."

"I'm sure it is, but you've put in so much hard work to get here and you're so close to finishing. It would be a real shame to quit now."

Alice looked down at her lap. "I've decided not to go into academia after all."

"When did you decide this?"

"It's something I've been thinking about for a while." That

at least was true. She'd been having doubts about it since before the situation with Gilchrist developed. "I like data gathering and analysis, but I've never liked teaching. I just don't think it's what I want to do for the rest of my life."

"I can understand that. It's not for everyone."

Alice avoided looking Dr. Frazier in the eye, too afraid of the disappointment she'd see there. "There are a lot of jobs I could get with my skill set. I could go into data science, for example."

"That's true. You've definitely got options outside of academia—but you'd have a lot more options if you finished your doctorate. It would be foolish to quit at this point. If you push through this last little part, it will open so many more doors for you."

"I just…" Alice gulped around the burning in the back of her throat. "I can't finish. I don't even think I want to."

"Which is it? You can't or don't want to?"

Alice's answer came out in a whisper. "I can't."

"Tell me why. Whatever the problem is, I can help. We'll figure it out together."

This was her opening. If she was going to tell Dr. Frazier about Dr. Gilchrist, now was the time to do it.

Alice stared at the kid art just beyond Dr. Frazier's left shoulder. It was a picture of a red horse, and it had five legs. A giant blue cloud hung ominously above it, as big as the orange sun next to it.

She'd spent the whole weekend trying to come up with a workaround, but this morning she'd realized it was pointless. Even if she could figure it out herself, or find someone else to help her, Gilchrist would still be on her committee. She'd have to see him. Seek his approval. Be interrogated by him in her defense.

She just couldn't do it. She couldn't even stand the thought of being in the same room with him, much less being questioned by him at the most important moment of her academic life.

"Well?" Dr. Frazier pressed.

Alice's hands twisted in her lap. She was tired of carrying this stain alone, but after so many months of silence, it was hard to make the words come out. "Dr. Gilchrist was supposed to help me with the network analysis for my dissertation…"

"Yes."

"I—" Alice swallowed down the lump in her throat. "I can't work with him."

Dr. Frazier was frowning. "Why can't you work with him? Was he uncooperative?"

Alice shook her head. "He makes me uncomfortable."

Dr. Frazier got up and closed her office door. Instead of going back to her desk, she sat down in the chair next to Alice. "Uncomfortable how?" Her expression was somber and urgent. "Did something happen?"

Alice looked into Dr. Frazier's dark, concerned eyes, took a deep breath, and told her everything.

GRIFFIN WAS ON HIS LAST SETUP OF THE DAY, A TWO-SHOT ON the doctor's lounge set with Alexandra Shaw, the actress playing his current love interest. The extras wouldn't be needed until they moved on to a later scene set in the hospital cafeteria, which meant Alice hadn't been in yet.

Whenever the director called cut, Griffin would look around to see if she'd arrived, anxious to hear how her meeting with her advisor had gone. It was ridiculous. Here he was, constantly checking his phone, a nervous wreck over someone else's problem. Someone he barely even knew. It was exactly the kind of distraction he'd been wanting to avoid—the opposite of a temporary business arrangement with no personal entanglements.

A couple of the other extras had wandered by, but so far no Alice.

He wished he'd asked her to text him as soon as she got out of the meeting to let him know how it went. Except…he wasn't sure he was entitled to that level of friendship. Sure, she'd confided in him this morning when he'd caught her in a moment of weakness, but that didn't mean she was on board to give him constant updates on her personal life.

On the other hand, she *had* asked his opinion. Didn't that give him a stake in the outcome?

He didn't spot her until after the seventh take. She'd already changed into nurse's scrubs, and she clutched a large to-go cup of coffee as she spoke to the second AD. Griffin caught her eye and gave her a questioning look.

She responded with a tentative smile and a nod—which meant what, exactly? Did the meeting go well? Had her advisor believed her? Was that douchebag professor getting his ass reported to the administration? Or was Alice just putting a good face on it all because she didn't want to talk to him about it at work?

Griffin's instincts urged him to go over there and pull her aside to make sure she really was okay. He nearly did, until the makeup artist popped up in front of him with a handful of brushes. Thwarted, Griffin spread his feet in order to lower his face to Janie's eye level so she could touch up his makeup.

They reset for another take, and Griffin tried not to think about Alice and her problems while he shared an intimate moment with his latest on-screen girlfriend—fully clothed, thank god. The current storyline was made slightly awkward by the fact that Griffin and Alexandra had briefly—*very* briefly—been involved last year. Fortunately, they were both professionals who could deal with it like adults.

Alexandra's character was his fifth love interest in seven seasons. The last couple years, the writers hadn't seemed to know what to do with his character other than throw actress after actress into his bed so they could show off Griffin's newly acquired six-pack. It wasn't exactly the character growth he'd been hoping for at this point in his tenure, a fact which had made his decision not to renew his contract easier.

Today's scene consisted of three pages of dialogue ending in a kiss that was meant to grow heated as the camera cut away. After the other setups they'd already done, it must have been his fiftieth time kissing Alexandra that morning. His lips were numb and swollen, and he could taste the eggs she'd had for breakfast beneath the Altoid she'd popped before they started shooting.

"Cut!" the director called out halfway through their lip-lock, and came over to talk to them. "I'm sure you two are as tired of kissing as I am of watching you kiss, but I've seen sibling figure skating pairs with more chemistry. Can we give it a little more oomph, please?"

"Sorry." Griffin shot an apologetic look at Alexandra. "That's on me. I'll get my head in the game."

The next take, Griffin shoved all the distractions—including Alice and his personal feelings about Alexandra and this particular storyline—into a box and dredged up more energy to sell the scene.

"Excellent!" the director said, followed by the magical words everyone loved to hear: "Let's move on!"

Released from purgatory for the day, Griffin immediately went in search of Alice. He found her by the craft services table, grazing on a big bowl of M&Ms. "Hey!" He pulled her slightly aside and lowered his voice. "How'd it go?"

"Good, actually." She glanced down to where his hand was still holding her arm and then back up at him with her eyebrows slightly raised.

Shit. "Sorry." He let go of her and shoved the errant hand into his back pocket so it wouldn't be tempted to touch her again. "What does 'good' mean?"

"Well—"

"Background!" the second AD shouted. "I need background over here!"

"I've gotta go," Alice said, edging away.

"I'm done for the day," Griffin said. "I'm about to head out."

"I guess I'll see you later, then." She gave him a tentative smile and snagged a handful of M&Ms before heading off to join the other extras.

Right. Later. He could wait to hear the details, he supposed. At least she'd said it was good. That was promising.

Griffin put in his two hours at the gym, then went home and spent the rest of the day killing time. As the evening turned into nighttime and ten o'clock approached, he started to get increasingly restless. He had a six o'clock call time in the morning and he ought to be going to bed soon. But he knew he wouldn't be able to sleep until he'd talked to Alice and found out how her meeting had gone.

At eleven he gave up and headed to bed anyway. For all he knew, she wouldn't be home for hours. He should at least try to sleep.

It was nearly midnight when he finally heard her come in. Griffin got up and followed Taco into the kitchen, where they found Alice staring into the open fridge. "Shooting ran long today," Griffin said, stifling a yawn.

She glanced his way and then back to the fridge. "Yeah. Alfie kept messing up his lines."

Alfie didn't have a lot of fucks left to give. He was almost sixty and hadn't exactly been good about memorizing his lines even when he'd still cared about this job.

"So?" Griffin said. "Tell me about the meeting this morning."

"Umm…" Alice still had her head buried in the fridge.

"What are you looking for?"

"I don't know. I have the munchies, but I haven't been to the store so there's nothing to snack on."

He nudged her aside and grabbed the Greek yogurt and coconut milk off his shelf. "I'll make you a smoothie."

She wrinkled up her nose. "I don't want one of your gross, goopy protein drinks."

"You're gonna like this. It's like a milkshake." He pulled a Ziploc bag of frozen bananas out of the freezer. "Trust me."

Alice gave the brown, mushy bananas a skeptical look.

"Go sit down," he ordered.

She hopped onto one of the stools at the counter and watched while he gathered the rest of his ingredients and carried them over to the blender with Taco following hopefully at his heels.

"So?" Griffin asked as he measured frozen berries into the canister. "Did you tell your advisor the truth?"

"Yes."

He didn't turn around, figuring it would be easier for her to talk about it if he wasn't looking at her. "Did she believe you?"

"Yeah, she did. She was surprised, I think, but she took it seriously."

"That's great. What's she going to do about it?"

"Well, first of all, we're kicking Dr. Gilchrist off my committee."

He glanced at her in surprise. "Just like that? She can do that?"

Alice was actually smiling. "Yeah, apparently. I just have to file some paperwork with the dean's office and it's done. Dr. Frazier said she'd find someone to replace him and smooth it over with the rest of the committee."

Griffin reached for the plastic honey bear and squeezed a dollop into the blender. Then, remembering Alice's sweet tooth, he added some more. "What about the stuff you needed his help for?" He hadn't really understood that part of it or what exactly it was she needed from him, but she'd made it sound like it was insurmountable.

"Dr. Frazier thinks I can leave it out. If I was pursuing a career in academia, it might give me an edge up on the tenure track, but since I'm not…"

Griffin glanced over his shoulder again. "You decided that for sure?"

Alice nodded. "We talked about it—a lot—and I convinced her that it's just not what I want anymore. I've never loved teaching, and there are a lot of data science jobs I can get with my PhD. I'd rather go into the private sector." She looked remarkably calm and at peace with her decision compared to this morning.

He turned back to the blender in relief. "But you're definitely finishing your PhD?"

"Yeah. Dr. Frazier's going to help me finish my dissertation —without having to interact with Dr. Gilchrist."

"That's great."

"Yeah."

He turned on the blender and the motorized racket filled the kitchen, cutting off further conversation. When it was finished, he reached for a silicone spatula and said, "What about Gilchrist? Is anything going to happen to him? Is she going to report him?"

Alice hesitated before answering. "I asked her not to. I don't want to get involved with a Title IX investigation. I just want to get my degree and get out of there."

Griffin nodded and got a glass down from the cabinet.

"Maybe that's selfish," she went on as he poured her smoothie. "But I just don't have it in me to take him on. If I go public with what he did, they'll put my whole life under a microscope. It's not just that everyone will know what he did to me—I would hate that, but I could stand it. It's that all my relationships, my sex life, everything I've ever said to anyone will get written up into an official report. It'll be humiliating and traumatic, and he'll probably still get off with a gentle slap on the wrist—if that. So what's the point?"

Griffin set the smoothie in front of her. "You don't have to convince me."

Alice stared at the smoothie and sighed. "I think I'm trying to convince myself."

"You need to protect yourself. First and foremost." When she didn't respond he went on. "Don't beat yourself up over this. You're a student. It's not your responsibility to fix the university's problems—they're supposed to protect *you*. You reported the harassment to your advisor, so now she's aware. She can keep an eye on this guy in case he tries his shit with anyone else."

Alice's chin lifted in a halfhearted nod. "Yeah. That's what she said. And I told her if someone else decided to make a report later, I'd be willing to go on the record to corroborate. I just don't want to be on my own with this, his word against mine."

"I get it. It's a shitty position to be in. No one should have to go through something like that."

"No one should, but they do. All the time."

Griffin's fingers twitched with an urge to reach across the counter and take Alice's hand. Instead, he balled his hand into a fist and nodded at the glass in front of her. "Drink your smoothie."

She reached for it and took a tentative sip, the skepticism written all over her face. A surprised smile fluttered to life as she licked her lips. "This is really good!"

He felt a warm rush of pleasure, which he hid behind a smirk. "I know."

She took another sip and her smile got wider. "It tastes like ice cream."

Griffin realized he was staring at her mouth like some moonstruck sap in a romcom, and went to wash the blender at the sink, stepping around Taco, who'd given up on getting a treat and laid down in the middle of the room. "And yet, it's full of stuff that's good for you," he tossed over his shoulder in an attempt to sound casual. "Calcium. Protein. Potassium. Plus a little cocoa powder and a *lot* of honey."

"That's why it tastes like ice cream."

He heard her get up, and when he turned around she was standing right beside him.

"Thank you," Alice said, and startled him by giving him a hug.

A soft rush of breath tickled his neck, and he felt the warmth of her body through her thin navy cardigan. Before he could respond, she'd already stepped back again, leaving a whiff of peach shampoo in her wake.

He swallowed, hoping his face didn't reflect his sudden rush of confused emotion, and deflected with a joke. "It's just a smoothie," he said, affecting a grin.

"No it's not." Alice gave him a shy smile before taking her smoothie and heading off to her room.

The scent of peaches lingered as Griffin watched her depart, and he chided himself for the inappropriate and unexpected thoughts that had begun to creep into his brain.

Don't be an ass. She's not for you.

nine

Dinner tonight? I'm cooking.

ALICE FOUND the Post-it on the coffeemaker when she got up Saturday morning, and it induced a surge of girlish excitement that she tried fruitlessly to squash.

Just when things were finally looking up in every other area of her life, she'd developed a new problem in the form of Griffin. Namely, all these feelings she was starting to have about him.

Ever since he'd caught her crying the other morning and been so sweet and supportive, she'd been struggling with what could only be described as a crush. It wasn't like it was *new* news that Griffin was an incredibly attractive man, but recognizing that someone was attractive and actually being *attracted* to them were two very different things that Alice's brain usually had no trouble compartmentalizing. What was happening to her now was definitely the latter, and she needed to cut it out immediately. The very last thing she needed was an unrequited crush on an inappropriate man.

Alice silently repeated the list of reasons she shouldn't be having feelings for Griffin: landlord, employer, actor, not her type, not *his* type, and altogether too much potential for heartbreak all around. She'd been repeating it on a loop for the last several days, but so far it hadn't done anything to dissuade her from her ill-advised preoccupation.

He was simply being friendly. Like a friend. A surprisingly good friend, but a friend nonetheless. There was no point torturing herself by reading any more into it than that.

When Griffin came home a couple hours later with an armful of grocery bags, Alice got up from the couch to help, because that was what friends and good roommates did for one another, and not at all because she wanted an excuse to be near him.

"What'd you get?" she asked, peeking into the reusable grocery bag he passed her. This one was full of his usual eggs and spinach, which gave her very little idea of his plans for dinner. Given how strict his diet was, she'd already reconciled herself to eating roasted lean meat with some sort of dire vegetable on the side.

Flashing her one of his endearing grins, he pulled a package of rib eyes and a pair of russet potatoes out of another bag. "My specialty: steaks and loaded baked potatoes."

Alice looked at him in surprise. "Can you eat that?"

"Today's my cheat day. I can eat what I want—within reason—and what I want is to throw a couple rib eyes on the grill and slather a baked potato with all the dairy products it can hold."

"Nice."

"I hope you like steak."

"I love steak." She almost never had it because it was too expensive for her budget, and in any case she wasn't a good enough cook to be entrusted with a pricey cut of meat. But she was willing to bet Griffin knew how to cook the perfect steak on that fancy grill on the deck.

He dug around in a bag and came out with a pint of Ben and Jerry's Cherry Garcia which he shoved into her hands. "That's for you."

Alice stared at it and then up at him. "You bought me ice cream?"

"I thought you could use a reward for facing your advisor and moving forward with your dissertation." He took it back from her and tucked it in the freezer, along with several bags of frozen vegetables.

She felt an embarrassing rush of heat crawl up her throat and turned to fold the grocery bags that had already been emptied. "You're going to share it with me though, right? Since it's your cheat day."

Griffin shook his head as he stacked four dozen eggs in the fridge. "Dessert's too hard to come back from if I let myself slip. I learned that the hard way."

"That sucks."

He shrugged. "I might have one bite. And then I'll just enjoy watching you eat the rest."

She felt herself color again and hid it with a laugh. "That's weird."

"Hey, I gotta take my pleasures where I can get 'em these days."

At five o'clock, Griffin went outside and started up the grill. Then he went to the fridge and opened two beers—one he brought to Alice on the couch and one for himself.

"Cheers," he said, and clinked his bottle against hers. The look on his face when he took his first taste was positively orgasmic, as was the groan that followed. "God, I miss beer."

She watched him, laughing. "Do you and your beer want to be alone?"

"No, we're open to a threesome." His eyes widened as he realized what he'd said. "Shit. I'm sorry! I didn't mean—"

"It's fine," she assured him. "I can take a joke when it's actually a joke and not a come-on with a threat hidden behind it."

He grimaced in embarrassment. "Just to be clear, I do not literally want to have sex with my beer. Although..." He held up his bottle and raised a speculative eyebrow. "With enough lube..."

Alice snort-laughed. "Okay, now you're creeping me out."

He collapsed onto the couch next to her with a bone-weary sigh. "I just miss beer so much." He gazed at the bottle as he smoothed the label with his thumb. "I know it's the main reason I was chubby, but *god* I wish I could have beer and an acting career at the same time."

She pulled her legs up underneath her and turned toward him. "I guess there's a lot you've had to give up for your job. Eating, drinking, your privacy."

He took another swig of beer and rested the bottle on his knee. "Losing my privacy was almost as bad as giving up beer. When I was at Whole Foods today, this gaggle of teenagers followed me around the store giggling and whispering to each other. It's hard to shop when you know someone's watching everything you put in your cart so they can report it on Twitter later."

"That must get old."

He shook his head, frowning. "I don't want to sound like an ungrateful asshole. I know how lucky I am to be doing as well as I am." His mouth curled in a half-smile. "It's kinda nice that people like my work enough to act like total weirdos around me when I go out in public."

"Do you ever wish you could go back to being invisible?"

He gave a one-shouldered shrug. "Sometimes. You don't really appreciate the luxury of anonymity until you lose it."

"I've seen some of the stuff people say about you online. It must creep you out to have people talking about you like that." Alice had always been morbidly fascinated by the way people treated celebrities online. The weird possessiveness and the othering. Like they were an inanimate object instead of a real person with feelings and insecurities like everyone else.

"A little." Griffin took another swig of beer. "Mostly I try not to look at that stuff. My Twitter mentions are insane. It's just a never-ending stream of people calling me 'Daddy.'" His lip twisted in revulsion. "Why?"

"Don't ask me. I'm baffled by it too." She shook her head as she sipped her beer.

"So gross."

"*So* gross," she agreed.

"Better prep the potatoes," he said, pushing himself to his feet. When he was done, he carried them out to the deck, along with his beer. "You coming?" he asked Alice.

She followed him outside, and they sat on the deck chatting as Taco lounged at their feet and the sunset painted the sky a thousand different shades of orange. It was hard to believe how normal this had already come to feel. Living with Griffin, sharing his space and his meals. Talking like friends.

Alice realized with a shock that she was completely relaxed, aside from the small inconvenience of her crush on him. It was an odd sensation, not feeling on edge or on guard around him. Not having to watch what she said or worry that she might laugh too loudly or at the wrong thing. Whether he'd suddenly turn on her and take offense—or worse, decide she'd been coming on to him.

She trusted him. Maybe she shouldn't, but she did. It wasn't something she would have thought possible a month ago, but here she was. Completely comfortable with Griffin Beach.

If only she could stop thinking about how attractive he was.

After forty-five minutes, the alarm on Griffin's phone trilled a series of ascending notes. "Steak time!" he announced, getting to his feet.

Alice grabbed their empty bottles and followed him into the kitchen. "Do you want another beer?" she asked as he started prepping the steaks.

He cast a longing look at the fridge. "Desperately, but I'd better not."

She decided not to have a second beer either. Instead, she got them both tall glasses of water and carried them out to the table on the deck. Then she went back inside for silverware, plates, napkins, and fixings for the baked potatoes: butter, shredded cheese, and sour cream—aka all the dairy they could hold.

By the time she had the table set, the steaks and potatoes were coming off the grill. Griffin brought them to the table, and they sat down to their feast.

"I hope you're ready to *steak* it to the limit," he said as he carved off a bite and waved it in the air.

Alice couldn't help laughing at his terrible wordplay. "Wow. Way to dad-joke."

He swallowed a mouthful of steak with a blissed-out expression. "Well, I never had a dad, so I had to make my own dad jokes."

"That's funny," she said as she loaded her potato with sour cream. "I didn't have a dad around either, and I never missed the jokes."

He winked at her as he tossed Taco a piece of steak. "You missed them. You just didn't *know* you were missing them."

Alice groaned, smiling as she cut into her steak.

Griffin wolfed down his own steak in about two minutes flat, then proceeded to make increasingly orgasmic expressions over every cheesy, sour cream-topped bite of baked potato. The more he did it, the more she laughed, and the more she laughed, the more he did it. "God, I love dairy." He sighed happily. "You have no idea."

"I think I've got a pretty good idea," Alice said, and slid half her potato onto his plate.

When Griffin had cleaned both their plates, they carried everything into the kitchen and loaded the dirty dishes into the dishwasher.

"Can I ask you something?" Alice ventured, feeling emboldened by their night of roommate bonding.

Griffin reached under the sink for the dishwasher detergent. "Shoot."

She leaned back against the counter with her hands grasping the edge behind her. "Would you have come back for another year if they'd renewed *LV Gen*?"

He glanced at her, then away again. "No."

"Did the network know that when they canceled it?"

Griffin got the ice cream out of the fridge and put it in Alice's hands without meeting her eye. "It's complicated."

"You don't have to answer if you don't want to." She hadn't meant to make him uncomfortable.

"We're not really supposed to talk about this stuff."

"That's okay. Pretend I never asked." It was the first time Alice had ever felt like she'd crossed a line with him. She got two spoons from the drawer and held one out as a peace offering.

Griffin hesitated before accepting it. "If you're asking if it's my fault the show's ending, the answer is...sort of."

Feeling bad for bringing up what was obviously a sore subject, she peeled open the ice cream and offered it to him. He stared at it like he was trying to make up his mind whether to have some or not. After a moment he reached for it, covering her hand with his to steady the container while he carved out a spoonful of the frozen treat.

"You can't tell anyone this, okay?"

Alice swallowed, her hand half frozen and half warmed by the contact with his. "Of course."

He let go and shoved the spoon of ice cream into his mouth. His eyes drifted closed for a second as he savored it, then he bent and put his spoon into the open dishwasher. "Alfie quit first. He told them he wasn't renewing his contract, no matter how much they sweetened the pot."

Alice could have guessed as much. It had been pretty obvious for a while that Alfie was eager to be free of his contract.

Griffin leaned against the counter beside her and shoved his hands in the pockets of his jeans. His eyes were hooded as they fixed on the opposite counter. "They came to me and offered me top billing and a substantial raise to re-up."

"And you said no?" Alice asked, stabbing the frozen ice cream with her spoon.

He nodded. "I almost said yes—for about five minutes." His eyes found hers guiltily. "But after I turned them down, they decided to cancel it. So it's my fault you're about to be out of a job."

She set the ice cream down between them and rubbed her cold hand on her jeans. "That's not why I was asking. And it's not your fault."

His mouth twisted. "Sure it is. If I'd said yes, three hundred people would have a job for another year—or more."

"They'll get other jobs," Alice told him. She hadn't expected him to feel such a strong sense of responsibility. "They'll be fine. Another show will come along and take its place. That's how the business works."

Griffin crossed his arms and nodded, clearly still feeling bad about it.

"Anyone would have done the same thing." She scooped a big bite of ice cream onto her spoon and held it out to him. "You're about to be a huge star—and I'm gonna be able to say I knew you before you were famous. How cool is that?"

A hint of a smile curved his lips as he accepted the spoon. "I'm actually pretty famous already. I don't know if you've noticed."

Alice suppressed a shiver as he licked the spoon clean and passed it back to her. She lowered her eyes and plunged it back into the ice cream. "See?" She struggled to keep her tone light and jokey. "You've already got the big head to go with your superstardom. You're ready."

"Hey!" He nudged her arm with his elbow. "My head is normal-sized, thank you very much."

She smiled, glad that things were back to being easy between them.

Other than all these random acts of feelings she had to be on constant guard against.

"ARE YOU SURE THIS ISN'T BOTHERING YOU?" GRIFFIN ASKED, casting an anxious glance at Alice during a commercial break. She was camped at the other end of the couch working on her dissertation while he watched TV, and the last thing he wanted to do was distract her.

She looked up from her laptop and smiled. The way she was sitting, sideways with her back against the armrest and her legs crossed underneath her, he was directly in her line of sight when she lifted her head. "No, I like it. It's the perfect white noise."

"Okay." He turned back to the TV. It was Easter Sunday and his only plans involved vegging in front of a baseball game. He'd never been a churchgoer, so with the candy and chocolate bunnies off-limits, Easter was just another day to him.

Alice had been camped on the couch all day in a pair of cutoff shorts, so he gathered it wasn't a big holiday for her either.

"My working here isn't bothering you, is it?"

He looked over at her again and lifted a mocking eyebrow. "Yeah, your quiet typing is really interfering with my sitting on my ass and watching the most boring game in the history of baseball."

"I just wanted to make sure."

"Don't be a dork."

She smiled again. "Fine."

Never in a million years would Griffin have imagined he'd actually like having a woman—or anybody for that matter—sharing his house with him. His memories of having room-mates were mostly of the bad stuff: the noise, the mess, the inconvenience, the smell. Living with Alice wasn't like that. She was considerate, clean, and quiet as a church mouse. But beyond that, there was something about having her around that made him feel...content. It was better than being alone, somehow. Even now, simply sitting beside her watching the game without talking, he felt more relaxed—happier, even—just having her nearby.

He actually *liked* having a roommate. Go figure.

Alice went back to her work, and Griffin turned his attention back to the game. Or he tried to, anyway. The score had been stuck at 1-0 since the first inning, and it wasn't really holding his interest. Every few minutes he'd find himself sneaking a glance her way.

Her blonde hair was piled on her head in a messy bun, with a few wavy tendrils slipping out. She kept pushing them behind her ear, and they kept falling right back into her face. Every once in a while, she'd pause and smile to herself like she was pleased with whatever she'd written. He liked seeing that smile. It lacked her usual self-consciousness, as if she wasn't even aware she was doing it. It felt like he was catching a glimpse of something rare that most people who knew her never got close enough to see.

Alice looked up and caught him staring at her. "What?"

"Nothing." He flashed the grin he used to diffuse awkward situations. "Do you want some coffee? I was thinking about making some." He hadn't been, but she seemed to drink a lot of coffee when she was working, so he thought she might like it.

Her face lit up. "I would *love* some if you're making it."

Griffin pushed himself to his feet and headed for the kitchen. "One pot of coffee, coming up."

Jesus Christ, he needed to get a grip. What was he doing creepily staring at her like that? *Not cool, dude.*

After he started the coffeemaker, he hung around the kitchen unloading the dishwasher and gave in to Taco's begging by tossing him a treat. When the coffee was ready, he filled two mugs and carried them into the living room.

"Yay, coffee!" Alice set her laptop aside as he approached. "Thank you," she said, gingerly accepting the hot mug from him and setting it on the coffee table.

"De nada." He took his own coffee back to the other end of the couch and sank into the cushions. He didn't really want coffee, but he also didn't want Alice to know he'd made it just for her.

While she waited for her coffee to cool, she reached her arms overhead and stretched, arching her back. Her breasts strained against the fabric of her favorite T-shirt. He knew it was her favorite because she always wore it first after doing laundry. It was white with a cartoon of a cat passed out on the floor above the words *Not Today.* He could see her pink bra through the thin cotton—the same pink lace bra he'd seen hanging in the laundry room the other day. He'd tried really hard not to look at it when he'd started his load of dirty gym clothes, but he'd seen it anyway.

And now he was staring at her breasts like an asshole.

Griffin jerked his head back toward the TV and forced himself to keep his eyes on the screen for the rest of the game.

Eventually Alice shut her laptop and set it on the coffee table, but she stayed on the couch with him and watched the last twenty minutes of the game. Neither the Pirates nor the Tigers had managed to score another run since that first one. When it was over, he slid the remote toward her. "It's your turn to pick something."

She didn't touch it. "Isn't there something else you want to watch?"

"Nope. It's all you. We can watch whatever you want."

Hesitantly, she reached for the remote. "I've been kind of wanting to start *This Is Us*. I don't know if you want to watch that though."

"I'm cool with whatever." It was one on a long list of shows Griffin had always meant to check out but had never gotten around to. With the long hours he worked, it could be hard to find time to keep up with all the shows he felt like he should watch, so he mostly didn't bother.

"Okay, if you're sure." Alice navigated to one of the streaming services and started up the first episode.

Griffin settled back into the couch, unable to remember the last time he'd sat around with someone else doing something as simple as watching a television show he hadn't worked on.

By the time they'd reached the twenty-minute mark, his throat had developed a permanent lump and Alice was teary-eyed and sniffling. By the time the pilot was over she was a blubbering mess. He glanced at her and swiped at his eyes when she wasn't looking.

"Oh my god," she said, hitting pause before the next

episode started. "I'm *so* sorry. I knew it was sad but I didn't realize it would be *that* sad."

Griffin cleared his throat. "It was really good though." His voice sounded hoarse, so he quietly cleared his throat again, hoping she wouldn't notice.

Alice was too busy rubbing her eyes to pay much attention to him. "I haven't cried like that since my mom died."

He glanced at her sharply. That was something they had in common, in addition to their absent fathers. They were both effectively orphans. He tried to clear his throat again, but it came out more of a grunt.

Alice went into the bathroom to blow her nose and brought the whole box of tissues back with her.

"When did your mom die?" Griffin asked.

She sank back onto the couch, clutching a tissue in her hand. Her nose and eyes were bright red. "When I was thirteen."

"Mine died almost ten years ago. Lung cancer." It was the worst thing that had ever happened to him. He'd dropped out of community college to help her through her treatment, foolishly thinking she'd be fine in six months or maybe a year at most. It hadn't occurred to him she would actually die. Not at the age of forty-four. But that's exactly what had happened. Instead of going back to school, Griffin had left Phoenix as soon as he'd tied up her affairs, and struck out for LA to pursue acting. Everything he'd accomplished in his life had happened because of her death, but he'd give it all up—the money, the fame, the acting career—if it meant he could have her back.

Alice nodded, her eyes fixed on the wall straight ahead. "Mine was in a car accident."

They shared a moment of silence in honor of their membership in the Dead Mom Club. Griffin wanted to ask Alice if she'd been in the car and what had happened to her after—if she'd gone to live with a relative or been put into foster care—but since she didn't volunteer anything further, he thought she might not want to talk about it.

"You want to watch another episode?" he asked instead.

Alice nodded. "Definitely."

"In that case I'm getting us some Gatorade," he said, getting up. "You'd better hydrate if there's going to be any more crying."

ten

ALICE HEARD the sound of laughter as soon as she opened the front door.

Did Griffin have a friend over? In the three weeks she'd been living with him, he hadn't once had another person over to the house. He didn't even seem to go out socially. She was starting to think the guy was a monk, contrary to what the gossip rags said about him.

Another burst of laughter echoed through the house as she shut the door behind her. She followed the sound to the kitchen, where she found Griffin and—*whoa*.

"Hey! You're home!" Griffin said, catching sight of her. "Alice, this is my buddy Boone. He's down from Vancouver for a couple days."

Boone Sheridan, star of the long-running Fox Network paranormal procedural *Abnormal Investigations*, beamed a dazzling smile at her. Alice had been slightly obsessed with the show—and Boone—in the early seasons when she was an undergrad, and it was surreal coming home and finding him casually hanging out in the kitchen.

In the flesh, Boone was smaller than she'd imagined him to

be—barely an inch taller than her with a slim build—but possibly even more handsome. But the most jarring thing—other than the fact that he was here—was that he wore a plain black T-shirt and Nikes rather than the plaid shirt and cowboy boots that were his character's trademark look on the show. It was all very disorienting.

"The famous Alice," Boone said, coming forward to shake her hand. "We meet at last."

What? Had Griffin been talking about her to *Boone Sheridan?* She'd had no idea they even knew each other.

"Nice to meet you," she managed as her brain slowly recovered from the shock. The words came out nearly an octave higher than her normal voice, and she felt her cheeks flush.

Boone quirked an eyebrow in amusement, causing the ghost of Alice's younger self to quiver in embarrassed excitement. "I've heard a lot about you," he said. "It's nice to put a face to the name."

So Griffin *had* been talking about her. Alice was afraid to even imagine what he might have said. She cast a questioning glance at Griffin, who was observing them with an unreadable look on his face. "That's funny. Griffin's never once mentioned you."

Boone rounded on Griffin in mock indignation. "Seriously, dude?"

Griffin shrugged. "I don't like to drop my famous friends' names."

"Whatever, *movie star.*"

"You ready for another beer?" Griffin asked, jerking open the fridge.

Boone waggled his bottle to check the level. "Yeah, hit me."

"Alice? You want one?"

There was a tightness to Griffin's expression that made her think maybe he'd prefer she made herself scarce, so she shook her head, clutching her laptop bag to her chest. "I'm just gonna head into my room to do some work and leave you guys to whatever it is you're doing."

"No way!" Boone said, laying his hand on her arm. "You just got here. You can't disappear on me already."

Alice looked at Griffin uncertainly and his expression softened. "Stay and hang out with us." He twisted the cap off a beer and held it out to her. "It's open now. You have to drink it."

"Well, I wouldn't want to let a beer go to waste." She accepted it and took a large swallow.

"That's my girl." Boone grinned and tipped his bottle in Griffin's direction. "We can trade notes on what it's like to have this guy for a roommate."

She looked at them in surprise. "You guys were roommates?"

Griffin snorted, leaning back against the counter. "More like co-tenants in purgatory."

"We lived in the same crash pad for about six months," Boone explained as he set his empty bottle next to the sink, "along with a rotating roster of four other down-on-their luck actors."

"It was vile," Griffin said, making a face.

Boone rolled his eyes. "He's exaggerating, because he's unnaturally persnickety."

Griffin crossed his arms, which happened to do amazing things for his biceps, and Alice wondered if it was a conscious —or unconscious—display to emphasize his muscular advantage over Boone. "If it's persnickety to expect people to wash a dish or pick up their trash every once in a while to keep the rats at bay, then I proudly own my persnickety-ness."

She was enjoying watching their back-and-forth banter, which had clearly been honed over years of friendship. It was a different side of Griffin than she'd seen before. She'd often seen him yukking it up with the guys on set, but she'd always gotten the sense that was at least partially for show. He wanted everyone to like him, yet he didn't seem to be genuinely close to anyone. But now here was Boone, the first and only person Griffin had invited to the house, and for once he didn't seem to be performing or trying to impress. It was like getting a glimpse into what Griffin had been like before the fame and money.

"Does he ride you all the time about cleaning up around the house?" Boone asked, turning to Alice.

"No," she answered honestly. "Not once."

"Seriously?" Boone shot an exaggerated look of surprise at Griffin, who simply shrugged.

"She cleans up after herself like a normal functioning adult. Go figure."

"I'm pretty fastidious about that stuff, actually." Alice nodded toward the sink. "Right now I'm having to physically restrain myself from rinsing out that bottle and putting it in the recycling bin.

Boone's mouth curved into a smirk. "Match made in heaven."

She saw something flash across Griffin's face before he turned away to refill his water bottle. When he turned back his expression was oddly blank. She took a big swallow of her beer, thinking maybe she shouldn't have stuck around after all. Did he not want her here? Was she imposing on his time with his friend?

"You know who else came through that crash pad while we were there?" Boone said to Alice. "Steward Vaughan."

"Really?" Steward Vaughan had won an Oscar last year for his portrayal of Frank Zappa in a recent biopic. Instead of an acceptance speech, he'd mumbled an indecipherable poem he'd written about global warming.

"Total weirdo," Griffin said with a nod. "Barely talked to anyone."

"And he ate nothing but Vienna sausages!" Boone shook his head. "I'll never forget the smell of them. He ate them so much he exuded them through his pores like some kind of giant, walking Vienna sausage in clothes. Remember that?"

"I've tried hard to forget." Griffin opened the fridge and pulled out a package of ground beef. "I'm grilling tonight. How many burgers does everyone want?"

Alice lifted her eyebrows in surprise. "You're eating a burger?"

"No, I'm grilling a chicken breast for me. But I'm making burgers for you two, because Boone has the metabolism of a hummingbird so the lucky bastard can eat what he wants, and as for you—" He fixed her with an accusing look. "I don't want you eating Pop-Tarts for dinner."

"Gimme two," Boone said, rubbing his washboard-flat stomach. "I don't have any more shirtless scenes left this season."

"Alice?" Griffin asked. "One or two?"

"One, please. Thank you."

"Were you really going to eat Pop-Tarts for dinner tonight?" Boone asked Alice.

"No!"

"What *were* you planning to eat?" Griffin asked, glancing over his shoulder at her as he formed the hamburger patties. "Go on, tell the class."

"Peanut butter and jelly," Alice mumbled into her beer.

"Wow," Boone said, grinning at her. "That's some A-plus adulting right there."

"I don't cook," Alice said with a shrug. "I never learned how."

Griffin's eyes met hers, and she could see him putting two and two together, realizing why she'd never learned to cook. *Dead mothers can't pass down treasured family recipes to their daughters.*

"It's basically her only flaw," he said, turning back to the counter. "Boone, get her another beer. I have hamburger hands."

"That's what she said," Boone shot back as he moved to the fridge, and Griffin snorted. Smirking, Boone twisted the cap off a beer and handed it to Alice. "M'lady."

If her past self could only see her now, having a beer with Boone Sheridan like it was an everyday occurrence. Now that the initial shock had worn off, it felt surprisingly normal. Working on a TV set had taken a lot of the shine off celebrity, and Boone wasn't quite what she'd expected. He was exactly as pretty as he seemed on TV, but in person he lacked some of the sex appeal his character emitted through the screen.

"We used to watch a lot of *The Office* back in the day," Boone told her as he leaned against the counter beside her. "Remember?" He flicked a glance at Griffin. "We'd have those Jim-offs."

"Oh, I remember," Griffin said without turning around.

"What's a Jim-off?" Alice asked.

"You've watched *The Office*, right?"

"Of course."

"So you know how the camera always cuts to Jim for a reaction when something ridiculous happens, and he makes a funny face?"

"Sure." It was so ubiquitous that "stares into the camera like on *The Office*" had become an internet meme.

"But it's a slightly different face every time, depending on the context and how Jim felt about what had happened. And because Krasinski was brilliant and we wanted to be just like him, Griff and I would sit around making Jim faces at each other until one of us broke."

"And I always won," Griffin piped up.

"You did," Boone agreed with a grin. "I was always the first to break. Still am. I get in trouble for it all the time on set."

Griffin finished forming the burgers, and they all pitched in to carry plates and condiments and buns to the back deck and set the table. While Griffin manned the grill, Boone tossed a ball for Taco, and Alice sat quietly sipping her beer as the two old friends chatted. It was all very pleasant and relaxed, and she wondered why Griffin didn't entertain more often. He certainly seemed to enjoy cooking for other people.

When the food was ready, they sat down to eat, and Boone practically inhaled the two burgers on his plate. Griffin shook his head as he skewered a bite of chicken breast. "I wish I had your metabolism."

"And I wish I had your career." Boone wadded his napkin up and dropped it onto his plate. "I used to be the successful one, remember?"

Abnormal Investigations had started a year before *Las Vegas General*, so Boone had been the first to get a steady TV gig, but Alice could detect no bitterness in his tone. Only more of the same friendly rivalry they'd been exhibiting all night.

"You do all right," Griffin said. "That show of yours is probably going to go for another ten years, and then you'll never have to work again."

"That's the dream." Boone leaned back in his chair, patting his stomach in contentment. "No one makes a burger like you do, man."

Griffin carved another bite off his plain grilled chicken breast. "I'm surprised you could even taste it. You're like an anaconda swallowing its prey whole."

Boone smirked and turned to Alice, hooking a thumb at Griffin. "We used to call Griff the den mother. He was the only one who ever tried to cook in that hell kitchen at the crash pad. The rest of us lived off ramen and cereal, but Griffin always wanted to cook, like, actual meals and shit." He swiveled his head to address Griffin again. "Remember that time you tried to make brownies?"

Griffin scowled. "Vividly. Someone had left a pair of old

tennis shoes in the oven, so I had to clean it first, and only after I'd spent an hour sanitizing the damn thing did I realize it didn't even work."

Boone chuckled. "But you'd already bought all the ingredients, so you made the batter anyway and we ate it raw. I've never had such a stomachache in my whole goddamn life."

Smiling, Griffin pushed his chair back. "If you'll excuse me, I've got to see a man about a horse."

Boone snorted. "Jesus, dude. You're still saying that?"

"Always," Griffin said, smirking as he headed inside.

"You know who else says that?" Boone yelled after him. "My pop pop!" When Griffin was out of sight, he swung back around to give Alice a speculative look. "You two seem to be getting along pretty well."

"Yep." She reached for her beer to hide her sudden shyness at being the focus of Boone's attention. "It's fun hearing stories about him as a struggling actor. I guess he's always liked cooking."

Boone leaned back in his chair. "I think a lot of his domestic streak is because of his mom."

"He told me she died of lung cancer."

Boone looked surprised. "He doesn't usually talk about her. But yeah. It was just the two of them. I think he got used to looking after her even before she got sick. She was a single mom who worked two jobs, so Griff did all the cooking and cleaning around the house. When she got sick, he was taking business classes at community college, but he dropped out to take care of her. Then after she died, he moved out here to be an actor instead."

"That's kind of an abrupt change from business school."

"I guess he figured he didn't have anyone to take care of anymore, so he could do what he wanted. And he'd always wanted to be an actor."

Alice tried to picture Griffin as a business major, going into some dull middle management office job. She had to think he would have been miserable living that life. "How long after that did you meet him?" she asked Boone.

"Like right after. I think he lived out of his car for a few weeks before he landed at the crash pad with me. All that den mother stuff and the cooking, it was what he was used to doing for his mom—but I think it was also him trying to hold on to a piece of her. To make a home out of that dump."

"That's so sad."

She remembered the way she'd felt after her own mom had died. How lost she'd been after losing her mother and the only home she'd ever known in one fell swoop. There had been no possibility of making a home for herself when she'd gone to live with her father and his new family. Her stepmother and stepsiblings had reminded Alice every minute of every day what an imposition she was and how unwanted. And from her father she'd gotten nothing but the same disinterest he'd always exhibited toward her. She was nothing but an obligation to them, and she hadn't been able to get away fast enough. Thank god she'd had the money from her mother's life insurance to pay for college out of state.

"It was a real bad time for him," Boone said, frowning as he scraped at the label on his beer bottle. "That's why he's got such negative memories of the place. I mean, yeah, it was a total shithole, but I've still got some nostalgia for that period of my life. There's something special about the friends you make when you're broke and desperate."

"Who's broke and desperate?" Griffin asked, rejoining them.

"We were," Boone said. "We're talking about the crash pad again."

"Ugh." Griffin's lip curled. "That place."

Boone shot Alice a sideways glance, lifting his eyebrows as if to say, *See?*

As Griffin started clearing the table, Alice felt an intense rush of affection for him and all his domestic tendencies. "I'll handle all the cleanup," she said, getting to her feet.

"I can do it," he protested.

She took the plates from his hands with a stern look. "Sit down and relax. That's an order."

He surrendered without further argument as Boone tried unsuccessfully to hide his amusement. Alice stacked all the dishes with the efficiency she'd learned waitressing her way through undergrad, and went to clean up the kitchen. Not because she felt she had to, but because she *wanted* to.

"I LIKE HER," BOONE SAID AS SOON AS ALICE WAS INSIDE THE house. "She doesn't take any shit off you."

Griffin leaned back in his chair, smiling. "I know."

"So what's going on there anyway?"

"Where?" Griffin asked, affecting a blank expression. He knew exactly what his friend was getting at, but chose not to acknowledge it.

"You and Alice." Boone fixed him with a penetrating look. "Come on, you've been shooting daggers in my direction all night."

"That's because I find you so annoying."

"Bullshit. You're smitten with her."

"I am not *smitten*," Griffin said. "Besides, if anyone's smitten, it's her with you."

She'd practically been rendered dumbstruck at the sight of Boone. You'd have thought Griffin had brought home fucking Elvis. She'd never once acted that starstruck around *him*.

Boone erupted into delighted laughter. "I can't believe it! You're actually jealous! Holy shit! When's the last time you liked a woman enough to get jealous?"

Griffin scowled, uncomfortable with the direction the conversation had taken. "It's not like that."

"Really?" Boone eyed him speculatively. "So if I wanted to take a shot, you'd be fine with it?"

It took an embarrassing amount of effort for Griffin to suppress the impulse to object. "I don't have any say in her romantic life," he replied tightly. He could actually feel a vein throbbing in his forehead.

"Come on, man, I'm just kidding!" Boone leaned over and gave his shoulder a shove. "That girl only has eyes for you."

"She definitely does not."

"Don't be dense."

"I'm not. That's just not how it is with us. Trust me." He shook his head, remembering how guarded Alice had been around him at first. "She barely even liked me when she moved in."

Boone snorted and took a swig of beer. "All she wants to talk about when you're not around is you. And the way she looks at you when you're not paying attention? That girl's head over heels for you."

Griffin found that impossible to believe. Sure, they'd reached a point where it felt like they were becoming friendly, if not actual friends, but that was it. Alice's interest in him was purely platonic. Of that, he was certain.

He leaned forward for his water, wishing like hell he could have a beer instead. "I told you, we're just friends."

Boone gave him a disbelieving look. "You're hopeless. I notice you're not denying you like her though."

Griffin opened his mouth to protest, then snapped it shut again. There was no point. If he tried to lie about it, Boone would see right through him.

His friend let out another peal of laughter. "Oh my god, you're in love with your dog sitter! I love it!"

"*Shhh*. Jesus." Griffin threw a glance at the house to satisfy himself that Alice wasn't within eavesdropping range. "It's not love," he insisted in a low voice. "It's just an infatuation or something. I'll get over it."

Boone looked at him like he'd just proposed taking a vow of celibacy. "Why would you want to do that?"

"Because I'm paying her to house sit. I'm not going to sleep with someone on my payroll. It's sleazy."

"Okay, but—"

"No buts," Griffin said firmly. "It's nonnegotiable." Not with the sexual harassment Alice had already had to deal with. No way was he going to risk crossing any boundaries.

"*But*," Boone continued with his usual stubbornness, "she's not going to be your house sitter forever."

That thought had occurred to Griffin. But it wasn't worth dwelling on. In a week he was leaving for three months, and who knew where they'd both be when he got back or how they'd feel about each other. They might drift apart in his absence. She could have a boyfriend by then, or take a job in another city. There was no point in pinning his hopes on the future.

Boone polished off the last of his beer and set the empty on the table. "Just for the record, I totally ship it. If you could see the way you two look at each other—you're like the living embodiments of the heart-eyes emoji." He stretched his legs out in front of him and tucked his hands behind his head, looking smug. "I can't believe Griffin Beach, the king of No Strings Attached, has a crush on a woman he hasn't slept with. I'm gonna need some time to let this sink in."

"Don't be a jackass."

Boone's expression turned uncharacteristically serious. "This is a big deal. As long as I've known you, you've been totally closed off to even the possibility of love."

Griffin frowned at him. "That's not true." He wasn't closed off. Just practical.

He had his priorities, and right now advancing his career took precedence over finding a life partner. He was still young; there would be plenty of time to fall in love later, once he had established himself and things had slowed down. Besides, it wasn't like true love had been knocking down his door and he'd been turning it away. He'd yet to meet a woman who'd stirred anything deeper than a temporary attraction.

That's all it was with Alice too. An infatuation that would probably fade as quickly as it had developed. There was no sense ruining a perfectly good friendship over it.

"Look, I get why," Boone went on as if Griffin hadn't even spoken. "You're scared of letting yourself care about someone and then losing them the way you lost your mom. But I'm telling you, that's no way to live, man."

Griffin shot him a mutinous glare. "You're so full of shit."

Boone's latest girlfriend was a therapist, and ever since they started dating six months ago, the guy thought he was Dr. Phil.

Griffin's mother had died over a decade ago, for chrissake. He wasn't still walking around like some broken shambles of a man who couldn't put it behind him.

The look Boone gave him was surprisingly earnest. "Just promise me you'll keep an open heart. That's all I'm asking." His gaze swung to the horizon with a wistful sigh. "It's hard to find someone who really gets you. Someone you can actually stand to be around who's willing to put up with all your bullshit."

On that point, at least, they were in total agreement.

eleven

THURSDAY WAS Alice's official last day on *Las Vegas General.* Griffin wrapped on Friday when she wasn't there, but he told her there was a cake he hadn't been able to eat and a lot of tearful hugging. There had been no cake for Alice or the other extras on their last day, but that was no surprise. There had been some tearful hugging, however.

The extras had actually been invited to the wrap party on Saturday though. They'd made plans to get together for a pre-party before they headed over to the official party later, and Diane, who'd been a background regular since season one, had volunteered to host it at her house.

Alice was having a good time at the pre-party. No, scratch that. She was having a *great* time. She couldn't remember the last time she'd had this much fun. Part of it was probably due to the punch Diane had made, which was delicious and *strong.* But it was more than just being buzzed. For the first time since she'd started working as an extra, she felt like a full-fledged part of the gang instead of the newbie—ironically, just as it was all coming to an end.

The other extras had always been friendly to her, but

before tonight they hadn't felt like *friends*. Sure, they all spent long hours together and chatted on set and had meals together in the catering tent, but it had felt more like coworkers forced into proximity than actual friends. They'd never socialized outside of work before—well, some of them had, but Alice was the newcomer and hadn't been included before tonight. Her feeling of being an outsider had been compounded by the fact that she wasn't in it to be an actor like most of the others, and didn't share their ambitions or a lot of their interests.

Bex and Tina shared an agent and were always touching up each other's makeup and hair between takes. Joy and Katie were Soul Cycle buddies. Mark and Pete went on ski trips together and talked incessantly about the powder in Big Bear. Some of the other guys played in a weekend basketball league and passed their lunch breaks shooting hoops behind the soundstage. Middle-aged empty-nester Diane spent her down-time knitting scarves she handed out as gifts to the other extras and crew—who wore them with pride whenever the weather turned cold—but Alice hadn't been there long enough to rate one yet.

Rachel was the next newest, having only worked on the show for half a season longer than Alice, and the two of them had naturally migrated to one another during the long days on set. There'd been talk occasionally of catching a movie or hitting a sale on the weekend, but concrete plans never seemed to materialize. Which was Alice's fault, maybe, for not following through or giving off the right signals. In truth, she'd been operating in a bit of a haze this last year, so busy hiding from her former life that she hadn't bothered to invest much in her current one.

Two cups of punch into the pre-party at Diane's Silver Lake house, Alice realized she'd done herself a disservice. Unconstrained by set protocol, facing the imminent end of their working relationship and loosened up by alcohol, everyone had become considerably more fun than Alice was used to. The realization struck her belatedly that she actually *liked* these people she'd been working with for the last nine months—and surprisingly, they actually seemed to like her back.

"Your hair looks so pretty!" Bex slurred affectionately as she patted Alice's hard-fought waves, which had cost thirty minutes of effort and two curling iron burns to achieve. Bex turned to Tina, sloshing punch out of her red Solo cup onto Diane's terra-cotta tile floor. "Doesn't her hair look amazing?"

Tina nodded as gravely as if they were discussing relations with North Korea. "*Amazing*," she echoed a little too loudly as she reached up to test the springiness of Alice's curls. "Is that Dry Bar?"

"I did it myself," Alice said, trying not to feel weird about having two different people's hands in her hair.

"Fantastic!" Bex saluted her with her cup, spilling more punch onto the floor and narrowly missing her own shoes. "And your lipstick! It's perfect with that dress."

"Thank you," Alice replied as she eased out of the splash zone.

"We should all go to Sephora," Tina declared.

"Yes! We'll do a makeover day. I want to see what Alice would look like in a plum lip stain." Bex turned to Tina. "Don't you think she'd look great in plum?"

Tina squinted at Alice's lips with another grave nod. "Definitely."

"A regular happy hour!" Mark announced, appearing beside Bex with Pete in tow. "What do you say? I'm thinking Saturdays."

Tina turned her squint on him. "What?"

"We've decided we should plan a regular get-together so we don't lose touch," Pete explained. "Saturday afternoon drinks work for everyone?"

Bex nodded with enthusiasm. "Oh, I like that!"

Mark jerked his head toward the kitchen, where there was a large group huddled around the punch bowl. "Joy and Katie have already agreed to switch to the early Saturday Soul Cycle class so they can make it."

"Well, then we have to do it," Tina said.

Pete turned to Alice, lifting his eyebrows expectantly. "What about you? Are you in?"

"Absolutely." Alice hadn't felt "in" anything in ages, and it felt good to say yes. She just wished they'd all gotten together like this months ago, before they were about to go their separate ways.

After giving Mark her number so he could set up a group text to coordinate the details, Alice spied Rachel beckoning to her from the kitchen and excused herself.

"Did you say yes?" Rachel asked, topping off Alice's cup with more punch. "To the happy hour?"

"I did."

"Oh, good!" She clinked her plastic cup against Alice's. "It'll be nice to keep in touch."

"It will," Alice agreed, feeling lighter than she had in months. For once, the stars seemed to be aligned in her favor. She had a sweet place to live, a game plan for finishing her dissertation and graduating, and a whole new group of friends, apparently. Life was pretty good.

Rachel leaned in close and lowered her voice. "Can I ask you something?"

"Sure."

"What do you think of Pete?"

Alice glanced back toward the living room, where Pete was talking up the happy hour to the basketball contingent. "I don't know him very well…" She didn't know any of them very well, but she didn't know anything against him either. "But he seems nice?"

"Do you think he's interested in me?" Rachel asked, lowering her voice even more.

"I have no idea," Alice answered honestly. "But I don't know why he shouldn't be. You're hot and awesome."

Rachel beamed. "I am hot and awesome, aren't I?"

"Is he single?" Alice couldn't recall him ever mentioning a wife or girlfriend, but then she hadn't been paying all that much attention to him. "And straight?"

"Yes," Rachel answered definitively. "And god I hope so." She bit her lip. "Do you think I should ask him out?"

"Absolutely." Alice nodded vigorously. "You should definitely do that."

"Maybe I will…sometime when we're all not so drunk."

"Good plan." They clinked cups again, dissolving into alcohol-fueled giggles.

"Oh, Alice! There you are!" Diane elbowed her way through the kitchen to reach them. "I've got something for you," she said, thrusting a brown paper gift bag at her.

Alice passed her cup to Rachel so she could peek into the bag. When she saw what was inside, her eyes started to water. "You knit me a scarf?"

"I was afraid I wasn't going to finish in time, but I stayed up late last night to bind off and put the tassels on."

Alice looped it around her neck proudly. "I love it! Thank you so much!"

"There," Rachel said. "You've been anointed by Diane. You're officially part of the family now."

Alice threw her arms around Diane. "Thank you for the scarf, and thank you for having us all at your house tonight!"

"It's my pleasure," Diane replied, hugging her back with affection.

"Diane, what is in this punch?" Rachel asked. "It's turning us all into blubbering idiots."

"Everclear," Diane said with a wink. "Guaranteed to knock you on your ass."

Rachel's mouth fell open. "Holy shit, Diane! That's like a hundred and fifty proof!"

The older woman simply smiled as she moved off to refill the chip and dip platter.

"Did you drive?" Rachel asked Alice as she handed her cup back to her.

Alice shook her head. "Ubered."

"Me too, thank god. Want to share a car to the wrap party?"

Alice helped herself to more of the Everclear punch. "Definitely."

GRIFFIN GLANCED TOWARD THE DOOR FOR WHAT MUST HAVE been the hundredth time in the last half hour.

"Expecting someone?" Alexandra asked, lifting a speculative eyebrow.

"Nope," he replied and turned his attention back to her, attempting to feign polite interest in whatever she'd been talking about.

The wrap party was in full swing around him as he nursed his club soda and lime, regrettably sober. He and Alice had come separately—she'd met up with some of the extras beforehand for a pre-party, while Griffin had attended another pre-party for the principal cast at Alexandra's house. The catered dinner and cocktails—none of which Griffin could consume— had been an odd mix of celebratory and mournful, and the feeling had followed him to the wrap party.

No one seemed able to decide whether they were more relieved to be free of the grind or sad that it was all coming to an end. It reminded Griffin of his high school graduation, except if high school had lasted seven years and consisted of fourteen-hour class days. Some people would undoubtedly be moving on to bigger and better things, but others might not see another job this steady for the duration of their careers. Hollywood was a brutal business that way—you never knew when your ticket was up.

Griffin felt a bit guilty being the one with the most obviously burgeoning career. While everyone else was scrambling to line up auditions for pilot season, he already had two starring roles in major studio films on his docket, and another in the works. He'd successfully climbed out of the television dungeon and broken through into the big leagues.

Assuming his first big-budget starring vehicle didn't flop, of course. One failure was all it took if it was the *wrong* failure. He wasn't yet successful enough—or confident enough—to believe it couldn't all slip through his fingers at any moment. He'd seen it happen too many times before, and could list two dozen actors who'd grasped the ring of stardom only to disappear into obscurity after a couple unremarkable films. Their names haunted him every night as he tried to sleep, like his own personal cadre of Marley's ghosts.

The more the cocktails flowed and the night wore on, the more people gave up trying to talk over the thumping music in favor of shaking their stuff on the impromptu dance floor that had formed in front of the stage. Fortunately, Griffin was too sober to be tempted into showing off his questionable dance moves this year. He was still trying to live down the vids of his drunken, sweaty rendition of "Single Ladies" that had hit social media after last year's wrap party. There was something good to be said for involuntary sobriety.

A whoop sounded from the door as a group of newcomers joined the party. The extras had started trickling in, and from the sound of it they were well lubricated from their pre-party.

Griffin craned his neck for a glimpse of Alice in the crowd. When he finally spotted her, his jaw dropped.

She'd still been getting ready when he'd called out his goodbye on the way out the door earlier that evening, so he hadn't seen what she was wearing tonight. In a dramatic departure from the sweatshirts and T-shirts she usually favored around the house, she wore a red strapless dress that hugged her hips. Her fine blonde hair had been transformed into silky, springy waves, her wide blue eyes dramatically lined, and her lips painted a bright crimson.

She was stunning.

Reluctantly, he forced himself to look away. No matter how attracted he was to Alice, she was his employee, and she'd dealt with more than enough of that kind of shit already. It felt like she was finally starting to trust him—to like him even—and he wasn't going to do anything to mess that up.

Alice was off-limits. Which was all kinds of too bad, because she was the first woman he'd actually *liked* in—fuck, he couldn't even remember how long it'd been since he'd actually been interested in a woman for more than just a one-night stand.

How pathetic was that? Maybe Boone was right. Maybe he had closed himself off.

Unfortunately for Griffin, his old strategy of drinking away his feelings was currently off the table, so there he stood, stone-cold sober, trying not to pay too much attention to Alice.

"Sulking?" Alfie asked, squeezing Griffin's shoulder as he sidled up beside him.

Griffin pasted on a smile and attempted to drag himself out of his funk. "About what?"

"You're thinking about how much you're going to miss all this."

"Yeah, I guess I am."

"That's okay." Alfie's eyes sparkled as they surveyed the

room. "That means it was a good job. I've had way too many I couldn't wait to get away from. Count yourself lucky."

Griffin nodded as he sipped his club soda. Alfie was right. He *was* lucky. Everything was going his way. He should probably stop moping in the corner and try to enjoy the party.

"It's not like you'll never see any of them again." Alfie gave him a hearty slap on the back. "Hollywood's not that big a town. You'll find a way to keep the ones that are important in your life."

"Sure." Griffin's gaze traveled across the room to where Alice was talking with some of the crew.

"Why don't you go over there and ask her to dance?"

Griffin snapped his attention back to Alfie. "Who?"

"That extra." He waved vaguely in Alice's direction. Alfie could never remember anyone's names. "The one you've been staring at for weeks."

"I haven't been staring at her." Not for weeks, anyway. Had he? *Shit.* If Alfie had noticed, others probably had too.

"Job's over, so if that's what's been holding you back—"

"It's not." Alice's other job was the problem. The one working for Griffin, which had barely even started. If it wasn't for that…maybe.

Except if it wasn't for that, she'd still be giving him the cold shoulder, probably.

"Oh, go on." Alfie gave him an ineffectual shove. "Gather ye rosebuds, my boy."

* * *

ALICE'S FIRST—AND LIKELY ONLY—WRAP PARTY WAS MORE than living up to her expectations.

The venue that had been rented out for the occasion was draped in fairy lights and dramatic swags of jewel-toned crepe, softening the dark, industrial space and giving it a gothic feel.

A smattering of high-top tables dotted the floor by the bar at one end of the room, while a DJ spun records from a stage at the other. In between, throngs of cast and crew crowded the space in varying states of intoxication. There was quite a lot of hugging, some dancing closer to the DJ, and an occasional shriek of laughter loud enough to pierce the thrum of music.

Alice gave herself a moment to soak it all in. For the first time since moving to Los Angeles five years ago, she was at a real Hollywood party with celebrities on the guest list. Granted, they were celebrities she'd worked with for the better part of a year—and in one particular case was currently sharing a house with—but still. The boisterous, noisy vibe of the evening made a striking contrast to the on-set atmosphere. Of course, even in the midst of a party, social hierarchies persisted. She didn't observe a whole lot of intermixing between the underlings and their betters. The bigwigs seemed to be sticking mainly with their own kind, and the crew were largely divided by department. So basically it was your typical office party.

"Come on," Rachel shouted, grabbing Alice by the hand and dragging her toward the bar. "Let's refuel."

Alice felt like they'd already had plenty of fuel, courtesy of Diane's killer punch, but didn't argue. Once they were armed with cold bottles of beer, Rachel scanned the crowd—presumably for Pete, who'd caught a ride in another car. Alice peered to their right and spotted Griffin. He'd been talking to Alfie a minute ago, but now he was standing by himself clutching a club soda. Poor guy. He was probably one of the few sober people here.

He lifted his chin in greeting when he caught her eye, and she offered a sympathetic smile in return. Just as Alice was on the verge of heading over to talk to him, he was joined by a posse of women from the makeup department. His face relaxed into a smile as they grouped around him, looking every bit as glamorous and beautiful as the actresses in attendance. Maybe he wasn't having such a terrible time after all. As she watched them flirt with him, Alice was reminded of all the famous actors who'd fallen in love with makeup artists— possibly because they spent so much time staring into one another's eyes at work.

Well, good for him. Alice wished them all luck tonight.

Frankly, she was surprised Griffin hadn't brought any women home since she'd moved in. Maybe he was self-conscious about bringing them to the house with her living there. For all she knew, he'd been hooking up elsewhere before coming home every night. Well, maybe not every night, but some nights possibly. It was another thing she felt guilty about. She didn't like the idea that she was crimping his love life.

Rachel's hand closed on her arm, tugging her over to a group of PAs, who greeted them with enthusiastic hugs and girlish shrieks. Most of the PAs were younger than Alice, but one day some of them would likely be successful directors and producers and writers. At the moment, however, they were all scrambling to find new jobs, just like everyone else in the cast and crew.

It was a frequent topic of conversation throughout the night. There was as much networking happening as drinking, with people sharing leads and inside tips on productions that were about to start hiring and positions that might be opening up.

Alice found herself a bit on the outside again in the midst of these conversations. She wasn't in desperate need of a job thanks to her arrangement with Griffin—which she was too self-conscious to mention to anyone—and she wasn't going to work in the entertainment industry again, assuming things went as planned with her degree and post-graduation career path. This genuinely was the last time she'd ever see most of these people, she realized with a pang.

She wasn't the only one feeling emotional. The hugs flowed as freely as the booze as the night wore on. People Alice had barely interacted with all season kept coming up to offer overly earnest good wishes and sweaty, affectionate hugs. Eventually the social barriers broke down enough that the cast and higher-ups in the production began doing some mingling with the lowlier members of the crew. The paradigm shift was instigated by Alfie, who might not have many fucks left to give about his acting career, but still took his role as number one on the call sheet and self-appointed friend of the everyman surprisingly seriously. Once he started making the rounds on a mission to shake hands with everyone there—whether he remembered their names or not—Griffin quickly followed suit. Never having been one to hold himself apart from the crew, he abandoned his club soda in favor of circulating with his phone in hand, requesting selfies with everyone to remember them by.

Once the imaginary lines had been breached, it turned into a selfie free-for-all. Even Alice worked up the nerve to snag a few with some of her favorite cast members—minus Griffin, who she avoided for reasons she couldn't articulate. Possibly because she was having trouble reconciling Work Griffin with Home Griffin. On the one hand there was the hot young actor plastered on billboards all over town who was worshipped by the crew, and on the other there was her shockingly normal roommate who she'd gotten used to wearing pajamas around. There was also a sense—correct or not—that their relationship transcended the need for a goodbye selfie. Unlike everyone else here, Alice would remain in regular contact with him after tonight.

Besides, whenever she glanced his way, he seemed to be flirting with a different female crew member. Which was fine. But she wasn't interested in competing for his attention.

Instead, she focused on having her own fun, dividing her time between the bar and the dance floor, which was now packed with bodies and took up almost half the room. At some point she lost track of how many drinks she'd had, how many people she'd talked to, or what time it was. She had a definite memory of doing a bump and grind with an Emmy-winning writer, but the rest of it was a blur. After a particularly vigorous dance-off to her favorite Bruno Mars song, the drinking and the exertion caught up with her, and she stumbled away from the throng of dancers writhing to Janelle Monáe, in search of some water and maybe a place to sit down and catch her breath.

As Alice elbowed her way through the crowd in front of the bar, an intoxicated producer's assistant accidentally hip-checked her, sending her careening directly into a startled Griffin.

"Whoa," he said, wrapping a hand around her arm to keep her from losing her balance. "You okay?"

"Fine." She tried to focus on his chest, because his face was too pretty to stare at this close—and also too blurry.

Yeah, okay, maybe she'd had a little too much to drink.

"You want some water?" He pressed a plastic bottle into her hand. It was blessedly cold, and she was seized by the urge to stick it down the front of her dress to cool herself off. Instead, she settled for drinking half of it in one long glug.

"Better?" Griffin asked with an amused look.

"Yes, much. Thank you."

She tried to give the bottle back to him but he shook his head. "Keep it. I've been hydrating all night, while you've been out there dehydrating."

In that case she *was* going to press the damn thing against her overheated chest, propriety be damned. She sighed in ecstasy as the cool plastic hit her skin, and saw Griffin's eyes flicker to her cleavage, then quickly away in embarrassment. It was gratifying to know he didn't just see her as a sexless dog sitter.

"Have you been having fun?" she yelled over the music. She was a little surprised he hadn't yet left with one of the many adoring and clearly willing women she'd seen him flirting with throughout the night.

His smile went glassy. "Yep. Great time."

She knew him well enough by now to recognize the lie. "I'm sorry it's not more fun for you."

He let his smile slip as he shrugged. "It's hard saying goodbye to everyone, and I don't have the advantage of being drunk to numb myself to it."

She suspected he was also still harboring guilt over the show ending. After all, there wouldn't be any goodbyes tonight if only he'd chucked his burgeoning film career and renewed his contract with a modestly-rated network drama with maybe another season or two left in its run before it was canceled for mediocre ratings. Not that anyone in their right mind would make such a choice. But he seemed to enjoy beating himself up over things that weren't his fault. Not that Alice would know anything about that.

A gaggle of people from the production office pushed past them, and Griffin reached a protective arm out to shift her toward him, using his mass to shield her from being jostled. "We haven't taken our selfie yet."

Alice covered her face with her hands and shook her head in horror. "I'm all sweaty and messy."

His fingers closed around hers, tugging her hands down. "Are you kidding? You look beautiful."

Her head jerked up and she found herself looking directly into his eyes. In the dim room they shone with pinpricks of light, like stars in the night sky. The way he was looking at her made her stomach knot and her heart clatter against the inside of her chest.

Alice shook her head again. Whatever she might think she saw in his eyes was only a product of her alcohol-fueled imagination. One embarrassed peek at her cleavage did not mean Griffin Beach was in any way interested in her. She turned her face away from his, feeling flustered. "My mascara's probably running down my face."

"Your mascara's fine. Look." He held his phone up so she could see herself in the camera app.

Shockingly, she didn't look that bad, even after a night of hard drinking and sweaty dancing. Three cheers for water-proof eyeliner. She hastily smoothed her hair and swiped under her eyes for good measure.

He took his phone back and draped a heavy arm around her shoulders. "I have to have something to remember you by," he said as he pulled her close enough that she could smell his aftershave, which she recognized from the whiffs that drifted down the hall from his bedroom. And here she was reeking of sweat and metabolized Everclear probably.

She let out a nervous laugh as she slipped her arm around his waist. "We literally live together."

He held his phone at arm's length and leaned his head against hers to fit both their faces in frame. "Only for another couple days. I'm leaving Monday."

She'd known of course, but until that moment it hadn't really hit her. Ever since she'd moved in, she'd been looking forward to having the house to herself and counting down the days until Griffin left. But now that it was imminent she found herself dreading his departure.

His head rested warmly against her temple. "Smile."

Alice looked into the camera and did her best.

"Perfect," he declared, presenting the photo to her for approval.

He looked predictably gorgeous, but she didn't look half bad either. The two of them appeared cozy and happy together beaming out of the screen. "Will you send me a copy of that?" she asked.

"Of course." Griffin let go of her, and she swayed a little. "You okay there?" he asked, lifting a concerned eyebrow.

She nodded too vigorously and the room tilted. Her hand shot out, clutching at his arm to steady herself. "Just a little dizzy. I don't want to shock you, but I think I may be drunk." Her voice sounded too loud, even over the music and the din of the crowd.

"How much have you had?"

"Mmmmm…" She tried to remember and quickly gave up. "No idea. A lot. But I'm fine. I can hold my liquor." She let go of him to prove her point, teetered, and attached herself to his arm again.

His mouth tugged into a smile. "I'm sure you can."

"The room's just annoyingly wobbly is all."

"The room is perfectly stationary. You're the one who's wobbly, tough guy."

"Po-tay-to, po-tah-to." Alice rubbed her temples, which had begun to throb in time with the music.

A frown wrinkled Griffin's forehead. "Maybe you should call it a night."

She glanced toward the dance floor, where some of the extras were shaking their groove things to "Shake Your Groove Thing." The thought of more dancing made her feel queasy. "I think you may be right about that."

"You didn't drive yourself, did you?"

"No, I shared an Uber with Rachel. I'll find her and see if she's ready to go." Still holding on to Griffin for balance, Alice rose up on her tiptoes and craned her neck, scanning the room for Rachel's purple dress and dark hair.

"She left an hour ago with Pete."

"She did?" Alice hadn't even noticed. Good for Rachel. And good for Pete. She hoped they were having magnificent sex.

Griffin extracted himself from Alice's grip and slipped a

steadying arm around her waist. "Come on. I'll drive you home."

A pang of guilt pierced her alcohol buzz as he steered her toward the door. "You don't have to leave the party on my account. I can get my own Uber."

"Believe me, I'm ready to go home."

She spared a moment to worry that someone would see them leaving together, then decided she didn't care. It was far easier to just lean on Griffin and let him lead her away.

The show was over, so they weren't coworkers anymore. Besides, everyone was too busy having their own good time to notice who she left with.

twelve

AN UNFAMILIAR FEELING burned in Griffin's chest as they waited for the valet to bring his car around. Whatever it was, he didn't like it.

Alice leaned against him, her cheek resting on his shoulder and her hair tickling his neck. That part he did like—intensely. He suspected the one feeling had a lot to do with the other, in a way he wasn't prepared to examine too closely at the moment.

A gust of wind sent goose bumps shivering over her skin and he instinctively slid his hand down her arm. She sighed and nuzzled closer, clasping her hands behind his back.

The feeling in Griffin's chest worked its way up to his throat. He swallowed and shifted Alice slightly to the side and away from his growing erection.

Oh thank god. The valet.

Griffin escorted Alice to the passenger's side and saw her tucked inside the car before handing the valet a tip and sliding behind the wheel.

"Seat belt," he reminded her as he fastened his own.

Alice's head swiveled toward him, and she smiled as if she

was surprised to find him sitting beside her in his own car. "Hmmm?"

"You need to put your seat belt on."

"Right-o." She twisted away from him and dug around beside the door looking for it. It took her an absurdly long time to locate it and stretch it across her body. Griffin let her fumble with the buckle for a few more seconds before taking it from her and clicking it into place himself.

"Thanks," she said, placing her hand over his and squeezing warmly.

Her skirt had slid up when she got in the car, exposing an expanse of smooth, creamy thigh. It was nothing he hadn't seen around the house plenty of times when she was wearing her favorite cutoff shorts, but somehow it felt more dangerous here in the car beneath her killer strapless dress.

Griffin fixed his eyes straight ahead and put both hands on the wheel.

Alice fiddled with the sound system for a few minutes, skipping through his playlists until she found one she liked. As a Sia song filled the car, she settled back in her seat with a sigh. "I didn't mean to drink so much tonight, but it was just so fun and so delicious."

Amusement curved his lips. "Don't worry about it. You deserve to cut loose and enjoy yourself."

"What about you?"

"What about me?"

She reached across the console and gave his leg an accusing poke. "You didn't cut loose. Or enjoy yourself."

Griffin kept his eyes on the road. "I don't have to cut loose to have a good time."

"But you didn't have a good time, did you? You pretended to, but it was all an act."

"I'm an actor. Acting's kind of my thing."

"Why didn't you have a good time?" she persisted.

He shrugged. "I don't like goodbyes."

"Yeah, me neither."

When he let himself glance over at her, she was staring out the window.

They passed the rest of the drive in silence. He was pretty sure Alice had fallen asleep until her head snapped up when he put the car in park. She rubbed her eyes and tried unsuccessfully to stifle a yawn.

Griffin unclipped his seat belt and leaned over to help her with hers. "Let's get you unbuckled."

"You're nice," she murmured drowsily. "I didn't think you would be, but you are."

He snorted. "Thanks...I think."

Her brow wrinkled with a frown. "You know what I mean. People don't always turn out to be nice. But you did."

He reached out to touch her face before he had a chance to think about what he was doing. Her head lolled against his palm, her lips forming a soft smile as her eyes fluttered closed. It felt so natural and she looked so lovely, he couldn't help stroking her cheek.

No.

Alice was drunk and she didn't know what she was doing. Griffin had some idea what it had taken for her to start trusting him, and he sure as shit wasn't going to repay that trust by taking advantage when her inhibitions were lowered.

"Come on," he said, retracting his hand. "Let's get you inside."

He got out of the car and walked around to her door, balling the hand that had touched her face into a tight fist, as if he could hold on to a piece of her that way.

When he opened the car door, she smiled up at him and extended a hand. He accepted it, resting his other hand on the back of her head to protect it as he helped her out of the car. As soon as she was on her feet she leaned against him again, as casually as if it were something she'd done a thousand times before. His heart thumped in his chest as he slipped his arm around her to guide her toward the house. *For her own protection*, he told himself. So she didn't stumble and fall on the dark, uneven walk to the door.

"You smell nice," she murmured into his chest.

"So do you." She smelled like peaches, and very slightly of sweat, but in a not-unpleasant way.

He suspected she'd be mortified tomorrow, assuming she remembered any of this. Meanwhile, Griffin was trying to burn the memory into his brain. To memorize how it felt to hold her body close to his, since it would probably never happen again.

When he got Alice into the house, she bent to pet Taco and wound up sliding to the living room floor in a heap. Griffin left her there for a minute while he went to grab a Gatorade out of the fridge. When he came back, she was stretched out on her back like she planned to fall asleep right there with Taco licking her face.

"Up," Griffin said, setting the Gatorade on the coffee table. "No passing out on the floor."

"But it's so comfy here."

"No, it's not." He stooped and grabbed her hands to pull her upright. The momentum carried her all the way into his arms, where she sagged against him.

"I take it back," she mumbled into his chest, holding on tight. "This is much comfier."

Wincing at the inappropriateness of their current position, he hug-walked Alice over to the couch, where he carefully lowered her down. "Sit."

"Sit," she repeated, grinning up at him.

When he was reasonably convinced she wasn't going to tip onto the floor again, he reached for the Gatorade. "Drink," he ordered, twisting the lid off and handing it to her.

She scrunched her nose up. "*Sit...drink.* I'm not a dog, you know."

"I know that, but you're taking as much micromanaging as one. And you need the electrolytes, so drink up." He sat down at the opposite end of the couch, leaving plenty of space between them.

She took a sip and made a face. "What flavor is this?"

"Blue."

"Blue's not a flavor, it's a color."

"I think it's supposed to be raspberry."

"Raspberries aren't blue. You know what's blue? Blueberries. Why is everything always blue raspberry, which doesn't exist, instead of blueberry, which does?"

Griffin felt himself smile. "I don't know. Maybe the guy who invented blue raspberry flavor really hated blueberries. Drink some more."

Alice managed a few more swallows, then wiped her mouth with the back of her hand and set the bottle on the coffee table. "Gross."

Griffin eyed her warily. "How're you feeling? You're not gonna ralph, are you?" If so, he preferred to get her into the bathroom now and save his upholstery. Blue raspberry left a bitch of a stain.

"Nope. The room's a little spinny, but otherwise I'm gooooood." Alice twisted around and lay back on the couch with her feet hanging over the armrest and her head in his lap.

Terrific. Griffin willed his body to relax, and tried to act like he wasn't feeling anything about having Alice so close.

She reached up and ran her fingers over his chin.

Breathe. This is fine.

"I wish you weren't leaving," she said as she traced his jawline. "I like being your roommate."

He caught her fingers, giving them a squeeze before placing them on her stomach. "I like being your roommate too." He didn't dare confess that he wanted to be more than just a roommate, even though she probably wouldn't remember. He couldn't risk damaging what they had.

She rolled toward him in an attempt to snuggle closer, and her head brushed against his dick.

Griffin practically sprang out from under her. "Time for you to go night-night," he said as he levered her to her feet.

"Boo." Her lower lip stuck out in an exaggerated pout, but she let him guide her to her bedroom.

He hadn't been in there since her first day in the house, when it had still been cluttered with suitcases. The room smelled like Alice now. Sweet and flowery with an undertone of peaches. The room was neat as a pin, except for some discarded clothes on the floor. He tried not to look at the lacy pink bra lying in plain sight as he led her to the bed.

She sank down on the end of the mattress and flopped backward with her arms stretched overhead, which did alarming things to the top of her strapless dress. Griffin averted his eyes from the hint of black lace peeking out, and instead focused on Alice's feet, which were clad in strappy black heels.

No way was he helping her out of her dress, but he could at least do her the favor of taking her shoes off for her before she fell asleep. He sat on the edge of the bed, lifted one of her feet into his lap, and began to unfasten the tiny buckle on the strap. The damn thing was *really* small, and his thick fingers had a bitch of a time. Alice's toes were painted the same crimson as her lips and dress, and they wiggled playfully as Griffin fought with the buckle. At least she wasn't ticklish. He remembered that much from the scene they'd done together, when he'd pretended to examine her ankle. The memory of her body, warm and small on the gurney under his, came back to him, and he pushed it back down deep.

By the second shoe, Griffin had started to get the hang of those infernal little buckles, so it went much faster than the first. When he eased it off he noticed an angry red blister forming on the ball of Alice's foot.

"Does that hurt?" he asked, prodding it gently to see if it required antiseptic.

"It's fine," she muttered, plucking at his arm. "Come here."

Griffin stood up and walked around to the side of the bed, standing over her uncertainly.

"Sit." Alice scooted higher on the bed and tugged on his hand.

Reluctantly, he let her pull him down to sit beside her on the edge of the mattress. "Do you need anything?" Maybe he should get her some aspirin or a glass of water—

"Just you."

Griffin was a decent fucking human being who didn't put the moves on women when they were drunk, but *goddamn*. The devil was really determined to test him tonight.

Alice was still holding on to his hand, stroking her thumb over his knuckles. He curled his fingers around hers and swallowed. His whole body tingled with an awareness of her that crackled in the air between them like a magnetic field. It would be so easy to close the distance between them and brush his lips against hers...

This was dangerous.

He let go of her hand and stood up, backing away. "I'll be right down the hall if you need anything."

She curled up on her side, tucking her hands beneath her cheek, and closed her eyes. Griffin unfolded the throw blanket from the foot of the bed and gingerly draped it over her. Then he backed out of the room, turning off the light before quietly shutting the door behind him.

Safely in the hall, with no one around to see, he rested his forehead against the door and smiled.

Alice's memories of the wrap party were hazy.

The part when Griffin had taken her home was somewhat clearer, surprisingly, but still frustratingly blurry. She couldn't remember much of their conversation, but had a distinct impression of nuzzling against his chest, which was acutely embarrassing. There were other vague memories as well: strong arms, gentle hands, soft eyes.

And one very clear image of lying on the couch with her head in his lap.

She was utterly mortified. Also annoyed. It was unfair that she'd somehow managed to cuddle with Griffin and could barely remember it.

She'd awoken on top of her comforter the next morning, still wearing her dress from the party and covered by a blanket she assumed she had Griffin to thank for. That was a bit embarrassing as well.

They both avoided speaking of it. Alice's head was throbbing with a massive hangover, and Griffin was busy packing. Aside from handing her a large bottle of Gatorade and two aspirin, he considerately left her alone to her misery and embarrassment.

She wanted to thank him for getting her home and into bed like a gentleman and a good friend, but was too ashamed to raise the subject. Far easier to pretend the whole night had never happened.

Unfortunately, someone *had* seen Alice leave the party with Griffin, and the news had made it through the crew gossip mill. There was even a blurry photo of them getting into Griffin's car on TMZ, but fortunately Alice's face was turned away from the camera.

Rachel called in the afternoon to get the scoop. "I want all the gory details. Spill."

"Huh?" Alice had been dozing on her bed when her phone rang, and her head was still feeling woolly.

"You and Griffin? Everyone knows you left with him last night."

Alice groaned and rolled onto her back. "It's not what you think."

"Tell me absolutely everything," Rachel rushed on. "Is he a good lay? Does he have the six-pack even when he hasn't done a water cut? How long is his dick? This one time he was wearing these tight slacks, and I swear to god it looked like the bulge went halfway down his thigh, but Tina insisted it was just the battery pack for his mic—so which is it?"

"Stop!" Alice begged, rubbing her temple. "I don't know any of the answers." Except the six-pack thing, which was a definite yes, but now was not the time to admit that.

"Come on. You did leave the party with him, didn't you?"

Alice got up and shut her bedroom door, in case Griffin was within earshot. "Yes, but nothing happened. I swear."

"How is that possible? He's a total man-slut. Wait—did you *turn him down?*" Rachel sounded aghast.

"No, I didn't have to," Alice tried to explain. "It's not like that. I'm…" His friend? His roommate? His dog sitter? All of the above?

"You're what?"

"I'm his house sitter, okay? I'm gonna be taking care of his dog and bringing in his mail while he's in Atlanta the next three months." She suddenly remembered he was leaving tomorrow and felt a knot form in her stomach.

"Oh." Rachel's voice deflated in disappointment. "Hang on. Are you staying at his place *now?*"

Alice winced. "Yeah."

"You're living together?" Rachel's voice was so piercing that Alice had to hold the phone away from her ear.

"I guess, yeah. As roommates, sort of."

"What's *that* like?"

Alice sank down on the corner of the bed. "It was kind of weird at first, but it's not so bad. He's a nice guy."

Rachel snorted. "That's not what I heard."

"What does that mean? What did you hear?"

"You know as well as I do he flirts with everything on two legs."

"That's just his personality. He's all bark and no bite."

"Yeah, that's not what Janie in makeup said. From what I've heard, the guy's slept with most of his female costars, half the hair and makeup departments, and he's made a pretty good dent in wardrobe too. He's practically a sex addict."

"That's an exaggeration." As far as Alice had been able to discern, Griffin had been effectively celibate for the last month. "Don't believe everything you hear."

"Are you telling me he's never once put the moves on you?"

"Never once."

"Oh." Rachel's tone was pitying.

Alice supposed it was sort of pitiful. On the one hand, she was grateful Griffin hadn't hit on her while she was living with him. But on the other…it was hard not to feel a little insulted. Why *hadn't* he? Was there something wrong with her? Was she not hot enough for him to try to sleep with?

Alice bit down on her thumbnail. "He doesn't see me that way, is all."

"Right. Gotcha." Rachel's voice was bitter. "Because we're not people, we're just extras, right? Even he won't lower himself that far."

"It's not like that." She and Griffin were friends—sort of. "He's my employer, technically. He probably just thinks it would be skeevy." Which it would. Further proof that he was a nice guy and not some out-of-control sex addict.

"So what's his house like?"

"Nice. It's not huge or anything. Just a regular two-bedroom in Studio City. Great view though."

"What's he like when he's not at work?"

"Pretty much the same as when he's at work, only quieter."

Rachel groaned in disappointment. "Come on, you've got to have *some* dirt to share."

"I don't. He's pretty boring, really. He's on this ridiculous diet for the movie he's about to do, so he mostly just eats protein and goes to the gym."

"That's depressing."

It was, a bit. On top of his hefty shooting schedule for *LV Gen*, Griffin spent two hours training at the gym every day and basically had to force himself to choke down ungodly amounts of protein. Now that Alice had seen how hard he worked for that body, she had even more respect for it. "He does have the abs though. Like, all the time."

"Nice! At least you're getting something out of this arrangement."

"Enough about me and my boring living arrangement," Alice said, changing the subject. "I want the scoop on you and Pete."

―――――――

GRIFFIN WAS KEPT BUSY ALL DAY WITH PACKING AND TRAVEL preparations. Three months was a long time to be away, and he bustled around the house with a harried expression as he made last-minute arrangements and wrote up lists for Alice with emergency phone numbers and reminders about things like paying the cleaning woman and the gardener.

That night, he grilled steaks for the two of them again, and after they'd eaten they sat on the back deck taking turns throwing a tennis ball for Taco as they watched the sun go down.

"I'm gonna miss this," Griffin said wistfully.

Alice told herself he was talking about Taco and the house,

not her specifically. Why would he miss her? She'd only been part of his life for a few weeks. She passed the tennis ball to him. "I bet you'll be so busy the time will fly. It'll be over before you know it."

He chucked the ball into the yard. "Do you think Taco'll forget about me? I'm not sure dogs have object permanence. As soon as I'm gone, he'll probably think I've winked out of existence."

Alice thought about it as Taco proudly returned the ball to his owner. "Maybe that's why dogs are always so happy to see you when you come home. Because they think you stop existing as soon as you're out of sight."

Griffin's brow furrowed as he tossed the ball again. "His brain *is* the size of a ping-pong ball, so maybe."

It was an interesting theory, but Alice didn't like the frown on Griffin's face. "He's not gonna forget about you. Are you kidding? Your scent's all over the house—and you've seen those videos of soldiers coming back and surprising their dogs. Those dogs definitely did not forget."

"That's true, I guess."

"It's gonna be fine," Alice said, noticing the way Griffin's fingers were clenched on the arm of the chair.

He nodded abstractly. "I hate starting a new job. Always do."

"Why?"

"Acting is…" He paused and rubbed a hand over the back of his neck. "It requires a certain amount of vulnerability. At least for me it does. Tapping into that in front of a bunch of strangers is always terrifying the first few days. It usually gets easier once I get to know people and start to feel more comfortable, but at first it's fucking awful. There's always this fear that I'm not good enough, that I don't deserve to be there and I'm about to show my ass. That everyone will realize how much I suck."

That was exactly how Alice had felt about graduate school. It was a shock to realize Griffin struggled just as much with imposter syndrome as she did. He'd always seemed so confident and laid back, but she was beginning to understand just how much effort he put into maintaining that appearance, and how much anxiety it disguised.

"You know that's just your brain telling you lies, right?" she said. "I know how hard it can be to shut out those negative emotions when they start snowballing—believe me—but I'm here to tell you that you don't suck. You're objectively awesome."

He reached a hand over his shoulder to scratch his back, looking uncomfortable. "Thanks. I really wasn't fishing for compliments though."

"I know. I wasn't complimenting you. I was just stating a fact."

He glanced over at her, a hint of a smile appearing at the corner of his mouth before his eyes darted away again. "Anyway, you'll probably be glad to get rid of me and have the place to yourself. I imagine you'll start throwing keggers as soon as I'm gone."

Alice leaned over to pick up the ball Taco had dropped between them. "Not really my style. I'm more of a high tea person."

"I guess it's all right if you want to throw a high tea."

"You sure? My high teas can get pretty wild. Sometimes I serve two kinds of jam with the scones." She faked a throw, but Taco was too smart to run after it. He stayed where he was, swishing his tail expectantly.

"Wow. Okay, Queen Victoria. Let's not go overboard."

She tossed the ball for real and turned her head toward Griffin. "You know I'm not going to throw any parties while you're gone, right?"

His impossibly blue eyes met hers. "You can have people over if you want. I trust you."

It felt good to know he trusted her, but it was the way he was looking at her when he said it that made her feel warm all over. She dropped her eyes to the beer in her hand. "I'll probably just work on my dissertation the whole time."

"How's that going?"

Her thumbnail scraped at the label. "Okay, I guess. It's hard, getting back into it after all these months, but I'm feeling more motivated than I have in a while." A circumstance she owed largely to Griffin. She wasn't sure how she'd ever repay him for this opportunity to throw herself back into her schoolwork worry-free.

"I expect you to have a PhD by the time I get back."

Alice snorted and took a swig of beer. "If only. At the earliest, I might be able to defend in time to graduate at the end of the summer. But more likely December."

"So you'll be Dr. Carlisle by Christmas."

"Maybe." It was hard to imagine the finish line after all this time, but it wasn't actually that far away anymore.

"I expect an invitation to your graduation."

She made a wry face. "Sure."

"I'm serious."

When she looked over at his earnest expression it made her chest feel tight, like someone had wrapped an Ace bandage around it. "I probably won't even go to the ceremony."

"Why the heck not?"

"Because they're boring. And it's not like I have any family who'll insist on being there." She had no desire to sit on a stage in a polyester gown for two hours, only to be greeted by a deafening silence when her name was called.

"When you said before you didn't have a dad—"

"I have a dad," she said. "He's alive and well. He just doesn't give a shit about me."

"Sorry if it's a sore subject."

She shook her head, not wanting Griffin to feel bad. "It's fine."

He gave her an appraising look. "Whatever it is, I don't think it's fine."

Alice shrugged. It wasn't that she minded talking about her father, so much as she minded that he'd ever been a part of her life at all. "My parents divorced when I was five, and my dad got remarried to a woman who had two kids. I barely ever saw him at all—until my mom died and I had to go live with him and his new family." She pressed her lips together, remembering the grudging manner in which she had been welcomed into her own father's home, and the cold, resentful interactions that had marked the next five years. "Let's just say we didn't click. They didn't want me there any more than I wanted to be there."

"I'm sorry. It must have been awful."

"I got through it." At this point, the pain felt distant, like an old injury that only ached when it rained. "I found a college out of state and I never went back." She shrugged again. "I haven't really talked to my father much since."

"And he hasn't tried to reach out to you?"

"Nope. I told you, he doesn't give a shit." She washed down the bitterness in her throat with a mouthful of beer.

Griffin's gaze remained fixed on her for a moment, his expression soft and thoughtful, before he turned away. His eyes seemed to focus on the distant skyline as he ran a hand through his hair. It was a nervous tic he'd been displaying all day as he prepared for his imminent departure, and it had left his hair an endearingly tousled mess.

"I never knew my father," he said quietly. "He didn't want anything to do with my mom after she got pregnant. But maybe I was better off that way—even though it sucked for my mom, having to raise me alone."

Alice took another swallow of beer. "Is it wrong that I wish I'd never known my dad?"

"No, I don't think it's wrong."

"I guess it means I would have gone to foster care when my mom died, but at least in foster care you know why they don't love you."

The eyes Griffin turned on her were almost as dark as the sky overhead where a few faint stars had begun to glimmer. "Your dad's an idiot."

She tried to muster a smile. "So's yours, for taking off before he got to meet you."

He held her gaze for a moment before shaking off the heavy mood and reaching for the water bottle that was never far from his fingertips. "Oh hey, speaking of family—you should probably know I put you down as my emergency contact. I hope that's okay."

Alice blinked at him. "Me?"

Shrugging, he leaned back in his chair again. "I don't have any family I'm close to, and you're here taking care of my dog and my house and all my stuff. I figure if they're gonna call anyone in an emergency, it should be you."

"Oh, sure." It was perfectly logical reasoning—which did not account for the very unreasonable rush of feelings it inspired.

"I thought about putting Boone down, but he's up in Vancouver three-quarters of the year, and anyway he'd be fucking useless in an emergency. At least you'll be able to keep a cool head and take care of shit."

"Did you know I actually got my master's degree in taking care of shit?"

Griffin's mouth curved into a smile. "If you're gonna be in charge of my personal affairs, I guess I should tell you my deep, dark secret."

"You have a deep, dark secret?"

He nodded with theatrical seriousness. "My last name isn't really Beach."

Alice played along, giving him a look of wide-eyed interest. "You don't say."

"It's Micklethwaite."

"Griffin Micklethwaite." She pronounced the syllables slowly, taking it for a test drive.

"Doesn't exactly roll off the tongue, does it?"

"No," she agreed. "But I like it."

It felt like he'd given her a gift. As if by sharing his real name he'd offered her a glimpse of his true self—the one he kept hidden behind his charming smiles and happy-go-lucky facade.

A lump formed in Alice's throat. Who'd have thought, when she first moved in with Griffin, that she'd ever come to feel this close to him? And now it was all about to end. She wasn't ready for that to happen.

Tomorrow he would get on a plane, and he'd be so busy adjusting to the new city and shooting his new movie that he'd forget all about her. Maybe she'd get a text from him occasionally to do with Taco or the house. But they wouldn't talk. Not like this.

And then when he came back, she'd have to move out and that would be that. He'd go back to his life and she'd go back to hers.

They'd probably never see each other—unless he needed a dog sitter again.

Monday morning, Alice got up early to see Griffin off and help him roll his bags out to the hired car that would take him to the airport. It was a sleek black Town Car driven by a blond Eastern European named Ignas who was entirely too cheerful for six o'clock in the morning.

"Call if you need anything," Griffin said as Ignas loaded the last bag into the sedan's cavernous trunk. "Anything at all."

"I will." Alice scooped Taco off the ground and held him up to her face. "We'll be fine though, won't we, buddy?"

Griffin reached out to ruffle the dog's head. "Be good. Don't chase the neighbor's cat or eat any poop while I'm gone."

"I'll do my best," Alice said, which got a faint smile out of Griffin. "Don't worry about us. Go do your movie star thing."

"Right."

Ignas had already shut the trunk and gotten behind the wheel, waiting to take Griffin away.

"You better get going," Alice said.

Griffin nodded. For a second, he looked like he might be about to hug her, then seemed to decide against it. He bent to kiss the top of Taco's head and gave her a jerky sort of goodbye nod instead.

Alice held Taco tight as Griffin walked to the car and got in the back seat. He paused with his hand on the door and looked back at her. "See you in three months."

She bit her lip and waved goodbye.

After the Town Car backed down the drive, Alice went into the house and flopped down on the couch. The place was all hers now. She ought to be excited about that. It was what she'd been waiting for ever since she moved in.

So why did she feel like she'd just lost something important?

thirteen

IT WAS beyond weird living in Griffin's house without
Griffin. Alice kept listening for the sound of him coming home
and then remembering he wouldn't *be* coming home. Not for
months.

The first week passed with agonizing slowness.

She'd never actually lived alone before. There had always
been a roommate, and before that her father's family, and
before that her mother. She had thought she'd enjoy the soli-
tude, but mostly it set her on edge.

She was restless during the days and had a hard time
sleeping at night. With her job on *Las Vegas General* over, Alice
found herself at loose ends. It was jarring to go from working
long hours to having her days completely empty. There was
literally nothing to keep her from staying in her pajamas all
day, except her own sense that it would probably be an
unhealthy habit to get into. A nagging voice in the back of her
mind kept telling her she was just one missed shower away
from sinking into a spiral of sloth and depression.

To combat the yawning abyss of inertia, she tried to keep
busy working on her dissertation, but the models took hours

and hours to run, which left her with a lot of time to fill in between. She started taking Taco for walks twice a day, exploring all the nearby parks and walking paths. She watched all of *The Crown* and fell into a Wikipedia k-hole reading about the Windsors. She even tried teaching herself to cook, with extremely mixed success.

Her house-sitting duties were light, but she took them seriously. Every few days she'd text Griffin a picture of Taco so he'd know his dog was alive and well. Usually he responded with a thumbs-up or maybe a brief comment, but that was pretty much the extent of their communication.

She'd gotten exactly one non-dog-related text from him since he'd left: a photo taken from the balcony of his midtown condo in Atlanta on the night he arrived. Alice had complimented him on the view, he'd texted back a thumbs-up emoji, and that was that. She assumed he was busy acclimating to his new surroundings and job. She wanted to ask him how it was going, but she was too afraid of bothering him when she knew he was probably busy, so she left him alone.

Saturday, at least, was drinks with the other extras, which got Alice out of the house and around other human beings. They teased her about "bagging" Griffin and her brush with TMZ fame until she explained the situation: that she'd simply traded one menial, celebrity-adjacent job for another. Diane made a Kato Kaelin crack that Mark explained to the rest of them courtesy of his obsession with *The People vs. O.J. Simpson*, but after that the conversation switched to other topics.

Pete had already gotten another background gig on a new Netflix show. Mark was in the running to be the writer's assistant on a network sitcom. Diane had taken an unpaid role in a student film, Bex had booked a commercial, and Tina had a callback next week for a speaking part in a Hallmark movie. Rachel was picking up shifts at Starbucks for the time being, but Pete was trying to get her onto his show.

Only a week since *Las Vegas General* had closed up shop, and they'd all moved on already.

Alice was glad to see everyone again, especially since she hadn't spoken to anyone but the dog and the cleaning woman since Griffin had left, but it was bittersweet. It was almost more depressing to be reminded of what she'd lost. She missed that stupid, boring job that had actually been pretty cool. She hadn't appreciated it enough at the time. She wished she'd made an effort to befriend the other extras sooner. Part of her even wished she could go back to the days when all she had to do was sit around a soundstage waiting for her turn to walk down a fake hallway, instead of spending hour after agonizing hour waiting on models that never seemed to converge.

ON MONDAY, ALICE HAD ANOTHER MEETING ON CAMPUS WITH Dr. Frazier. Even though they'd picked a day when Dr. Gilchrist didn't have any classes, Alice cast a nervous glance around the campus coffee shop as she slipped in the door. You never knew when or where he might turn up unexpectedly.

There was no sign of him inside Jo's Coffee, fortunately. Alice got in line behind a guy with a canvas backpack and genuinely tragic blond tips, and waited her turn to order.

"Alice?"

A hand touched Alice's arm, and she spun around to find Anh Vo staring at her. They'd both started in the sociology graduate program together five years ago. A lot of their cohort had already graduated and moved on, but apparently Anh was still around, just like Alice.

Anh's mouth dropped open, her eyes widening in surprise. "Oh my god, you're alive!"

"Anh! Hi!"

Anh's look of surprise transformed into a smile. "Where the heck have you been? We all thought you quit."

"Oh, um..." Alice cast her eyes at the front of the line, which hadn't moved an inch, thanks to an undergrad at the front having trouble with his Campus Cash card. "I did, sort of —for a while anyway. My fellowship ran out and I had to take a job off campus, and then I just sort of stagnated."

She avoided mentioning the real reason, because she wasn't prepared to go into the gory details right then—not taken unawares in the middle of Jo's before she'd had her morning coffee, for sure. Alice wasn't sure she'd ever be able to talk about it without getting upset all over again.

Anh nodded, her mouth compressing into a sour line. "I know that feeling. I'm starting to think I'm never going to get out of this place."

"Why? What happened?"

"The IRB just rejected my application—for the third time."

"Oh, man." The university's Institutional Review Board had to approve any research conducted on living creatures to ensure it followed strict ethical standards. Approvals were an annoying and arduous process, but the scrutiny was even stricter when the subjects were considered part of a protected or vulnerable class—and Anh's research on minors in institutional care definitely fit that bill.

She sighed as she twirled a strand of silky black hair around her finger. "I'm pretty sure I'm going to die of old age before I get the approval for my research."

"I'm sorry, that sucks."

"Eh." Her shoulders lifted in a shrug. "I knew when I chose this topic that it would be tough. I'll just have to resubmit again. It would help if they weren't so vague about the changes they wanted me to make to the study, but I'll get it eventually. Fourth time's the charm, right?"

"I'll keep my fingers crossed for you," Alice said, impressed by Anh's positive attitude. But that was who Anh had always been: a tiny, optimistic ray of sunshine.

The line moved forward finally, and they both shuffled closer to the counter. As Anh's eyes settled on Alice again they narrowed in concern.

"So you're okay, right? Matt was convinced you were pregnant, but I told him he was an idiot."

Alice laughed at the unlikelihood of that, given her nonexistent love life the past year. "I am definitely not pregnant—nor was I, at any point, ever."

"Do you have time to grab a table and catch up? I can fill you in on all the departmental gossip you've missed."

"I would love that, but I'm actually on my way to meet with Dr. Frazier. Rain check?"

"Totally." Anh smiled. "I'm glad you're back."

"Me too." Alice was surprised how much she meant it.

They continued to chat until they reached the front of the line, and Alice paid for Anh's coffee as a consolation gift for her IRB problems. Now that her first house-sitting paycheck from Griffin had hit her Venmo account, she could afford a little largesse—more than Anh could, probably.

When their coffees were ready, Alice bid Anh goodbye and took her extra-large cold brew to Dr. Frazier's office, where she found her committee chair bent under her desk, cursing up a storm under her breath. Alice called out a "Hello?" from the open doorway, and Dr. Frazier popped up like one of Mr. Rogers' puppets.

"Come in, come in! I'm just looking for my favorite pen."

Alice dropped into one of the wooden chairs, pulling her messenger bag into her lap and resting her iced coffee on top of it.

"So!" Dr. Frazier smiled brightly. "How does it feel to be back on campus?"

"Pretty good, actually." Once more, Alice found herself surprised by her own answer. Most of her nervousness had dissipated during the wait in the coffee shop. "I ran into Anh Vo just now at Jo's."

Dr. Frazier shook her head sadly. "It's awful how many hoops the IRB are making her jump through. She's a fighter though. She'll bounce back."

Unlike me, Alice couldn't help thinking. Hadn't she basically given up at the first bump in the road? At least she was back now finally, and trying to fix it. That had to count for something.

"Let's talk about you," Dr. Frazier said. "How are the new multilevel models going?"

"Pretty well, I think? Although I have some questions…" Alice set her coffee on the floor and slipped her laptop out. "The base models are running fine and I've been able to get a Level Two model with just the organization ID to run—"

"How long did that model take to run?"

Alice grimaced. "Twenty-two hours. But it converged okay."

Dr. Frazier matched Alice's grimace with one of her own. "It's just a big data set—it is what it is."

"The coefficients for that model all make sense, but I can't get a model that includes percent female on the organization's board to converge at all."

"How long are you letting that model run?"

"It's still going after forty-eight hours."

"Yeah, that thing's not going to converge at all," Dr. Frazier said. "Do you have the descriptives on percent female?"

Alice opened her laptop and passed it across the desk, coming around to stand at Dr. Frazier's side so they could look at it together.

Her advisor's fingers tapped a thoughtful rhythm on the desk as she frowned at the screen. "You know what I bet it is?

There's no variance in percentage female board members across the parent companies."

Alice's eyes widened as the light dawned. "There's no variation across companies because—"

"The companies only have one token woman on their boards," they finished in unison, sharing a look of sororal disgust.

"Here's what you do," Dr. Frazier said. "Go and verify that we're right—pick through each of the boards and see how many women there actually are. That will be tedious, but it won't be hard."

Alice nodded as she took her laptop back and sat down again.

"If we're right, there's no way to include that variable. But you can still talk about it—it's a weakness you can make a strength. The weakness is that you can't measure percent female. But the strength is that you can show why—it adds another layer to your story that the companies that own these media outlets don't have female input. Are you having trouble with other Level Two models?"

"I haven't tried a different one—I was trying to get percent female to converge." Alice bent down to retrieve her iced coffee from the floor.

"Go ahead and move on to a different model. It's going to take twenty-four hours to converge even if things go well, so you can be investigating this other possibility at the same time."

"Got it."

"Good." Dr. Frazier leaned back in her chair, pressing her lips together. "And now for the unpleasant stuff."

Alice sucked a mouthful of coffee through her straw, stiffening in dread.

"I'm not trying to push you one way or the other, but I wondered if you'd given any more thought to filing an official report. Now that you've had some more time to sit with your decision, I just wanted to check in and see if anything's changed."

Alice fidgeted in her seat. "I know I probably should...but I just don't think I can stand to go through all that."

In her downtime she'd done some research into Title IX investigations. What she found wasn't encouraging. More often than not, the results were inconclusive. Even when they ruled in the complainant's favor, the repercussions for the offender tended to be underwhelming. Like that baseball player in Texas who'd been found guilty of rape in a campus Title IX investigation and was right back on campus a semester later. A whole semester's suspension—for *rape*. After everything the woman he'd assaulted had put herself through to come forward and see justice done, she'd still had to change schools to avoid running into her rapist on campus. And he was just an undergrad athlete. He wasn't a tenured professor like Gilchrist.

What was the point of speaking up if no one was going to do anything substantive? Why should Alice put herself through hell so the school could give Gilchrist the equivalent of a stern talking to and let him go right back to harassing students?

"There's no 'should' in this situation," Dr. Frazier said firmly. "It's entirely up to you to decide what you're comfortable with."

Alice nodded unhappily, still feeling as though she'd disappointed her. "I guess—now that I've finally gotten myself back on track again, I really, *really* don't want to go back to thinking about him all the time, and that's what filing a report would feel like. At this point I just want to get on with my life."

"I completely understand."

"I do feel a little guilty about it though." Alice stared down at her cup, twisting the straw between her fingers. "Like I'm being selfish and thinking only of myself. I mean..." She looked up at Dr. Frazier miserably. "What if he does the exact same thing to someone else because I didn't make a formal report? My whole dissertation is about women being treated unfairly, and here I am perpetuating a system that allows men to harass and abuse women with impunity."

A crease formed across Dr. Frazier's brow, and she leaned forward, steepling her fingers as she rested her weight on her forearms. "Okay, first of all, it's not your responsibility to make sure the guilty are punished. As a sociologist, you're well aware of how imperfect systems are, but it is *not your job* to oil the gears of those systems with your blood. Your only job in this particular situation is to thrive, whatever that means for you. Finish your dissertation, get a job, be a wild success, and get yourself into a position to hire and promote more women. That's your revenge, and how you change the world."

Dr. Frazier's eyebrows lifted as she awaited acknowledgement, and Alice gave a reluctant nod of assent.

"Second of all," Dr. Frazier went on, tapping the desk in front of her for emphasis, "I believe very strongly that the best way to resist is to engage in self-care first. If you push yourself to do something that doesn't feel right, you may damage your ability to help in other ways. For instance, if it interferes with finishing your dissertation, thus inhibiting your professional advancement and taking you out of more powerful jobs where you might have a chance to actually improve a broken system."

Alice had to assume Dr. Frazier was speaking from personal experience. As the only black woman in the sociology department and one of only three in the entire school of social sciences, she must have dealt with a lot of microaggressions and discrimination over the course of her career.

"My number one priority right now is making sure you feel safe," Dr. Frazier said in a gentler voice. "And if a formal investigation isn't going to do that, I don't want you to feel pressured to go through with it. This isn't your problem to fix."

Alice's eyes went to the drawing of the five-legged horse with the big dark cloud over it. "But if everyone says that, the problem never gets fixed. Isn't it a little bit my fault if Gilchrist hurts someone else?"

"Absolutely not. It's *his* fault and his alone. No one is responsible for his actions but him. Least of all you."

Objectively, Alice knew that was true. But it didn't absolve her guilt. She still *felt* responsible.

Dr. Frazier reached for the coffee mug on her desk and knocked back the dregs with a grimace. "If it makes you feel any better, I've spoken to the director of graduate studies in the department, and she will not be signing off on any future committees for female students that include Dr. Gilchrist. I've also reported the situation to the department chair and he was appalled. I don't know what, if anything, he'll do about it, but Gilchrist is on everyone's radar now. The whisper network will be watching him very closely, and rest assured that if *I* witness any inappropriate behavior, I will not hesitate to file a formal report."

"But in the meantime, he probably gets away with it."

"There are unlikely to be official repercussions," Dr. Frazier admitted, pushing her empty coffee mug away. "But his actions will not be without consequence. More importantly, the internal workings of this department are not your problem or your business. Your business is finishing your dissertation, and it sounds like you're making some solid progress toward that."

Alice answered with a reluctant nod. It did feel like some sunlight had finally started peeking through the clouds. However much guilt she might feel, she wasn't willing to put her momentum at risk.

Dr. Frazier gave her an encouraging smile. "Let's keep it up, then, and not do anything to upset the apple cart, okay? I want to get you out of here with a doctorate in your hand as fast as we can."

That was exactly what Alice wanted too. More than anything.

GRIFFIN FLINCHED WHEN HE FELT AN OVERLY FAMILIAR HAND land on his shoulder.

"Easy, big guy!" Drew, the studio flunky who'd been assigned to the set, put up his hands in an exaggerated display of surrender.

Griffin forced a smile. "Sorry. You startled me." He tried to maintain a professional, friendly demeanor with everyone on set, but Drew had rubbed him the wrong way from their first encounter, when he'd made a passive aggressive crack about Griffin's muscles.

Guys like Drew were all too common in this business: puffed-up rulers of petty fiefdoms whose obsequious praise usually contained a thinly veiled put-down to remind you of the power they wielded. In this case, Drew happened to be Andrew Fulton III, son of Andrew Fulton II, the head of the studio financing the film. Which meant everyone had to suck up to him—except Jerry Duncan, who didn't suck up to anyone. Jerry and Drew were constantly butting heads over the budget, and had spent the morning shouting at each other over an expensive shot that Duncan wanted and the studio refused to pay for. The altercation had put them two hours behind schedule and left Jerry in an even more vile mood than usual, so Drew was especially high on Griffin's shit list today.

"In your own head space. I get it." Drew nodded sagely, as if he had a lot of acting experience under his belt—which Griffin felt sure he did not, unless pretending to have a valuable role to play in his daddy's business counted as acting. Drew's mouth curled into a smirk as he cocked his head toward the craft services table Griffin had been staring at. "You're not going for that candy, I hope."

Griffin frowned. "What? No."

Okay, maybe he'd been fantasizing about sneaking a

Snickers bar, but it wasn't like he actually would have done it. Probably. Also, it was none of Drew's fucking business.

"Good man. Don't want you turning back into a fatty on us." Drew reached out and gave Griffin's stomach a pinch, like he was gauging the body fat on a hog at the county fair.

Since breaking the son of the studio head's nose would definitely get him fired and end his career on the spot, Griffin gritted his teeth and resisted the urge to punch the guy in his smirky fucking face. "You need something, Drew?"

"Just checking in with the talent. Making sure you're happy. You're happy, right, Griff?"

"Sure," Griffin said, smiling thinly. "I'm delirious with joy."

"How's that new trainer working out?"

"Great." The studio had set Griffin up with a local trainer here in Atlanta to keep him in shape during production. He was kicking Griffin's ass five times a week, but that was what he was being paid to do, and he was doing a decent job of it.

"Stunt team's looking after you?"

"Yep."

"Good. Good." Drew leaned in close and lowered his voice. "We want you to feel safe. You ever have a problem with a stunt, I want you to come straight to me. I'll always take your call."

"Great. Thanks." Griffin's voice was so flat you could have melted it between two slices of Wonder bread and called it a grilled cheese sandwich.

The stunt coordinator, Ed, was a twenty-year industry veteran who took his job more seriously than anyone else on set. Griffin would—and did—trust Ed with his life. Drew? Not so much.

"And your trailer?" Drew asked. "You like your trailer? That's the top-of-the-line model we got you."

"Yeah, it's fantastic." Griffin hooked a thumb over his

shoulder as he edged away. "As a matter of fact, I'm headed there now—unless there was anything else?"

"Nope. You go on. Do your thing." Drew waved him off magnanimously. "Good talk."

"Dick cheese," Griffin muttered under his breath as he trudged off to his trailer.

It was a nice trailer, he had to give Drew that much. Good thing, because Griffin spent a lot of time in it. He flopped down on the couch and stared around discontentedly. He'd sooner eat nails than confide anything to Drew, but the truth was, Griffin was miserable.

Starring in a solo action vehicle was turning out to be kind of lonely. He was used to working on ensemble projects, where he shared a lot of screen time with his costars. But a lot of his scenes so far had been with day players who came and went faster than he could get to know them, or with the guys on the stunt crew, who were cool, but also a little cliquey. It was obvious they thought of Griffin as someone who had to be managed so he didn't hurt himself, which wasn't entirely inaccurate, but made him feel even more isolated.

The actress playing his daughter was fourteen and acted every bit of it. She spent all her time between scenes with earbuds in, so absorbed in her phone she probably wouldn't notice if the fire alarms went off. And then there was Richard Scardino, who was playing the drug lord villain of the movie. Sure, he had an Oscar nomination under his belt, but he was one of those method actors who stalked around the set in character, refusing to drop his fake Mexican accent and terrorizing the PAs like he thought he was actually the head of a cartel.

Kimberleigh Cress, who'd be playing Griffin's love interest, wasn't even due on set for another couple weeks, but he didn't have high hopes for their working relationship. She'd barely even acknowledged his existence at the table read, as if it was beneath her to socialize with a lowly television actor. Griffin imagined their upcoming scenes together would be about as much fun as a dental cleaning.

Atlanta was humid, the midtown condo they'd put him in had walls so thin his neighbors kept him up half the night, he was unhappy about a bunch of the last-minute script changes, and oh yeah, he fucking hated Jerry Duncan.

The man was a perfectionist micromanager who went out of his way to make Griffin feel like an incompetent, no-talent waste of space. Every day was a constant struggle to figure out what Jerry wanted from him, and Griffin's self-confidence was at an all-time low. He hadn't felt this uncertain of his abilities as an actor since the early days when he'd been fired from that beer commercial.

On top of all that, he missed his dog and he missed Alice. If he was being honest, he missed Alice even more than his dog.

He hadn't let himself call her, even though he wanted to. He figured she was probably glad to be rid of him, and she deserved to be left alone to focus on her dissertation without intrusions. But he hadn't talked to her in two weeks, and it was killing him a little. He was like a junkie, itching for a hit after going cold turkey.

Idiot, he berated himself. How had he let himself get infatuated with a girl who barely tolerated him? Who saw him as a person she had to be nice to because he'd given her a job and a place to live. If she knew how he really felt about her, she'd probably run for the goddamn hills. And she'd be right to, after all she'd been through.

He couldn't let her know. That was the real reason he hadn't let himself call her. He was feeling so low, he was afraid he might give himself away, and he had to hide his feelings at all costs. She needed this job and she needed this summer to be drama-free so she could concentrate on her dissertation and finish her degree. He wouldn't do anything to ruin it for her.

Maybe when he went back to LA, after he finished this damn movie. Maybe when she wasn't working for him anymore, he could tell her how he felt. Find out if she'd even be willing to give him a chance.

Or maybe not. Hadn't he learned his lesson in the past? He wasn't cut out to be a boyfriend. He'd only end up hurting her. If he really cared about her, he ought to just leave her alone. The last thing she needed was to deal with all his shit.

For lack of anything better to do, and because he was a masochist, Griffin opened the Twitter app on his phone. He'd noticed a few weeks ago that Alice had followed his Twitter account, which he almost never used. Now, he went into his followers and searched for her name to bring up her profile. It was mostly retweets of funny posts or political news. Only occasionally did she post original content. He'd hoped for some sort of window into her life in LA, maybe even a photo of Taco or a glimpse of his house, but there was nothing like that. She was probably protecting his privacy, which he appreciated, but right now he could really use the sight of something familiar.

She'd gone to see the new *Avengers* movie the other day and tweeted about it. She'd gone for bành mí and posted a picture of a delicious-looking open-faced sandwich. There was a photo of a graffitied wall he recognized from the park a mile from his house. Finally, he found a photo she'd posted of herself. It was a selfie taken at a bar with some of the extras from *Las Vegas General*. They were all smiling at the camera and holding up pint glasses of beer.

A pang of homesickness settled in Griffin's chest. He missed that stupid show, he missed feeling like he was part of a close-knit group like that, and he missed every face in that photo—but most of all he missed Alice.

He swiped to his text messages. She'd been texting him

photos of Taco every few days accompanied by cheerful notes. Smiling to himself, he reread the most recent one.

We had a great time on our walk today. Taco was very excited to bark at a squirrel but frustrated I wouldn't let him chase it. He misses you lots and lots and will be so happy to see you again when you come home.

A lump formed in his throat. Was it possible the heart-eyes emoji she'd tacked onto the end was meant to be from her? He wanted desperately to believe she wasn't just speaking for the dog—that maybe Alice missed him a little too, and would be happy to see him again when he finally came home.

He tapped on her contact info. He was supposed to be leaving her alone, but he'd had an exceptionally crappy day today. Jerry had browbeaten him for two hours this morning trying to get the exact emotional response he wanted, and it had been humiliating.

He just wanted to hear Alice's voice. Or better yet, see her face.

Maybe he could FaceTime and ask her to put Taco on. That wasn't asking too much, was it? He hadn't bothered her for days. He was entitled to check in and see his dog's dumb face every once in a while.

Before he could talk himself out of it, he pressed the icon for FaceTime.

fourteen

ALICE STARED at the sentence she'd just typed. The English language was starting to lose all meaning. The longer she stared at the words, the less sense they made. Groaning in frustration, she pushed her laptop away and laid her head down on the kitchen table.

When her phone buzzed right next to her ear, she startled upright so violently she almost knocked it across the room.

Griffin's face—a cropped version of their selfie from the wrap party—lit up the screen, along with the words *Griffin wants to FaceTime with you.*

Alice's heart leapt into her throat. Why was he calling instead of texting? And why on earth did he want to video chat when she was sitting here in a scummy old T-shirt with dirty hair and no bra? In a panic, she checked her chest for obvious food stains and refastened her messy bun into something slightly less messy before accepting the call.

"Hey!" She squinted at the screen as a live image of Griffin pixelated into focus. A large bloody gash on his forehead caused her eyes to widen in alarm. "Is everything okay?"

He smiled into the camera, and she felt a tingle like a surge of electricity travel down her spine. "Yeah. Great." He touched his forehead and his smile got wider. "This is just makeup."

"Oh, good." Of course it was makeup. He was on a movie set for crying out loud. It wasn't like he was out there in Atlanta getting into actual fistfights.

"I was just sitting in my trailer missing Taco's stupid furry face, so I thought maybe you could put him on camera so I could see him."

Seriously? How cute was that?

"Is that lame?" he asked shyly.

"No, of course not! Hang on, I'll get him."

Alice set the phone down and bent to scoop Taco off the floor at her feet. "You got a phone call, bud!" Settling the dog into her lap, she picked up the phone again and aimed it at him.

Griffin's face lit up as soon as Taco came into frame. "Hey, buddy! It's me!"

Taco looked at Alice and yawned.

"He's kind of sleepy," she said. "He just woke up." She tapped the screen and Taco's eyes followed her finger to the phone.

Griffin waved. "Hey, Taco! Did you miss me?"

The dog looked toward the living room and tilted his head.

"Do you think he can see me?" Griffin asked, frowning.

"I dunno. Can dogs see pictures on screens?"

"No idea."

"He can definitely hear you. His tail's wagging."

"That's something, I guess. Everything going okay there?"

Alice shifted in her seat, trying to aim the phone so Griffin could see Taco without her double chin or her unsecured breasts looming in the background. "Yeah. We're great. I've been taking him for walks twice a day. Oh, and we drove over to that dog park in Laurel Canyon."

"Nice. I'll bet he loves having someone around the house all day."

"Honestly, I think he's tired of me. He mostly just sleeps. I have to wake him up to go out."

"Well, he's not used to all that exercise."

Alice bit down on her lip. "Should I not walk him so much?"

"No, it's good for him. Get his lazy ass out of the house. He's gonna have a sleek, athlete's physique by the time I get home. All the girl dogs at the dog park will be throwing themselves at him. Right, buddy?"

Taco jumped off Alice's lap and trotted into the living room to curl up on his dog bed.

"Sorry," she said, aiming the camera at her face again.

"Nah, it's fine." Griffin let out a mock dramatic sigh. "I know where I stand."

Maybe it was just the makeup or the lighting in his trailer, but he seemed…tired. There was a hollowness around his eyes she wasn't used to seeing, even on the longest shooting days on *Las Vegas General*.

"How's it going there?" she asked.

"Good. Hard work, but good."

Because he was an actor, Griffin instinctively looked directly into the camera without getting distracted by the smaller image of his own face in the corner of the screen like most people did. Alice tried to follow his lead, refusing to look at her own pale and ghastly face lurking in the corner of her screen. "What's Richard Scardino like?"

Griffin gave a contemptuous snort. "He's like if Drakkar Noir was a person."

She laughed. "That bad?"

"His hair plugs have hair plugs. And he's method. Need I say more?"

"No." They'd had a couple method actors come through

LV Gen and they were always insufferable. "How is it working with Jerry Duncan?"

Griffin's smile took on a plasticky sheen. "It's great. He's brilliant."

"Why do I think you're lying right now?"

He blew out a long breath and leaned back, giving her a better view of the inside of his trailer. "I'm pretty sure he hates me and regrets giving me this part."

"I'll bet that's not true."

"No, I'm pretty sure it is."

Alice's stomach gave a little heave at the unhappiness that had leaked into his expression. "Come on. No one could hate you."

His eyes flickered away from the camera. "This guy does. He finds fault with everything I do. No matter how hard I try, I just can't figure out what he wants from me."

"Isn't it the director's job to communicate what he wants from the actors? If he's not doing that, it's on him, isn't it?" Alice was no expert, certainly, but she'd seen a lot of directors direct a lot of actors in her season on *Las Vegas General*, and she had some idea what separated the good ones from the bad ones.

Griffin's mouth twisted wryly. "I'll just tell Jerry fucking Duncan that he's a crap director, then. That sounds like a good career move."

"Hey, you're Griffin fucking Beach," she fired back. "He's lucky to have you in his dumb movie—not that this movie is dumb," she added quickly. "I'm sure it's going to be great."

"No, it's pretty dumb. I'm starting to think—" He stopped and shook his head, grimacing.

"What?"

"I think I might have made a mistake taking this part. The script wasn't exactly stellar to begin with, and the rewrites aren't making it any better. We're over budget and Jerry's constantly fighting with the studio and everyone else on set. It's not going well and everyone knows it."

"I'm sorry," Alice said, wishing she could do more. "That sucks."

"I think…" Griffin paused, shaking his head. "I'm afraid this might be Jerry Duncan's first big flop, and I'm the chump starring in it."

He looked so worried and miserable it made Alice's heart ache. She ran her finger along the edge of the phone, wishing she could reach out and hug him through the screen. "Isn't this par for the course for him, though? From what I've read, he's always a nightmare to work with, but then he manages to pull it together and turn out a huge hit anyway. People love his stupid movies."

"Maybe. Maybe I'm being oversensitive."

She recalled what he'd said before he left, about feeling vulnerable on a new set and worrying that he wasn't good enough, and it made her angry on his behalf. Fuck Jerry Duncan for playing into his fears and making him feel worse. "Listen," she said, "you're a great actor, and you wouldn't have this role if Jerry Duncan and a bunch of other people didn't want you there. If he can't get a good performance out of you, it's because he's not as good at his job as he thinks he is."

A smile peeked through the clouds on Griffin's face and she felt a little thrill of triumph. "That's enough whining out of me." His eyes found the camera again, giving the appearance they were looking directly into hers. "How's your dissertation going?"

Alice swallowed down a flare of self-consciousness at the inky intensity of his stare coming through the screen. "Okay, I think. I've almost got all my multilevel models done, and now I just need to finish picking through some of the data by hand before I start writing up my findings."

"I'm gonna be honest—I have no idea what any of that means."

Alice smiled. "It means I'm making progress. Slowly but surely."

"Awesome! When do you think you'll be done?"

"With the first draft? Maybe another month. Then I'll get comments back and have to revise everything they don't like, repeating ad nauseam until it's approved for defense. Which is the really scary part."

"What does the defense involve?"

"Presenting my research to an audience of faculty and fellow graduate students, explaining how it supports my hypotheses, and answering any questions they throw at me. Basically they rake me over the coals to see how I perform under pressure."

Griffin's face lit up in a grin. "But then you'll be a doctor."

Alice felt her cheeks warm and hoped it wasn't too obvious on his screen. "PhD. But yeah. Once I pass my defense, graduation's just a formality."

"I guess I should probably let you get back to work on it then, huh?"

She would have preferred to stay on the phone with Griffin, but she didn't want to take up too much of his time, so she made a noncommittal noise.

"Okay, well, enjoy the rest of your day," Griffin said, taking her waffling for agreement. He seemed to hesitate. "Do you think—would you mind if I called again in a few days so I could say hi to Taco?"

Alice tried to hold back her smile. "You can call as much as you want."

———

GRIFFIN FACETIMED AGAIN TWO DAYS LATER.

"You sure you don't mind doing this?" he asked as Alice called Taco over to the kitchen table to put him on camera. She'd answered the call on her laptop this time so she wouldn't have to juggle the phone and dog.

"Of course not. It's what I'm here for, right?" She hefted the dog into her lap and aimed the laptop camera at him. "Say hi to your daddy!"

Taco stared at her blankly.

"Ahh, don't worry about it," Griffin said. "At least I get to see his scruffy little face, even if he doesn't give two shits about me."

"He cares. He just doesn't understand screens. Or phone calls. Or long absences. But just wait—he'll be so psyched when you finally come home, you'll feel bad for ever doubting his loyalty."

Griffin smiled, leaning back on the couch in his rented condo. From what Alice could see, it was very stylishly furnished, with lots of dark wood and rich, jewel-toned fabrics. "So what'd you do today?" he asked.

"Well…" She set Taco back on the floor and carried her laptop into the living room. "I did about an hour of actual writing, and then I spent the next four hours trying to format one of my data tables." Sinking down on the couch, she balanced the computer in her lap and adjusted the tilt of the screen.

"Sounds hard."

"It's not that bad. I just wasn't focusing well today. To be honest, I spent at least half of that time reading Twitter instead of actually working."

He broke into a grin of boyish delight. "Busted."

"Hey, it's important to stay informed of current events."

"Is that what you do on Twitter?"

"Sure. That and memes."

Griffin leaned out of frame and reappeared with a smoothie shaker in his hand. "I don't understand memes."

"No one gets all of them. There are too many to keep up with these days."

"Do you know what a 'zaddy' is? Because now, in addition to being addressed as 'daddy' by strange women on Twitter, I'm also being called a 'zaddy,' whatever the hell that means. Is it gross? It's gross, isn't it?"

Alice laughed at his revolted expression. "No, actually, it's a compliment."

"But what's it mean?"

"It's hard to describe. Basically it means you're hot."

"Okay, what about 'thicc' with two c's? I get called that a lot too."

"Thicc is good," Alice assured him.

"It doesn't mean I'm fat?"

"No. It's more like…you know, muscular."

"Okay, I guess that's not bad."

"No, it's not bad at all."

"Kelly, my publicist, wants me to use social media more." Griffin took a drink from his smoothie shaker and scowled, but whether at the taste of the beige concoction or the topic of conversation, Alice couldn't tell.

"It is kind of weird that you never use your Twitter account, come to think about it." She'd followed him a few weeks ago, and he hadn't updated even once since. His last tweet was nearly six months ago.

"I hate social media. I don't want to have to write a report every time I have a cup of coffee or take a shit."

Alice laughed. "I feel like you could come up with something more interesting to tweet about than that. People love getting a peek into celebrities' lives."

Griffin's lip curled in distaste. "But that's exactly what I don't want to do—invite a bunch of internet randos into my private life."

"You can control what you share though. You just have to post the occasional inconsequential tidbit to make people feel like they're getting a glimpse of your life without giving them anything too personal or real."

"I always feel pressure to be smart and witty, but I'm not a writer." He reached up to run a hand over his head. "I don't think I can pull it off."

"You're really funny though, and charming. I'm sure you'd be fine on Twitter."

He shook his head, unconvinced. "It's one thing to make a joke off the cuff in a conversation, but writing it down and sending it out to hundreds of thousands of followers is scary as shit. Plus, there's this echo chamber effect where you get thousands of people liking every little turd of a comment you send out into the universe, and then you start to believe everything that comes out of your mouth is some precious drop of wisdom. You get addicted to the dopamine rush of approval and lose touch with reality."

"I don't think you're in danger of losing touch with reality." He was one of the most down-to-earth people she'd ever met, despite his fame.

"Everyone in this business is in danger of losing touch with reality."

"See, this right here is why you'll be fine," Alice told him. "Because you're actually worried about it. Honestly, I don't know how you do it."

"Do what?"

"Stay humble."

He snorted. "Crippling self-doubt?"

"Come on."

"I don't know." He leaned back and rested his hands behind his head. "I guess I just think about my mom and what kind of person she'd want me to be. Before I do anything, I always try to ask myself if it would make her proud of me, and if the answer is no, I do something different that would."

A wave of intense affection washed over Alice and she smiled at the screen. "Well, there you go. The ghost of your dead mom will keep you humble on Twitter. And if that doesn't work, the internet trolls definitely will."

He groaned. "That's another reason I don't like Twitter. I've made the mistake of doing a couple vanity searches, and it always fucks me up to hear people talking shit about me. I don't need all that poison delivered directly into my notifications. No, thank you. That's how you end up paranoid and isolated, thinking the whole world is against you. It's just one more thing to stress myself out about. I don't need the additional anxiety."

"I get that. But if your publicist thinks it's important…"

"Then I should probably make the effort," he finished, covering a yawn. "I know you're right."

Alice calculated the time difference between Los Angeles and the East Coast. "It's late there. Don't you need to get some sleep?"

"Probably," he conceded.

"I'll let you go, then."

Griffin's eyes seemed to look through the camera straight into hers as his lips curved in a soft smile. "Goodnight, Alice."

"Goodnight," she said, smiling back as she disconnected the call.

GRIFFIN STARTED CALLING ALICE EVERY FEW DAYS, AND HE didn't bother pretending anymore that he was calling for the dog. They'd video chat if he was at home or in his trailer, but sometimes he'd call when he was bored in the car being driven to and from set, or out at the grocery store. He liked to be on the phone when he was out in public, he said, because people were less likely to bother him that way.

Alice didn't mind being his telephone beard. Her schedule was flexible, so she was usually able to stop whatever she was doing to talk to him.

He'd tell her funny stories about the crew, who he liked, or complain about his costars, who he didn't particularly. Alice would report what the *LV Gen* extras were up to after she came back from one of their Saturday happy hours, and sometimes she and Griffin would reminisce about the good old days on the show. He kept in touch with some of the cast, and she kept in touch with some of the crew via social media, so they'd compare notes, keeping tabs on the old gang.

Griffin had been making more of an effort on Twitter, so she made sure to compliment him on his latest tweets. He'd been reposting some of the photos she'd sent him of Taco, with a countdown until he was reunited with his dog again.

"You think it's okay?" he asked nervously after the second one.

"It's great," Alice assured him. "People love dog pictures. Just make sure there's not like a piece of mail with your address on it in the background or anything."

"Don't worry, I vetted the shit out of those photos before I posted them."

Every time he posted a new dog photo bemoaning their separation, the internet went into ecstasies. He'd gained a hundred thousand Twitter followers in just the last two weeks.

Alice looked forward to Griffin's calls, checking her phone repeatedly throughout the day and scrambling for it whenever it lit up with his photo. She never called him though. She was afraid he'd think there was some emergency with the dog or the house, so she left it to him to initiate their conversations. Besides, his availability was too unpredictable when he was on set. The odds of getting his voicemail were high, and then he'd just have to call her back anyway.

When the series finale of *Las Vegas General* aired, six weeks into Griffin's Atlanta shoot, they watched it together over the phone.

"God, look at my hair," he moaned in embarrassment. "I don't know why they insisted on doing it like that." He'd called from his trailer, and she could hear the murmur of his television in the background, echoing hers.

"I liked it," Alice said, tossing a handful of popcorn in her mouth.

Dr. Ethan Convey's slightly nerdy middle part had given him a boyish, approachable appearance that Alice—and millions of other women—had found endearing. Griffin's current, shorter style was more fashionable and masculine, but she missed the floppier tousled look.

"Jesus, that dialogue!" he complained after his character delivered one of his all-time cheesiest lines in a show that had always been packed with lots of cheese. Finales were meant to be bigger and better, so they'd layered it on as thick as a block of Velveeta for this episode.

"You did your best with the tools you were given," Alice said.

"That's one way of putting it."

"Honestly, you were always too good for this show. I'm glad you've moved on to bigger and better things."

He snorted. "I'm not sure that's true. If you could hear some of the dialogue in this movie…"

"Okay, but millions more people will see you deliver cheesy lines in a Jerry Duncan movie than ever saw you on our modestly rated network medical drama."

"Fingers crossed," he replied with a sarcastic lilt.

"Anyway, this show's not that bad," Alice insisted. On the screen, two women in wedding dresses were having a screaming fistfight in the middle of the ER. "I used to watch it before I started working on it, you know. The melodrama could be a little over the top, but it had some nice moments. I always liked the characters."

"Which character was your favorite?"

"Duh. Obviously you."

Griffin laughed. "Are you just saying that because you're living in my house right now?"

"No," Alice answered honestly. "Ethan really was my favorite." She'd always liked him best because, unlike the other hotshot alpha male doctors, Ethan was sweet—a trait it had taken her too long to realize Griffin shared with his character.

They watched in silence as Alfie's character shared a series of poignant goodbyes with the other main characters on his last day working in the hospital. They'd written the episode around his retirement, but stolen a page from *M*A*S*H* by killing him unexpectedly offscreen at the end. Alice had a box of tissues ready at hand for when they got to that part.

"I guess this show wasn't *so* bad," Griffin conceded. "At least it brought us together, right?"

"That's true," Alice said, feeling her throat grow tight.

It had been years since she'd had a best friend, but in a weird way that's what it felt like she and Griffin were becoming. Except these weren't just friendly feelings she was having. Her crush on him had grown into something deeper and much more complicated. She wasn't sure she was ready to use the word *love*, but it was hovering in her peripheral vision. Taunting her.

His feelings were more difficult to read. At this point it was impossible to deny that he liked her, but just how much or in what way remained a mystery. Alice had absolutely no idea if Griffin was romantically attracted to her at all, and refused to let herself think too hard about it. There was no point, when he was so far away. Better to just enjoy what they had now and worry about the future when it came.

WITH ONLY A MONTH OF FILMING LEFT, GRIFFIN FIGURED HE could get away with having a few drinks. He deserved it, for dealing with Jerry Duncan's bullying and bad temper on a near-daily basis. As soon as he was done with this fucking film, he would never again set foot on one of Jerry's sets.

Only a few more weeks of this hell, and then he'd be headed home to Alice.

Griffin wasn't sure what was going to happen then, but he was feeling more optimistic about it. It seemed like she definitely liked him as a friend, which was a big win. The question was, would she want to be something more? And how could he find out without ruining what they had now?

Fuck it. That was a problem for another day. Tonight he was out having fun with his fellow cast members, at least two of whom he almost sort of liked. Kimberleigh had turned out to be perfectly pleasant to work with, if a little frosty, and halfway through the shoot Richard Scardino had finally dropped character enough to be practically tolerable.

The club tonight had been Scardino's idea. It was all polished marble and glittering chandeliers. Supposedly several local rap stars and the cast of *The Walking Dead* frequented the place, which explained the paparazzi loitering across the street. Ordinarily, Griffin avoided trendy clubs like this. He preferred a quiet night out with friends—or with one particular friend if he was looking to get laid—somewhere they could actually hear each other talk, with a lower probability of having his outing chronicled on a gossip site.

But this was where Scardino had wanted to come, so this was where Griffin was spending his Saturday night. It wasn't so bad, really. The DJ was good and the drinks were strong. Mostly, Griffin was just glad to be out of his condo, which had begun to feel like a prison after two months on this miserable shoot.

He'd lost track of how many scotch and sodas he'd had when Richard peeled off to charm a group of leggy blondes who appeared to be barely of age. Wanting no part of it and feeling suddenly tired, Griffin headed over to the VIP booth where Kimberleigh sat alone, staring at her phone.

She didn't look up when he joined her, and he was struck by an overwhelming wave of loneliness. "I wish Alice was here," he mumbled forlornly into his drink.

"Who's Alice?" Kimberleigh asked without shifting her attention from her phone.

"No one." He shook his head. "No, I didn't mean that—she's someone, obviously. Just no one you've heard of."

Her mouth curved in a knowing smirk. "Not an actress, you mean?"

"Yes. Exactly. She's not an actress."

Kimberleigh set her phone down and reached for her drink. "Is she your girlfriend?"

Griffin shook his head, wincing as the room swooped around him. "She's my friend, but that's as far as we've gotten."

"You want her to be your girlfriend though."

"Yes—maybe. I don't know. I like her, but I don't know if we're right for each other."

Kimberleigh tapped a manicured nail against her glass. "It's hard for people like us to date normals. They don't understand what it's like. The constant pressure of the spotlight."

Griffin nodded and swallowed another mouthful of scotch. "It's hard enough dating people who *do* work in the business."

Her mouth gave a bitter twist. "I'll drink to that." As she downed the last of her vodka rocks, Griffin was reminded that her most recent relationship had ended publicly and *very* messily when her actor boyfriend was photographed stepping out on her with a rising young pop starlet.

He set his drink down and stared morosely at the marble surface of the table. "How can I drag Alice into all this shit we have to deal with? It's not fair to her. Assuming she even wants it—me—which I'm not even sure of."

Kimberleigh offered a surprisingly sympathetic smile. "I don't know anything about her, but I'm willing to bet she wants you. That's part of the problem with being us. Everyone wants us—or thinks they do. Until they actually get to know us and the shine wears off."

"I think I'm drunk," Griffin said, surprised.

"Really?" Kimberleigh lifted a mocking eyebrow. "You mean you didn't do the 'Single Ladies' dance to Migos stone-cold sober?"

He narrowed his eyes at her. "How are you not drunk? You've been sucking down vodka like it was La Croix all night."

She rattled the ice in her glass, smirking. "Practice."

Griffin picked up his scotch again. "This is my first drink in…" He pressed the cool glass against his forehead while he did the math. "Almost three months."

"Griffin, sweetie. That's your fifth drink tonight."

"I don't mean this specific drink. I mean—you know what I mean. Tonight's the first time I've let myself drink."

"So you're not always this much of a lightweight, is what you're saying?"

"Definitely not."

Kimberleigh picked up her phone again and swiped her thumb across the screen. "Maybe we should get you home. This place is a little high-profile. If you're going to get maudlin, better to do it somewhere without two hundred cell phone cameras and a dozen paparazzi within pissing distance."

A wave of exhaustion rolled over Griffin and he rubbed his eyes with the heels of his hands. "Mmmm. You may have a point there."

Kimberleigh scooted her way out of the booth and hooked a hand under Griffin's elbow. "Come on, big boy. Let's put you into an Uber."

"I thought you hated me," he said as she steered him toward the door.

"It's nothing personal. I hate everyone."

The humidity slapped Griffin in the face like a wet towel as they stepped out onto the sidewalk. "Jesus, why is it so hot in this fucking state?"

Kimberleigh checked her phone and scanned the street for his Uber. "Only a few more weeks, then we can both fly away back to the desert where we belong."

Griffin watched her watching for his car. "Why do you hate everyone?"

She shrugged. "Force of habit."

Impulsively, he bent down and kissed her cheek. "I think you're secretly nice," he whispered into her ear. "I think it's all for show, to keep people at a distance."

The smile she gave him when he pulled away was amused but also slightly sad. "If only."

"It's a good act, but I'm not buying it."

She reached up to brush her hand through his hair. "You're sweet. I hope you get your Alice."

"I hope you get yours too."

A white Escalade pulled up to the curb and Kimberleigh corralled him toward it. "Here's your chariot, handsome." She blew him a kiss once he was inside, and went back into the club.

It was blissfully quiet and air-conditioned in the car. Griffin slouched down in his seat and listened to the soft jazz his driver was playing as they crawled through the streets of midtown Atlanta.

"The music okay?" the driver asked, glancing in the rearview mirror at a stoplight. She was young and black, with a dog-eared organic chemistry textbook wedged between her seat and the console.

"Yeah," Griffin told her. "It's great."

"Was that Kimberleigh Cress back there at the club with you?"

"It was."

"She your girlfriend or something?"

"Nope. Just someone I work with."

"What's she like?"

Griffin thought about it. "She's nice," he said, knowing Kimberleigh would hate it. "Really nice."

The driver's eyes found his in the mirror again when the car rolled to a stop at another light. He could see the moment recognition dawned. "You're that guy from that show."

"That's me," Griffin said, turning his face to the window.

"Cool. My mom watches that show."

"Then tell your mom I said thanks."

The light changed, and they drove the remaining six blocks to his building in silence.

"Have a good night," he told the driver as he got out of the car. "Good luck in school." He took out his phone as the car pulled away from the curb.

Made it home, he texted Kimberleigh. *Give her a good tip.*

He let himself into his apartment and made a beeline to the fridge for a Gatorade. Tomorrow morning he'd probably be full of regret, but right now he was still feeling pretty good.

He wandered into the bedroom and set the unopened Gatorade down on his nightstand. Kimberleigh's perfume was all over his clothes. He stripped his shirt off and tossed it across the room, but the smell still lingered in his nostrils.

Slipping his phone out of his pocket again, Griffin sank down on the edge of the bed and stared at the screen. What time was it in LA? It was one forty-five here, so that meant it was…something earlier on the West Coast. He was too drunk to do the math, but he figured Alice might still be awake.

A voice in the back of his head tried to warn him that now was not a good time to talk to the woman he was secretly in love with. He ignored it and hit *call*.

After three rings, he got Alice's voicemail. *Damn.*

He should just hang up. He didn't have anything important to say that couldn't wait until tomorrow.

He didn't hang up.

"Alice," he said after the tone. "Hey, Alice. It's me—Griffin. Uh…I was calling to talk to you, but I guess you're busy or asleep or something."

He paused, bending over to slip his shoes off as he considered what to say.

"I went out drinking tonight. And guess what? I got drunk. After only four drinks! I'm a lightweight now."

He lost his train of thought and frowned, trying to remember what he'd been meaning to say.

"Oh! Right. Anyway, the reason I'm calling is because I have to tell you something very important, in case you didn't know by now. So here it is: I like you. So much. I don't know if you knew that, but I thought maybe you should. I like the way you smell, and the way you smile at me when I walk in the door. The sound of your laugh—and the fact that I can make you laugh. I really hate being so far away from you. I miss you more than dairy, and you know how much I miss dairy."

He stopped and scratched the back of his head.

"Okay, sooo…that's it, really. That's what I wanted to say. I miss you. I'm gonna go to sleep now."

Feeling proud of himself, he dropped the phone and passed out facedown on his bed.

fifteen

I REALLY HATE BEING SO FAR AWAY *from you. I miss you more than dairy, and you know how much I miss dairy. Okay, sooo...that's it, really. That's what I wanted to say. I miss you. I'm gonna go to sleep now.*

Alice stared at her phone in shock and replayed Griffin's voicemail again from the beginning. Very slowly, she broke into a smile.

Griffin liked her.

Okay, so he had to be drunk to come right out and say it, but he definitely liked her. She had proof now.

But did he like her in a hot and bothered, want to mash their face holes together kind of way? Or in a platonic, let's just be best friends kind of way?

He wouldn't have drunk-dialed if it was the latter, right? That wouldn't be something he had to get liquored up to say. Unless he was just really, really bad at having friends.

But he wasn't. He was good at it, from everything she'd ever seen.

Stop trying to talk yourself out of this. Enjoy it. Bask in it. Let yourself feel happy.

It was hard. Alice was programmed to distrust compliments. She was always waiting for the other shoe to fall. For the backhanded blow that usually followed.

This was different though. Griffin wasn't like that. He'd called to tell her he liked her because he *actually* liked her. Just because he was drunk didn't mean he hadn't meant it. It just meant he was too nervous to say it sober.

How about that? Griffin Beach was nervous to tell her he liked her.

She thought about calling him back, but given the time-stamp on the voicemail and how drunk he'd been, she figured he was probably still sleeping it off.

Instead she called Rachel.

"That's funny," Rachel said, sounding not the least bit amused when Alice had finished telling her about the voicemail, which…was not the reaction she'd been expecting.

"Why is it funny?"

"Because Hot Hollywood Nights has a photo of him leaving some club in Atlanta last night with Kimberleigh Cress."

Alice's stomach dropped down to the floor. "What?"

"Google it. They looked pretty cozy to me."

She opened her laptop and found the photo a few posts down on the sleazy gossip site's home page. There was Griffin, clear as day, with his arm around Kimberleigh and his face pressed against her cheek. She was smiling and had her hand resting on his chest.

Alice swallowed down a wave of nausea. "He's just kissing her cheek. It could be nothing. I saw him kiss *your* cheek at the wrap party. He's a cheek kisser. He kisses everyone's cheeks." Except Alice's. He hadn't kissed her cheek that night. She was probably the only woman there he hadn't kissed.

"I'm sure you're right," Rachel said, sounding not at all sure but like she was trying to make Alice feel better.

"I mean—okay—it says they left together, but you know these sites get stuff wrong all the time. And even if they did leave together, it doesn't necessarily mean they slept together. Maybe they were just sharing a car."

"Sure." Rachel was clearly just humoring her.

Alice bit down on her lip. "If he was with Kimberleigh last night, you really think he would have called me? Like, did he crawl out of her bed to drunk-dial me? Seems unlikely."

"Unless he'd already skedaddled after they did the deed. He's not exactly known for sticking around to cuddle."

Alice enlarged the photo on her screen. They did look disturbingly…intimate.

"You're probably right, though," Rachel said. "It's probably blown out of proportion. That picture could be totally innocent."

It could be. But was it? Alice wasn't so sure.

"Why don't you just call him?" Rachel suggested. "Ask him straight out what the deal is."

"Maybe I will," Alice said, knowing she would do no such thing.

She didn't have any claim on him or his romantic attentions. Technically, he hadn't said anything in his voicemail that definitively proved he wanted to be more than just friends. She might have *inferred* more, but there was nothing that would stand up in court.

Not that they were going to adjudicate this in court. *Ugh.* This was so stupid. Why had she let herself go and fall for him? She'd been much better off before she had all these annoying *feelings*.

GRIFFIN CALLED LATER THAT AFTERNOON—A VOICE CALL, NOT a video chat. Alice wasn't sure what to read into that.

"Hi!" she chirped a little too loudly when she answered. So much for not acting weird.

"Hey." His voice sounded rough, like he was still recovering from his hangover. "So...I have this vague memory of—did I call you last night?"

She got up from the couch to pace around the living room. "You left me a voicemail." Taco's eyes followed her anxiously as she walked past his bed.

"Ohhhh shit." Griffin groaned. "I was pretty drunk."

"Yes, you were," Alice agreed.

"Did I say anything stupid or embarrassing? Do I need to apologize?"

She chewed on her lower lip. "No. You were fine."

"What did I say?"

The fact that he didn't remember meant the ball was in her court. She could tell him the truth and force a conversation about it...or she could rewrite history and pretend he'd never said the things he'd said.

Alice took the coward's way out, because that was how she rolled. "You mostly just told me you were drunk.'"

"Oh. Okay." He sounded relieved, and she wondered what he'd been afraid he might have said. "I didn't mean to get that wasted, but I'm a lightweight these days."

"That's exactly what you said in the message."

"I'm sorry."

"It's fine." She stopped pacing and took a breath before saying the next part. "I saw a picture of you from last night, actually, on Hot Hollywood Nights."

"Shit. Really? What was I doing? I wasn't dancing, was I?"

She squeezed the phone, which felt slippery in her hand. "Uh, no. You were kissing Kimberleigh Cress, actually."

"*What?*"

"On the cheek, it looks like."

"Whew. Okay."

"So?" Alice tried to sound lighthearted and teasing. "You and Kimberleigh, huh?"

"It's nothing."

"It says you went home together."

"We didn't," he said darkly. "Don't believe everything you read on the internet. Most of what they post on those sites is lies."

Her shoulders slumped in relief. "Yeah. That's what I figured."

"They're always making something out of nothing."

See? She was right. It was nothing.

"God. Only four more weeks." He blew out a breath like he'd just sat down. "And then I'll be back home. I can't wait. You have no idea."

"Yeah, about that..." Alice resumed her pacing. "I've been looking at apartments, and I found a decent prospect, but it's not available until the first of August, which means I'd be in your hair for an extra week and a half, and I wasn't sure if—"

"It's fine. There's no rush."

"Are you sure?"

"Yeah. I'm not in a hurry to get rid of you or anything."

Alice twisted a strand of hair around her finger. "I just thought you might like to have your house to yourself when you come back."

"Nah. It's cool. In fact, you don't have to move out at all."

"What?" She halted mid-step and pressed the phone to her ear.

"You can stay as long as you want."

Her heart thudded loudly against her rib cage. "What? Like as your roommate?"

"Why not?" She could picture him shrugging. "We get along great. It's not like it's a hardship."

"Yeah, but you don't want a roommate cramping your

style." *Do you? And what about a girlfriend? Would you like one of those? Would you like it to be me?*

He laughed. "You should know by now I don't have any style to cramp. And I don't mind having you around. I like it, actually."

"Oh." Alice walked over to the couch and sat down heavily, causing Taco's ears to perk up.

"It's totally up to you," Griffin continued. "But, you know, if it's easier for you to stay until you graduate or whatever, you're welcome to. For as long as you want."

"Wow, that's—are you sure?" She was even more confused now. Did he think of her as just a roommate, or did he want to keep her around because he *liked* her?

"Yeah. Totally sure." His tone was light and guileless. "You should stay."

"Okay," Alice said tentatively. "Well, thanks." Who was she to turn down free rent while she was still in school? If he was willing to have her, she'd be an idiot not to stay.

"It's settled, then!" He sounded happy. "Taco and I get to keep you."

"Ha ha, yeah." She swallowed down the nervous butterflies trying to flap their way out of her stomach.

"Oh, shit." He sounded farther away suddenly, as if he was holding the phone at arm's length.

"What?"

"My agent just texted." His voice sounded close again—so close she could hear the puff of his breath against the microphone. "I'd better call her back. I'll talk to you soon, okay?"

"Yep. Bye."

Alice set the phone down on the coffee table and folded forward, clutching her stomach with both arms.

Apparently she wasn't moving out after all. Which meant when Griffin came home—what?

She had no idea.

GRIFFIN'S AGENT WAS FLYING OUT TO ATLANTA TO TALK TO him. In person. That was ominous. Sabrina only ever delivered bad news in person. Good news she delivered over the phone, but with bad news she always felt the need to "manage" him. If she was flying two thousand miles, it must be pretty fucking bad.

She'd refused to tell him what it was about though. "It's nothing," she'd said lightly. "Don't panic. We'll talk when I get there."

Griffin was panicking.

He'd spent every minute since their conversation in a state of constant, stomach-churning anxiety. By the time Wednesday rolled around—the day of Sabrina's late-afternoon arrival—he was positive he was developing an ulcer.

At five thirty, one of the PAs—a sweet kid named Ashley with a bulldog tattoo on her ankle—let Griffin know his agent had been given a temporary pass at security and escorted to his trailer as he'd requested. He thanked her and popped another antacid as he waited for the director of photography and his crew to finish lighting the shot.

"You're sweating more than usual," his makeup artist, Zaundra, said, narrowing her sharp eyes at him as she blotted his brow and gave him an extra dusting of powder. "You feeling okay, hon?"

"Not really," Griffin said.

It was an hour and a half before they got the shot to Jerry's satisfaction and Griffin was able to get back to his trailer. Sabrina was waiting for him, having made herself at home by setting up a temporary workstation at his desk. She spun her chair around, sliding her reading glasses off as he let himself into the trailer.

"Aren't you looking fit as a bloody trout?" She rose and

greeted him with a double cheek kiss before giving him an appraising once-over.

"How was your flight?" Griffin asked, enduring her inspection for a count of three before going to the fridge for a protein drink.

"Horrid, but that's commercial travel for you." She slid back into her seat, reaching up to pat her sleek, straw-colored hair. Sabrina had to be well into her fifties, but thanks to the miracle of Botox, she hardly looked a day over thirty.

Griffin flopped down on the dark gray couch and cracked the seal on his drink. "So? Am I in trouble?"

She threw back her head and laughed. "Lord, no. Is that what you thought?"

"Something brought you all the way out here."

"I'm here because of Kimbergriff."

He stared at her like she'd started speaking in tongues. "What?"

"That's the portmanteau you and your costar have been given. I assume you know about the photo of you two leaving an Atlanta hotspot together?"

Griffin grimaced as he choked down a mouthful of protein drink. "I haven't seen it, but someone told me about it." He was still pissed Alice had seen that. She'd sounded weird on the phone, and he hadn't been able to figure out if it was because of that damned photo, or because of whatever it was he'd said in his drunken voicemail. Or maybe both.

"The two of you were looking very cozy outside that nightclub."

His shoulders lifted in a shrug. "It was a platonic goodbye kiss. If the paps caught it, then they also caught me getting into a car by myself and going home alone." Although they seemed to have conveniently forgotten that part when they sold the photo.

"Right now, it's just some speculation and a titillating photo."

"I wouldn't call a kiss on the cheek titillating." Griffin didn't understand what the big deal was. Even if it had been a real kiss, was it really worth flying all the way out here to berate him about it? What exactly was she worried about?

"The point is, it could be a serious story." Sabrina paused for dramatic effect. "If we made it one."

He froze with his drink halfway to his mouth. "What does that mean?"

"The comments are overwhelmingly positive. People are excited at the idea of you and Kimberleigh together."

Griffin snorted. "Too bad we're not together, I guess."

Sabrina arched a perfectly penciled eyebrow. "What if you were?"

"What if we were what?" An uneasy prickle traveled down the back of his neck.

"Together. As far as the public knew."

He stared at her in growing horror. "You're not suggesting—"

"I am."

"No way."

Sabrina was silent, appearing to consider her approach. "*Hit and Amiss* had a one-hundred-fifty-million-dollar opening this weekend. Do you know why?"

"Because it's a cool-looking movie everyone wants to see?"

She flicked a dismissive hand. "Don't be ridiculous. It's trash. That film had no buzz until one half of 2015's couple of the year left his wife and jumped into bed with his costar. *That's* what got people talking about it. Suddenly, everyone wanted to see the movie 2018's couple of the year fell in love filming." Sabrina stared at Griffin pointedly.

He felt his hackles rise. "I don't have a wife to leave and I'm not in love with Kimberleigh."

Sabrina rolled her eyes. "I'm not telling you to fall in love with her. I'm simply proposing a series of staged photo ops that give the impression you're dating. Accompanied by a few feeder stories, of course. Possibly followed by an exclusive interview or two."

Griffin's mouth opened and closed like a goldfish.

"If you were simply seen together a few more times," Sabrina went on. "If the public were led to believe you were an item, it would do wonders for your visibility—and the film's. It's win-win."

"It's going too far, is what it is," Griffin said when he'd recovered from his shock enough to speak. "My personal life is not for public consumption."

The look Sabrina gave him was both affectionate and pitying, the way you'd look at a whiny toddler or a three-legged dog. "Don't be naive. Of course it is. You're a commodity, and everything the public thinks they know about you is part of your brand. If you want to play with the big boys, we need to improve your brand."

"I thought my brand was pretty good," Griffin said defensively.

"It's all right, but it could be better. Your star is rising right now, and we need to capitalize on that momentum before something else comes along and knocks you out of the sky. You're likable, but not as much as you could be. I know you value your privacy, but frankly you're a bit of a blank slate. You need to give the public a reason to care about you if you want to win their hearts and minds."

"I've been using social media more, and I think it's going pretty well."

"Yes, that's fine, but I'm talking about something big. Social media isn't going to launch you into the stratosphere unless you put your foot in it and make yourself into a pariah—which is *not* the kind of attention we want."

"Then I'll do more interviews or something."

Sabrina shook her head. "Interviews can only get you so far if you don't have an interesting story to sell. You need to give the public a reason to get invested in you."

"You think a girlfriend makes me interesting?"

"It does if the girlfriend is Kimberleigh Cress."

"She's a little young for me, don't you think?" Griffin was almost thirty-one and Kimberleigh wasn't even old enough to rent a car, for all that she had the world weariness of someone twice her age.

"Hardly," Sabrina scoffed.

Griffin felt his lip curl. It was one thing for a twenty-two-year-old to be cast as his love interest on-screen—that decision was out of his hands. But if people thought they were dating in real life, that made him a grown-ass man in his thirties whose taste ran to girls barely past drinking age.

"I'll be blunt," Sabrina said, her wrinkle-free face settling into the closest it could get to a frown. "The early buzz on this project is not great. No one's excited about this movie. It's got the worst IMDb popularity score of any Jerry Duncan film in the last decade."

"We're still in principal photography," Griffin protested.

"*The Nock* was in the top two hundred at this stage of production. Right now, this project is hovering around three thousand."

"Jesus." Griffin rested his head in his hands. Sabrina had just confirmed the fears he'd been trying to pep talk himself out of for weeks.

"It's barely registering a blip on the Rotten Tomatoes radar," Sabrina went on, putting more nails in the coffin. "There's nothing but resounding silence on Reddit, Twitter, and Facebook. The only place anyone is talking about this film is Kimberleigh's tag on Tumblr, and even her die-hard fans aren't particularly excited about it."

Griffin set his jaw stubbornly. "I'm not pimping myself out to save Jerry Duncan's ass." It wasn't his fault this film was a steaming turd, and there was a part of him that wanted to see Jerry fail after the hell he'd put Griffin through.

"What about your own arse, then? Because if this ship goes down, you're going down with it. I can promise you the narrative Jerry will spin to the studio is that you're not a big enough name to carry this film. They will hang this flop around your neck, and you'll never see another major starring role."

Griffin had always tried to surround himself with people who'd call him out on his shit—he didn't want to turn into one of those fame monsters who bought into their own hype—but he wasn't prepared for that level of bluntness. Sabrina had always been honest with him, but usually she tried to bolster his confidence rather than tear it down.

The expression on his face must really have been something, because she got up and came over to sit beside him, laying her hand over his. "I'm sorry, darling. I don't mean to be harsh, but you need to face reality and stop being such a prude. All we're really talking about is a few carefully orchestrated appearances and some interviews. It's not asking the moon."

Griffin knew she was probably right, but he still didn't want to do it. "Kimberleigh will never agree to it."

"She already has."

He swiveled his head and blinked at her. "What?"

Sabrina offered a casual shrug. "You don't think I'd fly out here on a pipe dream, do you? I didn't even bring this to you until I knew I had her team on board."

"And you just assumed you'd be able to convince me?"

"Yes. Because you're a sensible man who cares about his career. Haven't we built some trust by now? You know I wouldn't suggest something like this on a whim."

"And Kimberleigh's seriously willing to do this?"

"She's in if you are."

Griffin slumped back against the couch and rubbed his temples. "Do you really think this film's going to flop?"

"Not if you save it," Sabrina said. "This is your shot, Griffin. Your narrow window of opportunity. You need to make sure it sticks—unless you don't mind sliding back into television obscurity."

He sighed. "Fine. What do I have to do exactly?"

Sabrina beamed a triumphant smile at him. "I knew you'd see sense! You won't regret it."

"Oh, I'm pretty sure I will."

sixteen

New Couple Alert! Kimberleigh Cress Hits the Town with TV Hunk Griffin Beach

Things are heating up between Kimberleigh Cress and her costar in the upcoming Jerry Duncan blockbuster *Prepare for War*—none other than former *Las Vegas General* heartthrob Griffin Beach.

A source confirms the two spent a romantic Fourth of July together, stepping out for a dinner date at a Japanese restaurant in Atlanta, where Cress was photographed breaking out in laughter as she held hands with Beach. After dinner, they continued their outing at celeb hot spot Hunky Dory, where they were seen enjoying cocktails and each other's company until 1:30 a.m.

The pair sparked romance rumors two weeks ago when they were papped leaving an Atlanta nightclub together and looking very much like a couple.

The source told us that Kimbergriff have been

spending a lot of time together in Atlanta after finding love on the set of the film they're shooting there. Cress plays Beach's on-screen love interest in the hotly antici-pated *Prepare for War*, and the couple have been sizzling in real life as well as in front of the camera.

"They recently started hanging out, but it's still very new," the insider said. "They're both deliriously happy and just seeing where things go for now."

I'M SO SORRY, Rachel had texted Alice, along with the link to the Hot Hollywood Nights piece.

Alice didn't know what to believe. Two weeks ago Griffin had sworn there was nothing going on with Kimberleigh. But this didn't sound like nothing. They'd even quoted a source. They wouldn't just lie about something like that, would they?

There were photographs of the two of them holding hands. And getting into the same car. They'd even given them their own portmanteau.

Kimbergriff.

Alice wanted to vomit.

She might be able to write it off as a couple of friends going out to dinner if it weren't for the hand-holding. You didn't hold hands with people who were just your friends. She and Griffin were just friends and he'd never tried to hold her hand. Of course, they'd never gone out to dinner together either—because they weren't that kind of friends.

Clearly they also weren't the kind of friends who told each other when they started dating someone. Because he hadn't once mentioned Kimberleigh or the fact that he was appar-ently dating her now, despite his previous denial.

He didn't mention it the next time he called either. Alice kept waiting for him to say something. Offer some sort of explanation for denying it before, or at least admit he'd had a change of heart and relationship status.

Nothing. Not a word.

Alice was too chicken to raise the subject herself. If he didn't want to talk about it, that must mean he thought it was none of her business. And if they weren't the kind of friends who told each other things like that, she wasn't sure what kind of friends they were. Or if they even were friends, really.

She wasn't sure whether she was more hurt that he'd started dating someone so soon after leaving her that drunken voicemail, or that they weren't close enough for him to share major developments in his personal life.

Either way, he obviously didn't have feelings for her, or he wouldn't have started dating someone else two weeks before he was due to come home.

"I'M HOME!" GRIFFIN CALLED OUT AS HE BURST THROUGH THE front door.

Taco barked in excitement, waggling his whole body as he spun in circles. Griffin left his bags by the door and scooped the dog off the floor, rubbing his face into the soft, familiar fur as he went in search of Alice.

She wasn't there. The house was dark and empty.

What had he expected? That she'd be waiting at the door to greet him alongside the dog?

A bit, yeah. Griffin had hoped maybe Alice had missed him as much as he'd missed her. That she'd want to see him as soon as he got back. But maybe that was asking too much.

It was a Friday night, after all, and she had a life that didn't involve him. If she wanted to go out with friends—or even on a date, for all he knew—she was free to do so. She didn't owe him anything, wasn't even technically his employee anymore as of tonight.

He might *want* her to be his girlfriend, but she wasn't. He didn't have any right to expect her to be here on the night he came home.

Feeling like the high he'd been riding all day had been punctured, Griffin set Taco down and dragged his bags to his room. It was still a huge relief to be home, back in his own space, but without Alice it felt like something was missing.

Taco hovered at his heel as he unpacked and started a load of laundry. When that was done, Griffin wandered into the kitchen, wondering what to do about dinner. That was where he found the Post-it note Alice had left him.

Welcome back!
Taco's already had dinner.
I'll be back late.
—A

Well, that was something. Confirmation she'd at least remembered he was coming home tonight. It didn't explain where she was, or why she'd chosen to go out, but she didn't really owe him an explanation.

She could do as she chose, and what she'd chosen was not to be home to greet him.

Griffin tossed Taco a dog treat, grabbed a beer for himself, and collapsed onto the couch, feeling dejected.

Alice finally came home three hours later, while he was watching *SportsCenter*.

"You're back," she said, stepping into the living room.

Griffin got to his feet, planning to hug her, but stopped when she didn't move toward him. He stuck his hands in his pockets and smiled instead. "I'm back."

"How was your flight?"

"Good. Fine."

This wasn't the enthusiastic reunion Griffin had been looking forward to. He hadn't spoken to Alice as much these last couple weeks, in part because the intensity of his schedule had started catching up with him, leaving him drained and exhausted, but also because he'd been avoiding telling her about the arrangement he'd made with Kimberleigh. He'd been trying to avoid even *thinking* about the Kimberleigh thing, because with everything else stressing him out, it had been too much to deal with.

But now he was back and it felt like Alice had pulled away from him. Like they'd somehow grown apart over the last few weeks when he wasn't looking, and he hated it.

"I'll bet Taco was happy to see you," she said.

"He was." *Are you?* Griffin bit down on his lip to keep the words from slipping out.

"The house is still standing." She gestured around them. "As you can see."

"Looks like you took good care of it."

"I tried."

"Where were you?" He tried not to let it sound like an accusation.

"Campus."

He thought she hated going to campus. But maybe that had changed while he was gone. He guessed maybe a lot had changed while he was gone. "How's the dissertation?"

She shrugged. "You know. Coming along." Her gaze fell on the pizza box sitting open on the coffee table and her eyebrows lifted. "Pizza, huh?"

"The diet for the next movie starts Monday. I figured I deserved to treat myself in the meantime."

"You definitely do."

"You want some?"

She shook her head. "Thanks, but I think I'm just gonna head to bed."

His head dipped in a single nod. "Sure."

She hesitated, like she wanted to say something else, and he held his breath, waiting.

"I'll see you in the morning." Alice disappeared down the hall, leaving Griffin alone and confused.

ALICE WAS FULLY AWARE SHE WAS BEING PETULANT.

She'd gone to campus tonight specifically to avoid being home when Griffin got back, even though she hated working on campus. But she was still smarting over the Kimbergriff news, and yeah, she'd wanted to punish him a little. To show him that her life didn't revolve around him any more than his clearly didn't revolve around her.

It had worked too. Even though he didn't say anything, she could tell he was hurt that she hadn't been there to greet him when he got home.

Good. He deserved a little of his own medicine.

Except it wasn't good, because it made her feel awful. She didn't want to hurt him. She wanted to throw herself into his arms and tell him how glad she was to have him back.

But she couldn't, because he had a girlfriend now—a girl-friend whose existence he still hadn't bothered to mention to her—and it made everything feel weird and terrible.

He hadn't called as much over the last few weeks, in case Alice needed further confirmation that his attention had moved elsewhere. The few times they had talked, Griffin had sounded distracted and in a hurry to get off the phone again. He'd made it pretty clear where Alice stood. Avoiding him wasn't just about pettiness. She needed to put some distance between them for her own protection.

Is he back? Rachel texted as Alice was getting into bed.
Yeah.
Well? How'd it go? What'd he have to say about Kimberleigh?
Nothing. We didn't really talk.
I'm sorry.
It's fine, Alice replied, even though it was nowhere near fine.

She switched her phone to Do Not Disturb and tried to sleep.

GRIFFIN WAS UP AND MOVING AROUND THE HOUSE BRIGHT AND early in the morning. Alice woke to the sound of him banging around in the kitchen, and the smell of bacon.

She tried to stay in bed, but her stomach rumbled in protest. It was Saturday, and if Griffin was off his diet until Monday, he was probably off the gym too. Which meant he'd most likely be around the house all day, and she'd have to face him. Maybe even talk about things, like the fact that he had a new girlfriend and whether it would be better for everyone if Alice moved out after all. Surely they wouldn't want her around now. Too bad she'd missed her window on that apartment she'd been looking at. She'd have to start her search over again.

They definitely needed to talk about it. Today was probably as good a day as any—unless Griffin had plans with Kimberleigh today. She must be back in LA now too. God, what if he wanted to have her over to the house? What if that was who he was making breakfast for?

Alice couldn't deal with that. No way did she want to hide in her room while Griffin and Kimberleigh fed each other bacon and canoodled on the couch. Or whatever it was they did when they were together.

She needed to get out of the house again.

Brunch? she texted Rachel. *My treat.*

Rachel responded in the affirmative, and they agreed to meet at their favorite breakfast place in one hour. Quietly as she could, Alice slipped across the hall to shower and get dressed, then crept back to her room for her shoes and laptop bag. Only when she was all ready to go did she venture into the kitchen, car keys in hand, to face Griffin.

He was sitting at the breakfast table smiling at his phone. At the sound of her approach he looked up, and his smile grew wider. "Morning! I made pancakes and bacon. They should still be warm. Well, maybe not warm. Warmish. Possibly cold, but cold pancakes and bacon are still pretty good."

"Thanks," Alice said. "But I'm meeting Rachel for brunch." She felt a pang of guilt as his face fell. "Sorry."

He shrugged and flashed a plasticky smile. "More for me."

"I'm going to head back over to campus after that, so you'll have the house to yourself for the day." *If you want to have your girlfriend over*, she didn't say aloud, but assumed he'd infer.

"Hey, Alice," Griffin said, stopping her as she turned to go. "Do you have plans tonight?"

"Um…" What did he want her to say? Was he hoping she'd make herself scarce all night too? Because there was only so much time she could stand to spend on campus.

"'Cause I was thinking," he went on, "if you're free, I'd make us dinner and we maybe could watch some more *This Is Us.*"

She was even more confused now. He was sure acting like he still wanted to be friends, but friends told each other about the significant others in their lives. So if he was cozying up to her while hiding the fact that he was dating someone…well, there was only one reason she could think of why he'd do that, and it wasn't a reason that made her like him very much.

"Um," she said again, because he was looking at her expectantly, and she had no idea what to say. "The thing is…"

"You're busy."

"No, it's not that. It's just—I thought you'd rather spend time with your girlfriend."

His face froze, like a kid who'd been caught pocketing candy.

Alice's fingers clenched around the strap of her laptop bag. "Kimbergriff? There was another piece about the two of you on Hot Hollywood Nights."

"Oh god." His face twisted into a scowl. "That."

"Yeah," Alice said. "*That.* You were holding hands with her, so I assume it's true this time." Deep down inside, she couldn't help nurturing a small sliver of hope that it would all turn out to be some kooky misunderstanding, and he'd explain that he wasn't dating Kimberleigh after all. Somehow.

His mouth hung open—exactly like a man caught in a lie and trying to think of another lie to take its place. "It's complicated."

And there it was. Hopes: smashed. She'd thought Griffin was different. Better. But it must have all been an act.

"Right, then. Thanks for the Facebook status update." Alice turned and headed for the door, needing to get away from there. Away from him.

"Hey! Alice, wait." He jumped up from the table and followed her to the door, arriving there at the same time she did. "Why are you so pissed at me?"

She thrust out her chin. "I'm not."

"Liar. You've barely said two words to me since I got back. What's going on? What did I do?"

"It's nothing," she said, refusing to meet his eyes.

"It's obviously not nothing. Will you please just talk to me?"

She blinked away the tears blurring her vision, embarrassed by how childish she felt. "You made me think we were friends." God, she even sounded like a child. No wonder he didn't want to date her.

"We *are* friends."

Sucking in a breath, she turned her face up to his. "Then why didn't you mention that you'd started dating Kimberleigh Cress? If we're really friends, why wouldn't you tell me that? And now you're offering to make me dinner like she doesn't exist? What am I supposed to make of that?"

His eyes skated away guiltily. "I was going to tell you."

"When? Before or after Netflix and chill tonight?"

"I was planning to tell you about it last night, but I only saw you for thirty seconds!" He flung it at her like an accusation, as if it was somehow *her* fault he'd been keeping his girlfriend a secret for two weeks.

"Why didn't you tell me when it started?"

Griffin gnawed at his bottom lip, looking everywhere but at her. "Because I was ashamed."

Alice didn't try to hide her disbelief. "Of dating Kimberleigh Cress?"

"It's not what you think. She's not my girlfriend."

"The internet begs to differ."

"I told you not to believe what you read on the internet." His eyes met hers finally. "It's fake. It's all for show."

She stared at him. "What?"

"My agent cooked it up. She had my publicist make the dinner reservation and tip off the paparazzi so we'd be photographed together. The whole thing is a PR strategy."

"You mean like Hiddleswift?" Alice couldn't believe he'd do something like that. Obviously his career was important to him, but he'd always seemed to care more about the work than artificially inflating his viral appeal.

Griffin winced. "Sort of, yeah. Only I hope we'll be a little more believable than that."

"But…" She had so many questions, but she elected to start with, "Why?"

He hunched his shoulders as his face flushed. "Because

everyone's so afraid this movie's going to flop, they decided we needed to create a distraction—a reason for people to buy tickets besides the movie itself. The reason I didn't tell you was that I was embarrassed I'd agreed to such a cheap stunt. I wasn't trying to hide it, I just wanted to tell you in person instead of over the phone. And I was hoping maybe you hadn't seen the story—you really shouldn't read those crappy gossip sites, you know. I told you not to believe anything they said."

Alice felt some of her anger drain away. "Is the movie really that bad?"

"Yeah. It is." He looked pained.

"I'm sorry."

He shrugged, unsuccessfully trying to banish his emotions. "That's why I didn't want to talk about it. Not over the phone, anyway."

Stupid, stoic, insecure man. Too afraid to show any weakness or failings. Not that Alice had a lot of room to judge in that department.

"You could have told me," she said.

He visibly swallowed. "I was afraid you'd think even worse of me."

"Worse than what?"

"Worse than you already do."

Her head spun, trying to make sense of his words. Is that what he really thought? That she didn't think well of him? "I— I don't—" she stammered. "I wouldn't."

Griffin cleared his throat and looked down at the floor. "Anyway, that's why. I'm sorry I didn't tell you sooner, but I was going to tell you, I swear. I just wanted to do it in person, so—I don't know, I just thought it would be easier to explain in person, but I guess maybe it's not." He shoved his hands in the pockets of his athletic shorts. "And—uh—it's obviously important that everyone thinks it's real, so please don't tell anybody."

"I won't." Alice laid her hand on his arm, giving it a tentative squeeze.

The eyes he lifted to hers were heavy with emotion. "Are we okay?"

She nodded, suddenly very aware of the sound of her own heartbeat.

"Good." He gave her a regretful smile. "You've got to go."

For a split second, she thought he was throwing her out, before it came to her: Rachel. *Shit.* Would it be terrible to cancel? Yes, yes it would. It was too last minute. She'd already be on her way to the restaurant by now. *Damn.*

"What about tonight?" Griffin said. "Are you free?"

Alice nodded, and that small sliver of hope fluttered back to life inside her. "As a matter of fact, I am."

His smile got even wider. "Then I'll see you tonight." He stepped back and pulled the door open for her. "It's a date."

---

*I*T'S *A DATE?*

What the hell had possessed him to say that?

He had definitely freaked Alice out. He could tell by the look she'd had on her face—and just when they'd almost seemed to be okay again.

Griffin knew he'd fucked up by not telling her about the Kimberleigh situation. He could see that now, but at the time he simply hadn't given it that much thought. As far as he was concerned, it was just another tedious part of his job, like publicity shoots and press interviews. But of course Alice hadn't known that. All she'd known was what she'd seen on the internet, because he hadn't told her otherwise. And because he'd avoided going on the internet or reading any of his press the last few weeks, he hadn't realized just how much traction the story had gotten.

This was why he was terrible at relationships. He got so caught up in his own shit that he didn't always think about how it affected the people around him. It was just like his last ex had said: he was a self-involved asshole.

If he'd taken even a second to think about all this from Alice's perspective, he would have realized how shitty it seemed. Of course Alice would be hurt when she read about it in the news instead of hearing it from him. And of course she'd assume there was a slimy reason he was hiding the Kimberleigh thing from her when he offered to make her dinner.

He was such an idiot.

You made me think we were friends.

The hurt in her voice when she'd said that had sliced through him like a hot knife. He hated himself for making her doubt their friendship. Christ, she was his *best* friend. Maybe it was crazy, but there was no one else he'd rather talk to about anything. He wasn't someone who enjoyed opening up or letting himself be vulnerable in front of anyone, but for Alice? He'd gladly lay himself bare. He'd do anything for her. Anything.

He was going to prove it. And he was going to start by making her the best damn dinner she'd ever had. Griffin mentally sifted through every conversation they'd ever had for clues to her favorite foods. She tended to eat a lot of junk food and takeout, but he needed tonight to be special. He wanted to wow her.

It might be wishful thinking, but he couldn't let go of the impression that she'd been relieved when he told her he wasn't really dating Kimberleigh. Had she actually been... jealous? Maybe she *was* interested in him as more than just a friend.

Or maybe not. Either way, tonight would be a celebration. He'd show her how much she meant to him, how much he valued her friendship, and how glad he was to spend time with her again.

Italian.

She'd mentioned once that she loved Italian food. Not just pizza, but actual authentic Italian. He knew just the recipe to knock her socks off.

Smiling, Griffin pulled out his phone and started making a shopping list.

IT'S A DATE.

Alice couldn't stop replaying the words in her head. They'd been bouncing around in her brain all day, growing larger and more distracting with each passing hour. She was fixated. It was like an earworm, but instead of a song it was three little words that made her heart feel like it was going to burst.

Whyyyy had she said she was going to work on campus all day? She could have kicked herself. Why hadn't she just told Griffin she'd changed her mind and she'd be back after brunch?

For that matter, why not just go home right now instead of sitting in this study carrel, totally failing to get any work done?

Because of those three little words.

It's a date.

Had he meant it? Or had it just been an expression? Now that she knew he wasn't actually dating Kimberleigh, Alice was back to being completely confused by the signals he was sending her. He'd said they were friends, but did that mean they were *just* friends? She couldn't shake the sense that maybe he wanted more—but also she was afraid to let herself hope for something like that. But then there was the drunken voice-mail he'd left her. It had to have meant something, right?

Alice had been the worst brunch companion ever this

morning. She'd barely spoken beyond monosyllables, and poor Rachel had spent the whole meal trying to cheer her up, thinking she was upset about Griffin and Kimberleigh.

When Rachel had asked about it, Alice had been forced to lie. She'd told her that Griffin had owned up to dating Kimberleigh and that it was fine—which Rachel obviously didn't buy, given Alice's distracted state of mind.

It sucked not to be able to tell Rachel the truth. She needed someone to talk to about all this uncertainty she was feeling—she needed someone to tell her if she was insane to hope something might actually happen between her and Griffin. But she couldn't tell anyone anything. She'd promised Griffin not to say a word, and she wouldn't jeopardize his career by blabbing something he'd told her in confidence.

Instead, Alice had drowned her troubles in maple syrup and bacon waffles. She couldn't even have more than one mimosa, because she'd driven, and because she was going to campus straight after brunch to try to get some work done.

Ha. Not likely. Not in her current state of mind.

Instead, she was sitting here in the library, idly scrolling through Twitter after giving up on working altogether.

"Alice?"

The familiar voice dragged her out of her own thoughts and triggered an icy surge of fear.

It was *him.*

Dr. Gilchrist.

seventeen

"IS THAT YOU?" Dr. Gilchrist said behind her.

Panic bubbled in Alice's chest as she slowly turned to face him, feeling like a cornered animal.

"I thought it was you. You really are back." Gilchrist's mouth curved into a predatory half-smile. "Look at you."

Ugly, unclean feelings skittered over Alice's skin as his gaze trailed down her body. Everything about him repulsed her. His too-long-for-his-age hair and his trying-too-hard-to-be-cool clothes. His arrogant, smirky smile. His *smell*.

The too-familiar cologne burned in her sinuses, and Alice shifted away from him, remembering the way the scent had clung to her clothes and lingered in her nose after their meetings in his office. Her gorge rose and she swallowed, struggling to keep her eyes on him.

Don't look away. Don't give him the satisfaction of knowing you're scared of him.

"Dr. Gilchrist." At least being in the library gave her an excuse to speak in a whisper. She wasn't sure she could have managed much more.

His eyebrows lifted slightly. "I used to be Neil. What's the matter? Aren't we friends anymore?"

She didn't respond, conscious of all the students around them. The guy at the next carrel had earbuds in, but the tapping of his pen against the desk reminded her of his proximity and made her feel marginally safer.

"You disappeared on me," Gilchrist said. "I was worried."

She bet he was. Alice looked down at her phone, refusing to give him the satisfaction of her full attention. "I took some time off for personal reasons."

"I hope everything's okay?"

Her lips pressed into a thin smile. "Perfectly fine."

"I'm glad. It's good to see you back at it." She said nothing, and they gazed at one another for a pregnant moment before he continued. "Apparently I'm not on your committee anymore?"

"That's right."

"Can I ask why?"

She looked up at him with her blandest, most innocent expression. "Didn't Dr. Frazier talk to you?"

"I'd like to hear it from you."

"I've decided to go a different way."

A pair of passing students waved at Gilchrist on their way to one of the group study rooms and he gave them an acknowledging nod. "I'll be right there." Turning back to Alice, his eyes narrowed slightly, which gave him an even more weasely appearance than usual. "What about the network analysis? You don't need help with it anymore?"

She lifted her chin in a display of confidence she didn't quite feel. "Dr. Frazier and I decided it wasn't necessary after all. I'm doing a multilevel analysis instead."

"Really?" The patronizing smugness of his tone set her teeth on edge. "Are you sure that's in your best interest?"

"I guess we'll see." She didn't tell him she'd decided to leave academia and therefore it didn't matter how many articles she could get out of her dissertation, because it was none of his business. She didn't want him thinking her decision had anything to do with him. For that matter, she didn't want him thinking about her at all.

"Well. Regina knows best, I suppose. Good luck. I imagine I'll see you around."

She certainly hoped not.

He subjected her to one last appraising stare, followed by a smirky nod, before he headed to the study room. Alice watched him go, waiting until he'd disappeared inside before gathering her things and fleeing the library.

Her hands were shaking and her lungs heaving as she got into her car. She clenched the steering wheel as she tried to calm down. Her eyes darted to the rearview mirror to make sure he hadn't followed her, even though she knew it was unlikely. He had a study room full of students waiting for him, and no legitimate reason to chase after Alice. They were done, professionally. She never needed to interact with him again.

She was free.

He couldn't force her to do anything anymore. She'd faced him and walked away under her own power. Taken back some of the control he'd used against her.

Alice took a few more slow, deep breaths, making sure she was calm enough to drive before starting the car. By the time she got home her heart had stopped pounding so hard, but the sour feeling in the pit of her stomach still persisted.

Taco greeted her at the door, wagging his tail as he trotted at her heel. She found Griffin in the kitchen, in the midst of making dinner. A pan bubbled on the stove behind him, fresh produce and spices covered the counters, and delicious smells filled the house.

After the unpleasantness in the library, walking into such a homey, comforting scene felt like waking from a nightmare to realize you were snug and safe in your own bed.

Griffin had changed from the T-shirt and shorts he'd been wearing this morning into a pair of expensive-looking dark-washed jeans and a light blue button-down. Alice remembered, for the first time since Gilchrist had spoken her name, that Griffin had called tonight a date.

When he looked up from the vegetables he was chopping and smiled at her, she felt her eyes sting at the intense rush of feelings. He was so gorgeous and sweet, and he'd gone to all this trouble for her. What had she ever done to deserve this? How was this her life?

She tried to return his smile, but her lip trembled, betraying her.

Griffin froze. "What's wrong?"

"Nothing." She tried to make it sound convincing, but based on the deepening creases in his forehead, she didn't seem to have pulled it off.

He set the knife down and wiped his hands on a dishtowel before moving toward her with a concerned frown. "Are you still pissed at me?"

"No! I promise. It's not—" She shook her head. "It doesn't have anything to do with you."

"It has to do with me if you're upset." He jammed his hands into his back pockets like he didn't know what else to do with them. "What happened?"

"I'm fine." She didn't want to talk about it because it felt like that would be bringing Gilchrist home with her. Letting him infect even more of her life. She didn't want one stupid encounter with him ruining the whole night.

"You look spooked, like you've seen a UFO or something."

She blew a breath between her teeth. "I would be *thrilled* to see a UFO. A UFO would be awesome."

"Something bad did happen."

She sighed. Griffin obviously wasn't going to let it go until she told him. "I saw *him*. When I was on campus."

"Him?" She could see the moment he realized who she meant, because his expression went hard. "You mean that professor who—"

"Yeah."

He took a step toward her, reaching out to give her arm a tentative touch. "Did he see you?"

She nodded. "I was in the library, and he came up behind me."

Griffin's eyes widened. "Did he touch you?"

"No." *Thank god.* She felt sick even thinking about the possibility. "We were in the middle of the library, surrounded by other people. He just talked to me."

She was lucky, really, that the encounter had happened in such a public place, somewhere they'd be overheard and observed. Someplace with witnesses. If she'd run into him in an empty hallway, or a stairwell, it might have been different.

Strong arms enveloped her as Griffin pulled her into a protective embrace. Alice felt her whole body sigh with relief as she wrapped her arms around his waist, enjoying the closeness. Taco danced around them, butting his nose against their ankles as he tried to get between them. She shuffled closer, boxing the jealous dog out, and felt Griffin's arms tighten around her.

"Are you okay?" His hand stroked up her back, coming to rest in her hair.

She nodded against his chest. "Yeah."

And she was, she realized. Surprisingly so. Gilchrist didn't have any power over her anymore. He couldn't pressure her to meet with him in private, or force her to jump through hoops in order to finish her dissertation, or prevent her from getting her degree. He was nothing to her anymore. Just an annoyance that could be sidestepped. In a few short months, she'd be free of the university altogether, and she'd never have to see his repulsive face again.

Griffin's arms fell away from her, and Alice let go of him, missing the comfort of his touch even as she tried to put an appropriate amount of distance between them again. He didn't let her get far though. His hands grasped her shoulders as his eyes, bluer and softer than she'd ever seen them, searched her face.

She tried to smile for him. "I really am okay, I think."

"Are you?"

"It wasn't as bad as I thought it would be. And now that I've faced him and lived to tell the tale, I feel better, actually. Stronger."

"Good." Griffin's hands stroked down her arms, raising goose bumps on the surface of her skin. "What can I do?"

This, Alice thought. *Keep doing what you're doing right now and never stop.*

"Nothing," she told him. "I just want to forget about it and have a nice, relaxing night at home with you."

His eyes twinkled as his face split into a heart-melting smile. "I can do that."

Griffin watched Alice take her first bite with a trepidation he usually reserved for watching his own acting in dailies. When her face lit up in an approving smile, he nearly fainted with relief.

"This is amazing!" she said. "How did you manage to make chicken taste so good?"

A *lot* of butter. More than he liked to think about. He didn't mention that part though. "Pound it thin, bread it with parmesan cheese, and serve it with a lemon artichoke sauce."

"It's incredible." Alice cut another bite and placed it on her tongue. "Oh my god. I don't think I've ever tasted anything this good outside of a restaurant."

Griffin reached for his wineglass to hide how pleased he was. They were eating in the dining room, which he wasn't sure he'd ever actually used for entertaining since he bought the house. He'd certainly never gone to this much effort to cook dinner for a woman before. He'd even dug out placemats and cloth napkins, and bought fresh flowers to decorate the table. Candles had briefly been considered, then discarded as too clichéd and weighted with intention. He didn't want Alice to feel any pressure; he just wanted to make her like him.

It was kind of shameful how woefully underdeveloped his wooing skills were. Griffin wasn't used to trying this hard with women. He didn't usually need to. The women he usually chose to sleep with were the ones who were eager and looking for a short-term hookup just like he was. He didn't need to woo them. They understood just as well as he did that it didn't mean anything.

This was completely different, because this *meant* something. It frightened him a little, how much Alice had come to mean to him. He couldn't afford to screw this up. Better to go too slow than too fast. Better to only have a small part of her than push too far and lose everything.

He figured he'd start with dinner. Cooking was the best way he knew to show someone he cared about them. A way to prove how much he valued her presence in his life. They'd have dinner tonight, talk, maybe watch some TV, and hopefully it would smooth over any lingering awkwardness from this morning.

Then maybe he'd have a better sense of whether she seemed interested in taking things to the next level. He was willing to wait. Forever, if need be. If it turned out she only looked at him as a friend, well, he could find a way to live with that. As long as she was in his life, he could live with anything.

At least Alice seemed to be enjoying the dinner he'd made. That was a good start.

She touched her napkin to her lips before taking a sip of wine. "You've got a whole month off until you start your next shoot, right?"

"Something like that." *Troublemakers 5* started principal photography in LA at the end of August. "But I've got rehearsals and wardrobe fittings and stunt training in the meantime."

"Still, all that stuff will be a cakewalk compared to your usual schedule. When's the last time you even had time off between projects?"

"Three years ago." It would have been the hiatus before he was cast in *Troublemakers 4*. It felt like a million years ago. Like another life.

"Whatever will you do with yourself?" She forked another bite of chicken into her mouth, and her eyes fluttered briefly closed in ecstasy.

"Maybe I'll spend all my time cooking for you." If she was going to get that look on her face every time, he would gladly act as her personal chef. He wondered what else he could do to inspire that particular expression, and felt his pulse quicken as his mind supplied a variety of appealing ideas.

The space between Alice's freckles took on a rosy glow. "I'm serious."

"So am I."

Her eyes seemed to sparkle as she broke into an unrestrained grin. "Have I mentioned how happy I am that you're back?"

Griffin's heart nearly leapt out of his chest to do a lambada with the salt shaker right there on the table. "Have I mentioned how happy I am to be back?" he said, matching her grin with one of his own.

It felt like a barometric shift was taking place. Like something unfamiliar and new was unfolding between them. Something both terrifying and wonderful.

He couldn't wait to see what came next.

eighteen

GRIFFIN HAD BEEN STARING at her all night. Not just looking at her—they'd been sitting directly across from each other at the table, so obviously he'd been looking at her. This was different. This was *staring*. Like—she couldn't quite describe it. It wasn't quite as if he was seeing her for the first time—although that wasn't too far off. It was more like he was *letting himself* look at her for the first time.

Alice had never really felt the full weight of Griffin's attention before—not in such a concentrated beam of dazzling intensity. It was a *lot*. In the past, she'd always had the sense he was trying not to look at her too much. Like he was giving her plenty of space. A safe buffer zone. But now it felt like the buffer had melted away, and the air between them was growing thinner by the minute.

They'd chatted casually enough over dinner—which was quite possibly the best homemade meal she'd ever had—but the whole time she'd been conscious of his searing gaze, which made her feel things she'd been afraid to hope for. When he got up to clear the table, it was almost a relief not to feel his eyes on her for a few minutes.

227

He refused to let her help with the dishes, so she poured them both more wine as he told her stories about the stunt team he'd worked with in Atlanta, and how he'd taken them all out for karaoke his last weekend there.

"I didn't know you were a karaoke guy," Alice said, leaning back against the counter.

"I'm not." Griffin slotted the last plate in the dishwasher. "That's how much I liked these guys—I actually let them drag me to a karaoke bar!"

Tossing her old *no ogling* rule out the window, she shamelessly enjoyed the view as he bent over to retrieve the detergent. "Did you sing?"

"You have to sing. It's karaoke."

"*Can* you sing?"

Griffin threw an affronted look over his shoulder. "I'm no Josh Groban, but I've had voice lessons. I can hold my own."

"What song did you do?"

"Wouldn't you like to know?" He slammed the dishwasher closed and turned to face her with a smirk on his face.

"Yes, I would. That's why I asked."

"You'll laugh."

"Only if it's funny."

His smirk got wider. "'We Are Never Ever Getting Back Together.'"

Alice barked out a laugh before she could slap a hand over her mouth.

Griffin tried to look hurt but couldn't seem to stop smiling. "You laughed."

"It was funny!" She crossed the kitchen and gave his arm a conciliatory squeeze. "Come on, Taylor Swift? Please tell me someone videoed it."

"Not a chance." His gaze dropped to where she'd touched his arm, and Alice drew her hand back.

"Too bad," she said, wondering what would happen if she kissed him right now. "I'd pay good money to see that."

"Maybe I'll do a command performance for you one day."

"Is that a promise?"

Griffin's eyes found hers and held. The air between them felt charged, like it was liable to start throwing off visible sparks any second now. That was when the clouds of doubt finally parted. Alice wasn't the only one feeling something. That was an *I want to kiss you* look on his face if she'd ever seen one.

And then it was gone. Griffin stiffened, shaking his head slightly as if shaking away bad thoughts, and started to step away.

Alice's hand closed around his wrist. "Don't."

Emotions warred on his face. "You've had a traumatic day."

It took her a moment to realize what he meant. She'd actually forgotten. Her happiness at being with Griffin had superseded the trauma of the encounter in the library. Even now, thinking about it, it felt distant and blurred. Inconsequential.

She gave his wrist a squeeze. "It hasn't been that bad. This last part's been pretty great, actually."

Still, he hesitated, and she had an appalling thought. "Unless…unless you don't want…" God, if she'd read him wrong, she was going to drive straight to the beach and throw herself into the Pacific Ocean. She'd never be able to face him again. She'd—

Griffin's mouth closed over hers. The shock of it hit her like an electric jolt, and she let out an involuntary squeak of surprise.

He jerked back, forehead creasing in confusion. "Did you not mean—"

"No." Her hand curled around the back of his neck. "I did. I do."

He tilted his head, eyes narrowing. "Just to be clear, we're talking about kissing right now?"

"Yes."

"And you *want* me to kiss you?"

"Yes!"

His eyes sparked with mischief. "You're sure?"

Alice laughed, giving him a little shake. "Oh my god, yes! Kiss me!"

He did.

It was tender and warm. Almost careful, as if he was testing her, waiting for her to stop him.

She didn't want him to stop. *Ever*. Her tongue stroked the seam of his lips and they parted for her. The pads of his fingers touched her jaw, exerting light pressure to tilt her head back more. Need bubbled up inside her as the pressure of his mouth increased.

Alice grabbed his shoulders to steady herself and pressed her body into his, wanting to feel more of him. Griffin answered with a moan, followed by a rough tongue thrust that sent a thrill shooting through her core. His lips crushed hers, bruising and searing as their breaths intermingled in desperate pants. As the intensity increased, so did Alice's body temperature, and she shrugged out of her cardigan, letting it fall to the floor. Rough, callused fingers slid over her bare arms, raising shivers of pleasure over the surface of her skin.

"Alice." Griffin spoke her name in a low rasp as his hands dropped to cup her ass, his fingers kneading the soft flesh. "I can't believe—"

He broke off, groaning, when she ground her pelvis against his, craving more delicious friction. More contact. More heat.

His fingers dug into the backs of her upper thighs, and she gasped in surprise as he picked her up and settled her high on his hips. Laughing, she wrapped her legs around his waist, and he carried her into the living room.

Supporting her body with his strong arms, Griffin laid her gently on the couch. The thick muscle of his thigh pressed between her legs as he leaned over to kiss her, one hand cupping her face and the other holding himself above her.

His lips grazed hers, lightly teasing before moving to her throat. As he kissed a trail down her neck, his index finger traced her collarbone, then traveled down her breastbone, drawing a tortuous, singeing line between her breasts.

Alice wriggled beneath him, longing for more of his touch, and he smiled as he pressed a kiss to the hollow beneath her collarbone. His hand curved around her hip, then slid up over her tank top to cup her breast. Her hips arched beneath him when his thumb grazed her oversensitive nipple. As he smirked in satisfaction, his fingers snaked under the hem of her top. He lifted it up, stopping just under her bra, and bent to kiss her stomach.

She was a writhing, aching mess beneath him, desperate for more, and Griffin was loving every bit of it. Laughing, he pulled her tank top up, exposing her pink bra. His expression grew serious as he hooked his fingers inside the lacy fabric and tugged it aside.

"You're so beautiful," he murmured, lowering his mouth to her nipple.

Alice's heart shot into her throat, and she curled her fingers into his hair as all rational thought abandoned her. She drifted on a cloud of blissful unreality, trying to come to grips with the fact that this was really happening.

Surely this must be a dream—an incredibly *hot* dream, but a dream nonetheless.

But it wasn't a dream. She hissed her pleasure as Griffin's teeth grazed her nipple, and he responded with a gentle lave of his tongue. A tug on his hair brought his mouth back to hers, and their tongues slid together, playful and searching.

Her hands explored everywhere, stroking his face and his

body, following the lines of hard muscle and bone. When they found the waistband of his jeans and flicked open the button, his whole body seemed to tense, then he scooped her up and flipped her over so he was lying on his back with her straddling him.

Alice enjoyed the shifting kaleidoscope of expressions on Griffin's face as she shifted her hips against his. He curled a hand around the back of her neck and roughly pulled her mouth down to his. As their lips slid together, frantic and devouring, her hands wandered under his shirt. She needed to touch those abs she'd glimpsed on her first morning in the house—the ones he had been so careful not to flash in her presence ever since.

"Off," she grumbled, fumbling with the buttons, and Griffin smiled against her mouth as he reached up to unfasten them for her. While he shrugged out of his shirt, Alice sat back to properly admire the taut muscles beneath the tanned, waxed perfection of his skin. "Wow."

He watched her watching him, a small smile at the corner of his lips. "I hope so. I worked fucking hard for this body."

"It definitely paid off." Alice reached out to trail her fingers over his stomach muscles and he twitched. She smiled as a hypothesis presented itself, and touched him again—just a light brush of her fingers. Griffin's whole torso contracted like he was trying not to flinch away. Her smile got wider at the confirmation of her theory. "You're not ticklish, are you?"

"A little, yeah." He grimaced. "You're going to use this against me, aren't you?"

Alice affected an air of somber consideration. "Mmmmm. Depends."

"On what?"

"Whether you behave." She pressed the flat of her palm against his stomach, and this time he didn't try to twitch away. "Better?"

He nodded, his breath hitching a little. She slid her hand firmly over the hard ridges of his abs, appreciating the way the muscles contracted at her touch. When her fingers got near his waist, he flinched. She changed direction, and when she got to the other side of his waist he flinched again.

"Having fun?" he asked, lifting an eyebrow.

"Yes. Loads." She continued to explore his torso, mentally cataloging all the sensitive spots like a cartographer mapping a newly discovered continent. His nipples, she discovered to her delight, were particularly sensitive. Especially when she used her tongue.

"God, Alice, you're killing me."

His hand fisted in her hair, pulling her away from his chest, and his mouth clamped over hers. He kissed her with even more urgency than before, his teeth dragging across her lips and his tongue plunging hungrily into her mouth. His hands slid down her waist and over her hips to the outside of her thighs, then back up again to her breasts.

They were both breathing raggedly, gasping into each other's mouths. Alice could feel the wetness pooling between her thighs and the pressure building inside her, in desperate need of release. She pressed her palms against Griffin's torso again, careful not to graze any of the ticklish spots and ruin the mood.

When she unfastened the button of his pants, his hand closed over hers. "We don't have to."

"Of course we don't," she replied impatiently. "But we want to." A stab of doubt caused her to draw back. "Don't we?"

"I do." He squeezed her hand, and she breathed out in relief. "It's just…"

Her fingers twined with his. "What?"

"I just want to make sure—" He stopped and sucked in a

breath. "Our friendship is important to me, and I don't want to screw that up."

"You're afraid having sex will screw it up?"

"No." He frowned. "Well, maybe."

Alice reached up to touch his face, her fingertips pressing against his cheek as her thumb dragged over his lips. "I hate to tell you this, but after all that making out we just did, there's no way we can go back to how things were. We passed the point of no return about fifteen minutes ago when you stuck your tongue in my mouth."

Griffin winced. "It's just...I don't have the greatest track record with relationships. I'm not sure I'm cut out for them."

"Oh," she said, dropping her hand from his face. "Right."

"No." His hand captured hers again, squeezing. "I don't mean that. This isn't just a hookup for me. I just mean there's a decent chance I'm going to fuck this up."

Alice bent to press a tender kiss to the corner of his mouth. "You're important to me too," she whispered against his skin. "It'll be okay."

She felt the tension drain out of him and he curled a possessive hand in her hair, capturing her lips with his own. Their mouths clashed together, and she shivered as his fingers traced down her spine. His hands clasped the bottom of her tank top and pulled it off over her head. He kissed the top of both her breasts, then reached around to unclasp her bra.

Griffin's heated gaze seared into her skin, then his arms wrapped around her, tightened, and he flipped her onto her back again. As he lowered his mouth to hers, Alice's chest heaved with restrained lust, her nipples firm and erect. Every breath dragged them against his bare skin, and it was both not enough friction and too much at the same time.

Arousal thrummed in her veins, pushing everything but her own need and Griffin's out of her awareness as his lips slid down her throat to her breasts. His soft lips caressed her inflamed skin, his stubble deliciously rough as it grazed a prickly path. Heat radiated off him, igniting her everywhere their bodies touched.

Her hands glided over the planes of his back, then down to squeeze his ass through his jeans, pulling him closer. His erection pressed against her leg, and she pressed back, desperate and craving.

"Fuck." Griffin groaned, the vibration humming through both their bodies.

Alice dug her fingernails into his skin. "That's the idea."

Something cold and wet touched the bare skin of her waist, and she jolted in shock.

"What?" Griffin asked, pausing the attentions he was lavishing on her left breast.

Taco stood beside the couch, exhaling a rancid cloud of dog breath as he wagged his tail at them.

"Dog," Alice said, shifting away from the edge of the couch.

"Right." Griffin scooped her up, cradling her against his chest as he carried her down the hall to his bedroom. "You stay out there," he admonished the dog, and kicked the door closed before laying Alice on the bed.

She'd only been in Griffin's bedroom once before, when she was searching for a dog toy. During the three months he was gone, she'd avoided coming in here out of respect for his privacy, though the door had remained open to give Taco access to his second-favorite nap spot.

The furniture in Griffin's room was very plain and very Scandinavian. All golden beechwood against plain white walls, with accents of charcoal gray and primary red. Masculine, but in an understated way.

Alice watched Griffin dig around in a bedside table drawer until he came away with a strip of condom packets. Her whole body was wound so tight, it was all she could do to lie still until he came back over to her, tossing the condoms on the king-size mattress beside her as he lowered his body over hers. His fingers caressed her jaw, and he placed a tender kiss on her forehead.

"What do you want?" he asked in a raw, husky voice.

"You," she said. "Between my thighs. Now."

She felt him smile against her brow. "As you wish."

His tongue trailed a path down her body until it reached the waistband of her jeans. Her hips bucked in anticipation as he unfastened them. Only then did it occur to her that the landscaping situation down there probably wasn't up to his usual standards. In fact, she realized in growing horror as she stared at Griffin's perfectly smooth and hairless torso, he'd definitely waxed more recently than she had.

"What's wrong?" he asked, sensing her hesitation.

"Nothing."

He kissed her stomach, then rubbed his bristly chin on the delicate skin at her hip to make her squirm. "Alice."

"I didn't exactly plan for this, so…"

He smirked at her. "A little bushy in the pleasure garden?"

"Oh my god!" She clapped a hand over her face to hide her embarrassment.

His fingers slid inside the waistband of her underwear, pulling it away from her skin so he could peek inside. "I like it."

The desire in Griffin's expression banished all self-consciousness as he peeled her pants and underwear off. He ran his hands up her legs, then heaved them over his shoulders, lifting her hips as he closed his mouth over her sensitive folds.

Sensation jolted through her, and Alice moaned as his tongue traced delicate and then intensifying circles. When his fingers slipped inside her, she couldn't help thrusting against his face. Pleasure carried her away as he increased the pressure, building to a steady rhythm.

She was so primed already, it didn't take long before she

was shuddering and breaking apart in his hands. His kisses gentled as she rode the wave of an orgasm so intense it rocked her to her core, leaving her a boneless, quivering puddle.

When Alice finally came back to her senses, Griffin was grinning up at her. "I love watching you do that."

She made grabby hands at him. "Come here."

He crawled up her body and she pulled his face to hers, licking the traces of her juices off his lips. "Goddammit, Alice," he growled.

"Pants off," she ordered. "Now."

Griffin pushed off the bed, and she propped herself up on her elbows to watch as he shoved his pants and underwear down in one hurried motion. When his dick popped free, she bit her lip and sat up on the edge of the mattress, reaching for him. His eyes closed, his legs trembling as her hand wrapped around his shaft. But when she started to slide off the bed and kneel before him, he stopped her, grasping her arms with both hands.

"No way. Not unless you want me to embarrass myself by coming in two seconds like a teenager. I've waited too long for this." He guided her back onto the bed, leaning down to grab a condom as she splayed out beneath him with her legs spread in eager anticipation. It surprised Alice how unselfconscious she felt. How comfortable. All her thoughts were on Griffin, and how badly she needed him inside her. There was no room to think about anything else.

The wrapper crinkled as he tore the condom open, and she watched hungrily as he rolled it on and settled himself between her legs.

"You okay?" he murmured, nuzzling a kiss against her temple.

"Mmmm." As he pressed against her opening, she shifted her hips for easier entry. Slowly, cautiously, he filled her up, until the pressure was just on the edge of being too much.

"God, Alice," he breathed.

"Griffin." Her hands smoothed over his shoulders. "You're shaking." She pulled his mouth to hers and kissed him, slow and deep.

As he started to move inside her, she quivered beneath the solid weight of him, her fingernails scraping over his skin. His eyes met hers, and the raw emotion she saw in them made her heart thump against the wall of her chest.

He lifted one of her legs for a deeper angle, and as his thrusts increased in urgency her world narrowed to the feel of him inside her and the slick friction of their bodies sliding together. He held her tightly, his breath hitching as the pressure built. She tried to match his movements, forgetting about her own pleasure as she focused on his, and felt his rhythm falter, his muscles trembling as he strained to hold himself back.

"Let go," she ordered, grinding against him ruthlessly. "I want you to come."

He groaned and let more of his weight fall on her, crushing her into the mattress. "Jesus, Alice. Fuck, you feel so good."

His thrusts sped up, becoming more frenzied and precise. The sudden increase in intensity went straight to her core, sending her tumbling unexpectedly over the edge as Griffin shuddered above her, gasping out her name. They clung to one another in their shared ecstasy, chests heaving and sweaty limbs entangled.

"Can't breathe," Alice squeaked after a moment, prodding Griffin's shoulder. Her lungs felt like they were going to explode.

He lifted himself up and brushed a kiss against her forehead before flopping onto his back.

She sucked in a ragged breath, feeling like she'd just run a hundred-yard dash. "Shit, I'm out of shape. I think I'm dying."

"I hope not," Griffin said, twisting to give her another kiss before levering himself off the bed and disappearing into the bathroom. While he was gone, Alice took the opportunity to run down the hall and use her own bathroom.

When she returned, he'd peeled back the comforter and was lying on his back beneath a single white sheet with his hands behind his head. She slipped into the bed next to him, and he rolled over to curl his body around hers. "You okay?"

She turned her face toward his, nodding. "Perfect."

"God, I missed you." He reached up to brush her hair out of her face. "I never told you, but I missed you like crazy when I was in Atlanta."

She smiled, remembering his drunken voicemail. "You did tell me, actually."

"I did?"

"When you drunk-dialed me that night. That's why you said you'd called. To tell me how much you missed me. You said you missed me more than dairy."

His cheeks dimpled as he laughed. "That's an awful lot. But it's true."

"I thought…" Alice stopped as a rush of unexpected emotion overcame her.

Griffin's brows pulled together. "What?"

"When you left that voicemail, I thought it meant you *liked* me, liked me. But then the next day there was that photo of you and Kimberleigh leaving the bar together."

"That was a lie. I swear, I went home by myself that night."

"Yeah, but then two weeks later, there was a photo of the two of you holding hands along with that story about your new relationship."

"I'm sorry. I should have—" He grimaced and kissed her forehead. "I didn't realize—I should have, but I didn't think. I didn't know what I'd said in the voicemail, or what you were thinking. I didn't know you'd care."

"I did." She stroked her finger over his brow, overwhelmed by just how much she did care.

"Why didn't you just ask me about it? I would have told you the truth."

"I was afraid to, I guess. I didn't want official confirmation that you were sleeping with someone else when you left me that voicemail."

"I wasn't sleeping with her."

Alice nodded. She knew that now, but— "It made me feel like the friendship I thought we had wasn't real. That I was someone you could throw away as soon as you didn't need me anymore."

Griffin's palm cupped her cheek. "I wouldn't do that."

She blinked against the tears stinging her eyes and nodded again.

He pulled her closer, and his lips brushed against hers. "Alice, there's no one in my life more important than you."

Her eyes flew open, searching his.

"Maybe that sounds crazy," he said. "I'm not very good at being close to people, I guess."

"I'm not either," she admitted.

He took her hand and placed it over his heart. "Then we can be not good at it together."

She pulled his mouth to hers, unable to believe how lucky she was. Any moment, she feared, this implausibly perfect bubble would burst, and reality would come crashing in to ruin everything.

But it didn't. Instead, he pulled her onto his chest, wrapped his arms around her, and held her until they both drifted off to sleep.

nineteen

"YOU'RE RIDICULOUS," Alice said, feeling drowsy and content as she watched Griffin move around the bedroom.

He stopped in the middle of pulling his pants up and turned toward the bed where she still lay curled up under the sheets. "What?" He'd just come out of the shower, and his skin was glistening and so perfect it was unreal.

Alice lifted her arm, gesturing from his head to his feet. "All of this. No one should be this hot. I'm filing a complaint."

Griffin broke into a grin, yanked his pants up, and came over to the bed, stooping to kiss her. "I could let myself get fat again if it bothers you. Quit waxing and getting spray tans and expensive haircuts."

She caressed his nonexistent love handles. "You were never fat, but I wouldn't care if you were or if you never did any of that stuff again. You'd still be gorgeous, as far as I'm concerned."

"If only my agent or literally anyone else in the world agreed with you."

Alice's fingers inadvertently grazed a ticklish spot, and he backed away from the bed, shaking a scolding finger at her.

"What time is it?" she asked as he turned his back to flip through the shirts in his closet.

"After eleven."

She sat up and rubbed her eyes. Her hair probably looked like something you'd pull out of the shower drain, but somehow she didn't mind Griffin seeing her like that. He was the one who'd messed it up, after all. "I can't believe I slept so late."

"You were out like a coma patient. I got up and took Taco outside, made a smoothie, showered, and you hadn't so much as shifted in your sleep. I almost called 911, but you were still breathing so I figured you were fine."

"Someone wore me out last night."

A few hours after dozing off the first time, she'd awakened to the sensation of Griffin kissing her neck, and they'd had another round of slightly more languid, but no less satisfying sex. Alice felt like she'd run a marathon. Or what she imagined it must feel like, since she wasn't a runner and wouldn't be able to run a marathon even if she was being chased by a zombie horde. Perhaps she should consider taking up running? If she was going to be having sex with Griffin on a regular basis, some more cardiovascular endurance might come in handy.

"Which shirt should I wear?" He turned around, holding up two button-downs, one with gray stripes and the other with blue checks on it.

"Wear to what?"

"I've got that brunch with Kimberleigh. Remember? I told you about it last night over dinner."

Alice felt herself go cold. "You're still doing that?"

"Yeah."

"You're not breaking up with her?"

He dropped his arms, letting the shirts trail on the floor. "We're not together. You know that."

"But everyone thinks you are. Which makes me the other woman."

"Only if they find out about you. Which they won't."

She swallowed around the giant lump in the back of her throat. "Right."

He shoved the striped shirt back into the closet and pulled the checked one off the hanger. "It's kind of perfect, if you think about it."

"How is you publicly dating another woman while sleeping with me perfect?" Alice asked as she watched him slide the shirt over his shoulders.

"I'm not dating her." Griffin turned back to face her, straightening the collar of his shirt. "Everyone just thinks I am, which is the perfect cover. This way, we can keep us to ourselves."

"Why do we have to keep it to ourselves?"

"Because going public will make everything a million times worse."

For who? Alice wondered.

Griffin finished buttoning his shirt and came over to sit on the edge of the bed. "Trust me. The last thing you want is to be publicly connected to me." He reached for her hand and entwined their fingers. "The paps will follow you, the entertainment press will dig into every detail of your life, and a bunch of strangers who've never met you will tear you apart on the internet, criticizing everything you say or do."

Alice nodded numbly. She knew all that was true. It wasn't like she thought it would be pleasant, but she was willing to put up with it if the reward was having Griffin in her life.

He cupped her jaw and pulled her toward him for a kiss. "If everyone thinks I'm dating Kimberleigh, they'll leave you alone." His thumb caressed her cheek. "We can be together on our terms."

It didn't sound to Alice like her terms. It sounded like Griffin's terms, and his publicist's, and Kimberleigh's. It sounded like what *she* wanted fell somewhere much farther down the priority list.

"I've got to go," he said regretfully. "Please tell me you're okay with this."

Alice reminded herself how ashamed and upset he'd been about the Kimbergriff arrangement in the first place. He was only doing this because he believed it was necessary to keep the movie from flopping and damaging his career.

Griffin needed this, which meant he needed her to go along with it.

"It's fine," she said, mustering a smile for him. "Go."

He kissed her again and pressed his forehead against hers. "I'll be back in a couple hours, and then we'll have the whole day together. Think about what you want to do, okay?"

Their noses rubbed when Alice nodded her assent. Griffin kissed her forehead and stood up, smoothing out his shirt. "How do I look? There's going to be photographers there."

"Gorgeous." She gave him an encouraging smile despite the sour taste in her mouth.

"SORRY I'M LATE," GRIFFIN SAID WHEN KIMBERLEIGH OPENED the door of her Brentwood home.

"Whatever." She stepped outside and locked the door behind her. "The paps will be more eager if they have to wait for it."

She was dressed more softly than he was used to seeing her, in a loose flowered dress and light pink lipstick, with her hair carefully arranged in an elaborate "messy" bun. The perfect low-key celebrity photo op brunch attire. Although she hadn't chucked her trademark heels, he noted as she teetered over to his Range Rover. Kimberleigh was only five-foot-four, so the heels helped even out the six-inch height difference between them.

He offered his hand to help her into the car, waiting until she'd artfully arranged herself inside before walking around to slide behind the wheel. When he started the engine, the Drake album he'd been listening to on the way over blasted out of the speakers.

"Sorry," Griffin said as he thumbed the volume down to a more reasonable level.

Kimberleigh rolled her eyes and plucked her phone from her handbag.

That was the extent of their conversation on the half-hour drive to their noon reservation at Taste on Melrose. Griffin didn't care. He was still riding the high from his night with Alice, and Kimberleigh's frostiness couldn't touch him today. In a couple hours, this annoying little venture would be over, and he would be on his way back home to spend the whole rest of the day with Alice. He couldn't wait.

When they stopped at a light a few intersections away from the restaurant, Griffin's eyes drifted over to Kimberleigh. She was still glued to her phone, and he wondered how their date was going to look if they couldn't even make eye contact, much less carry on a conversation.

"We're gonna have to actually talk in the restaurant," he said to her. "We're supposed to be in the throes of new love, not one of those old married couples who sit in silence across the table from one another because they've run out of things to say."

"I'm aware of my role," Kimberleigh said without looking away from whatever was so engrossing on her phone.

"Are you mad about something?" Griffin asked, frowning. "You seem pissier than usual."

"No."

"Okay." He shrugged and drove on as the light changed.

He heard her let out an annoyed sigh. "I'm just not thrilled about giving up my Sunday for this." When he glanced at her again, she was staring out the window.

"Well, that makes two of us," he said, clenching his fist around the steering wheel. He supposed it was some consolation that he wasn't alone in his misery.

As soon as they pulled up to the valet stand, Kimberleigh's whole attitude changed, like an invisible director had called out "action." Suddenly, she was smiling and warm, looking into Griffin's eyes and clinging to his arm as she pretended to shy away from the attention they'd attracted.

There were at least two photographers loitering across the street. Griffin made sure they got plenty of good shots as he led Kimberleigh into the restaurant.

They were seated on the patio, as arranged, so they could be photographed throughout the meal. Griffin wasn't thrilled about having his picture snapped while he was eating, but that was the job. He ordered the protein scramble, and Kimberleigh asked for a fruit cup and plain egg white omelet to go with the bottle of prosecco she'd requested.

The business of reading menus and ordering had occupied their first few minutes ably, but now that the waiter was gone and they had their drinks, the pressure was on to make this look good.

Griffin needn't have worried. Kimberleigh immediately launched into a bubbly monologue about some ridiculous exercise her trainer had tried to get her to do. Griffin affected his best listening face, nodding along and laughing at the appropriate moments.

"Your turn," Kimberleigh said, leaning back with her champagne flute when she'd reached the end of her anecdote.

He countered with a story about his own trainer, and the time he'd convinced Griffin to try parkour with hilarious and painful results. Kimberleigh's tinkly laugh rose above the din of conversation around them, and Griffin pretended not to notice when some of their fellow diners not-so-sneakily used their phones to take photos of them. The whole thing felt a little like being a zoo animal, if zoo animals actually cared whether they were seen scratching their junk or dribbling food down their chins.

"See?" Kimberleigh said when he'd finished his story. "It's not hard, is it?"

Griffin reached for his prosecco. "I take it you've done this before?"

"Uh, yeah. So many times."

As he sipped his drink, Griffin thought about all the men Kimberleigh had been romantically linked with in the press. "Were any of your relationships real?" he asked, lowering his voice.

She laughed. "Only the ones you never heard about."

"Is it hard? Keeping your love life under the radar?"

Her green eyes darkened, belying the pleasant smile she kept fixed in place. "Everything's hard. But it's easier to watch the press and your fans tear apart someone you don't care about than someone you do. Believe me."

A tremor of unease traveled down Griffin's back, and he swallowed another mouthful of prosecco.

Alice would be his first attempt at a real relationship since his *Troublemakers* debut and the accelerated level of fame that had come with it. The increased public scrutiny wasn't the only reason he'd avoided letting anyone into his life, but it was certainly a factor. He realized, as he sat in a restaurant having his picture taken with one of the most popular young film actresses in the world, that he really didn't have any idea how to navigate all of this. How to protect Alice or himself.

The waiter brought their food and topped off their champagne flutes before retreating again. Grateful for the distraction, Griffin set himself to the task of eating his scramble without dripping ranchero sauce down the front of his shirt.

"Whatever happened with that girl?" Kimberleigh asked unexpectedly. "Arleen?"

"Alice." He stabbed a forkful of shredded chicken and shoved it into his mouth.

"Right. Did you kids ever get together?"

Griffin glanced at Kimberleigh, then back down at his plate when he felt his cheeks start to heat. "Yeah, actually."

"Really? Are you still…"

He swallowed and met her gaze across the table. "Yes."

She lifted her glass in salute. "Well! Look at you, Harry Potter, dating a muggle."

"Very funny."

Kimberleigh leaned forward, resting her forearms on the table. "Are you sure you know what you're getting into, dating a normal? What you're getting *her* into? Does she?"

Griffin shrugged. "I guess we'll find out." He shoveled another bite of chicken in his mouth. It tasted like paper, but he couldn't tell if the fault lay with the restaurant or his mood.

"I hope it works out for you," Kimberleigh said in a slightly softer voice. "I really do."

He reached across the table and speared a cube of pineapple off her plate, which she'd yet to touch. "Got any tips?"

She laughed and took a long swig of prosecco. "I'm the last person you should ask for advice."

"Why?"

"Because I've never had a relationship that didn't crash and burn—other than the fake ones, of course."

"I'm sorry," Griffin said.

Kimberleigh turned her face to the street, affecting a synthetic smile as she gazed at the paparazzi camped on the opposite sidewalk. "It's a hard world we've chosen for ourselves, sweetie. Make sure you keep your armor on."

———

"I'm back!" Griffin shouted as he let himself in the front door.

The only greeting he received was from the dog. After stooping to give Taco a scratch, he made his way into the living room and found Alice ensconced on the couch with her laptop. She looked up as he came toward her. "How was your brunch?"

"Unpleasant." He bent to kiss her, but she stopped him with a hand on his chest. "What?"

Her lips pressed into a thin line. "You've got lipstick around your mouth."

"Shit. Sorry. I thought I'd gotten it all." He scrubbed his lips with the back of his hand. "We did a fake kiss for the cameras as we waited for the car."

"I know." Alice turned her laptop so he could see it.

On the screen was a slightly blurry photo of him kissing Kimberleigh outside Taste. His hand rested on the back of her neck, and both her arms were wound around his waist. He was impressed by how cozy they looked, given how decidedly *not* cozy they were. Sabrina would be pleased at least.

"That was fast," he said. "I didn't think it'd hit the gossip sites until tomorrow."

"It hasn't." Alice took the laptop back and closed the photo. "Some people who were at the restaurant posted to social media. It's all over both your mentions."

Griffin grinned. "Been Twitter-stalking me?"

Alice's gaze stayed fixed on her laptop screen. "If you're wondering, the response is mostly positive. People seem pretty psyched about Kimbergriff."

He rolled his eyes at the stupid name. "Well, at least I'm not doing all this for nothing." When Alice continued to stare at her laptop, he nudged her leg with his. "Are you too grossed out to kiss me now? Am I damaged goods?"

She looked up at him and offered a small smile, finally. "No, of course not."

Griffin sank onto the couch next to her, moved her laptop aside, and took her face in both his hands. "I only ever want to have brunch with you. You know that, right? This is just work."

Alice nodded, and he kissed her, pouring into it exactly how much he'd missed her. He felt her start to relax into him, then she stiffened again, pulling away.

"Is that her perfume?"

Horrified, Griffin sniffed his shirt. *Ugh.* He pushed himself to his feet. "I'm gonna go take a Silkwood shower and wash away every molecule of that fucking brunch. I'll be right back."

He went straight to the shower and washed himself from head to toe—twice.

When he made his way back to the living room ten minutes later, Alice was staring at her laptop again. Griffin leaned against the doorway and posed, wearing only a towel slung low around his hips. "Hey."

She looked up and smiled, just like he'd hoped she would.

He waggled his eyebrows suggestively. "Permission to approach?"

Alice's teeth bit down on her lower lip, and his dick pulsed in response. "I don't know. Are you sure you didn't miss a spot?" She twirled her index finger in the air. "Spin."

Griffin strutted to the center of the room like a runway model and slowly spun around, giving her an eyeful of him from every angle. "What do you think?"

The corner of her mouth twitched. "Not bad."

"Not bad? That's all I get?"

She shut her laptop and set it on the coffee table. "Maybe I need a closer look."

That was more like it. He stood directly in front of her.

"Lose the towel," she ordered.

He did, giving it a flourish before chucking it over his shoulder.

Her gaze traveled up and down his body appraisingly, like a judge evaluating a show horse. Her smile grew wider. "*Very* nice."

Griffin dropped to his knees in front of her. Alice locked eyes with him as he fit his hips between her legs and leaned forward to kiss her. It was supposed to be a slow, seductive kiss, but the taste of her mouth stoked his hunger and short-circuited his brain. All he could think about was how much he wanted her. He devoured her with hungry strokes of his tongue, curling his hand into her hair as her fingernails scraped down his chest.

When her hips arched against him, he reached down to palm her through her cutoff jeans shorts. God, those fucking shorts. He loved the way they showed off her thighs and the curve of her ass. His fingers dipped inside the leg opening, exactly the way he'd fantasized about a hundred times before, and he stroked her through her underwear. "Fuck," he said when he realized how wet she was already.

Alice bucked her hips against him, as eager for him as he was for her, and he unfastened her shorts. He'd been in too much of a hurry last night, too eager to have her, but this time as he stripped off her clothes, he did it slowly, noticing everything. The single freckle near her belly button. How pale her skin looked in the sunlight pouring through the patio door. The way she whimpered in the back of her throat when he stroked her.

He ran his hands down her inner thighs to spread her wider as he bent his face to her slippery folds. Breathing deep, he flicked his tongue against her, smiling at the way she squirmed in frustration at the light touch. A closed-mouth kiss followed, then another, light and teasing.

When it seemed like she couldn't stand the anticipation anymore, he buried his face in her and hummed with pleasure. So soft, so warm, so delicious. He reached up to squeeze her breast with one hand, pinching her nipple gently while his other hand slid under her hips to lift them for better access. His tongue stroked her, eagerly lapping at her juices, then his lips closed around her clitoris and he sucked, drawing a moan of ecstasy from her.

He wanted to spend the rest of the day making her moan like this. Just exactly like she'd moaned beneath him last night. There were so many things he wanted to do to her, so many ways he wanted to touch her.

But even more than that, he wanted to make her smile. To make her laugh. To spend a whole day with her, just the two of them. Hold her in his arms. Cook for her. Watch TV with her. Even just sit near her while she worked on her computer.

He wanted her *here*. In his house. In his life. His Alice.

twenty

OVER THE NEXT FEW WEEKS, Alice and Griffin fell into a cozy domestic routine: he'd get up early, go for a run, then come back and make breakfast for the two of them. He was on a diet again, but he always made some kind of carbs for her—toast, or a bagel, or pancakes when he was feeling extra energetic—to go with the poached eggs he ate every day.

Alice had actually started to like poached eggs—or maybe it was just Griffin's eggs she liked. And no, that was not a euphemism, but maybe it should have been.

After breakfast, they'd clean up together, then Griffin would try to stay out of her way for the next few hours so she could get some work done. Unfortunately, she didn't always make a lot of progress. She was too aware of him in the next room, and she'd get distracted listening for sounds of him moving around the house—or even just staring into space daydreaming about him.

The pull between them was irresistible. It was like a tangible force that crackled in the air whenever they were within a hundred feet of each other. Even locked away in her room, the knowledge that Griffin was just on the other side of the wall presented a permanent distraction that itched at the back of Alice's skull, tempting her to chuck it all and go see what he was doing.

She needed to work. She was so close to the light at the end of the tunnel that she could practically taste it, but it remained persistently out of reach. Working was next to impossible when she knew Griffin was at loose ends in the next room, just waiting for her to emerge and hang out with him. The temptation to blow it all off and snuggle on the couch with him was too great.

He had consumed her whole life. She couldn't stop thinking about him. Wanting him. She was obsessed, in a way she'd never been obsessed over a man before. They had sex like rabbits, all over the house: his room, her room, the living room, the kitchen, even the deck, may his neighbors forgive them.

It was amazing. She'd never in her life experienced anything like this before.

Was this what love felt like?

Alice was afraid to let herself go too far down that road. As doting as Griffin seemed when they were together, she couldn't be certain his feelings were as strong as hers. After he'd pledged his affections that first night, he hadn't repeated the sentiments —not in actual words, anyway. It didn't seem to be his style. He wasn't the guy who whispered sweet nothings or wrote love notes.

Instead, he gave her mind-blowing orgasms and made her laugh until she nearly peed. He cooked for her, bought her favorite flavor of ice cream, and let her pick what movie they watched.

She had nothing whatsoever to complain about. Except for this tiny, gnawing insecurity that wouldn't go away.

Griffin was always Mr. Happy-Go-Lucky, so how was she supposed to know when all that happy ease signaled something deeper than just a good time? Just because she'd fallen like a ton of bricks didn't mean he had. He'd already admitted he didn't have a good track record with serious, lasting relationships. Maybe it wasn't his thing.

But maybe it could be. There were times, when they were together—the way he looked at her or touched her made it easy to believe he might love her, even if he didn't come right out and say the words.

There were other times, though, that left her doubting. He didn't seem to have any trouble compartmentalizing, for one thing. When he needed to go off and learn his lines for a rehearsal, he went off and learned his lines with no problem. And when he was supposed to be letting her work, he left her alone. Just like that. As easy as flipping a switch. He didn't seem nearly as distracted and obsessed as she was, and that worried her. Did it mean he wasn't as invested, or was it simply that he was better at prioritizing than she was?

The absolute worst, though, was when he had a date with Kimberleigh. Alice would watch him picking out his clothes, styling his hair, and trimming his stubble to the perfect fashionable length, carefree as ever while he performed these pre-date rituals he'd never once performed for her benefit. He didn't think twice about the fact that he was going out on dates with another woman. Holding hands with another woman. *Kissing* another woman. All the things he was supposed to save for Alice, he was doing with someone else. And he didn't even seem to feel bad about it.

She told herself it was because he was an actor, and this was just another role to him. Alice didn't think it would have bothered her so much if that were actually true. If he was doing it under lights on a soundstage in front of grips and teamsters, with a lav mic tucked under his shirt, she would have been fine with it. That was work.

What he was doing with Kimberleigh was something else. They were unsupervised, out on their own in public. Worst of all, everyone in the world believed they were in love. Even Alice's closest friends.

It made her feel like Griffin's dirty secret. Worse than that, it made her feel isolated and alone.

GRIFFIN WAS DOING A LIVE Q&A FROM THE DINING ROOM. Alice could hear the garbled voices of the fans videoing in to ask questions, and Griffin's cheerful, jokey answers. It was some charity thing his publicist had set up to bring attention to a good cause, in this case a home for cancer patients and their families who had to travel for treatment. But it was also meant to polish Griffin's star a little and help push him—*and* Kimberleigh—into the next entertainment news cycle.

He was getting a lot of questions about her, of course. Alice's jaw clenched every time she heard him say Kimberleigh's name. Why were the walls in this house so goddamned thin?

Also, why had she left her phone in the living room? Now she couldn't get it without walking through the middle of Griffin's Q&A. She was trapped in the back of the house until he finished. Not that she really needed her phone when she was supposed to be working, but she *wanted* it. It wasn't like she was actually getting any writing done right now, so she might as well be playing Pokémon Quest.

Alice opened her bedroom door and peeked out. It didn't sound like Griffin was even getting close to wrapping up out there. She crept down the hall. When she got to the end, she dropped to her hands and knees and started crawling.

She'd almost made it through the dining room when she heard Griffin laugh. "That's my dog sitter crawling past back there. Everyone say hi to her!"

Alice fast-crawled the rest of the way out of the shot, then got to her feet to glare at him. He gave her a shrug and a lopsided grin, then went right back to answering fan questions. Annoyed, she snatched her phone off the coffee table and went out to the deck. At least out there she didn't have to listen to him answering insipid questions about his love life with bald-faced lies.

Twenty minutes later, Alice heard the patio door slide open and Griffin's hands settled on her shoulders. "Hey," he said, pressing a kiss to the top of her head. "I'm all done."

She kept her eyes on her phone and didn't say a word.

He sat down on the lounge chair, nudging her legs aside to make room. "Alice? Hello?" He waved his hand in front of her face.

"What?" she asked, lowering her phone.

His brow furrowed. "Are you mad?"

"No." She got up and went inside to the kitchen, then jerked the refrigerator door open and grabbed a bottle of water.

Griffin trailed after her, looking irritated. "Can we not play this game? Just tell me what the fuck the problem is."

She slammed the fridge door. "Why would I have a problem? Because you made me look like a fool in front of god-only-knows how many people on the internet?"

"I didn't make you crawl through the background. You decided to do that all on your own."

"No, you just called me your dog sitter."

He ran a frustrated hand through his hair. "What did you want me to say instead?"

"I don't know, since I guess the truth is too much to expect."

Griffin stared at her. "You think I should have just casually announced in the middle of a live Q&A that Kimberleigh and I are a sham and you're my real live-in girlfriend? Is that actually what you expected me to do? After all the effort I and other people have put into selling my relationship with Kimberleigh for the press?"

As Alice stared back at him, she felt some of her anger drain away, only to be replaced by a sense of despondency. "*Am* I your girlfriend? Because it doesn't really feel like it sometimes."

Dismay washed over Griffin's face. "Alice." He stepped forward and grasped her arms. "Of course you're my girlfriend."

She nodded numbly, and he surrounded her with his arms.

"I know this situation sucks for you, and I'm sorry." He clasped her face in his hands, gazing at her tenderly. "I'm sorry, okay?" He brushed a silken kiss against her lips. "You're not just my dog sitter. You're so much more important than that." As he kissed her again, the warm, intoxicating sensation curled around her like a protective cocoon. It was so easy to let herself be carried away by the soft, insistent pull of his lips. To forget everything else…

Alice put her hands on Griffin's chest and drew her head back to look at him. "Are we ever going to talk about this Kimberleigh thing? Do I ever get a say in any of this, or am I just expected to go along with it like a good little soldier?"

Confusion creased his brow. "What do you mean? We did talk about it—that first morning, when I left for brunch."

"We talked about it for forty seconds when you were halfway out the door already."

"You said you were okay with it. I didn't know we needed to do more talking."

"You asked me to tell you I was okay with it because you had to leave, so I told you what you wanted to hear instead of making a scene."

He stiffened and let go of her. "Are you saying you want me to back out of this agreement with Kimberleigh? Is that what you're asking me to do?"

Yes, Alice thought, and *If I was, would you? Would you even do that for me?*

She didn't want to know the answer. She would never ask him to do it anyway. This was his career, and she had no right to interfere in it. Would he ask her to quit school for him? Would she even consider it if he did?

Definitely not. She'd walk right out the door as soon as the request left his lips, is what she'd do.

"No," she told him, "of course not."

"Are you sure?" Deep furrows sprouted across his forehead. "Because if so, that's something we need to talk about."

She shook her head, terrified suddenly of losing him, and reached for his hand. Wetness blurred her eyes as she entwined her fingers with his. "That's not what I'm asking."

He took a breath and released it. Closing the distance between them, he tipped her chin up and gazed at her with troubled blue eyes. "Then what? Talk to me."

It was hard to look directly at him while admitting this, but she forced herself to do it. "I guess I—" She swallowed. "I don't trust this."

Hurt flashed in his eyes. "You mean you don't trust me."

Alice looked away. "I'm not sure I have it in me to trust anyone anymore."

Griffin sighed deeply and pulled her against his chest. "I guess I understand why. I just wish I could take all that pain away." His heart thumped against her cheek as he swept his hands over her tense back. "I swear to you, I won't ever hurt you."

It should have made her feel better, hearing that. Instead, it set her even more on edge.

People always hurt each other eventually, even if they didn't mean to. Even if Griffin's intentions were pure and good, it didn't mean he wouldn't ever break her heart one day. Alice honestly didn't know how people did it, trusting each other. Enjoying happiness without thinking about the pain that might lie around the next corner.

Griffin kissed the top of her head, then her temple, nuzzling her hair. His fingers caressed her cheekbone and jaw, and he angled her head back. She squeezed her eyes shut against the sincerity she couldn't bear to see in his expression. His nose grazed her cheek, and he brushed a gentle kiss against her lips.

"Alice." His voice was rough with tenderness and pain. Another aching kiss pressed against her lips. "There's no one but you. I'm not going anywhere."

She drew a hitching breath, fisting her hands against his chest. "You say that now, but—"

"But nothing." He sounded so sure, but he didn't understand. He couldn't know how quickly everything you cared about could slip away.

Alice shook her head, trying to explain, but her chest felt like it was bursting and she didn't know how to put what she was feeling into words. "People get tired of each other, or they meet new people, or—"

"That's not going to happen."

"—*things change*, and you can't predict it or stop it from happening. I'm scared this is all too much, too fast, because the way I feel about you isn't casual or temporary, and when you're done with me I don't know how I'm going to recover from that."

"*When I'm done with you?*" Griffin stared at her, incredulous. "Alice, you dummy, I'm in love with you."

She stopped breathing.

Love?

Had he really just said—

She blinked at him. "Say it again without the dummy part."

Smiling, he lifted her hand to his lips and kissed her knuckles. "I'm in love with you."

Her heart stumbled in her chest. She tugged him closer and rested her forehead against his. "I'm in love with you too."

Griffin's arms banded around her and he sealed his lips over hers, crushing her with his urgency. Heat seared through her as she clawed at his clothes. She needed him—that connection, that closeness—so much it felt like her skin was sizzling and he was the only thing that could put out the fire.

Rough hands pulled her shirt over her head and pushed her yoga pants down to pool around her ankles. Alice pushed his T-shirt off and ripped his jeans open as he dug in the junk drawer for a condom. When he'd rolled it on, Griffin lifted her up onto the counter.

Their eyes locked as he slid into her, and she saw her own raw vulnerability reflected in his expression. She wasn't alone. She had him, and he had her.

twenty-one

GRIFFIN LIKED WATCHING Alice walk around his house in her cutoff shorts. She was doing a lot of walking at the moment, and he was enjoying it immensely.

She was supposed to be writing, but instead she was pacing around the living room. Everyone had their process, he supposed. He liked to practice his lines in the shower, so he was in no position to judge.

"Is it working?" he asked after another minute.

Alice stopped and looked at him. "What?"

"The pacing. Is it inspiring any ideas?"

She resumed pacing. "No."

"Would it help if I left the house?"

Frowning, she shook her head. "It's your house. You don't have to leave. If anyone has to leave, it'll be me. I can go to the library if I have to. I just don't want to."

"I don't mind. I can make myself scarce for a few hours if it will help."

She loosed her hair from its ponytail and refastened it into a new one. "I don't want you to leave. I just want to figure out how to describe my conclusions in this one section without anyone having to leave the house."

"What if you tried talking it through with me?"

"That won't help."

Griffin tried not to be insulted by the way she'd brushed aside his suggestion. He was well aware that he wasn't as smart or as educated as she was. It still amazed him that a woman about to earn a doctorate could actually want to spend time with a man who only had a high school diploma and a few community college classes to his name. Most of what she did went way over his head, even when she tried to give him the Dummies version.

Alice halted her circuit of the room and changed direction. "I'm going to clean up all this old mail on the table," she announced, heading for the front entry with renewed purpose.

It wasn't that Griffin didn't think she could finish her dissertation. It was just...he was starting to worry about her a little. She didn't seem to be getting much done, from what he could see. He didn't know what it had been like when he was away, but the last few weeks she'd spent more time not working than working. He was starting to get anxious on her behalf.

But he didn't know what he could do to help. He'd offered to leave her alone, but she didn't seem to want that. But maybe he should do it anyway? Just make plans to be out of the house all day so he wouldn't pose a distraction.

Alice reappeared with an envelope in her hand and a puzzled look on her face. "You got an invitation to Alfie's birthday party?"

"Yeah."

"The party's this weekend. Why didn't you mention it?"

"I don't know. I forgot, I guess."

She dropped the invitation on the coffee table and flopped down on the couch beside him. "Are you going?"

"Probably not."

Her head came to rest on his shoulder. "Why?"

Griffin breathed in the peach scent of her hair as he twined his fingers with hers. "I don't feel like going alone."

"You could take me with you."

That was exactly why he hadn't mentioned it. Because he didn't want to have this conversation. He kissed the top of her head, hoping it would soften the blow. "That's probably not a good idea."

She pulled away and sat up to face him. "It's at Alfie's house. It's not like there'll be paparazzi there."

"I can't bring you as my date without telling people we're together."

"So?"

Griffin grimaced at the challenge in her tone. "So the more people who know about us, the greater the risk that it will get out."

"So we can just never go out anywhere together or tell anyone we know about us?"

"Not *never*."

"For how long, then?"

Good question. Sabrina hadn't been specific, and Griffin hadn't asked for clarification on that point. Alice hadn't been a consideration when he'd initially agreed to all this, so he'd assumed he'd go along with it for as long as Sabrina wanted him to. But *Prepare for War* wouldn't come out for another year. Surely he wasn't expected to keep up this charade all that time. Was he?

A few months ought to be long enough to build up some buzz for the film. Once the momentum kicked in, he could propose they orchestrate a diplomatic breakup with Kimberleigh. Hopefully.

"I don't know how long," he told Alice honestly. "But it won't be forever. I swear."

She twisted away and sank back into the couch, leaving at

least a foot of space between them. Her shoulders curled in on themselves as she crossed her arms across her chest.

He hated seeing her like this and knowing it was his fault. He hated this whole fucking Kimbergriff situation and wished there was a way out of it. But he'd made a professional commitment. People were counting on him to hold up his end —not to mention the fact that his own career was at stake. He couldn't just bail because it had become inconvenient.

"Hey." He scooted closer, draping his arm around Alice's shoulders. "You know if it was up to me, I'd tell the whole world about us?"

Her eyes shifted in his direction, full of doubt. "Would you?"

There were those trust issues again. It was like she was always half expecting him to disappoint her. She just couldn't seem to believe he wanted to stick around.

"Of course I would." He turned her face toward his, stroking his fingers across her cheekbone.

Her lips compressed into a thin line. "I guess you could take Kimberleigh to the party."

He sighed and dropped his hand to the couch. "I wouldn't do that. I don't want to have to lie to my friends about her."

Alice nodded glumly.

He leaned over to brush a kiss against her temple. "I'd rather stay home than go somewhere without you."

"Don't you ever get tired of staying home and hiding?"

Never. Griffin loved staying home, because he could be himself at home, away from the privacy-invading stares and cellphone cameras that waited for him everywhere he went. Maybe if he could run out for a coffee or a package of toilet paper without constantly feeling everyone's eyes on him, he'd enjoy going out more. But he'd lost that ability years ago.

"Do *you*?" he asked Alice.

"Sometimes." Her finger traced and retraced a figure eight

pattern in the couch cushion. "I can't be seen with you anywhere in public, I have to be careful what pictures I post on social media, and I don't even have anyone I can talk to about all of this—the good parts or the bad parts."

He captured her hand to stop its nervous fidgeting and ran his thumb over her knuckles. "You can talk to me."

"No, I can't. If I complain or act unhappy, you get that pitiful, guilty look that just makes me feel bad for making you feel bad."

He drew back, stung by her words. "I do feel bad for making you feel bad."

"I'm sorry." She buried her face in her hands, letting out a long, ragged sigh. "I know you hate this as much as I do. I'm just feeling sorry for myself."

Griffin slid an arm under Alice's knees and swung her into his lap. Cradling her against his chest, he stroked his hand down the back of her neck. "It's okay. It's gonna be okay."

She turned her face into his chest and nodded.

His fingers kneaded her neck and shoulders, trying to work away some of the tension. "Is there something else wrong? Is it your dissertation?" He felt her tense up again.

"It's fine." The white-knuckled fists she had clenched in his shirt said otherwise.

His hand smoothed over her hair. "It seems like you've been having some trouble focusing."

"It's just harder than I thought it would be. All this time, I told myself it was Gilchrist keeping me from making progress. Only it turns out, it wasn't just him. It was me." She unclenched her fists and plucked at the bottom of Griffin's T-shirt. "Even with him out of the picture, I'm not sure I can do it."

"You'll get it done."

"Sure."

He gave her a little shake. "You will. I believe in you."

"I'm glad someone does."

"Hey." He studied her troubled features, trying to think of some way to cheer her up. "What if..." She lifted hopeful eyes to his. God, he was such a sucker for her, he'd do anything if she batted those big blue eyes at him. "Maybe we could go to Alfie's party together."

"Really? Are you sure?"

"Yeah. It's probably fine." Chances were good he was just being overly paranoid. No one invited to Alfie's house was going to go telling tales out of school. He needed to relax and stop worrying so much.

Alice rewarded him with a smile, and he brushed his thumb over her bottom lip. When she caught it between her teeth and sucked it into her mouth, he exhaled sharply, letting out a small growl in the back of his throat. Tipping her head back, he claimed her mouth with possessive strokes of his tongue as he swept a hand up the inside of her thigh, once more appreciating the easy access provided by her cutoff shorts. Her legs parted for him, and her teeth bit down playfully on his lower lip.

By the time she'd worked his pants open, Griffin had forgotten all about the churn of unease in the pit of his stomach.

THE SECOND ALICE STEPPED INSIDE ALFIE CROSBY'S Mediterranean-style Malibu home, she realized she'd made a mistake wanting to come. A quick scan of the room confirmed her worst fears: everyone else there was either famous, beautiful, rich, or some combination of the three. They weren't quite *all* actors—at least half the guests were writers, directors, producers, and other Hollywood heavy hitters—but it sure seemed that way.

Feeling mousy and out of place in her three-year-old off-the-rack cocktail dress, Alice hung back as Louis Blanchard, the former showrunner of *Las Vegas General*, greeted Griffin. Blanchard had never deigned to notice Alice before, and apparently had no intention of breaking that streak now, as he proceeded to chat with Griffin about his next show, utterly ignoring her presence.

"It was good catching up with you," Griffin said, extracting himself from the conversation after a few minutes. "We'd better go pay our respects to the birthday boy."

He rested his hand at the small of Alice's back as he guided her deeper into the house. "Sorry. That guy's a real gasbag."

After elbowing their way past an Oscar nominee, two Emmy winners, and a Broadway actress well on her way to a coveted EGOT, they found Alfie in the kitchen playing bartender. He returned Griffin's hug with enthusiasm before turning a quizzical eye on Alice.

"You remember Alice, of course," Griffin supplied. "She worked as an extra on the show."

"Right," Alfie said with a nod of recognition. "You're the one who threw all those scalpels at that other kid."

Since Alfie was notorious for forgetting people's names—there was a story going around that he'd once failed to recognize his ex-daughter-in-law at an industry event—Alice decided to put this in the win column.

"You have a lovely home," she told him. She'd never been to Malibu before, and the Pacific views from the back of the house were stunning, although the interior was surprisingly modest and down-to-earth with its floral couches and rough-hewn wood furniture.

"Thank you," Alfie replied genially. "I had nothing whatsoever to do with it."

"He's lying," said a strikingly beautiful woman who'd just come into the kitchen with a bag of ice. "He picked all the furniture himself. Agonized over it for months until it was just right."

Alfie shook an affectionately chiding finger at her. "Don't give away my embarrassing secrets, woman."

The woman set the ice down and turned to greet Griffin. "We're so glad you were able to come."

He gave her a kiss on the cheek before making the introductions. "Alice, meet Alfie's wife, Lynn."

"It's nice to meet you," Alice said, taking Lynn's perfectly manicured hand. Alfie's wife looked at least thirty years his junior, but according to the *Vanity Fair* profile Alice had read last year, their actual age difference was closer to ten years. Whoever her plastic surgeon was, he was a wizard.

"Alice worked on the show," Alfie added. "As an extra."

Lynn turned to Griffin with a raised eyebrow. "Are you two…?" She wagged a finger between him and Alice.

Since that was the million-dollar question, Alice looked at Griffin to see what he would say.

"Yeah," he said, after only a brief hesitation. "We are." He curled his arm around Alice's waist, tugging her closer, and she exhaled some of her tension.

"How lovely." Lynn smiled and turned to Alfie. "Isn't that lovely?"

"Mmm," he grunted, as if he couldn't care less who was dating who, and nodded at Alice. "What can I get you to drink, my dear?"

"Red wine would be great," she said, choosing the closest, easiest thing at hand.

"What about you, kiddo?" Alfie asked Griffin as he poured Alice's wine.

"Just water for me," Griffin said, patting his stomach. "I'm on another diet."

"Course you are." Alfie handed Alice her glass of wine and

cocked his head toward the back door. "There's a cooler full of sparkling water outside on the deck. Go crazy."

Alfie was drinking a La Croix himself. His battle with alcoholism and subsequent recovery twenty years ago was a well-documented chapter of his bio, so Alice wasn't surprised to see that he wasn't imbibing the drinks he was serving.

She and Griffin bid Alfie and his wife goodbye and headed outside in search of the aforementioned cooler. Once Griffin had equipped himself with his favorite flavor of La Croix, they joined a group of *Las Vegas General* cast members who had congregated by the pool. Griffin was greeted with enthusiasm, and Alice with unspoken curiosity and a few raised eyebrows. She attempted small talk for the next twenty minutes, but wound up mostly standing silently at Griffin's side, until Alexandra Shaw addressed her with an over-wide smile. "What are *you* up to these days, Alice? Have you moved on to another background job?"

"Um." Alice switched her now-empty wineglass from one hand to the other. "No. Actually—"

"She's finishing her PhD," Griffin supplied for her.

"Really?" Alexandra looked impressed. "In what?"

"Sociology."

"How thrilling!"

It wasn't exactly the word Alice would have chosen, but she smiled her agreement, prepared to explain the subject of her dissertation research.

No one asked about Alice's research, however. Instead, Alexandra turned back to Griffin, her eyes narrowing slightly. "And what's all this I've been reading lately about you and Kimberleigh Cress?"

Alice squeezed her wineglass, desperately wishing she had some left to gulp down.

Griffin shrugged. "Don't believe everything you read."

"But you two did just finish shooting that Jerry Duncan

movie together?" Alexandra persisted.

Belatedly, Alice remembered that Alexandra was one of the women Griffin was rumored to have slept with, then immediately wished she hadn't remembered that particular fact.

"That's right." Griffin took a swig of his cherry lime La Croix, seemingly unfazed.

"Let me guess—the studio put you up to it for the publicity."

"Something like that."

"But you're with Alice now?" Alexandra's smile had a tinge of disbelief to it.

"What was it like working with Jerry Duncan?" piped up Brendan Parrish, who'd played one of the other doctors on the show. Alice breathed a silent sigh of relief as the conversation turned away from her and her relationship with Griffin.

A few minutes later, she excused herself to get a refill on her wine.

"Grab me another La Croix?" Griffin requested cheerfully.

Alice headed inside and topped off her glass from one of the open bottles in the kitchen, which was full of people she didn't know. On her way back outside to the cooler of sparkling water, she was waylaid by Janie, one of the makeup artists on the show.

"Oh my god, Alice! I didn't expect to see you here!"

Alice was just as surprised to see Janie, until she remembered that Janie was Alfie's niece. Nepotism got you a long way in Hollywood.

"Janie, hi!" Alice tried not to spill her wine as Janie gave her an enthusiastic hug. "Yeah. I came with Griffin."

Janie's eyes widened. "Griffin Beach?"

Shit. Of course Janie was one of the makeup artists Griffin had slept with. And she had that same look of disbelief Alice had seen on Alexandra's face a few minutes ago. How many of his exes were here, exactly?

"Yeah. That's right." Alice gulped down a mouthful of wine.

Janie's eyes skated in Griffin's direction. "What about all that Kimbergriff stuff?"

"Oh. Um. It's complicated."

"Ha! I *knew* it!" Janie said. "I knew it was too good to be true. I said there's no way Griffin Beach had settled down. Guys like him don't change."

Alice tried to laugh like she was in on the joke. "Ha ha. Yeah."

"Don't get me wrong. He's a sweetie—but I don't have to tell you that. I had fun while it lasted, you know?"

Alice nodded, feeling queasy. "Can I ask…how long were you guys…?"

"Oh, just like a month or two."

"Two months…wow." She swallowed another mouthful of wine.

"He wanted to keep it all hush-hush. He said it was because we worked together, but I think he was more concerned about his privacy, to be honest. Plus, the fewer people who knew, the easier it was for him to extract himself when he was done."

Alice tried to swallow around the dryness in her throat. "Is that what he did? Just end it?"

Janie shrugged. "I mean, there wasn't all that much to end. It's not like we were dating, if you know what I mean. We never went anywhere together—I didn't even get an invite to his house. He'd just text me a couple times a week and ask if he could come over."

"Wow." At least Alice had access to Griffin's house. That was something, right? It paid to be the domestic help.

"It was fine." Janie shrugged again and her eyes traveled to where Griffin was standing. "I knew exactly who he was when it started, and I went into it with both eyes open. And like I said, it was fun while it lasted." She looked at Alice and grinned. "I'm sure you know what I'm talking about."

Before Alice could come up with a response, they were joined by one of Janie's cousins, who turned out to be Alfie's eldest son. While the two of them talked about Janie's new job on an indie film, Alice excused herself and wandered away.

Why had she ever thought she wanted to come to this party? What exactly about being judged and found wanting by all of Griffin's industry friends and ex-lovers had sounded like fun to her? All of them wondering why she was here, what Griffin was doing with her, when he'd get tired of her like he got tired of everyone else.

"There you are!" Griffin said, coming up behind her and squeezing the back of her neck. "I was about to send a search party."

Alice forced a smile as she turned toward him. "I was talking to Janie."

"Ah."

She tried to read his reaction, but he didn't seem to have one. He was his usual pleasantly blank slate.

He gestured at her glass, which was nearly empty again. "Did you get more wine?"

"Yeah." She looked down at what was left of her wine, then back up at him. "I'm ready to go whenever you want."

His forehead crinkled. "So soon? Aren't you having a good time?"

"Not particularly. But if you're having a good time we can stay."

He leaned toward her, his hand stroking down her arm. "Did Janie say something to you?"

"No." Nothing she hadn't already known—or should have known. "I just didn't think about how many women you've slept with that would be here." Griffin winced, and she reached up to touch his face. "It's okay, I just feel out of my element."

"Why?"

"Everyone here is on this whole other strata. It feels like they're all wondering why someone like you is with someone like me."

"Hey! What's wrong with someone like you?"

"I'm just a regular mortal who's not in the entertainment business—and even when I was, I was at the very bottom of the food chain."

"Alfie's wife isn't in the business. Neither are a lot of the plus-ones here."

"But they've all assimilated with the beautiful people and learned to walk the walk. Meanwhile, I'm over here like a dandelion in a rose garden."

He pushed her hair out of her face and touched his lips to hers. "Listen to me. You are by far the most beautiful woman here. You're more like a wild orchid surrounded by cheap plastic daisies. *And* you're about to be a doctor, so you're almost definitely the most brilliant person here. You have no reason to feel intimidated by anyone."

Alice couldn't help smiling. He was just so…sweet. And hot. And lovable. And he loved *her*, over everyone else. How had she gotten so lucky?

Griffin's hand skimmed down her arm, soothing and warming with his touch. "But we can go whenever you want. These industry parties are always boring as shit."

She rose up to kiss his cheek, and her lips lingered near his ear. *"Take me to bed or lose me forever."*

Top Gun was his favorite movie, as she'd discovered recently when she'd flipped past it on cable and he'd physically removed the remote from her hand and insisted they watch it. He knew every line of dialogue by heart and recited them along with the actors on-screen like a performer at *The Rocky Horror Picture Show*, to Alice's eternal amusement.

Griffin broke into a broad grin, his blue eyes sparking with pleasure. *"Show me the way home, honey."*

In bed much later that night, Alice watched the slow rise and fall of Griffin's chest while he slept beside her. His face was even more boyish looking in sleep, and she wondered what teenaged Griffin Micklethwaite had been like before Hollywood and his mother's illness had molded him into the man she knew. She trailed her fingertips down his arm, following the smooth hills and valleys of muscle, and he mumbled something incoherent in his sleep. Rolling over and pulling his arm across her, she snuggled against him and felt his body shift, seeking hers out instinctively.

Alice closed her eyes, and with Griffin's solid warmth at her back, fell into a deep and serene sleep.

ALICE DIDN'T STIR WHEN GRIFFIN SLIPPED OUT OF BED THE next morning. She wasn't a morning person like him, and she kept students' hours now that she wasn't working on the show. Fortunately, she was also a deep sleeper, so she didn't wake as he got up and pulled on his clothes before taking Taco outside for his morning constitutional.

It was going to be a hellaciously hot day, he could tell already. The state was in the midst of yet another drought, and the sky was hazy from the wildfires burning east of the city.

Griffin startled when his phone vibrated in his pocket—one long buzz to indicate a phone call rather than a shorter one for a text—surprised that anyone would be calling him before seven a.m. Even the fake IRS spammers didn't usually start this early in the morning.

He frowned at the name on the screen as he swiped to accept the call. "Sabrina? What's up?"

"You're awake." Her voiced was clipped and businesslike—

never a good sign. "Have you looked at your social media this morning?"

His frown deepened. "No. Why?"

"Look at your Twitter mentions."

"Hang on." He opened the Twitter app on his phone and tapped to view his mentions. They were coming in so fast, he could barely read them. Apparently there was a picture everyone was talking about? He scrolled down until he finally found it.

Fuck.

It was a photo of him and Alice from the party yesterday. It was grainy and out of focus, like someone had zoomed in and cropped it, but you could see their faces clearly enough to identify them. Kissing. Griffin's hand was on Alice's cheek and she was smiling slightly against his lips, her face tilted up to his.

It would have been a beautiful photo of the two of them, if it wasn't such a huge fucking problem.

"How the hell—"

"Alfie's daughter posted some photos from the party to her Instagram and you were caught in the background of one." Sabrina's voice was dangerously calm, the way she got when she was angry. Sabrina didn't yell, ever. In the best British tradition, she merely grew cooler and more polite. "Some of your fans were scouring social media for photos of you from the party and that's what they found."

"Jesus. I didn't think—"

"Clearly."

Griffin ran a hand through his hair, tugging at the roots. "It was a private party at Alfie's house, for god's sake."

"How many times have I told you there's no such thing as privacy in this business?"

Too many.

"I and a lot of other people have worked very hard to make the public believe in your relationship with Kimberleigh, and you've just gone and undermined all of it with one ill-timed kiss."

His rubbed his chest, which had begun to feel painfully tight. "I should probably call her." He owed Kimberleigh an apology, at the very least. She was unlikely to appreciate being cast in the role of the scorned woman—again.

"I've already been in touch with her people," Sabrina said. "We'll smooth it over."

"Is she pissed?"

"She's asleep. She doesn't even know yet. But she will soon enough."

Griffin sank down on the end of a lounge chair and rubbed his forehead with the heel of his hand. "I don't know what to say. I'm sorry, Sabrina. I fucked everything up."

"You certainly did." She sighed, and her voice softened infinitesimally. "But in the grand scheme of celebrity fuckups, this is just a minor hiccup. It's not the end of the world."

"What do you want me to do?"

"Damage control. Lots of it."

"What does that mean?" He stood up again, too anxious to sit.

"I'll email a list of instructions. Do us both a favor and follow them very precisely."

"Yeah, of course. Whatever you say." He heard a footstep behind him and turned to see Alice standing in the doorway. She must have overheard part of his conversation because her face was drawn in concern. The creases in her forehead deepened even farther at his expression, and she came forward to take his hand. "Thanks, Sabrina. I'll talk to you soon." Griffin ended the call and let the hand holding the phone drop to his side.

"What's wrong?" Alice asked, wide-eyed and innocent. "What's happened?"

twenty-two

ALICE'S PHOTO was all over the internet: Twitter, Facebook, Tumblr, Reddit, and who knew how many other wretched hives of scum and villainy. It hadn't hit the gossip blogs yet, but it was just a matter of time. *#GriffinBeach* was already trending in the US, along with *#Kimbergriff* and *#BeachesSlut*, which was the moniker Alice had been assigned, much to her personal and grammatical consternation.

Well, he wanted to generate publicity, Alice thought bitterly. *Now he has it.*

Only this was the wrong kind of publicity. It made both Griffin and Kimberleigh look bad: him for being a cheating scumbag, and her for being in love with a cheating scumbag. But that was nothing compared to what people were saying about Alice.

She scrolled through the hashtags, feeling increasingly sick.

Fuck that s2pid asshole bitch go die n hell u horney piece of shit I hop u get hit by a buss ugly motherfucker

The spelling in a lot of the tweets left something to be

278

desired, but managed to convey the general sentiment none-theless.

Greedy cunt prolly gives lots of blowjobs with that ugly pug face but that don't mean Griffin gives 2 shits about her lol.

They went on like that forever. Insulting every possible aspect of Alice's appearance while calling her some version of a whore or a bitch for stealing Kimberleigh's boyfriend.

The general feeling on the internet streets seemed to be that Alice was too fat, too plain, too manly, too ugly, too slutty, too tall, too much of a lesbian, too un-rape-able, or too all of the above to deserve Griffin, in addition to being a home-wrecking gold digger who deserved to either kill herself or be murdered in a variety of creative ways. Good thing she was un-rape-able, so at least she had no worries in that department. Griffin, meanwhile, was trash who didn't deserve Kimberleigh, and Kimberleigh was stupid to have ever thought Griffin would change his ways.

Rachel had already called to express her condolences and outrage on Alice's behalf, but beneath the words of support Alice had detected an undercurrent of hurt. She was Alice's closest friend, and she hadn't known about the most important relationship in her life until it had gone viral—which said something genuinely depressing about the state of Alice's life and relationships.

Alice had apologized, citing the need for secrecy—which was at least well supported by the social media firestorm the news had incited. Rachel had seemed understanding about not being let in on the secret, and had even offered to create an army of sockpuppet accounts and take to the internet in Alice's defense. It was a sweet gesture, but since it seemed likely to do more harm than good, Alice had reluctantly declined.

The internet vitriol only ramped up as the day wore on and

the picture spread. Occasionally someone would attempt to come to Alice's defense, pointing out the inherent wrongness of slut-shaming and attacking her appearance, but they were mostly drowned out by the sheer volume of haters.

Haters.

Alice actually had haters now. Lots of them. She'd never imagined she'd one day be someone who inspired such strong negative emotions in total strangers. Her one consolation was that they didn't know who she was. They had no name or identity at which to focus their ire. She was merely an anonymous blonde in a blurry photo.

Griffin flopped down on the opposite end of the couch with a protein shake and shot her a disapproving look. "Stop reading that shit. It'll make you crazy."

"How can you *not* read it?" She'd been glued to her phone all day. She couldn't look away. It was like a toothache she couldn't quit worrying with her tongue.

"Because it makes me sick, and I don't want to feel sick all the time." Griffin reached for the remote and switched on the TV.

"I can't just pretend it's not happening. Literally thousands of people hate me enough to go on the internet and shout about it. How am I supposed to ignore that?"

He took a swig of protein shake and changed the channel to ESPN. "You'll get used to it."

What if she didn't want to? That didn't seem like something anyone should ever have to get used to.

"How can you be so calm?" she asked him.

"I'm not calm. Believe me."

He seemed calm. But then she'd never seen him any other way. Alice had never known anyone whose emotions were on such an even keel. Or maybe they were just tamped down so hard it seemed that way. Was he Zen or just repressed? She never really knew what was going on in his head.

"*This basic bitch is the human personification of an Applebee's,*" Alice read out loud. "I'm supposed to just ignore that people are saying things like that?"

Griffin leaned over, grabbed her phone out of her hand, and set it on the coffee table. "Yes." He directed his attention back to the baseball game on TV.

Alice tried to make herself watch the game. Griffin had been dealing with things like this a lot longer than her and probably knew what he was talking about. She'd never really given much thought to how little he used social media, but she had a better understanding of it now. Twitter wasn't quite as much fun when it was full of strangers attacking you over lies someone else had made up.

It was disturbing, really, the level of investment people had in a relationship that didn't even exist between two strangers they'd never met. Kudos to the publicists, she supposed. A whole Kimbergriff fan community had been inspired by their supposed relationship. They seemed to spend all their time on the internet poring over photos, constructing elaborate fantasy narratives by filling in the gaps with details supplied by their imaginations, and then behaving as if those made-up details were absolute, incontrovertible truth. Confronted with a photo that threw their fantasies into doubt, they'd turned on the former objects of their obsession with an alarming speed and ferocity. Some of them almost seemed excited by this excuse to hate Griffin, as if they'd put him up on a pedestal purely for the pleasure of knocking him down.

Alice's phone buzzed on the table. It was lying facedown so she couldn't see the notification. She started to reach for it, but stopped at the look Griffin gave her.

"Fine." She sank back on the couch with a sigh.

Her phone vibrated again.

And again, a few seconds later.

Ignoring Griffin's glare, she leaned forward and snatched it off the table. "It might be Rachel."

It wasn't Rachel. It was a Twitter notification. As she stared at the screen, trying to make sense of the words being directed at her, another notification came in. And another.

Alice's blood went cold. "Oh my god."

"What is it?"

She stared at her phone in horror. "They know who I am. They identified me somehow and found my Twitter account." Which was linked to her Instagram and Facebook, so they'd be able to find those too.

"What? How?" Griffin took the phone from her. "Jesus." He shoved the phone back into her hands. "Lock it down. Right now. Set your account to private. Set all your social media accounts to private."

"Fuck, fuck, fuck," Alice muttered under her breath as she scrambled to navigate the settings and lock her account down. She'd gained a hundred new followers in just the last few minutes, which meant she was locking the gates after the Trojans had already wheeled their horse inside the city walls. *Fuck.*

"How the hell did they find you?" Griffin demanded.

"I don't know."

Okay. Twitter was locked, Facebook was locked, Instagram was locked. She went through her most recent followers, blocking all of them until she got to a name she recognized as an actual acquaintance.

Griffin started pacing in front of the TV, looking a lot less calm than before, and Taco got up to pace alongside him. "You didn't post anything, did you? I told you not to post to any of your social media accounts until we figured out what to do."

"I didn't!"

"Are you sure?" Behind him, one of the Washington

Nationals popped a fly ball directly into the glove of the Cubs' centerfielder to retire the side.

"Yes, I'm sure," Alice said through clenched teeth. She powered her phone off and shoved it into her back pocket before it could transmit any more devastating news. "This isn't my fault."

Griffin exhaled a harsh breath and scrubbed a hand through his hair. "I can't believe my whole career is at risk right now because you insisted on going to some stupid party."

Alice stared at him. "You think it's *my fault* all this is happening?"

"We never would have been photographed if you hadn't manipulated me into taking you someplace people would be taking pictures."

Whoa.

She was on her feet before she was conscious of making the decision to stand. "I *manipulated* you?" Her hands balled into fists at her side. "Being upset isn't manipulation. It's called having emotions—which I realize is a foreign concept to you."

"Hey!" He actually had the nerve to look hurt—after he'd flung the word *manipulate* at her like a weapon. "That's not fair."

"What's not fair is you conveniently leaving out the fact that we wouldn't be in this situation in the first place if you hadn't agreed to this ridiculous publicity stunt of a relationship!"

Taco looked back and forth between them and whined under his breath, upset by their raised voices.

A muscle ticked in Griffin's jaw. "I didn't have a choice."

"Of course you did," Alice shot back. "All you had to do was say no."

"My career is actually important to me, so no, I didn't have a choice. And we weren't even together when I agreed to it."

"But you didn't put an end to it after we were together. You forced me into the role of the Other Woman and made our relationship seem like something tawdry that had to be hidden."

"I'd made a professional commitment! Which I realize is a foreign concept to you."

Alice recoiled, shocked that he'd throw that particular barb at her when he knew perfectly well why she'd abandoned her dissertation, how hard she'd worked to get back on track, and how much of a sore spot it was.

Numbing tendrils of ice traveled down her spine, turning her voice glacial. "Fuck you."

They stared at each other for a moment, then Alice turned her back on him, grabbed her purse and keys off the table, and headed for the front door.

"Where are you going?" Griffin shouted after her. "You can't be seen out in public right now!"

"You don't get to decide what I can and can't do," she shouted back as she slammed the door behind her.

"I'M SORRY," RACHEL SAID, TOPPING OFF ALICE'S WINEGLASS. "All of this sucks so hard."

"It really does," Alice agreed.

She'd come straight to Rachel's when she stormed out of Griffin's house. Thank god Rachel had been home, because Alice hadn't had anywhere else to go. As much as it rankled her, Griffin had been right that she couldn't afford to be seen in public right now.

Rachel had welcomed her with a hug, canceled her plans with Pete for the evening, and opened a bottle of wine that the two of them shared while Alice spilled the whole wretched story from the beginning.

Rachel shook her head as she brought her glass to her lips.

"I can't believe Kimbergriff is fake. Do you think all celeb romances are fake?"

"I don't know," Alice said. "Maybe. Maybe everything's fake with actors."

"Hey!" Rachel protested, giving her a friendly shove. "We're not all like that."

"I know, I'm sorry."

Rachel's expression grew serious again. "You don't think Griffin's feelings for you were fake, do you?"

Alice shook her head. "I don't know what to think anymore."

That wasn't strictly true. She knew Griffin cared about her in his own way. She just wasn't sure his way was enough. He'd sworn there was no one in his life more important than her, but there was one person who would always be Griffin's number one priority: Griffin. His career was everything to him, and woe unto anyone who got in the way.

All Alice had wanted was for someone to put her first, for once in her life. She didn't think that was too much to ask of a person who was supposed to love you.

Her phone vibrated on the table, and she and Rachel both glanced at it warily. A second later it vibrated again, and then twice more before falling silent.

Rachel had been the one to figure out how Alice's identity was uncovered. Some obsessive fan had apparently scoured the accounts of everyone Griffin followed on Twitter until they'd found her. Alice had foolishly assumed she was safe since Griffin had never followed her back, but he did follow Robert, the show's old second AD, who also followed Alice. Right there in Robert's photo stream was a picture he'd taken with Alice and some of the other extras on their last day, just waiting to be discovered by one of the goddamn Sherlock Holmeses on the internet. And of course he'd tagged her and she'd commented on it. That was all it took for them to trace her back to her own account and splash her real name and Twitter handle all over the place.

She'd changed the name on her profile to something that wasn't her actual name, and was pretty sure she'd weeded out all the weirdos who'd followed her before she locked her account down, but the information was already a matter of public record for anyone who wanted it. Her identity had been outed to the world.

She felt numb. It was hard to believe this was really happening to her. How had she gotten herself into this mess?

Griffin had said she'd get used to this kind of negative attention. But what if she didn't? What if she wasn't capable of getting used to living like this? Maybe she wasn't cut out for this kind of life. Maybe it wasn't worth it.

She could understand why Griffin put up with it. It was the cost of fame. He'd chosen this life because he loved acting and wanted to live this way. But she hadn't chosen this. She wasn't looking for celebrity. There was no upside for her. She just wanted to be left alone to live her life in obscurity, but Griffin's adoring public would never let her do that. Not as long as she was with him.

"You want me to see what it says?" Rachel offered, gesturing at Alice's phone.

"Yes, please." Alice had turned off all her social media notifications, but she'd been getting texts and emails from old acquaintances and distant relatives all day. Now that she was infamous, everyone she'd ever gone to school with or gotten a birthday card from was crawling out of the woodwork to get the scoop on her celebrity relationship.

She had no desire whatsoever to reconnect with any of them at the moment. On the other hand, if someone was trying to alert her to some new social media disaster that was unfolding, she should probably know about it.

Rachel picked up the phone. "It's a bunch of texts from Griffin."

Alice's heart stuttered in her chest.

"Do you want to see them?" Rachel asked, biting her lip.

Alice swallowed a mouthful of wine. "I don't know. You tell me."

"He's apologizing."

After a moment's hesitation, Alice held out her hand. She might as well see what he had to say.

I'm sorry.

I was upset and I shouldn't have taken it out on you.

Can we talk?

Please?

"What are you going to do?" Rachel asked.

"I guess I'll talk to him."

Not tonight though. She was way too drunk to have a serious conversation tonight, much less drive.

Tomorrow, she typed back. *I'm too tired tonight.*

Are you okay? Where are you?

I'm at Rachel's. I'll come by tomorrow and we'll talk.

I'm glad you're with a friend. I love you.

Alice didn't reply back.

KIMBERLEIGH HAD SENT ALICE FLOWERS: A GIANT BOUQUET OF buttery yellow roses that Griffin didn't know what to do with. He stared at the card, wondering what it could possibly say, and whether it would make things worse between him and Alice. For a brief moment, he toyed with tossing the flowers straight into the big garbage can outside. Instead, he set them on the coffee table and went back to cleaning the house.

The house didn't need cleaning; his cleaning woman had been there only three days before. But Alice was coming over and Griffin was a nervous wreck. Cleaning soothed his nerves. It was something productive he could do to distract himself from the acid whirlpool currently ravaging his stomach lining.

He'd completely freaked when Sabrina told him about the photo yesterday. The thought of everything he'd worked for going down the shitter over a single careless mistake had sent him into a panic, and he'd taken that panic out on Alice in a way she hadn't deserved. He hadn't expected her to walk out like that though. It wasn't until after she'd left that the enormity of his mistake had sunk in. He'd been so focused on his own problems, he hadn't given enough thought to what she was going through.

He could have been more understanding. He should have tried to help her deal with her sudden infamy instead of lashing out at her over it. He would have gotten there eventually, if they'd talked it out last night. But instead Alice had gotten angry and left.

He'd thought they were just arguing. That they'd vent at each other a little until they'd gotten it out of their systems, and then they'd make up. But instead of staying to work it out, she'd run away. Walked out on him before he'd even grasped that it was happening.

He hadn't appreciated how upset she was, because once again he'd had his head too far up his own ass to look beyond his own immediate crisis. All he'd been able to think about was how it affected him, and his career, and his professional relationships. She probably thought that was all he cared about, because in the moment it was all he'd thought about. He really was shit at this relationship stuff.

In the emptiness Alice's absence had left behind, that one stupid photo didn't feel so important anymore. His career didn't feel so important anymore, if it caused him to lose her.

Griffin wiped down the kitchen counters, scrubbed the sink, ran the dust mop over the floor, and fluffed all the cushions on the couch. One of the roses had already dropped a petal. He plucked it off the coffee table and rubbed the velvety material between his fingers as he carried it to the kitchen. By the time he dropped it in the trash, it looked like a used dryer sheet.

Taco jumped up from his bed and ran to the sliding door, wagging his tail expectantly, which must mean Alice had pulled up.

Griffin stood in the kitchen and waited.

He startled at the knock on the front door. He'd expected her to come in through the sliding door, the way she always did when she knew he was home. And why was she knocking instead of using her key?

He had a feeling he knew why, and he really hoped he was wrong. His heart beat a jerky rhythm in his chest as he walked to the door. He paused with his hand on the knob for a second, drawing a breath before he pulled it open.

Alice looked pale and unhappy. Her skin had a papery translucence and her eyes were sunken, with a reddish cast as if she'd been crying.

Instinctively, he started to reach for her, then stopped himself. "Alice—"

She stepped into his arms, her hands sliding around his waist and fisting in the back of his shirt. The comforting, familiar scent of her worked like an aerosolized tranquilizer to banish his anxieties. He blew out a long breath as he wrapped her up, burying his face in her hair.

It would be okay. She still loved him. They could work the rest of it out. Together.

He'd break off the arrangement with Kimberleigh if that's what Alice wanted. Deal with the publicity from the fake breakup of his fake relationship and whatever that might mean for his career. As long as he had Alice, he could navigate the rest of it.

She took a deep, shuddering breath and pulled out of his arms. Her spine was rigid and her expression pained. That was when he realized. He'd read the situation all wrong. She hadn't come to make up with him at all.

She walked past him into the house, and he stood there staring helplessly out the open doorway like someone who'd just gotten on the wrong subway train and was watching the station recede in the distance.

After another moment he shut the door and followed Alice inside.

She'd stopped in the middle of the living room to stare at the roses. "Did you—"

"No," he said. "Kimberleigh sent them."

"Why?"

"I don't know. You'll have to read the card."

Alice walked over and took the tiny envelope from its plastic holder. He watched her expression carefully as she peeled it open and read the card inside. Blotchy pink spots formed on her cheeks, and she pressed her lips together.

"What does it say?"

She tucked the card in her purse. "That she's sorry for all this mess."

"I'm sorry too, if that counts for anything."

She turned to face him, and a feeling of cold dread settled in his limbs. "It does." She shook her head. "But not enough."

Griffin took an unsteady breath and released it. "I love you. Isn't that enough?"

Her eyes gleamed, but she blinked the tears away before they could fall. "I don't think so."

"Why? Because of Kimberleigh? I'll get out of that, if it's what you want."

Alice's mouth took on a bitter twist. "It's a little too late to put that toothpaste back in the tube. Whether you're in that relationship or out, the damage is done."

"Look, I know it seems bad now—"

"It doesn't just *seem* bad."

"We can get past this. Just give it time." He was desperate now. Pleading. "I know I didn't handle any of this well, and I'm sorry. But don't do this. Please, Alice. Let me fix it." There was a tremor in his voice.

"It's not your fault. I—" She took a step toward him and seemed about to reach out before she stopped herself with a little head shake. "It's not just about Kimberleigh or the photo. I just think all this was too much for me. Living together. Not being able to go out or talk to anyone." She made a jerky gesture in his direction. "Your whole lifestyle. I'm not like you. I can't deal with all this attention and craziness. I don't want it."

What she was really saying was that she didn't want him. Not enough to put up with all the downsides.

Kimberleigh had been right. She'd tried to warn Griffin back in Atlanta that it wouldn't work out. The glare of the spotlight was too harsh for those who hadn't chosen this kind of life.

Alice reached up to smooth her ponytail over her shoulder. She looked miserable. That was how being with him made her feel—miserable. "I just want to have a normal, quiet life and be in a normal relationship with a normal person. I deserve that."

Griffin nodded, surprised at how calm he was able to be while his whole world was crumbling. "I'll never be able to give you that. Even if this stuff with Kimberleigh had never happened—"

"People would still judge me," Alice said. "I know. I'll never be able to be seen with you without being photographed, scrutinized, and compared to some unreasonable standard."

He looked down at the floor. "There's nothing I can do to make any of that go away. It's part of the package with me."

"I can't live like that." Her voice hitched. "I could barely even deal with it when I wasn't part of the narrative. When we were together—"

Griffin's throat closed at her use of the past tense, as if the breakup was already final.

"—I couldn't focus. I couldn't get any work done. It was like I turned into this other person who was so caught up in you and your life that my own life didn't feel real anymore. And I didn't like being that person very much."

He thought it was unfair to blame him for her inability to focus, but he also knew it didn't matter whose fault it was. If being with him prevented her from living her life and accomplishing her goals, well then being with him wasn't very good for her, was it?

And if he wasn't good for her, then he needed to let her go.

"So what are you saying?" he asked, knowing perfectly well what she was saying. He needed to hear the words spoken aloud. For his own sense of closure.

"I guess I'm saying I can't be in your life anymore."

"Okay." He had to force the words out. "If that's what you want."

She did reach out for him then, wrapping her fingers around his wrist. "I think it's what I need."

He clutched at her hand and pulled her toward him, hoping she'd allow him one last embrace.

She fell willingly into his arms. Griffin breathed her in, knowing it might be the last time he ever got to hold her like this. Her chest hitched, and he laid his hand on the back of her head.

"Alice—" *I love you. I need you. Please don't do this to me. I don't know how to live my life without you.* He could have said all that and a lot more, but he choked it back. "I just want you to be happy."

She nodded against his chest, the tears she wouldn't let him see making his shirt damp.

They stood that way for a long time before she finally pushed herself away. Letting her go was one of the hardest things he'd ever done.

She gestured toward the bedroom. "I'm gonna go pack up my things."

"Do you need help?"

She shook her head. "It's probably easier if I do it alone."

Griffin sank down on the couch after she'd disappeared into the back. It only took her fifteen minutes to pack up all her things. He'd felt like their lives were inextricably bound together these last few months, but the truth was she'd never completely moved in. Not permanently. It shocked him how quickly she was able to remove all traces of herself.

He helped her carry it all outside and load it into her car. When the last of it was done, she bent to pick up Taco, who'd been anxiously trotting at her heel. He'd seen Griffin's suitcases often enough, he probably knew what they meant.

"I'm gonna miss you, little fur ball," she whispered, hugging the dog to her chest. Taco licked the dried tears from her face, and she squeezed her eyes shut.

Griffin looked away. It was too fucking hard to watch, and he didn't want to lose his shit until after she was gone.

He heard her set the dog down and step toward him. "Thank you—"

"Don't do that." He shook his head, grimacing at the bile in the back of his throat. "Don't thank me."

"You saved me."

Her voice sounded so rough, he had to look at her. A single tear stood out on her cheek. He reached out an unsteady hand and rubbed it away with his thumb.

Her eyes fell shut. "You really did. You were my knight in shining armor."

Was it his imagination, or had she leaned into his touch? "Are you sure we can't—" He stopped when she shook her head.

She moved his hand off her face. "I have to save myself this time."

He didn't like to think *he* was what she had to save herself from. But that was the truth, wasn't it? Maybe if he'd been an accountant or a car salesman, the two of them could have made it work. They could have had a happy, normal life together. But he was who he was, and the fame he'd fought so hard for was like a drug addiction. It brought a lot of highs, but the long-term effects were toxic—to everyone around him.

He held on to her hand, entwining their fingers. "If you need anything—ever—I'm right here. I meant what I said. I'm not going anywhere. I'll always—" He swallowed thickly. "I'll always be here for you."

She tilted her head up and pressed trembling lips against his. It wasn't so much a kiss as a wordless goodbye.

Her fingers slipped out of his grasp, and he watched her get in her car and drive away.

twenty-three

"ARE YOU GOING TO CAMPUS TODAY?" Rachel called out from the kitchen.

"Uhhh...probably not," Alice answered without looking up from her laptop.

Rachel's head leaned out of the kitchen. "But you are planning on getting dressed at some point, right?"

Alice rolled her eyes. "Yes, Mom. I'll remember to shower while you're at work."

She'd been crashing on Rachel's couch for the last month, thanks to Rachel's generosity and Rachel's roommate's propensity to spend most of her time at her boyfriend's apartment. Not for much longer though. Soon, Alice would be moving to a new place with her very own room and a brand-new set of roommates.

Her apartment search had gone much better this time around. One good thing about having your life publicly crash and burn was that it helped you figure out who your friends were. A surprising number of people had stepped forward, not to gawk at the traffic accident that was her romantic life, but to offer real assistance.

Rachel had offered a temporary place to stay with the full blessing of her roommate, who hadn't even known Alice before she'd volunteered her couch. Alice's grad school friend Anh had hooked her up with someone who was studying search engines and mediated internet interactions, who'd had lots of advice for scrubbing Alice's online footprint. Mike had said he knew of a producer on the hunt for a house sitter if Alice wanted to give that another go, but she had vetoed the idea straightaway—the last thing she needed in her life was more celebrity. Fortunately, Pete had come through by knowing a guy who knew a guy who needed to sublet his room in a three-bedroom apartment he shared with two other people.

The sublet was only for six months, but by then—fingers crossed—Alice would have graduated and found a full-time data science job, and would be in a position to afford a decent place of her own. She'd already started looking into a few companies who were hiring—two local and one in Austin, though she couldn't really see herself moving to Texas—and the market seemed promising. Far more promising than the higher education market, in point of fact.

"When was the last time you left the apartment?" Rachel asked, wandering out of the kitchen with a granola bar in one hand and travel mug of coffee in the other.

"Yesterday. When I went to the grocery store."

"That was two days ago."

"Whatever." Alice shrugged. "I've got to finish formatting all these references so I can submit the draft to my committee by tomorrow."

"Do you have a date for your defense yet?"

"Not yet. That's why I have to finish all this stupid format-ting. So I can get my approval to defend and they'll finally set a date."

"Well, let me know. I'll take off work that day."

Alice looked up from her computer, more grateful than she could articulate for her friend. "You don't have to do that."

"I know I don't, but I'm doing it anyway." Rachel threaded the hand holding the granola bar through her purse straps as she stepped into a pair of shoes beside the door. "Lock the door behind me, okay?"

Alice gave her a thumbs-up. "Have a good day!"

When Rachel was gone, Alice got up and locked the apartment door as instructed, then headed into the kitchen for another cup of coffee. She still had a lot to do before she turned in her draft tomorrow, but overall she felt positive about her chances of finishing.

She was feeling a lot better about everything these days, though it had been pretty rough going for a while there. Rachel had good reason to be concerned. There'd been more than a few days when Alice hadn't budged from the cocoon she'd made for herself on the couch—much less showered or gotten dressed.

It hadn't helped matters that *Troublemakers 4* was in heavy rotation on one of the cable networks. Getting over someone was made more complicated when you could turn on the television at almost any time and see their face in crystal clear 1080p HD. Alice was ashamed to admit how many times she'd watched it while Rachel was at work.

She'd always start out telling herself she was only in it for the scene where Griffin's character emerges shirtless and soaking wet from the decontamination shower, but then she'd end up glued to the screen until the end when he cries over the woman he wasn't able to save. Griffin cried really well on-screen. Not all actors were great criers. Some of them, their faces would get too snotty, too red, or too twisted up in pain. Griffin was perfect, striking just the right balance between emotional vulnerability and handsome suffering. Probably because it was completely fake. He wasn't a crier at all in real life.

In real life Griffin was stoic and resigned. He'd never cry over a woman. Alice watched the movie over and over because he displayed more emotion in that stupid movie than he ever had with her.

Alice had cried constantly for the first few days post-breakup. After that she'd managed not to cry so much, but she'd still felt like crying all the time. Even now, she risked tearing up if she let herself think about him too much.

The only time she didn't feel like crying was when she was working. Her productivity had skyrocketed since she'd moved out of Griffin's house and onto Rachel's couch. That had to mean something, right? Even with her whole life in a state of upheaval, she was getting more accomplished now than when she'd been with Griffin. It seemed a clear sign that the situation hadn't been good for her—for her goals, her career, or her state of mind.

As much as she loved him, they just didn't work. Their lives were fundamentally incompatible. She wasn't cut out to be a celebrity's girlfriend. He'd be much better off with someone at his side who knew how to navigate his world competently. It was for the best this way.

She'd been telling herself that every day, and every day she got a little closer to believing it.

Her new therapist was helping her understand that she hadn't been ready to jump into a serious relationship. The stuff with Gilchrist had saddled her with a whole baggage carousel of trust issues, and a self-involved actor who went through women like coffee filters probably hadn't been the best choice for her first attempt at a post-harassment relationship.

No, scratch that. That was her bitterness talking. It wasn't fair to Griffin.

He had a lot of great qualities, and she believed he'd meant well—even genuinely loved her. They'd just wanted different things out of life, and had very different expectations of one another. They moved in different worlds, and she should have known better than to think he'd make a place for her in his.

It was definitely for the best this way. No matter how much it might still hurt.

If there was one thing Alice had learned in her life, it was that pain faded over time. You got used to the new status quo, even if you didn't like it. You could get used to *anything* in time.

Even this Griffin-shaped hole in her chest.

Work. Work was her focus now. Her priority. Finishing her dissertation was the key to everything. To graduating and getting a job outside of academia. To moving on and starting the next phase of her life.

She'd finally taken Griffin's advice about ignoring what was being said about her online, and had deleted all her old social media accounts, creating new, completely private and anonymous ones that she only told her friends and real-life acquaintances about. She'd also stopped obsessively following hashtags and reading gossip sites to see what people were saying about her.

Lucky for Alice, internet infamy didn't necessarily translate to real world celebrity. She could still go out in public without being recognized or noticed. Being outed in a few online fan enclaves wasn't enough to turn her into a public figure outside the internet echo chamber. The photo of her and Griffin had made it onto a few of the tawdrier gossip sites, but they'd kept her name out of it, and the bigger entertainment news sites had ignored the story altogether. Alice assumed she had Griffin and Kimberleigh's publicists to thank for that. They'd probably pressured the mainstream entertainment press to overlook the photo in exchange for promises of some future scoop or access.

Kimbergriff was still going strong, apparently. The rough patch had been smoothed over by a well-timed shopping trip to

Cartier. The stories about Griffin's infidelity had been drowned out by speculation that they were looking at engagement rings.

Alice knew it was all bullshit. No way was Griffin getting married—especially not to Kimberleigh. She still had the card Kimberleigh had sent with the flowers. Occasionally, she'd pull it out and read it again.

I'm sorry you got caught up in this mess. Griffin seems like one of the rare good ones. Don't let all the made-up drama scare you away from something real.
—K

It was a kind gesture. Kimberleigh actually seemed pretty nice, but that didn't mean Alice should take life advice from her. No matter how well intentioned.

Leaving Griffin had definitely been the right decision to make under the circumstances.

She was ninety-five percent certain. Maybe ninety. But that was still pretty darned certain.

Sure, she wished sometimes that he'd fought harder for her —for them. But for the most part she was relieved it had all been handled so maturely. A clean break. No fuss, no muss. Everyone walking away with their dignity intact—more or less.

A conscious uncoupling.

Wasn't that what all the celebrities did nowadays?

———

"You look like warmed-over shit," Chuck Hammer said, looming over Griffin's chair.

Griffin acknowledged his costar with a scowl that felt appropriate for the five a.m. call time. "Thanks."

"Hey, the worse you look, the better I look." The aging

action star lowered himself into the chair next to Griffin with a hearty chuckle. "Keep it up, kid."

Griffin was glad to be back at work again, and doubly glad to be back with the familiar *Troublemakers* crew, but he was not in the mood for Chuck's ribbing this morning. Or any morning, lately. Ever since Alice had left, insomnia had become Griffin's new roommate, and the two weren't exactly getting along.

Chuck nudged Griffin with a massive forearm. "You used to be funny. Remember when you were funny?"

"Not really," Griffin muttered.

He hadn't been funny since Alice had walked out of his life. Worse, he seemed to have lost the knack of pretending. It was fine when he was acting—when he had someone else's words to say. It was coming up with his own jokes where he hit a wall. He just didn't find much of anything humorous anymore.

"Leave him alone." Merit Lebese wandered over with a forty-ounce tumbler of iced coffee. At forty-one, the handsome South African was the odds-on favorite to be the first black James Bond now that Idris Elba had turned the part down. "Didn't you hear? He's got woman troubles."

Griffin's scowl deepened.

"What sort of troubles?" Chuck swiveled in his chair and rested his chin in his hands. "Do tell."

Merit smirked as he sipped his jumbo-sized coffee. "His little girlfriend's been stepping out on him."

That was another thing souring Griffin's mood lately. After all the crow-eating he'd done over the photo with Alice, and everything Sabrina had made him do to smooth things over, they were right back in the same place, only with the roles reversed. Once all the publicity over his alleged affair with Alice had finally died down, everyone—meaning his publicist and Kimberleigh's publicist—decided it had died down *too* much. People had started to lose interest in Kimbergriff once it looked like they'd worked everything out. So they'd cooked up some new drama with Kimberleigh's ex—also fake—to keep the public interested.

Griffin was pissed because it made him look like a chump —although he supposed turnabout was fair play in that regard —but also because it was starting to feel like the whole exercise had been a waste of time and he'd lost Alice for nothing.

Chuck clicked his tongue sympathetically. "Cheating on pretty boy here? Surely not."

"I need more coffee," Griffin growled, pushing himself to his feet and leaving his two laughing costars behind him.

He knew they didn't mean anything by it. They were just taking the piss, as Merit would say. On the last movie, Griffin had loved being included in their friendly hazing, because it had made him feel like one of them.

It wasn't their fault he had such a short fuse these days. He had only himself to thank for that.

Chuck and Merit both knew his relationship with Kimberleigh was all for show, so they couldn't have known how close their taunting had come to the bone. A woman *had* left him a shattered mess.

It had been six weeks since Alice had walked out of his life, and her absence was like a wound that wouldn't heal. Everything in his house reminded him of her. His couch, his bed, even his dog. *Especially* his dog. Taco had been in almost as much of a funk as Griffin since she'd left.

The house didn't feel as much like home anymore, and Griffin didn't understand why. It was still the same house it had been before she arrived in his life. It hadn't changed at all. Alice had slipped in and back out again without leaving a trace. Not a tangible one, anyway. Somehow, her ghost lurked in every room, her absence crowding every corner.

Griffin had never felt this way after a breakup before, but then he'd never broken up with someone he'd been in love with before. The force of his feelings had caught him off guard. He didn't just miss Alice, he mourned for her and for the life he'd thought they would have. They'd only been together for a few weeks as a couple, but apparently in that short time he'd managed to pin all his hopes and dreams on her.

What a mistake that had turned out to be. Never again.

I am enough.

He repeated the mantra his therapist had given him, even though he wasn't sure repeating memorized phrases in his head was getting him any closer to internalizing the idea behind them. But he repeated them all the same, because it was better than doing nothing.

He'd find himself bowled over by grief at the oddest times these days. In response to TV commercials, offhand remarks, or things that were supposed to be funny—like Chuck and Merit's teasing. Something completely random would make him think of Alice, and then Griffin would find himself at the bottom of the well again.

The last time he'd felt this lost was after his mother died. He tried not to feel ashamed of that, that he was almost as upset over a girlfriend as he had been over his mother's death.

I have a right to my own feelings.

That was another one of his therapist's gems that he had a hard time accepting.

He couldn't even keep tabs on Alice via social media anymore. She'd deleted all her old accounts, cutting the last lifelines to her he'd had. But when some of the old *Las Vegas General* crew started following a new, private account with the username @SocGrrl18, he knew it was her.

He didn't dare send a follow request, so he couldn't see anything but the profile photo, which was a close-up of Alice's favorite coffee mug. He'd stare at that tiny round photo sometimes, remembering when he'd bring her coffee in that mug.

How she'd sit next to him in bed drinking out of it in the mornings.

"Griff!" Dylan Warren, the mild-mannered director of the second through fifth *Troublemakers* films, joined Griffin at the craft services table where he was perusing the selection of protein bars.

Steve Houghton, the film's tattooed stunt coordinator, followed close on Dylan's heels.

"How are you feeling about the stunt today?" Dylan's expression, as always, hovered somewhere between vaguely stressed and vaguely concerned—a refreshing change from Jerry Duncan's perpetual rage-stroke. "Still think you want to do it yourself?"

"Kyle's prepped and keen to step in," Steve said, hooking a thumb at Griffin's stunt double, who was loitering on the opposite side of the soundstage. "Guy really hates sitting around, so if you want to make him happy and give him something to do…"

"Nah, I'm good," Griffin said, selecting a turkey and cranberry meat bar. One nice thing about the *Troublemakers* sets was there was always plenty of protein lying around for the muscle-bound cast—although the soundstage did tend to reek of ball sweat and meat farts by the end of the day. "Piece of cake."

He hated using a stunt double for anything but the most technical, pants-shittingly terrifying stunts. Today was just a simple jump from a twenty-foot platform onto the hood of a parked car. If the car were moving that'd be one thing, but something this simple Griffin could do himself. So what if he wasn't wild about heights? He'd be wearing a harness, and it wasn't that drastic a drop. No problem.

Another of his therapist's mantras—*It's okay to say no*—floated through Griffin's head, and he swept it aside. Better to keep busy. A little fear was preferable to boredom. It would be harder to think about just how empty his life felt without Alice when he was swinging from a testicle-crushing rig two stories in the air.

———

Alice laid a hand on her knee to stop its errant jiggling. Her stomach felt like it was trying to crawl up through her esophagus and strangle her.

She'd just completed her dissertation defense—a brief talk to present her research followed by forty minutes of questioning by the five members of her committee—and had been ushered into the hall to wait while her committee deliberated.

Regina had told her not to stress too much. A good committee would never let the defense go forward if the work wasn't up to muster. That was the whole point of all the proposals and meetings and revisions she'd had to go through in order to get here.

Still, Alice was convinced she would be the exception who got into the room and totally bombed. She'd spent hours yesterday practicing her talk, but despite her preparation, today had been the most incoherent performance she'd ever given. The questions had all been reasonable, but she had almost certainly come off like a blithering idiot as her petrified brain struggled to formulate intelligent responses. She'd sweated through her blouse as her tongue tripped over itself and her mouth grew progressively drier no matter how much water she sipped.

And then it had been over. Regina had thanked her, and invited her to step out into the hall while the committee deliberated. "Don't wander too far off," she'd advised, as if Alice were in any danger of deciding now was a good time to run out for a burger or some light shopping.

She *had* run straight to the restroom to relieve her over-taxed bladder after all the water she'd consumed in her nervousness. Rachel and Anh had saved her a seat between them in the hall, and the three now sat in a tense row, listening to the indistinct murmur of voices drifting through the closed conference room door. At this very moment, Alice's committee could be discussing previously unidentified errors and omissions in the articulation of her methodology and the linkages of theory to her data. They could be asking themselves how she'd ever been allowed to get this far, and strategizing how to let her down gently.

At this point Alice would gladly take a "pass with revisions," even if it meant more work lay ahead of her instead of the sweet freedom she'd been hoping for. Anything was better than a fail. *God, please don't let it be a fail.*

A burst of laughter came from inside the conference room, and Alice exchanged an uncertain glance with Anh. Was that a good sign? Or were they laughing at her pathetic effort to pass off PhD-quality work?

Oh, god, she needed to pee again.

Before she could dash off to the restroom, the conference room door opened and Regina came out. She broke into a smile as her eyes found Alice. "Congratulations, Dr. Carlisle."

Whoops and cheers broke out around her. Alice was only dully aware of Rachel and Anh's celebratory exclamations as they hugged her before Regina led her back into the conference room. The other three committee members were smiling and coming forward to congratulate her. There was paperwork to fill out. The department secretary had brought cookies.

She had done it.

Alice had earned her doctorate. She was finished with school forever. She wouldn't officially graduate until December, but as of today she had completed the requirements for her PhD. There were some minor revisions to be made before submission through the university system, but the biggest hurdle was behind her. She could focus on her job search and the next phase of her professional life. She was free.

They were taking her out for drinks. Anh and Rachel were discussing where everyone should meet. Some of the other graduate students were coming, and Pete would join them later. While they argued over whether the margaritas were better at La Fuente or El Corazon, Alice checked her phone, which had been powered off for the last hour. There was a new voicemail message from a number she didn't recognize. Probably another spam call. She'd been getting a lot of weird robo-calls in Chinese, whatever that was about.

"The nachos are better at El Corazon," Alice offered to break the tie, her attention only half on her phone as she hit play and held it to her ear.

Hello, I'm calling for Alice Carlisle, who's listed as the emergency contact for Griffin Micklethwaite. I'm calling from Regnant Studios to inform you that there's been an accident and Mr. Micklethwaite has been taken to the emergency room at Cedars-Sinai. If you could call me back when you get this message—

twenty-four

ALICE FELT a chill as she stepped through the doors and into the emergency room at Cedars. The last time she'd been inside a real hospital—as opposed to the fake hospital set she used to work on—was when her mother had died. The associations it brought back were not pleasant.

She'd been halfway to the hospital when her brain had caught up with the panicked impulse that had literally driven her there in a state of highway hypnosis. Possibly she should have had someone else drive her, given her shaking hands and distracted state of mind, but that ship had already sailed.

"Griffin Micklethwaite?" she said to the woman behind the reception desk in the ER.

Her inquiry was regarded with narrowed eyes. "And you are?"

"Family," she answered without hesitation. "I'm Alice, his emergency contact. I got a call—"

"Come through," the receptionist said, waving her toward the security desk.

Alice was admitted into a hall that branched at a right angle, lined with exam rooms that faced a nurse's station in the middle. "Room ten, straight ahead on your right," one of the nurses told her, waving her in the right direction.

When Alice had tried to call back the person from the studio, she'd been shuttled to her voicemail, so she had no idea what to expect—what kind of accident it was, or how badly Griffin was injured. It couldn't be too bad if he was still in the ER, right? At least they hadn't immediately taken him to surgery or anything drastic like that. Still, she was terrified of what she would find as she approached.

The rooms all had large sliding glass doors that opened onto the corridor, but the curtains inside Griffin's had been pulled for privacy. Through a gap in the curtain, Alice could see that the room was dim except for the pale light of a small fluorescent above the bed where Griffin lay fast asleep.

At least she assumed he was asleep and not unconscious, based on the lack of medical apparatus attached to him. There were no visible marks or signs of injury, and Alice let out a long, shuddering breath at the sight of him seemingly in one piece.

She hadn't realized exactly how much she loved him until she'd been forced to imagine a world without him in it.

Tears clouded her vision, and she covered her mouth to stifle the sob of relief that threatened to erupt.

"He's gonna be fine," said a gruff voice.

Alice hadn't even registered that there was someone else in the room. Belatedly, she spotted the very large and very recognizable man sitting in a chair beside the bed.

Chuck Hammer, former professional wrestler and star of the *Troublemakers* franchise as well as nearly a dozen other action films, was kicked back with one booted foot propped on Griffin's bed, peering at her from beneath his heavy brow. "You're Alice, aren't you?"

She managed a jerky nod, swallowing against the burning in her throat.

"He took a bad landing during a stunt and got a bit of a bump on his head," Chuck explained. "Nothing too serious though. They've already done a CT scan and cleared him to go home today."

Alice's eyes darted back to Griffin, her stomach twisting as her mind conjured images of his body bouncing like a rag doll off the cement floor of a soundstage. She took a hesitant step toward him, then stopped herself before she followed through on the impulse to crawl into the bed beside him and cradle him in her arms.

Chuck got up from the chair and cleared his throat. "I'm gonna go grab something to eat. Why don't you sit with him for a while?" On his way out, he gave Alice a gentle push toward the bed.

She sank into the chair Chuck Hammer had just vacated. Now that she was closer, she could see smudges of dirt and blood on Griffin's skin and clothes, but whether it was stage makeup or from the accident she couldn't tell. After a moment's hesitation, she leaned forward and took his hand, clasping it between hers.

Her chest constricted, and with a muffled sob she crumpled forward, pressing her cheek against his hand.

THE CONCUSSION WAS CONSPIRING WITH HIS INSOMNIA TO MAKE him groggy. That was the only reason Griffin had been able to fall asleep in front of Chuck while they were waiting for the doctor to come back and approve his discharge.

To be honest, Griffin was a little embarrassed Chuck had insisted on accompanying him to the hospital after the accident. He was fine. He didn't want people making it into a big deal. The worst injury was to his pride. He was grateful Chuck had shooed away the people from the studio and the insurance company though. He'd be happy to explain to everyone that it was his own clumsiness and no fault of the stunt and safety teams that caused his footing to slip on the hood of the car, but maybe after his head had stopped throbbing.

The concussion must be giving him hallucinations too. Griffin could swear he'd heard someone say Alice's name, and then he'd felt her take his hand. For a moment, he lay there, trying to stay in the pleasant fantasy his injured brain had conjured. He knew when he opened his eyes she wouldn't be there, and he wasn't in a hurry to return to that reality.

But then he heard a stifled sob that sounded painfully familiar, and felt something wet on his hand. His eyes flew open, and a head of beautiful blonde hair swirled into focus, bent over the bed beside him.

Griffin blinked, afraid that when his vision cleared she'd be gone.

But it was really Alice. She was here.

He spoke her name in a raspy whisper, and her head popped up. Her tearstained eyes met his, and what he saw in them sent a tremor of hope surging through him.

Her grip on his hand tightened. "Are you really okay?"

"I'm fine." He tried to sound reassuring so she'd stop looking so scared. "It's just a mild concussion."

Her lips pursed in a disapproving frown. "You say that like there's any such thing as *just* a concussion. If you'd seen the research on brain injury and—"

"I'm okay. Really. They gave me all these tests and it's so minor they don't even want to keep me overnight."

Alice's chin quivered as her lips tried to form a watery smile. "I'm still your emergency contact?" Her hands were still clenched around his, refusing to let go, and his tremor of hope swelled into a tidal current.

Griffin exhaled a shaky breath as he squeezed her fingers. "I was gonna change it, but then I thought, if I was in trouble, who would I want with me? And it was you, Alice. It's always going to be you."

Her eyes filled with fresh tears, and she propelled herself onto the bed and buried her face in his neck. His arms wrapped around her, crushing her to his chest as her body hitched with sobs.

"I was so scared," she choked through her tears. "They left me a voicemail that there had been an accident and I didn't know what had happened or how serious it was."

Griffin's grip on her tightened. "I'm fine. It's okay. Everything's okay now." He threaded his fingers through her hair, and the knots in his chest loosened as he breathed in the familiar scent of peaches.

She had rushed to the hospital in a panic when she heard he'd been in an accident. That had to mean something. Maybe even that she still loved him.

Pushing herself upright again, Alice touched his cheek, her eyes searching his as her fingertips wandered over his face. "You're crying." She sounded surprised.

He covered her hand with his and brought it to his lips. "I missed you," he said. "God, I missed you. So much."

She pressed her lips against his cheek, kissing the tears from his face. "I missed you too." Her mouth found his, and everything else fell away.

The hospital room, the grogginess, the pulsing ache in his head—all of it disappeared as their mouths met in a slow, sumptuous slide. Relief blew through Griffin like a gust of sea air, and the last six weeks of loneliness, their last fight, all of their problems receded in the distance. None of it mattered as long as Alice was here. He'd been blessed with a second chance to make things right. And he would, somehow. He'd make a safe space for her in his life, and this time he'd protect it with everything he had.

Alice's fingers dug into his shoulders, fierce and possessive, as she pressed her body against his. His hand curled around the back of her neck, and he swept his tongue into her mouth, intoxicated by the taste of her. A low moan formed in the back of his throat as she shifted against him, straining for more contact.

"Ahem."

They startled apart, and Griffin grinned at his doctor, who stood in the doorway with an amused look on her face. When Alice tried to move away from the bed, Griffin captured her wrist to stay her retreat. He wasn't letting her out of his reach, not even for a moment.

Dr. Ortiz arched a speculative eyebrow at Alice. "You know he's going to be fine, right? I hope he didn't try to tell you he was dying or anything."

Alice's red cheeks turned an even brighter shade of scarlet as she ducked her head.

The doctor's attention shifted back to Griffin. "I gather you're feeling better?"

"Much," Griffin told her. "When can I get out of here?"

Dr. Ortiz glanced down at the tablet in her hand. "Sure you don't want to stay for dinner?" she asked as she swiped through Griffin's chart. "I hear we've got a nice bland meatloaf and some soggy, unsalted broccoli on the menu tonight."

"I'll pass, if that's all right." He gave Alice's wrist a tug, pulling her back down onto the bed beside him.

Dr. Ortiz nodded. "Right. Well, I'm prepared to let you go now, provided you have someone to drive you home and stay with you tonight, just to make sure your symptoms don't worsen."

"I'll do it," Alice said. Her eyes met Griffin's uncertainly. "If that's okay with you?"

His heart was so full, all he could do was nod and smile dumbly at her in response.

"Perfect," Dr. Ortiz said. "The nurse will be in soon with

your discharge instructions. It's been a pleasure meeting you, Mr. Micklethwaite. Try not to bounce off any more cars."

"Thanks, Doctor," Griffin said, already pulling Alice in for another kiss.

She smiled against his lips. "That was embarrassing."

"I'm sure she'll recover."

Alice gave his arm a gentle pinch. "I meant for me." Her expression clouded. "What if she tells people she saw us?"

"Pretty sure that would be a HIPAA violation. But also, I don't care. Let her."

"But you and Kimberleigh—"

"I'm done with that," he said decisively. "I'll tell Sabrina tomorrow, so she doesn't think it's the brain injury talking, but I'm telling her. That's over. She can figure out how to handle it with Kimberleigh and the press, but I'm not pretending anymore."

"You don't have to do that for me." Alice looked on the verge of tears again, and his heart nearly broke in two.

"I want to." His hold on her tightened convulsively. "Alice, I'm so sorry. I didn't handle things well, but I can do better. If you'll just give me another—"

She cut him off with a kiss, wrapping her arms around his neck, and his whole body breathed out in relief.

Her forehead pressed against his, their noses rubbing as she laid her hand over his heart. "I didn't handle it that great either," she said. "I've got some issues I'm still working through. But I love you too much not to try to make this work."

He felt his face split into a grin as he tangled his fingers in her hair. "Taco's gonna be so fucking glad to see you."

As Alice's laughter filled the sterile coldness of the hospital room, Griffin felt, deep in his bones, for the first time in he couldn't even remember how long, that everything was going to be just fine.

epilogue

ALICE GAZED out the tinted glass window of the limo and tried to make herself relax.

You've got this.

She'd been professionally dressed and styled: her hair swept into an elaborate do, her face transformed by so much makeup she almost didn't recognize herself in the mirror, and her body sausaged into Spanx to create a smooth silhouette beneath her designer peach chiffon gown. She'd even had lessons on how to get in and out of the car gracefully, how to walk in her stiletto heels, and how to pose on the red carpet. Quite literally, Alice had been taught how to walk the walk.

She was all armored up and ready for the Golden Globes red carpet that lay ahead.

Griffin was presenting tonight, and she was attending as his date. It would be their first voluntary public appearance together in front of the press. They'd been snapped by paparazzi several times since Griffin's supposed breakup with Kimberleigh, but tonight they would be parading hand-in-hand down a red carpet in front of flashing cameras, entertainment reporters, and a television audience that numbered in the millions. It was their official, very public coming-out as a couple.

Beside her, Griffin took her hand and lifted it to his lips. "You sure about this? It's not too late to back out and stay in the car."

Tempting as that might be, Alice had made a decision and she intended to follow through on it. No more running away. Besides, it wasn't as if she'd have to talk to anyone on camera. It had been decided that she and Griffin would walk the step and repeat gauntlet together, posing for photos, and then Alice would hang back with his publicist while he did the red carpet interviews solo. On the other hand...

"Are *you* sure?" she asked Griffin, noting the tension etched into his expression. "I can always sneak inside on my own while you do the red carpet."

"Not a chance." He gave her hand a possessive squeeze. "I'd much rather have you at my side, if you're comfortable being there."

Alice reached up to smooth his brow. "I don't think either of us are likely to be comfortable, but at least we'll be uncomfortable together, right?"

"You two are so cute you're gonna make me vomit," piped up Griffin's publicist, Kelly, who sat across from them in the back of the limo with her phone's camera aimed in their direction. "I've definitely gotta post this one on Griffin's social media."

She handed the phone to Griffin for his approval, and Alice leaned over for a look. The candid shot had managed to capture them gazing at one another with love shining out of their eyes. Griffin's fans would go wild.

Kelly had been managing the public face of their relationship for them. The narrative she'd spun was that Kimberleigh and Griffin had never been more than a casual on-again-off-again thing, and they'd both amicably moved on to other, more serious relationships while remaining friends. Kimber-leigh was by all accounts happily back with her ex, while Griffin was now with Alice. He'd done a lengthy interview that had appeared in *GQ* last week—timed to drop just before his Globes appearance—in which he'd spoken candidly about his friendship with a former extra that had, over the course of a year, grown into a true partnership and the most important relationship in his life.

The response, for the most part, had been a collective female swoon. There would always be some disgruntled fans and haters out there, but Kelly had crafted a convincing love story, and people were gaga for this new Griffin Beach, a reformed womanizer who'd been smitten by the love bug.

He smiled down at Kelly's phone, then up at Alice. "You look beautiful, Doc."

He'd been calling her that ever since her hooding cere-mony in December. Griffin loved telling people she was a doctor, which Alice found amusing, considering that when they met he'd been the one playing a doctor.

"Ah ah," Kelly warned as Alice leaned forward to kiss him. "Lipstick. No kissing until after the red carpet." She retrieved her phone from Griffin's hand and bent her head as her flying fingers composed a caption to go with the photo. Kelly—or one of her assistants—handled all Griffin's social media now. She'd even created new, public accounts for Alice that she managed as well, allowing Kelly to better oversee their couple brand.

She'd chosen to play up Alice's advanced degree and burgeoning career as a data scientist to counteract accusations of gold-digging, casting Alice and Griffin as a sort of second coming of Amal and George Clooney—minus the international humanitarian accomplishments and stratospheric superstardom, obviously. Alice's job with a local software company was a far cry from the United Nations, but Kelly had managed to spin the idea that Griffin was dating up by falling for a brainy PhD with a professional career of her own.

Alice wasn't entirely happy with the implication that Griffin was any less smart or professional than she was, but he'd lent his full-throated support to Kelly's fiction, making off-the-cuff remarks in the press about his own lack of formal education. It truly didn't seem to bother him, so Alice had stopped arguing against it. On the bright side, it had helped her get over some of the feeling that everyone was wondering what Griffin was doing with her.

She'd made her peace with being spotlight adjacent, and was learning strategies to navigate her new lifestyle. There were sacrifices, obviously, and downsides aplenty, but they paled in comparison to the reward: sharing a life with the man she loved. Griffin good-naturedly suffered through his share of social events with verbose postdocs and nerdy software engineers; the least Alice could do was nut up and strike a pose for a few red carpet pics.

"We're here," Kelly announced cheerfully. "Remember: chin up, look straight down the camera lens, and stand tall."

Alice felt her stomach lurch with last-minute nerves, but then Griffin was squeezing her hand, and when she looked into his bright blue eyes her apprehension fell away. She wasn't alone. They were in this together, and they'd meet whatever challenges lay ahead as a team.

The door of the limo opened to a glare of blinding flashbulbs and a roar of crowd noise. Hand in hand, drawing courage from each other, they stepped out to face the public.

Griffin's actor friend Boone will be back in **LUCKY STAR**, *the next book in the Starstruck series…*

author's note

I started plotting *Rising Star* not long after the Harvey Weinstein story broke, just as the *#MeToo* and *#TimesUp* movements were gaining momentum in the national conversation. Because sexual misconduct is as much a problem in academia as everywhere else, and because almost every woman I know has been harmed by it at some point in her life, I was inspired to write it into Alice's story.

The more research I did, and the more people I talked to, the more I went back and forth on how to resolve the situation with Dr. Gilchrist.

There's always an element of fantasy to the happy endings romances provide. But in order to make the fantasy more believable, I try to make the world my stories are set in as realistic as I can. There are no easy answers or simple solutions to life's problems. True love is a balm for the soul, but it is not a Magic Eraser for all our troubles.

As we've seen over and over, not just this year, but every year I've lived on this earth, it's never as simple as speaking up about the wrong that has been done to you and seeing the wrongdoer punished for his actions. For that reason, I was reluctant to wrap up this particular aspect of the story in too neat a bow.

Maybe one day, if we keep talking about these issues enough, we'll create a world in which women will no longer fear to speak up. When they needn't sacrifice their physical or professional safety in order to call out their abusers. When survivors are believed, and justice is done.

But that is not the world we live in now.

For more information on these issues, or to show your support for those who've been affected by sexual harassment and sexual violence, consider checking out the following resources:

Just Be Inc., started by #MeToo founder Tarana Burke

TIME'S UP Legal Defense Fund, started by a group of over 300 women in Hollywood

RAINN (Rape, Abuse & Incest National Network), the nation's largest anti-sexual violence organization, which operates the National Sexual Assault Hotline (800.656.HOPE) in partnership with more than a thousand local sexual assault service providers across the country.

Thank you for reading,
Susannah Nix

acknowledgments

This book would not exist without the assistance of my dear friend and sociology guru, Mikaela Dufur. Not only did she plant the idea that Alice should be a graduate student trapped in ABD limbo, she came up with Alice's dissertation topic, helped me figure out why Alice was having so much trouble finishing, and provided the majority of Dr. Frazier's wisdom. Thank you, friend, for writing detailed responses to my many questions and spending so much time talking through the plot with me when we could have been watching British mystery shows instead!

I am also indebted to my wonderful beta readers: Meredith Zylberberg, Danielle Dupré, Joanna Cotter, Dena Miccolis, and Bethany Gronberg. Thank you for your brilliant insights, and for helping me get the details right.

Speaking of getting the details right, I am eternally grateful for my editor, Julia Ganis, whose keen eye and expert suggestions made this book far better than it would have been without her intervention.

I have always had an amazing cheering squad of friends who have pushed, supported, and inspired me on my writing journey. I wish I had the space name every one of you, but know that you are each treasured.

Finally, and most important of all, I want to thank my husband, Dave, for encouraging me when I needed a boost of confidence, leaving me alone when I needed to concentrate, and loving me even when I was cranky and distracted while writing this book.

about the author

SUSANNAH NIX is a RITA® Award-winning and *USA Today* bestselling author of rom-coms and contemporary romances who lives in Texas with her husband. On the rare occasions she's not writing, she can be found reading, knitting, lifting weights, drinking wine, or obsessively watching *Ted Lasso* on repeat to stave off existential angst.

TO LEARN MORE ABOUT SUSANNAH NIX, VISIT:

susannahnix.com

OR FOLLOW HER ON SOCIAL MEDIA:

facebook.com/SusannahNix

twitter.com/Susannah_Nix

instagram.com/susannahnixauthor

bookbub.com/profile/susannah-nix

goodreads.com/susannah_nix